rh

TOMORROW THERE WILL BE APRICOTS

Tomorrow There Will Be Apricots

A NOVEL

Jessica Soffer

Houghton Mifflin Harcourt
BOSTON • NEW YORK
2013

www.hmhbooks.com

Library of Congress Cataloging-in-Publication Data
Soffer, Jessica.
Tomorrow there will be apricots : a novel / Jessica Soffer.
pages cm
ISBN 978-0-547-75926-5
I. Title.
PS3619.037975T66 2013
813'.6—dc23
2012042187

Book design by Melissa Lotfy

Printed in the United States of America
DOC 10 9 8 7 6 5 4 3 2 1

For my father, who taught me to sit still and imagine.

For my mother, who taught me to stop sitting around and to put my imagination to words. This book is because of you.

And for Alex, my heart.

TOMORROW THERE WILL BE APRICOTS

Lorca

I WAS PRETENDING to read the paper. I thought that if I didn't say anything, my mother might stop glaring at me, burning a hole in my face.

I was home from school. I'd been sent home.

And though I hadn't gotten myself caught on purpose, as soon as Principal Hidalgo said "suspended," my first thought was of my mother waking to the smell of homemade croissants. I'd be in an apron, piling the hot pastries high in a breadbasket, just beside the cranberry-sage brown butter I'd whipped up. I was suddenly happy, hopeful, thinking of the time we could spend together.

Then I came home. The fact that she refused to look me in the eye made me feel more like a nuisance than a disappointment.

"Kanetha told your teacher that you looked drugged," said my mother, biting a nail, then examining it, the picture of calm on the couch, as if we were talking about leftovers. She had a green towel slumped on her head, and her long shiny legs were spotted with freckles I'd never have. I'd never have her perfect eyebrows either. They were like the feathery fins of her famous pan-roasted sea bass.

I went quiet. She did too. I had to remind myself not to say a word. I talked too much when I was upset. I had a habit of asking her if she loved me. She had a habit of not answering.

"Kanetha's a sneak," I said. "She writes equations on tissues and pretends to blow her nose during tests."

More words bristled against my tongue. My mother's silence baited me. I wanted to tell her that Kanetha didn't always wear underwear and that she flashed the boys during American History II. Kanetha Jackson, eighth-grade busybody. She said I'd been standing in the stall and not "making." So she'd kicked open the door with her neon sneaker. I hadn't even known she was in the bathroom. The stupid thing didn't lock. She found me with my skirt up, my tights down, my shoeless foot on the toilet seat, the paring knife to my thigh. Her lips were stained with fruit punch.

I wanted to ask my mother if she knew the paring knife was hers. The Tojiro DP petty knife, her second favorite. I'd taken it off the counter that morning.

"I wasn't drugged," I said. "I've never done drugs."

I held my breath and looked down at the obituaries. "Mort Kramish, Celebrated Hematologist and Master Pickler, Dies at 79." Still, silence. I could feel it without looking: my mother's low, growly simmer. I gave in.

"I'm fine," I said, wanting and not wanting her to believe it. "I won't do it again." I wanted her to ask me to promise. I waited for it. She swatted the newspaper out of my hands. It cracked as it closed against my knee. She stood up. Her hands were heads of garlic, tight to her sides.

"I could have left you in New Hampshire, you know. You could have grown up with nothing, no one."

She meant that she could have left me with my father. Sometimes, she called him pudding. "He's as useful as box pudding," she would say.

"I'm a good mother," she said so quietly it was like stirring the air.

"I know," I said. "You're a great mother. That's not the point."

Stop. Stop. Stop. Stop talking.

I was sorry and I wasn't. I had the urge to hug her and I didn't. I told myself to be less selfish. She was so busy. She had a "staff of thirty-five and an untarnished culinary reputation to uphold."

The towel sat like a turtle on her head, its feet pushing and bending her ear. She had perfect ankles. Her eyes were the color of ripe pine trees. She made no sound when she cried. Like women in the movies. I was a blubberer. Full of watery snot. Aunt Lou said that when I cried it looked like I was about to throw up.

I put my hand on my thigh, willing her to forget. The scabs were pomegranate seeds, tiny and engorged.

"You've always been like this," she said.

My mother said I was sensitive even as a baby. After every fight, after she'd screamed, thrown a jar of niçoise olives against the wall, or poured—she actually did this once—a full bottle of thyme oil over my father's head, she'd go to my crib. I'd be on my back. Everything right except for my tiny fingers and toes. They were curled into themselves as tight as fiddleheads. She had to uncoil them, one by one. My nails left mini purple crannies in the fleshy parts of my palms. She didn't know where that strength came from in such a little thing.

"I hoped you'd grow out of it," she said and I wished myself to be small again.

I could have been more careful. I should have picked a stall that locked.

Now she went to the freezer and for a second I was bolstered. I thought, *She's about to forgive me. She's about to take out puff pastry. We're about to make cinnamon palmiers.* Instead, she grabbed a bottle of vodka and put it into her robe pocket. Whenever it seemed like she was going to scream, she didn't.

"You have no idea," she said. "This is so much more than I bargained for."

Nausea pulsed in my throat. I'd never meant to be more than she could handle. I did her laundry. I folded her socks into peacocks or hares. Civet of hare. Hare *à la royale*.

"I'm sending you to boarding school," she said. "Principal Hidalgo has a contact. There's a spot reserved for second semester, which gives you all of December to get your ducks in a row."

"No, I—" I started. Already, my mother's back was to me.

I wanted to sit down but realized I was already sitting. I couldn't breathe.

She grabbed the portable phone from the kitchen counter and dialed like this was all the phone's fault. She was calling Aunt Lou. She didn't say a word until she was in the other room. I wanted to tell her I was sorry. I would change. I bit down on my bottom lip until it almost popped. I shuddered. I noticed a spot on the couch that was darkened from where my mother must have been resting her head. I put my face into it. The dusty sweetness of her shampoo.

"Please keep me."

Just then, as if she'd heard me, my mother shouted from the other room, "And don't even think of hurting yourself while I'm in here."

The first time, I was six. I was making a cake for my mother's birthday and slipped on some grease when I was putting it in the oven. I seared both hands on the middle rack. For a second, the pain surprised me, took me, lifted me as if by a wave. I trapped the scream in my throat but tears busted out of my face. I was all shock until I heard my mother's footsteps and realized that I'd put out my hands to do it again, touch the heat again, be lifted again, when the rack collapsed. The undone cake splattered like vomit. There were fresh raspberries in the batter. She came in.

"Jesus, Lorca," she said, looking at the mess.

She acted like I'd gotten peanut butter on her blouse, just "Oh honey, get an ice pack." She had the obits in one hand, a peeled carrot in the other. I wanted to ask her if she loved me. She yelled for my father. He'd been outside chopping wood. His front was covered in splinters and chips. He made me put my hands on the counter, show him the damage.

"Hush, baby. Hush-hush," he said. I didn't need his sympathy but he needed to give it. His eyes were watery, just looking. "Oh, ouch, baby."

My mother was gone.

"Don't worry," I told him. "I promise, don't worry."

He meant well, but I couldn't have cared less. In a moment, I was running up the stairs, pretending I had to pee, trying to remember how I'd done it. I was aching to burn my skin again. And again.

After that there were light bulbs, tire spokes, vacuums. There were car doors, glue guns, and broken bottles winking to me from the side of the road. There was the grill in summer that could stay piping hot well after dinner, well after everyone had fallen asleep.

Back then, I couldn't say what it was about. I couldn't wrap my head around the need, the craving. Now I imagine that if my mother had just taken out the ice pack, tucked it into a towel, and held me on her lap, rocking me, whispering in my hair, cooling my fingers, things would have been different. The pain would have subsided normally, been reabsorbed normally. It wouldn't have remained forever, hovering over me, terrorizing me like an angry wasp, cruising for the exact right second to strike.

My parents fought like crazy. For the eight years of my life that they lived together in New Hampshire, I remembered their voices going scratchy and dull as the sun rose. The fights weren't about me. They were about them, each complaining about the other. My mother called my father pappy, not like "father," but like "old fruit." My father asked my mother please not to be so cruel. He begged her. I would listen carefully, waiting for them to mention me, to say my name. But they never did.

"How can you stand such a minuscule life?" she'd say.

"It's not minuscule," he'd answer, trying to whisper. "This is the country. You wanted to live here."

"It's like we don't even exist out here," she'd say. "How am I supposed to feel? How am I supposed to survive?"

In second-grade science, we watched water boil on hot plates. When the steam shot out from the beaker, I leaned forward onto the table. I let the heat lick my neck. It was so strong it made me gag. I nearly fell off my stool, reeling. The long corridor to the principal's office was quiet but for my footsteps on the nubby gray carpet and the wild sound of my pulse against the burn. I put my fingers to it. Blisters formed like uncooked egg yolks. Soon it would be recess. I walked faster.

My mother came and got me. She didn't say a word. I couldn't shut up.

I told her someone pushed me from behind.

Then I told her that I slipped and fell onto it.

Then I told her that I was reaching for something.

Then I told her my teacher told me to do it.

She was walking five steps ahead of me in the parking lot. Her bag was swinging against her legs. I was scrambling to keep up.

I told her it was an accident and she stopped, turned around, and looked at me. She said, "Ha," sarcastic, but also like she was expelling a popcorn kernel from her throat, and then she didn't say another thing.

If I had a dime for every time I told her that—it was an accident—I could buy all the cheese at Saxelby's. If anything could have made my mother happy, it would have been that. She liked the smelly kind the best, the kind that made your mouth pucker and buzz.

One winter morning maybe a year later, I woke to their shouting. I raced into the kitchen. My father's colorless hands were clenched as he slammed them on the countertop. He hit a green cough drop and it skidded and crashed into a million pieces on the floor.

"Enough," he said. "Enough, goddamn it."

My mother said my father walked out that time, the final time, because she had spent eight hundred dollars at the French Hen in Manchester—she'd special-ordered lox and toro and paddlefish caviar—and he wanted her to be miserable. And because she wasn't about to let him have the last word—"No way in hell," she'd said—*she* started packing.

I went deep into the woods behind our house and screamed until I was panting and lightheaded and falling on my knees. The trees were bare above me, reaching like roads on a map. My mother pointed out the redness in my eyes when I came home and I told her I'd been practicing headstands on the moss; the little vessels must have burst.

She was stuffing our clothing into garbage bags, telling me how she'd been wanting to dye her hair darker but my father had been against it. She pinched her cheeks in the mirror.

"Definitely," she said. "I'm definitely going to go dark."

I kept thinking that I wished I had a warm cat so it could sit on my lap. My mother was allergic to cats and she hated them. "You can't even fry them into an appetizer," she said. "So what's the use?"

She called her parents just before we left the house.

"Daddy," she said. I'd never heard her use that word before. "I am going to need some money. Lorca and I are making changes. We've had enough."

We drove to New York City from New Hampshire that day with my mother's pots and knives and induction pans seat-belted to the back seat, and the garbage bags piled so high in the rear of the car that they blocked the sun.

I told her, "I have a book report due on Monday."

She said, "This isn't an issue of life and death."

I told her she was right, remembering how she'd said "we" to her father. How that had flattered me. How I didn't want to let her down.

Outside it was March gray, and the windows were fogging up. As soon as I started writing something in the frost, she switched the defroster on and off a million times. It made a whirring sound as if it were speaking French. She said there was no reason for us to stay in Cow Hampshire. She called it that, Cow Hampshire. It drove my father nuts. He grew up in Cow Hampshire. My mother said she wanted to be in the food world again, where Pizza Hut wasn't considered gourmet. Find a life again. Put me in a school where all the kids weren't related and where the parents had teeth. She kept giving me this look with her eyes like we needed to be hopeful but the sides of her mouth were quivering. I could see them.

"Do you love me?" she asked. "You know, everything's going to be okay."

If I said it wouldn't, she would turn on me too.

"Everything's okay already," I said, holding my breath so my voice would stop shaking.

"Everything except your father," she said. "He's a wimp. Never fall for a wimp. Love someone stronger, or love no one at all."

I nodded.

I kept the lox and caviar and toro in freezer bags on my lap; they looked like my stomach turned inside out. I pinched the back of my thigh until my face turned hot pink. I could see it in the side mirror. My mother looked straight ahead, her knuckles white, like tapioca pearls, over the wheel.

"Wimp," she kept saying. "Goddamn wimp."

I missed the rest of third grade.

We moved in with Aunt Lou, who wasn't my mother's real sister, because my mother was adopted and Aunt Lou wasn't. My mother liked to say that explained everything—even though they grew up in the same house on Long Island with the same mother and father who loaned them money, going to the same schools, eating the same gloppy dinners and Chinese on Sundays.

Aunt Lou lived on the Upper West Side in a two-bedroom that smelled of supermarket candles and dust. She'd been renting a room to a foreign student, and as it happened, he'd just moved out. I slept where he had, in a small dark room whose rattling window stared into the fluorescent-lit staircase of a building across the way. I found matchbooks and ginger-candy wrappers he'd left behind. Aunt Lou never cleaned. My mother slept in the living room, which was the kitchen, den, foyer, and dining room too.

Our first night there, I got up at three and went into the living room, where they were still talking, and asked if they were tired. They made a scene of hugging each other.

"Are you going to mother us already?" Aunt Lou said. "You just got here, for chrissake."

They laughed, the two of them. My mother could have said something in my defense. She didn't. I'd been about to offer to make her an *omelette au fromage* just the way she liked. I didn't. I told myself that living there was only temporary.

In bed, I chewed the sides of my fingernails until I tasted blood. I recited my book report to myself over and over until I fell asleep. *Bridge to Terabithia.* Leslie was the new kid too. When she drowned, it broke Jesse's heart.

That night, they stayed up till dawn, drinking glass after glass of red wine. My mother tried out the same recipe seven different ways, jotting things down and getting pastry flour on her elbows. Aunt Lou gossiped about the wife of her boss and tapped her ashes into the pages of the *TV Guide.*

I woke up to the beeping sound of a truck backing up.

I said "Dad?" before I remembered where I was. My father had an old pickup so covered in rust that the rear bumper hung off like a broken jaw. When we left, the right headlight was smashed too. Everything he had was broken.

In the living room, there was a spatula wedged into the couch, the smell of butter and onion in the air, potato skins tracked onto the carpet, pans stacked above the lip of the sink. My mother shoved a steaming wooden spoon at me before I could say a word.

I tasted it. "More chives," I said, hoping.

She nodded gravely.

For a moment, we were in cahoots.

My mother had gone to the best culinary school, won a James Beard, and had "quite a reputation" before she married my father and moved to Cow Hampshire. So when we moved to New York, she got a job faster than you could say *vichyssoise.* Head chef and creative director of Le Canard Capricieux. *Zagat* had given it a 27. That year, Gael Greene wrote that my mother had "restored the Croque Monsieur to its long-lost position of dignity."

She found me a home tutor for the summer, a girl who insisted I call her by her first name, Neon. She smelled like skunk and she never stayed for as long as my mother paid her to. She'd say, "You know all this," as she whizzed through the textbook pages.

I kept asking where I'd go to school in the fall.

"Sprout," my mother said, "this is something I need to do."

I hadn't asked.

"Every woman should have a career. A life."

I hadn't asked.

"Your father made it so impossible."

I didn't want her to talk about him again.

"He demeaned my career. You can't be a chef in New Hampshire. Everybody knows that. He knew that. But he liked New Hampshire. His roots. His roots. Blah-blah-blah. His stupid, trashy roots. It was New Hampshire or nothing. He kept saying I wasn't trying hard enough."

She would be just about yelling then. His roots were my grandpa, who lived in a home for the elderly, called everyone Linda, and smelled like scented toilet paper. I'd met him twice and both times my mother's arms were wound so tightly around me that when I leaned forward to hug him, she came with me. She said he was uneducated, but I didn't know what that meant.

"Do you think I didn't try?" she asked but wasn't really asking. "I tried harder than anyone."

I nodded like crazy until it felt something like whiplash.

"It's what I have to do for myself," she said. "For women everywhere."

She talked a lot about women.

"Here's my credit card. I want you to sign yourself up for some ballet classes."

"I just wanted to know where I'll be going to school," I said.

She threw her hands up. I tried to barricade the crying in my chest before it could get to my face.

• • •

The September after we moved to New York I started fourth grade at PS 84, where there were bars or chains on everything, a metal detector, and not a tree in sight. The security guard told me I better wear my red raincoat inside out if I didn't want to be a target for the Crips, who were still active in the neighborhood, for my information. "Crisps?" I asked.

"Oh Jesus," the guard said, shaking her head, putting her palms together in prayer.

Because I was white and Jewish and the only white and Jewish girl going to public school in our neighborhood, they called me Latke, but not in a nice way. Everyone thought I was a suck-up because I started talking about Federico García Lorca when the teacher asked me to introduce myself. A boy named Jesús yelled from the back, "Does poetry make you horny?" Everyone was in hysterics. It didn't help that I brought an artisanal-cheese plate for lunch and the *époisses* stunk up the entire cafeteria.

On the way home from my first day of school, I wore no raincoat even though it was pouring. I treated myself to a ceramic knife at Williams-Sonoma. You could buy two for twenty dollars. They were delicate but they had the sharpest little tips. I'd use them whenever my mother was out too late, didn't ask about my homework, didn't kiss me goodbye when I kissed her, didn't notice when I made her four flavors of ice cream from scratch on her birthday, with everything organic.

Eventually my teacher, Mrs. Weiss, called, concerned, just making sure everything was all right at home. I should have known she would. Twice she'd asked me why there was blood on my spelling tests. It was from my wrists. "Change in altitude," I'd lied, touching my nose. She was no dummy. She'd looked around for used tissues and asked if we'd lived on a mountain in New Hampshire. "Mmm-hmm," I lied. "Absolutely."

Aunt Lou grounded me, sent me to my room. "Why are teachers calling us?" she said, as if I'd revealed some big secret: we were breeding endangered species of birds or keeping human body parts in the freezer. It was her house and she had a point, my mother said, shrugging as she fingered the newest Mario Batali book. "Listen to your aunt. She's doing us an enormous favor, letting us stay here. The least we can do is not be a bother."

"It's my pleasure," Lou said, but I knew the pleasure was only with regard to my mother.

We never moved out of Aunt Lou's. Not after my mother got a raise. Not even after she got two. It didn't take me long to figure out it had nothing to do with money. I wasn't stupid. My mother loved that Lou waited up for her at night, a couple of glasses and a bottle of red wine resting next to her. It didn't matter what time my mother got home. Or what time Lou had to be all business in a skirt suit at the legal-secretary job she'd never leave. Lou would drink an entire pot of coffee just to keep herself awake and prepared for anything my mother might want to talk about. The thing was (the thing that nobody cared about so much) was that I was waiting up too. I wasn't tired. I didn't need coffee. And I would have made her *chocolat chaud* just the way she liked, with a hefty pinch of salt.

Things pretty much stayed the same from then on. There were good years and bad years. My mother was warm in flickers and then very cold. All the while, I waited. Hope was lit and hope was extinguished incessantly. On and off. On and off. But my urge was constant. Like a band of moths stuck between the screen and the window but in my chest instead. I wanted the pain. Wanted it. Wanted it. It was the only consistent thing. It helped me breathe and sometimes more than that. Sometimes it gave me breath. And peace and comfort and something to look forward to. *Come,* it said to me. And I did. I raced. *Come here and rest your head.*

If someone had cared to search my room, this is what she

would have found: painter's razors in the cuffs of my old jeans, surgical tweezers—two pairs—tucked below the insoles of my old sneakers, lighters under my bed, and matches pretending to be bookmarks in a book that I hadn't touched in forever. With a flame, I could make leisurely circles around my bellybutton until I just about died.

Now, home from school because of Kanetha Jackson, I heard my mother on the bedroom phone with Aunt Lou.

"You're so right. I have tried my best. I've tried everything. I have to give up and let someone else step in."

I felt more exhausted than I'd ever felt. I lay down. I thought of myself at boarding school and of all the stalls that wouldn't lock. I thought of running three miles down a dark, windy road littered with wet leaves, just to get some quiet. Just to rip off my glove and make little cuts with a pocketknife on the tips of my fingers, like scoring dough. Then I thought of my mother, alone with Aunt Lou, who had no idea how to take care of her. I was the one who replaced her spices when they ran low. I took her hair out of the shower drain. I prepared a glass of cucumber water for her at night. It was always empty by morning.

I went into Lou's room with two cups of steaming tea. My mother was sprawled on Lou's dramatic bed amid one hundred rows of shiny, overstuffed pillows. Her feet were flexed and her hand was over her eyes as if she were blocking a glare. A sleeping mask was in the crook of her arm, defrosting onto the gold sheet. Wolfgang Puck was on TV, selling pans, aprons, and steak knives. I needed to convince her it was the last time she would have to deal with this. I wouldn't embarrass her again. But also, I needed to convince her that she couldn't live without me.

"Please don't start," she said before I'd opened my mouth.

"I brought tea," I said.

She sat up. I gave her the one with the nicer shade of brown.

She took it delicately into her hands, as if she were very sick and frail, and sipped. Only I got to see this side of her, undone and vulnerable, slow-moving and weepy, a French lace cookie. In the world, she was something else entirely. She shouted orders at the restaurant. And as she walked outside she took long steps, so deliberate that each time her foot came to the ground, people looked to see if she was signaling something important in the concrete.

But not with me. With me, she was different, softer, looser, which was only one of the many reasons I could never leave her. I needed to protect her secret side. If I couldn't, it might disappear, and then what? I wouldn't let that happen. That was my job as her daughter. That is what I told myself.

Now she smiled around the liquid in her mouth and I felt lifted. She could do that: make me feel like I'd lit up a room, if only for a second. Already I'd forgotten about boarding school. Now, remembering, I got a little frantic. I sat on the bed and put my bare feet next to hers so they were touching. I was casual about it, imagining that this was something we did often.

She moved away.

"Don't make me go," I said, only realizing once I'd said it that there was no way not to sound desperate.

"You're a danger to yourself and to others," she said, waving off an imaginary fly.

"I'm not—" I began, but stopped. I was better off quiet. If I'd learned anything in my entire life, it was that.

"You should see how they look at me," she said. "All those administrators with their ironed pants." She brought the mug to her face and inhaled. I waited for her to say something about the tea so I could run with it. I knew a lot about Earl Grey—she just needed to get me started.

"I had to give them comps to the restaurant," she said.

She shook her head. I dropped mine. I gathered my feet beneath me and made myself into the tiniest ball I could, wanting to intrude less on her space but not desert her. She didn't like to be alone. Sometimes, even when I'd made her mad, she'd ask me to sit by her—and then she'd pretend I wasn't there. A half punishment, really.

"Can't I just see the school psychologist again?" I asked. I'd done it before, but it turned my mother into a nervous wreck. She kept wanting to know what the lady asked me, what I told her, what she said in response. I knew there was a secret I'd better be keeping; I just wasn't sure what it was. So I told the lady next to nothing. "It was just a phase," she'd said in the end, signing a paper for me to give to my teacher. "And I do think you're so much better."

"Just a phase!" I'd exclaimed in agreement.

"Lorca, Lorca, Lorca," my mother said now. "If that worked, would we really be here again? You're in eighth grade. This is not a joke."

I had been so careful. I'd gotten away with it so many other times. Hundreds of times. Gajillions, it felt like.

"Yes," I said, pretending it was nothing at all. "Sure."

My mother ignored me as she looked for the remote. She turned up the volume on the TV until she wouldn't have been able to hear me even if I'd shouted. She watched intently with her back curled, the tea hovering at her mouth. Aunt Lou's room reeked of artificial vanilla.

"I'm sorry," I said into the enormous TV noise.

"I'm sorry," I said louder.

"Mom!" I said, but still nothing.

"I'm so sorry!" I yelled. "Don't make me go."

She must have heard me then, but she did nothing about it. And I didn't dare touch her, not wanting to scare her. Then she lowered the sound.

She lay down. I did too, but her face didn't get weird and melted like mine. Her internal structure was made of something stronger, something that made her beautiful even in the mornings, in unbearable heat and cold, when she was upside down.

"I could live with Dad," I said.

She made a noise like she'd been punched in the chest.

"Right," she said. "Because he's so effective. He'd let you kill yourself, for chrissakes, while he was outside whittling a goddamn tree into a stupid giraffe."

It was just a suggestion. I knew she was going to say no.

"Why is everything so hard for me?" she said and turned her head away.

The truth was, my mother was a magician. She could make herself disappear. If I had any hope of staying with her, I had to find a reason for her to come back.

There was one thing that made my mother truly happy: food. In New Hampshire, to save money, she turned off the heat and kept on the oven while she made four varieties of roasted beet soup. She wore pomegranate perfume. At the supermarket, she was like an ant building a hill. At night, she slept with yogurt and honey smeared on her face.

Food was my mother's life. Sometimes, I wondered if she'd married my father because of his last name: Seltzer. Her maiden name wasn't really her own. She was adopted. So she took a last name that represented the only part of herself that felt true: food. And seltzer was her secret to delicate crepes, the perfect French onion tart, and fried chicken that actually glittered.

If I were normal I would have:

1. called Principal Hidalgo;
2. begged to be forgiven;
3. promised to see the school psychologist twice a week (and promised my mother I would not say anything incriminating about my home life);

4. written a note to Kanetha Jackson that looked identical to a sincere apology for having scared her;
5. composed a speech explaining that kids went through phases, tried things, stupid things, and after screwing up and learning valuable lessons, they returned to normal—like I would—and then recited that speech to my mother and Aunt Lou.

Instead, I went to bed early. I was hopeless. Earlier that evening, I'd made a wild mushroom quiche, just to see if it could prove to my mother that I was worth keeping around. I made the crust from scratch. When she removed a woody thyme stem from her teeth, she didn't even say anything. She didn't have to.

Because of a gnarly herb, I was still going to boarding school.

I tossed and turned. My mother and Lou were watching television in the living room, but not really watching, and they didn't turn it down.

Aunt Lou said, "Nance, these things happen for a reason."

And I heard my mother say, "What reason?"

Aunt Lou liked that phrase. She said it a lot. When she was angry—like if she lost her MetroCard or dyed her hair and it didn't come out right—she closed her eyes and took a deep yoga breath. She called it that. She'd taken one class twenty years ago, but she acted like it had changed her life.

"Everything happens for a reason," she always said with her back very straight, her thumbs and forefingers curled into Os. "Everything happens for a reason."

And then, because I'd been practicing listening for years and years and years, I could hear Aunt Lou whisper, "Shhh." I could hear the sweep of her hand running up and down my mother's back. My own back began to itch. I tried to do the same sweep for myself but it was physically impossible.

I looked at the cut on my thigh, and the guilt made me sick. I flipped onto my stomach and shoved my face into the pillow.

When Aunt Lou had nothing to say to my mother, she played a game that she'd learned from me.

"If you could eat only one thing for the rest of your life, what would it be?" she asked now.

"Country bread, buttered, with heaps of black truffles."

"If you were on a deserted island, what item could you not live without?"

"A paring knife."

"If you could have lunch with anyone, who would it be?"

"Julia Child's husband, because she obviously didn't drive him nuts," my mother said.

"What is the best thing you've ever eaten?"

Poulet rôti. I was sure that my mother was going to say the poulet rôti from L'Ami Louis in Paris because she'd sat next to Jacques Chirac there and he'd said that since she was a chef, perhaps she would cook something for him. And so she did. She went right back into the kitchen and whipped up something fabulous. After that, they used goose as well as duck fat when frying their potatoes, because it had been her way.

I mouthed *Poulet rôti* into the pillow. But my mother was quiet. She could have made conversation, little noises while she was thinking. But she didn't. Lou didn't care.

"Masgouf," she said. "From an Iraqi restaurant that's closed now."

I sat up. I opened my mouth. I almost yelled, *What?* But she was still talking.

"I went there with her dad years and years ago." I imagined her jerking her thumb in the direction of my room. "The company was like watching paint dry, but the food was fantastic. Out of this world."

"And?" Lou said.

"And," my mother said, "I went back a couple of years ago, just to see, and it was closed up. Totally empty and sad. One silver tray sat in the middle of the place, I remember. Broke my heart to pieces."

"Masgouf?" Lou said.

I was already out of bed, sockless and by the bookshelf, zipping through the index of *The Joy of Cooking,* then *Cook Everything,* then, finally, *Recipes from All Over.* I found it. "'Traditional Iraqi fish dish, grilled with tamarind and/or lemon, salt, and pepper,'" I whispered, shocked.

"It was heaven," my mother said. "Literally heaven. I've tried to replicate it, I can't tell you how many times."

For a second, I saw spots. I would have bet my life on it—on the poulet rôti.

"You know how they say that life imitates art?" my mother said. "Well, life imitated masgouf. The fish was so good, so tender, and we ate it with our fingers. For a little while, I convinced myself that life could be so simple."

Which meant happiness. Masgouf was my mother's happiness.

Suddenly, I felt like I'd missed everything. Had I never asked her? Had I never asked her directly the question of questions, about her favorite of favorites? Maybe not. Maybe I'd just assumed. What else had I assumed? Was it just to Lou that she told the absolute truth? Maybe with me, she gave the answer that required the least fussing on her part. When I'd asked her more about L'Ami Louis, she'd said, "*Vanity Fair* did a brilliant piece on it. Have a look at that."

And then it hit me. If I wanted to make my mother happy and remind her why I was essential to her happiness, all I had to do was find the recipe and make the dish. It would make things better. I could be worth keeping around. I could give her the one dish she had loved the most, that had given her the most happiness.

A couple of years ago, I'd been all bustling like this. We'd had two blizzards and it was only December and my mother said if it snowed one more time she would skewer herself on a butterfly knife. That's when it occurred to me that we could move to California, and for about ten seconds, I felt like a genius. We could have avocado trees and Honeybell orange juice every morning. We could drive up the coast on weekends and be treated like royalty at the French Laundry. She could open a new kind of bistro that married haute French cuisine with New American. Alice Waters would make us brunch at her place and would be blown away by the dessert that my mother baked with four varieties of heirloom plum. But then, California had been a ridiculous idea. She would never have left Aunt Lou. It would never be the two of us. Another option would have been to move to Florida, which was like California. But the problem with that, of course, was Bubbie. They didn't get along. My mother always said, "I need her like I need a sharp stick in the eye. Not a creative bone in her body." And yet, every week, Bubbie called once, twice, three times and left messages on the machine—especially now that Pops was dead. My mother would make a face like someone had just caused her soufflé to drop and she'd say, "She doesn't understand me. She never could."

My mother had not tried to find her biological parents. She hadn't wanted to, Lou said. Lou had offered to help, said the two of them could run away and find them together. But my mother said no. She must have been so angry at them. People always said, "I would never want to be on your mother's bad side." Meat keeps cooking when you take it off the flame; my mother could turn herself off in an instant.

Lou had admitted to me that she thought it was better this way. "We'd miss her," she said. "Wouldn't we? If she found her parents, we wouldn't be the most important people in her life anymore. They'd be shiny and new and we'd still be us."

• • •

I'd always had stupid ideas, until now. This was something brilliant. The masgouf was perfect. Simple. It wasn't ridiculous. It was doable. And it could make her happy. I'd been suspended indefinitely, meaning at least through winter break, which started in two weeks. That gave me plenty of time to get my ducks in a row. Just like she'd said.

That night I fell asleep scheming—and in my dreams, I wasn't acting alone. Blot, a boy who worked at the bookstore on Eighty-Fourth, was my sidekick. I'd never said his name out loud but if anyone had bothered to ask me if I was into someone, I would have said easily, "Yes, actually. I'm into Blot." Just thinking it made me feel like my insides had been replaced with rhubarb freezer jam—sugary and squishy and all pulp—except at my throat, which got tight and dry, like an overdone English muffin.

In my fantasy, we wear brown leather backpacks and canvas sneakers and race through Central Park and Times Square at night, popping into Middle Eastern restaurants, shoving little bits of this and little bits of that into our mouths and jotting things down on yellow notepads. Our bags bop along like happy toddlers on our backs and when I get home late in the evening, flushed, spent, my mother wants desperately to know what I've been up to. I tell her it's a surprise, and she says, "Really?," like I'm doing her a favor. She is both patient and proud. She holds my face to get a good look at me and I'm the one who drops her eyes first, blushing. I've done good and we both know it.

Victoria

I ASKED JOSEPH if he wanted to go for a walk. It was Friday, and he'd been in bed all day, hands folded over his chest as if he were napping beneath some enormous lemon tree. He shook his head, shut his eyes, and cinched his mouth. His skin, which used to look like it was preserved with olive oil, had become matte and flaking. His blue saucer eyes were milky puddles, and his silver beard, once dense as a broom, was a light dusting of powdered sugar.

"No," he said. "I'd never find my way back."

I'd wanted him to say yes. I'd mouthed *yes* before he'd said a thing. I wanted to ask him if he planned to stay in that bed forever. I wanted to ask him if I seemed like a spring chicken. I'm fifty million years old. But look at me. I'm up. I'm at 'em.

I thought, *If he loves me enough, he'll get up on the count of three. If he wants to go on living, he'll feed himself on Thursday. He'll get dressed. He'll rinse a glass. He'll walk fifteen steps. He'll ask for the paper. He'll pee standing up. He'll turn off the light. He'll grip my shoulders and say exactly this with an ironic grin: "I love you so much that I cannot live without you. So I won't die. I'll live so we can live together."*

I looked at him now. I loved him so much it made my hands tremble.

I used all my strength to sit him up and pour water into his mouth. I grunted but hid it with a cough. It would have killed him to see my face wincing as I moved him from the bed to the chair, to know the way it shot hot daggers down my back.

"Hello there," I said. He looked around. He was a child, lost in Central Park. I waited, expectantly.

"If I went out," he said, "who would let me back in?"

Suddenly, I had the urge to yell at him. Then I had the urge to weep. The guilt always came later, an aftershock. He was home, I wanted to tell him. He was in his study with two walls of fraying brown cookbooks mixed in with Rumi, Rudaki, Hafez, Bellow, and Roth. But it wouldn't help to explain it. I wasn't delusional about that. In my head, I said, *Please. Figure it out.*

His eyes darted around, looking for clues. I adjusted the brown blanket I'd knitted myself around his shoulders. "Remember this?" I said, pulling a corner to his face. Nothing.

I motioned toward the set of framed eighteenth-century spoons. "Remember these?" I asked. Again, nothing. It wasn't dementia. Nothing as simple as that. It was cancer, pain meds, depression, exhaustion. It was that sometimes he couldn't bear to be present, to look down at himself and see what he saw. So he checked out. Gone fishing. I'd almost punched a nurse when she said, "Here one minute, gone the next," but she had a point. He was like a bulb, flickering on and off according to some erratic electrical current inside of him that I was desperate to rewire and fix.

I brought him the photo of his father's chicken stall in the Baghdadi market. There were white snowflakes against the lens. "Remember them?" I asked. I looked at Joseph but he wasn't looking at the picture. He'd begun to stare past things with his dull, weak eyes — a selective blindness.

On particularly bad days, I'd wonder if my only hope, his only hope, was to bring up our deepest secret, the one thing we never discussed, never mentioned. I didn't want to, dreaded it. It was desperate, a last resort, but we were at that point. If there was ever a time for candor, it was now. Forgiveness, now. Regrets, confessions, concessions, empathy, desperation, and exaggeration: now.

I wondered if everyone had a secret like this, something slightly wretched, bent and corroded with time, like a lost key that might not even unlock anything anymore. And if, in the end, it might be the only thing that mattered.

All those years ago, I gave up our baby. Joseph didn't want to. Hated it. I said it was to protect us, what we had. But she followed us everywhere, like a chill that we could not shake. I tried never to miss her. Joseph must have done the same. It was what kept us together and broke us apart. How much of what we said was an attempt to not say something else? It was so easy to talk about everything—and so we did. Bad lettuce, broken sidewalks, static on the television, the way our fingers swelled in the summer. We became who we became because of what wasn't there. What wasn't there became what was.

Still, on these new very bad days, I considered bringing her up in order to awaken him. I would ask him if he missed her. If he'd ever looked for her. Most of all, I wanted to know what I'd done, what I'd stolen—to hear it from him. What we were was never enough.

But I'd never asked him about her. I was too afraid. I imagined saying *our daughter,* and his eyes lighting up.

Where is she? he would ask then. I had a recurring dream of him passing away in her arms, his face full of emotion, hers too, together.

He leaned back and I ran my fingers over his head, waiting for him to fall asleep. I sang a song that he used to sing to me when I was pregnant. It was the only time we used Arabic in America, in song. Even in our home, on quiet evenings alone on our couch, we insisted on being Americans. We made latkes for Hanukkah. We practiced our vowels. We listened to Buddy Holly and

Sinatra, and we watched *The Honeymooners*. Some nights, I'd fall asleep crying for Elizabeth Eckford.

"Okay," he said out of nowhere. "Let's go for a walk."

If I were ten years younger, I would have jumped up and clapped my hands. I would have given him a giant kiss on the mouth. But I didn't. We hadn't walked together in months.

I said to him, "Great." It sounded pathetic, weak. But my age had caught up to me recently. My mother used to say, "Only the wearer knows where the shoe pinches." It's true. I never imagined that one day my brain would be racing and my body would be unable to keep up. Like trying to start a car that won't turn over. I was so used to asking him constantly and hearing no response that the very exercise of asking felt like enough positive effort. Expectations change. And then again.

"Fantastic!" I said and gave a double thumbs-up, grateful that he wasn't looking at me but at the carpet, at the long trek to the door.

I prepared a small bag with water and painkillers and a granola bar. I carried an extra fleece in my arms and cab money in my shoe. I put on a backpack that concealed a collapsible chair.

Joseph was wearing navy sweatpants, one of my old cashmere sweaters, and a down coat that slumped onto his shoulders. He was a tiny cardboard cutout of himself. His outdoor slippers flapped against his feet. In the elevator, he held the rail so tightly that his knuckles lost their color. It bolstered me. He still had some strength, somewhere. I imagined him hugging me. I imagined that I wouldn't be able to get out of his embrace if I tried.

"Isn't this something?" I said. He blinked.

We began down Frederick Douglass Boulevard. The air was unseasonably warm for early December. The sun was all through setting. The outdoor restaurant on our corner smelled of garlic. People strolled. Their leather handbags shimmered in the streetlights. They smiled at me. They could see it too, these strangers. How old he'd gotten. How I'd been left. I wanted them not to walk so quickly. I wouldn't have minded if they'd stopped, said we were a handsome couple. We looked like we belonged together. It had been so long since I'd heard something nice. I found myself craving it, begging silently for it.

Joseph had had the spirit of a twenty-year-old until around his birthday a few years ago, when the cancer settled into his prostate like a snake curling into his lap. That was the year after we closed our restaurant; the year the winter was so cold we stayed in the house for days ordering in boxes of black tea, paper towels, and Chinese; the year we stopped cooking together.

His pace was so slow, so achingly slow, and soon my leg cramped because of it.

"I'm so proud of you," I said.

As he pushed forward, Joseph did a kind of back-and-forth maneuvering, an attempt to keep all his parts intact, to keep them from deserting him. After half a block, he stopped.

"What?" I asked, looking around.

He looked at me like I was breaking his heart.

"Shall we turn back?" I asked. In my head, I had the answer all ready. I wanted him to go on. I wanted him to walk steps ahead of me, to turn around and say, *C'mon, slowpoke. Hup two.*

"No," he growled instead. "We're walking."

I tightened my grip. He was giving it all he had. He continued his shuffle. I was rooting for him. We were going to make it.

"Damn it," he said.

"What?"

I smelled it before I saw it. Urine blooming like an ink stain on his sweatpants. I was suddenly exhausted. I wanted to be home. I hated myself for having been so selfish, for making him walk just for me. The wind had picked up. I hailed a cab. He collapsed into it, mouth gaping, chest heaving. I patted at the wet patch with a tissue.

"No, Victoria," he said. "Let it be."

We had to loop four blocks to get back. I passed a twenty to the driver as we got out. The meter hadn't even been started.

"Keep it," he said in Arabic. His face was angular and dark, like a strong-jawed animal's, like Joseph's when he was young. I had the urge to ask him if he'd ever been to Iraq. He was Egyptian, I could tell, but still. Joseph's father was alive when I left, and in hiding. For a moment, I imagined that he was living in the beautiful house in Sal-hee-yah where I'd grown up. That when he came downstairs our maid, Daisy, was rolling out *shakrlama* dough in the kitchen. She'd become his caretaker. I imagined we'd left him in good hands. Joseph never tried to contact him from America. He didn't have to. He said, "A son just knows."

Back on the sidewalk, Joseph put his arm around my shoulders.

"Sorry," he said quietly. "I was going to buy you a FrozFruit."

He took a five-dollar bill out of his pocket, God knows where it was from, and handed it to me. I wanted to ask him, as if it mattered, what kind he would have bought for me. Lime or cantaloupe. If he still remembered.

I put my head down, let the tears mass behind my eyes.

"Come," he said, nudging me toward our building with his weight.

We took the elevator up. It clicked along, slower than ever, smelling of steak.

On our landing stood Dottie, our upstairs neighbor of more than thirty years. She posed, her hands on her hips, and she wore one of her ridiculous robes, a hideous purple thing with giant velvet flowers like tarantulas around her neck. What was left of her orange hair was wrapped around tiny curlers. Seeing Joseph, she covered her head with her hands.

"Oh!" she said. "I wasn't expecting you to be up and about. For a handsome young man, I would have dressed."

She winked. I rolled my eyes and pretended to gag. It drove me mad, the way she swooped in with her sense of humor, making me look somber, un-fun, a killjoy. And Joseph reacted to it. He straightened up, really smiled. I wanted to tell her that she hadn't touched his catheter. *Do that,* I wanted to say, *and then let's see you chipper.*

"You were indisposed," Dottie said. "I stopped in for your *TV Guide.*" She shook it in the air. "Thank you."

I narrowed my eyes, trying to vanish her. I wanted to be home, just the two of us. Over the years, Joseph had been kind to Dottie, making it impossible for me to shut her out entirely—and I'd grown to tolerate her. And because in her whole life, she'd probably never been more than tolerated, she considered me her all and everything. Still, we couldn't have been more different. Her cosmetics, her Southern mannerisms, her taste in television. Sometimes I'd tell Joseph to imagine her in Baghdad, imagine her with no microwave or shimmering body lotion. "Don't be mean," he'd say, laughing. "She wouldn't hurt a fly." But there was something about her—a kind of entitlement to be anywhere, say anything that I had yet to get over. We'd never felt powerful like her. This country wasn't set up like that for us. Decades later, and the only reason I continued to mind my manners around her was so Joseph wouldn't find me cruel. Again.

His weight was getting heavier and heavier on me. My legs had begun to shake.

"Onward," I said. I grabbed around his body to get a better grip and sort of hoisted him, preparing for the final stretch. "Almost there."

"So," Dottie said, stalling us. "If we're all awake, would you like to invite me in?"

Then she stopped. Her face, always peppy and alert, fighting against the wrinkles, fell in on itself. She gasped.

"Oh my gracious," she said and covered her mouth.

I looked at her eyes, followed them down. I'd forgotten. How could I? I'd lifted Joseph's jacket and exposed him. His accident.

He was still soaked. He hadn't even complained. I wondered if he'd caught a chill, if I'd given my husband pneumonia.

"Dottie!" I said, suddenly enraged at her.

"Whoopsie-doo," she said, turning around and scooting up the stairs faster than I'd seen her move in years. "I'll be seeing y'all," she called back. "Happy dreams!"

I watched her, wanting to throw the collapsible chair at her strutting hips. I wanted to wrap Joseph up in my arms and hide him. Did she know what kind of pain he was in? Did she know what he'd been through? And this was how she treated him? Old age scared her, most of all when it crept up on her perception of herself. We'd known her for a million years. She'd aged too.

"I'm so sorry," I whispered to him. "She's a terrible witch."

"No," he said, kindest man in the world. "She is who she is."

I was imagining really telling Dottie off, screaming at her with my fist in her face.

"It's not her fault," he said and I wondered what I'd said out loud. He hadn't been this lucid in months. He was right, I thought. I wasn't angry at her. It wasn't real anger that I felt. But anger kept a lid on the sadness, kept me from feeling like the stewed prunes I fed my husband, that he couldn't feed himself.

In the study, I helped him onto the bed. He sighed when he was on his back. His eyes were closed. I turned off the lamp and lay with him with my shoes on. Outside the window, the sky was a deep blue yawn.

This room used to be nothing but books. Now pills and pill bottles had elbowed their way onto the shelves. Crumpled tissues and half-drunk glasses of red juice too. There were three active humidifiers perched on piles of books. There were four vases of browning flowers in dull water. Would it be so hard, so very taxing, for me to change them?

Later, in the living room, I took out the newspaper and stared at the headlines until they turned into gray froth. Ada, rabbit of a nurse, big-eared, round-eyed, and upright, arrived with her medicine bag.

"You relax," she said before I could offer to make coffee. "I'll take it from here."

She was my favorite. She didn't go on about her family problems or try to get Joseph to be lively for visitors like the others did. She brought interesting fruits from Chinatown, rubbed the skins, and asked him to smell her hands. She read our books while he slept. She hummed and burned candles to fight against the plasticky, unaired stink of the place. If I was sick, I'd like to have her sit by me, her hand on my head.

I opened the newspaper to an opinion piece that started with *Baghdad. Baghdad,* I thought. It was like a dream that became harder and harder to remember. There were whole sections of the city that I couldn't bring to mind. My memory had gotten woolly. Old-lady pilly, scratchy, woolly.

I read the first line three times, trying desperately to sort it out, but my mind was too thick. I wasn't what I used to be. I used to read ravenously. Now it felt as though the words got stuck behind my eyes. I'd tried to get back into cooking too, but I couldn't lift the heavy Dutch oven, and soup wasn't soup without it. The smell of shellfish made me sick. It didn't help that there were pills everywhere — on the cutting board, balancing on the sugar jar, always in danger of falling into something or being lost. I'd become superstitious. I didn't move them, feeling as though they bore some ghostly weight and that any sudden shift might provoke a temperamental force that had been relatively good to us so far, keeping Joseph alive.

I could do very little but walk. Sometimes in Central Park. Sometimes down Central Park West, over to Columbus, and all the way down to the La Fortuna bakery on Seventy-First Street. I'd plop onto a chair and order two mini cannolis but eat only one. On the way back, I'd rest on a bench and watch the elderly couples from the nursing home shuffle by, leaning into each other as if against some fierce wind only they could feel. Peas in a pod. Yogurt and cucumber. Dates and almonds. How things should be. We should have gotten old at the same rate, I thought. That's what you hope for, that's luck: not waiting around.

Now, in our apartment, the air wafted in from the street, refreshing and bright. I decided to go out again. I'd get a FrozFruit for Joseph in case he remembered later. Ada was reading him a Bellow story. She didn't laugh at the right parts but neither did he. His face was smiling. I loved how it could do that: smile without moving. Someone else, some stranger, would never have known that he was happy inside. But I did.

"I'm going for a walk," I said.

I put my cheek to his face. He didn't kiss me though I waited for it. It wasn't easy on the muscles, but I waited, hoping. He was gone again. Finally, disappointed and in a full-body cramp, I left. More than fifty years together and I was still telling myself not to take these things personally.

I headed south. The street was quiet and wet, the air thick. I'd been inside for only an hour, but it had hailed in that time. Little puddles winked along the curb. The buildings seemed bigger at night. For a moment, I imagined one crumbling, out of nowhere. Just crashing. Me getting trapped. It wasn't the pain I wondered about. It was Joseph. If he would miss me. If he would even know.

The moon was a butter smudge. I allowed myself to imagine our daughter looking at the same moon. It's such a cliché, everyone under the same sky. But it wasn't just that for me. I wanted to know that the sky was hopeful for her, that it seemed limitless and promising. I wanted to know that she didn't mind being vulnerable and that someone was holding her even when she looked away, despite me giving her up. That maybe she was loved even more for it, because of who she'd become. Call me an old goon but I imagined that one day she'd just show up—her feet turned in but her body strong like a dancer's—and that she wouldn't be angry. She'd be as curious as we were, maybe even grateful. Proof I'd been watching too much television.

I walked past doormen who nodded their heads, businessmen whose shoes clacked as they stepped out of cabs, streetlamps that poured down orange light, big dogs, little dogs, empty bags of chips that lifted with a tiny gust of wind, a dead tomato with half its skin beside it. People still dropped tomatoes. People still stepped on other people's garbage, I thought. Everything despite everything and maybe because of it—because my Joseph was dying.

And then it hit me, just when I was feeling most sorry for myself. He'd been smiling for her. For Ada. He didn't give me a kiss but he'd been smiling for her. I picked up my pace. For a moment, I thought of all the things he could be doing. If he could smile, what else could he do? Make his own tea? Help me sort papers? Maybe I didn't push him enough, but not everything was my fault.

I was angry. I walked until I hardly realized I was walking anymore. I was really moving. I sped up. I gave it my all. I didn't care how old I looked—that I had to swing my arms like I was putting out a fire, that you could hear my huffy breathing from here to Hoboken. Sweat broke out on my back and grabbed at my sweater. My chest pounded harder and harder. It was exhilarating. Two more blocks. I could do it. I felt part of the world again, for the first time in months, destructible and indestructible. These emotions, this anger. Jealousy is invigorating in small doses. I knew I'd read that somewhere. This was part of a relationship. Part of being alive. It thrilled me for a second to think that we were still active in something, both of us. Still him and her.

For a moment, I was caught in a memory of a place that no longer existed. I was eighteen years old, combing my mother's hair in her bedroom. Two days before, she'd thrown herself from our balcony, desperate for my father to notice her, something. She was so sick then, her truths oozing out of her like a night sweat. My father had turned his back to speak to her, her face ravaged by the fall. "You look like a bad watermelon, rotten," he'd said. "I cannot bear to look at you." She begged him to stay with her but he left. He was a wearing a perfectly ironed shirt, English-tailored and white. I remember thinking, *I will never love a man who looks this civilized, this kempt.* As I combed her hair that morning, I looked out the window. There was Joseph, two steps behind his father, following the call of the *shamash,* shouting, *"Abu rahmin!"* Kicked-up sand coated just the backs of his pant legs, as if he'd fallen into a spill of Bedouin yogurt. I'd seen him before on his way from the Hinnuni bazaar. Our eyes locked. He didn't look away. He stopped walking altogether. For a moment, I thought he was going to throw something at me. But he didn't. We just stayed like that, looking. Joseph squinted his eyes—was that a smile?—and put his hand on his belly. With the other hand, he wiggled his fingers. It was a smile. It was a wave. He wiggled some more. I gasped, laughed out loud. He mouthed, *Are you all right?* He must have heard. I nodded. He pointed to the sun, then to where it would be at around four o'clock. Then he pointed to where he was standing. I would meet him here. *Yes.* I nodded. Thank you.

Our love affair lasted nearly a year in Baghdad. Often, we met at the Suq el-Haraj, where my family never shopped and where no one would recognize me. We walked along al-Mutanabbi Street, pretending we had important business. We stood together on the summer riverbed when the Tigris and the Euphrates had fully receded. When my father was at the Mee-Dan until the wee hours of the morning, we could be alone on the roof on my bed (which we'd brought up for the season), drawing invisible lines between the formations of stars. We loved to watch the stars. Joseph gave me everything I'd never had: affection, attention, hope. All the while, our relationship was a secret. We weren't the same, he and I. My father would never have let us marry. "An aggressive rooster," he liked to say, "yells when he is still in the shell." Joseph was poor but good. His heart was the purring engine in his chest, motivating everything he ever did. My father would never have understood. TB took my mother two months after we met.

Joseph went to the United States before me, preemptively, sure of what Baghdad was about to become. I wanted to go with him, of course. My father said over his dead body. So it was. He was a wealthy Jew, my father, and so suspected of Zionism. He was too proud. He'd always been too proud. I left the day before he was hanged. The only bit of kindness he ever showed me was when he woke me in the dead of night and pointed to the car across the street. "Go," he said. He'd sewn my mother's gold into the hem of my coat. There was nothing left for me. "Go," he said again. I went. I crept into the car packed with strangers. We sat in that car like matches in a matchbox and were driven for what felt like forever. When a baby coughed, his mother put her hand over his mouth. She didn't mean to but she killed him. Can you believe that? She didn't even cry out when she could no longer feel his pulse. She choked on her own breath and it sounded like her insides were drowning. Later, I woke up to a Bedouin with a dagger over my face. "Give me your sweater," he said. God knows why he didn't want my coat. And the whole time, from the moment I left to the moment I arrived at Ellis Island, I kept thinking of Joseph. Happy, bright thoughts that prevented my body from shaking with cold and the grief of leaving everything I ever knew. Sometimes I think I would have shivered to death without him.

In New York, everything changed. I thought love would come easily and I'd be good at it. I'd waited my whole life. We had nothing except for the clothes on our backs, feelings of betrayal and anger and nostalgia for a country that refused to keep us, and a rental with so many roaches that I slept with the covers over my head. I worked nights as a restaurant hostess and developed an allergy to peanuts. And though I was happy to be with Joseph, I couldn't bear feeling so vulnerable. The idea of love doesn't account for a fear of loss. In loving him, I grew afraid of losing him, more and more by the day. New York glittered; each light, I thought, was something else to take him from me. Something else for him to love more than me. Without him, I would be worse than just alone—I'd be alone after not being alone. It was possible, I realized, to hold on to something too tight, to suffocate it. In Baghdad, it had been different. Nothing was so precious. But in New York, I held on too tight. I'm not sure how to explain the feeling that's left when love is sacrificed in the name of love. Surely it's something hollowed out and dry.

That place where I'd watched him from my window was long gone. I could find it on a map but that was all. And there were so many maps of it, twinkling with blue arrows and American-flag graphics on the television. A battleground now. A writhing sandstorm. A grainy whirl of limbs; eyebrows as thick as mine over eyes peeking out from a broken window; blood and enormous green tanks creeping along like crocodiles until—*boom!*—another fountain of sand burst from the earth and floated down like glitter. Another twenty-one, fifty-four, eighty-six, thirty-three, sixty-two dead, said that banner gliding across the bottom of the screen. You cannot glide across sand. Another forty-five, seventy-eight, one hundred Baghdadi citizens dead, it said. And here we were with unbroken windows all around us.

On the day before Joseph left for the United States, I snuck to that place that's no longer there to see Joseph Shohet at his father's stall. *Shohet* means "chicken slaughterer." Before Joseph and his father killed the chicken, they felt under the feathers, checking for good meat. Legally, they had to kill it in one stroke. It sounded like a whip. Joseph's hands were sticky and so he kept them folded behind his back when he came to me. He put his toes over my toes. We were barefoot. He didn't kiss me. He hovered his lips over my lips. His nose over my nose. We stayed there like that, training ourselves. It might be a while until we'd see each other again. He would go first. We didn't know how long it might take. We were hiding behind a huge white wall covered in rose vines. Later, at home, I found a chicken feather stuck to my ankle. I arrived at Ellis Island more than a year later with the feather stuffed into my shirt, parallel to my spine, a mere needle then, barely recognizable.

I was almost home. Three tight knots of dog poo were perched on the sidewalk, as if from an icing piper. I stepped off the curb, around the broken hydrant, and to the railings. A couple of beer cans lay crushed in the flower bed. The smell of boric acid was strong in the lobby. I thought I'd heard the five-hundred-pound exterminator yesterday.

I walked to the elevator. Six steps and always six. Once it was four. The elevator light passed from the fourth to fifth floor, where it stopped, stalled, broken for the hundredth time this year. I walked up the three flights as slowly as can be, a little pain in my chest. There was graffiti on the second floor from the rascals in 2B who never got their hair cut. *JanICE,* the graffiti said. They could have been more creative. Silly boys, always on their skateboards, banging into our door and startling my heart. And the landing lights were broken again. The TV yammered in Dottie's apartment above us. *Survivor.* What else do you need to know about her?

Ada was waiting at the door. The single curl of gray hair at her left eye. She put her arms around my shoulders and pulled me to her. Dear heavens, she was strong. She did yoga, surely. Chin-ups too, I bet.

"Miss Victoria," she whispered in my ear.

She held me. I was everywhere else. Down the hall, green rain boots, welcome mat, umbrella, slash marks on a door from a crowbar, and next door, the door frame, white paint with a tan rectangle from where old lady Kratzner's mezuzah once was. We didn't have one. We didn't want the attention. I blamed that now. We should have. I blamed everything.

I knew from the words. Of course I did. From the way that she said them. It was that easy. I wasn't stupid.

"Miss Victoria, Miss Victoria," she said.

Miss who?

Miss me?

How long had that mezuzah been gone? It would have taken so little to fix the door frame. A dollop of paint. Wite-Out, for goodness' sake. Toothpaste even. Ada's gray curl played leapfrog now. She was moving her head around like she was an unhappy cow. She had lovely eyes like one too. A nutty brown. Long lashes. She didn't need to say it. She had experience in this. The eyes did it for her. What a waste of words, of good, useful breath.

"He has passed," she said.

Her mouth moved. Her teeth were the color of white lilies. Her lips the color of something more tropical. A gentle sprinkling of dark freckles was cast across her nose and cheekbones. Any face can become enchanting if you stare at it long enough.

"So so sorry," she said.

I was a tall building crumbling. I was a tall building with the insides ripped out. I thought I might faint.

Once, years ago, I fainted. I never told Joseph. Couldn't. It might have been dehydration. That's what the doctor insisted. I'd been in the hospital. I'd given birth. Given. Funny, you give. I gave birth. I gave her up. A few days later, I was walking down the street alone—I saw a child, I smelled dairy, the baby smell, and the blackness came. The sudden wispiness of the world around me. The chilly cold. And down I'd gone, collapsing like the ingénue in a musical. When I came to, a stranger told me he'd thought I was faking. My hand went to my forehead, he said. A high-pitched sigh. I fell as if I were dancing, as if someone had forgotten to catch me. I couldn't tell Joseph. It would have been the crack in my armor.

Now the blackness came toward me in a sequence of shots. Ink from a squid. I felt soaked and heavy. But Ada was here. She was keeping me upright. I stepped out of her embrace. The corridor wobbled. I put out my arms for balance and whacked my wrist against the door frame. I went into the study, saw him: the cashew color of his face, the sluglike scar on the left side of his nose. The oriental carpet was a heap of autumn colors. The metal mechanism that turned the sofa into a bed was exposed where the sheet had lifted, skeletal. He was on his back. He was lying on his back.

Joseph didn't move. He hadn't moved. It was Ada's fault. It had to be. I had not done this. My heart was pumping in my throat and in my wrists and in my gums and in the hairless spaces behind my ears.

He wasn't dead. He could not be dead. I watched, waiting for his belly to lift.

"Say *Victoria,* Joseph." I might have said this out loud, or maybe not. I might have tried it in Arabic after that. If I'd known how to speak Russian, I would have tried that too.

This is it, I thought. The moment I'd been waiting for. I had not been waiting for him to get better. For months, this was all I'd imagined, all the time. Scenario after scenario of how I'd find out that he was gone—the sound I'd make, the socks I'd be wearing, if I'd just have opened a can of seltzer and if I'd drop it or waste time finding a place to put it down, if my heart would stop along with his. I'd imagined it, but it hadn't come. Now it was here and I was alive.

What I hadn't imagined was this eerie stillness of his body. The sudden absence.

"Joseph?" I said it impatiently, like I was calling him for dinner.

"He is gone," Ada said.

"Gone where?" I said that out loud. Gone to the store. Gone to bed. Gone to heaven. Gone to the store to buy the bed that sits in heaven. Suddenly, I believed in heaven.

"I will take care of everything," I whispered, as if words might be enough to lure him back. I promised him that I'd open an Iraqi pastry shop. I lied.

"We will sell the vanilla cake with pomegranate sauce, the date truffles, the cardamom cookies, the *shakrlama*." All the things he loved. Things we had served night after night at the restaurant. Things that might have, if anything could have, perked him up, brought him back. I said this as if all of a sudden he might open his eyes and say he'd love a cookie, thank you very much. And I would have raced to the kitchen and there would have been a platter of them, piled high and hot.

"Everything will be all right," I said. I was aware of the weight of the sky, the blood careering through my veins, the cold slippery feeling of my feet, a bus somewhere down the street, its long, labored exhale. Lucky breath.

And then I was saying, "I will find our daughter." I didn't care if Ada could hear. She'd known nothing. Now she knew everything. I wasn't thinking of myself. "I promise," I said.

This was where it happened—on a pull-out couch after sunset on a Friday, with the smell of latex gloves in the room, of browning garlic outside, dirty white socks on the floor stiff as old bones, our old old building clanking like a madman was inside the pipes, two books on the shelf tipped toward each other and making room for a vase of dead purple flowers, me on my knees with my face on an unbeating heart while everything else around us continued to move, in its way, or be moved, for something hopeful in the future.

"I will find her," I said, meaning it. "It wasn't your fault. It was mine. She will love you still."

Lorca

I DIDN'T SLEEP a wink. The morning after overhearing my mother reveal her favorite meal of life, I lay in bed, awake before everybody, hoping desperately that a brilliant idea about how to track down the masgouf recipe would dawn on me. My hope was that my mother had written various versions somewhere as she tried to perfect it and stashed away the best one on a tiny piece of paper so all I had to do was find it, master it, and *fini!* that would be that. But there were three problems with this. First, my mother kept very few things. You couldn't find a single one of my kid drawings or report cards if you tried. I doubt she even had her own Social Security card. Second, what she did keep, she kept in a box below the couch where she slept. Where she was sleeping now. Third, my mother had said that even she couldn't replicate the dish, so if she'd written it down, and if by some miracle I was able to find it, the odds of my making something halfway decent from that recipe were slim to none. Closer to none.

Still, hopelessness is about as useful as rotten eggs. I hadn't had a good idea since the maple bacon and caramelized banana ice cream sandwiches that were now included on the brunch menu at Le Canard Capricieux, and my mother would be home all day, so I told myself that if I was going to do something, I'd better do it now. If I waited till she woke up, I'd wait for hours. When I couldn't stay in bed any longer, I went into the living room, got down on my hands and knees, and crawled across the floor. If she woke up from my movement, I'd just say I was de-fuzzing the carpet. Staying flat was harder than I'd expected; my arms quivered. But at this time of day, my mother was very sensitive to light. I couldn't move too quickly and I couldn't stand up. If even a piece of a shadow crossed her face, I'd be toast. I put one elbow in front of the other. She hiccupped. I went flat. I waited a minute. I kept going. When I was two feet from the couch, out of nowhere, very loudly and very clearly, my mother said, "Christ." I was sure she was awake and about to ask me what I thought I was doing, but she just flipped onto her left side, away from the room and me.

I looked at my elbows. They were covered in rug fuzz. I reached my arm under the couch. Just then, Lou's alarm went off in her bedroom. My heart stopped. I knocked my chin on the floor and bit my tongue. Only when I heard the shower turn on and Lou get in did I resume my quest. I had to stick half my body beneath the couch to reach the little shoebox. I grabbed it and raced to my bedroom, jumping when the door slammed behind me.

I poured everything onto the bed. There were dozens of napkins stamped with the names of my mother's favorite restaurants—most of which I recognized, none of which sounded Middle Eastern. I went through every single one. There was a replica of one of Julia Child's mixing spoons, a tiny burned thing, that my father bought from the Smithsonian gift shop. There was a small bouquet of dried lavender whose flowers were now spewed all over my bed like fleas. The only good news was that there was a photo of my mother as a child, which I stuffed into the flap of my father's old lumberjack hat to examine later. She hated photos of herself, and the only picture I could remember seeing was one my father had taken when they'd gone to the

Berkshires. Her face was like something from an old movie. I'd found a treasure, and yet, no recipe. No restaurant. No nothing.

I shook everything out again before I put it all back, just to be sure I wasn't missing something. I gently nudged the box back under the couch just as Lou turned off the shower and turned on her electric toothbrush.

Next, I scoured the Internet, searching for the restaurant, for any Iraqi restaurant in New York—for anything about it, reviews or photos or menus. Then for any Middle Eastern restaurant that had closed years ago. Nothing. Then for any Middle Eastern restaurant that hadn't closed. Nothing helpful. I found lots of street carts and distribution corporations in Brooklyn. *New York* magazine mentioned a Syrian place in the theater district. So I took the portable phone and, balancing the laptop in one arm and opening the door silently with the other, went out of the apartment and into the hallway. Then I called, even though it was six thirty in the morning.

I plopped down next to the elevator.

When someone picked up and said hello, I was deep in the archives of Chowhound and almost forgot to respond.

"Hello," he said again in a very nonprofessional, non-restaurant-host voice. He had thick throat congestion and a heavy accent. I wanted to say *A-hem* before we continued. I imagined my mother. *Lorca! Manners!* But at Le Canard Capricieux, the GM hired the hostess based on her phone voice: *GoodeveninglecanardcapricieuxhowmayIassistyou?*

"Sorry," I said. "Maybe I have the wrong number? I'm looking for a restaurant."

"This is a restaurant," he said. "We're not open for breakfast. We're not open for lunch either. And soon, we're not open for dinner."

"Are you closing?" I said and because I didn't think it through, I got hopeful.

"Department of Health says we've got rats. I don't think that's the end of the world but they do and so does my wife."

"Oh," I said. "I'm sorry. Do you make masgouf?" I whispered the word, not wanting my mother to hear.

"Masgouf!" he yelled back. "Syria has only forty-four kilometers of the Tigris. Iraq has the whole thing. Masgouf is from the Tigris. Fish from freshwater Tigris water. We don't have any masgouf here."

"Okay, and—" I started but he interrupted me.

"Are you a critic? I can make you masgouf. You want masgouf? Do you have funding?"

"No," I said. "Sorry."

He said, "I'm sorry too. Have a happy holiday."

It wasn't a holiday as far as I knew but he hung up before I could ask him about it.

Chowhound turned up nothing on masgouf. Neither did MenuPages. I searched through Indian and Turkish restaurants. I called the Syrian guy back and asked him if he knew of any Iraqi restaurants in Manhattan and he said, "First, you want Iraqi dish. Now you want Iraqi restaurant. We're Syrian! What can we do about it?"

I said sorry and hung up for the second time.

I went back into the apartment.

Lou walked into the living room with her blouse on inside out. I was about to tell her when she put a finger over her lips, telling me to shush. She pointed to my sleeping mother. She put on her coat and rustled her keys. On her way out, she let the door slam. She opened it again.

"Sorry, Nance," she half whispered and blew my mother a kiss.

Oh, and T.G.I.F., she mouthed to me before it occurred to her that I hadn't left for school, and then she remembered what had happened yesterday. When she did, she threw her hands up as if to say that we'd once been on the same team and I'd deserted her. But we hadn't been. Ever.

I learned online that the previous month, the restaurant in Baghdad with the best masgouf had been blown up by a car bomb. It killed thirty-five people. There was a photo of a little boy crouching next to a corpse. His knees were wide, like he was about to jump up for leapfrog. His hair was still parted perfectly like little boys' hair can be only when their mothers spend extra time. His hands were wrapped around the dead man's feet, covered in blood like water-soaked oven mitts.

I closed the screen.

I couldn't look at other people's blood. Only mine.

It was nearly noon when I decided I'd done all the research that I could possibly do at home—and I was no closer to finding the masgouf. For a moment, I wondered if somehow my mother was tricking me, trying to distract me. There might be no restaurant at all, no sacred recipe. This was all just to keep me busy and out of her way until I was sent to boarding school. You could never be sure with my mother. I wouldn't give up so easily.

I put my hair up and down and up and down four times before I managed to get out the door and to the bookstore. I wasn't usually so fussy, but I was thinking of Blot. Finally, I braided it tight the way that my dad used to like and then took it out a short while later so it was crimpy. I brushed my teeth and flossed and used the tongue scraper even though it wasn't like I was planning on kissing him. Not even a little.

Before I left, I told my mother I was going out. She was lying on her back on the couch and she flipped her head toward me. It was like an oven opening, the sudden gush of flushed light. Ever since I was a child, I'd wanted to savor that exact moment when I was leaving, the brief second in which she looked at me, acknowledging that tiny bit of mystery in my departure, *my* leaving *her,* for a change, the possibility that I might not come back. It had always seemed to me that I might never see her again—even when I was with her, it felt constantly like she was just coming or going.

Of course, I'd probably do better at the library, find out more, but Blot didn't work at a library.

At the bookstore, I collected three books: one on Middle Eastern cuisine, one on favorite fish dishes of Manhattan, and one with two hundred applications for watercress. My mother loved watercress.

It was quieter than usual even for a Friday. There was a reading going on in the children's section. The mothers were bouncing their legs. Strollers were positioned in a line. I slunk around the store as if I might get in trouble for being school age and not in school.

I went to the third floor's standardized-test section because it was deserted. Also because the books were big enough to reach the fronts of the shelves, so when I sat and leaned back against them, it wasn't like leaning back against the top of a picket fence. Sometimes I wanted to say to someone—and the someone was always my mother—*Look. See? It isn't all the time. I can help myself. I'm not a danger to myself or to others. There's no reason to send me away. Look at me just sitting here. Look at me trying to be comfortable.*

The week before, I'd read a whole book on mushrooms, and later I'd said something to my mother about morels and she'd said, "Hey now! Look at you, daughter of my heart." My chest tingled with bubbles until she went ballistic on the phone to one of her sous-chefs, who'd quit. And on a Saturday. If I'd picked up first I would have told him that it was not a good idea and that he should trust me because if I knew anything, I knew my mother. After that, she said she couldn't even speak. She turned on the TV so loud that I had to move some of the pieces in Aunt Lou's porcelain poodle collection so they wouldn't shimmy off

nd shatter. The sous-chef debacle cut off my morel
t had even begun.

here because Blot's desk was no more than ten steps away.

I had plopped down in a nice little spot where I could see him. My pulse did jumping jacks. He was in charge of this section—self-help, test-taking, *libros en español*. He had blond hair, flushed cheeks, and roughed-up leather boots that looked like they belonged to a different century. The bottoms of his pants were stained with black but he rolled them up so that it looked like dark cuffs. It occurred to me that maybe this was intentional, like he was too busy reading to take the stuff to the laundry. He wasn't dirty. A number of times, I had imagined myself smelling his chest, but I tried to stop thinking that way, realizing how insane it was. He kept a book in his back pocket and a pencil behind his ear. His hair was long enough that he was always touching it, swatting it away from his face like some kind of stubborn bug. I wondered what it looked like wet, if it stuck to his head like a little kid's, like mine. Now I imagined him leading me to a very secret place in Central Park with the biggest trees you've ever seen and a twig canopy. He'd read from a book and for some reason it was in Portuguese, which for some reason I understood. I told myself to get a grip, which is like trying to sear scallops in liquid.

He wore his nametag on his collar, and I loved how his name was stranger than mine. I liked to think it was a loving nickname, maybe from his baby sister who couldn't pronounce Blake or Blaise, though he didn't look like either of those. He used to have a skateboard that he tooled around on until his manager said, "Hey." I could tell, though, adults couldn't stay mad at him. In that way, he was the opposite of me.

He carried a huge stack of shiny books wrapped in plastic, and when he walked by he gave me a little wave, keeping his elbow tight to his side. I looked around. There was no one but me. Me? I looked at my lap. I looked up. He was waiting. It was the first time he'd waved. Usually, he'd tighten his lower lip, a kind of acknowledgment, as I'd been here a thousand times. I'd tighten mine back. I practiced it in the mirror to be sure I didn't look like a duck. *Now what,* I thought. I had already done my lip thing. Or had I? I couldn't remember now. So I did it again but my mouth was stiff like I'd been sucking on frozen peach slices. I was relieved when he started walking again. At least I hadn't done something hugely ridiculous like yelling a *Hey, Blot!* and waving with octopus arms. It occurred to me that I'd been staring at him for far too long. Probably he had to wave. Probably he was just being polite.

I needed to start looking for the recipe, but I was distracted.

I was sweating. I shouldn't have walked so quickly. My mother liked to say that I scurried like a pigeon. I took off my backpack and sweater. The bandage on my leg was thin, and, I noticed, the blood had leaked through. A dot of purple stained the pants on my thigh. Stupid Kanetha Jackson. She'd startled me. Made the knife go straight in. I went to the nurse. They made me. I was fine. The nurse was mousy. She never looked me in the eye and must have thought that I was some kind of vamp nut. But when the goose bumps came, she put her hand flat out on my thigh and kept it there, as if blessing me. I wanted to put my fingers between her clean, unfancy mother hands. I wondered about her own children, about whether she sat with them in the mornings and watched them eat breakfast. I bet she did. I bet she made them eat oatmeal—or pancakes, if they must, but blueberry buckwheat. *Something with a little heft,* she'd say, opening the fridge and reaching for the milk.

My mother was always sleeping in the mornings; I'd become a professional tiptoe. A professional silent French-toast maker too. You couldn't blame her for being tired. She had a staff of thirty-five but some of them were so unprofessional. Sometimes a prep chef would just not show up. I wanted to tell them what they did to her. How they wore on her nerves.

I put my jacket over my legs, put on my sweater, and made sure Blot hadn't seen the blood, which he hadn't. I didn't even know where he'd gone.

I took out my notebook and opened the book about Middle Eastern cuisine. It was divided up by region. Iraq took up only six pages, and three of them were recipes for desserts. I was about to get up when Blot's shoe appeared on the gray carpet beside my leg. My heart did that sighing thing again, and out of nowhere I felt like I had to pee. I glanced up and held my jaw tight so I didn't look like a smiling dimwit. I narrowed my eyes, pretending something was bright. It kept the grinning at bay.

"What are you doing?" he asked. "You always look so busy."

"What am I doing?" I repeated, no better than an intelligent parrot. "I'm researching," I said. I gestured to my notebook and hoped that he couldn't see my notes. I'd drawn his shoe one day, next to a recipe for Ina Garten's savory coeur à la crème. I thought, *It wouldn't take much to recognize your own shoe.* I got lightheaded. I covered the pages with my hands.

"Researching what?" he asked.

"I don't know. Stuff," I said too harshly. I hoped he wouldn't go away.

He sat down next to me and rested his arms on his knees. His legs were so long and thin that he could have tied them into knots. He moved his hair out of his face. He smelled of detergent and deli, which meant bacon. I took this as a very good sign. I was into bacon. My mother had said, one day when she loved me, "I want to wrap you up in bacon and put you on a silver tray."

"Stuff," he repeated. He rubbed his chin, pretending to be

old, though he was probably only nineteen, five long years older than me.

"You know," I said. "Like, stuff." It felt like there was cheesecloth between my brain and me.

"I'm a stuff specialist," he said. "So if you need any help, I'm Blot."

"I know," I said, and in a moment of rare clarity, I pointed to his nametag so I didn't seem like a stalker who might also know his birthday, address, and mother's maiden name. He smiled. He didn't ask me my name. He just sat there, not really waiting for anything, just sort of being there, with or without me. Quiet. I'd never been good at that. Aunt Lou said that a lady should refrain from blurting but I couldn't help it: I'd become someone who snuffed out silence.

I blurted, "I'm Lorca." Blot's dimples flashed but didn't make him look young. I had nowhere to look, so I looked at his fingers. Black lines were under his nails as if he'd scraped off all the words of a book, page by page by page. He put his hands into his pockets. I wanted to tell him that I wasn't grossed out, that he shouldn't be embarrassed, and that I was always embarrassed too. I wanted to tell him that I would like to see his fingers again. I hadn't meant to make him uncomfortable.

"Lorca," he said softly to his shoes. No one had ever said my name like that. "Wasn't Lorca the gay one?" he asked, out of nowhere. "Wasn't he the one they shot?"

"No," I snapped, hating myself for a second but also not needing Blot to think that my parents wanted me dead.

"Yes," he said. "I know I read that somewhere."

"No," I said again. And then: "Yes." When the sound repeated in my head, it was impatient and rude.

"That's cool, though," Blot said. "It's cool to be named after a poet guy."

I wanted to tell him, but didn't, that my father had named me after Federico García Lorca because he wrote about the moon's white petticoats and the gypsies. (I didn't speak Spanish, but I memorized the whole poem in its original language when I was seven, and when I recited it to my father, tears came to his eyes and he kissed my face all over, again and again. *El niño la mira, mira.*) And because my mother had still loved my father then, when I was born, she'd let him choose my name.

I wanted to ask Blot what he knew about Lorca. Why else a father might have named his daughter after him. Maybe, I thought, I could feel closer to him, knowing those things. Blot got up. I whispered, "Wait," but reconsidered and did a pretty good cover-up:

"His first play," I said, "was actually *El maleficio de la mariposa,* not *Mariana Pineda.* It's about a cockroach and a butterfly who fall in love. It's a common misconception that it was *Mariana Pineda.*"

I was an idiot. Where did I get this stuff? He must know that I loved him. What else?

"Cool," Blot said. There went the dimples again. They made me forget to breathe out.

"Thank you," I said. Stupid. Moron. Idiot.

Just as Blot was walking away, it occurred to me that if I really wanted to find the recipe and save myself, I couldn't waste any time.

"Hey," I blurted, a little spit flying. "Do you have any older issues of *Zagat*?" My face went hot and numb as it occurred to me that this was a bookstore and not a library and why would they?

"Well, no," he said. "We replace them every year. We have the newest one downstairs."

Obviously. Then I lied. "Oh, the old ones are very valuable," I said. "The Strand has some in their rare-book collection."

"We don't," he said. "Are you looking for something specific?"

Specifically, I wanted to know if he wanted to search for the masgouf with me. If he wanted to traipse around the city and hold my hand and maybe eat a hundred different dishes until we found the one that would make my mother go bananas, in a good way. His presence would change everything. That was the specific question I wanted to ask him. And the specific answer I was looking for was *I'd love to. I can't wait.* That's what I wanted him to say.

Then, carefully, I explained the situation to him—excluding all the parts about getting in trouble, boarding school, hurting myself, and the romantic bits featuring him. He said, "Is it a special birthday or something? Is that why you want to make your mother the fish?" I hadn't expected that. I hadn't expected that it might seem strange that I would go to Mars and back for my mother for no good reason. You'd think I'd have realized how weird this was earlier, years before, but I hadn't.

My mother was an enigma, fickle, unknowable, like a giant fish. She loved me in fits and spurts. Lou said that she was how she was because she was adopted. "Someone didn't love her enough. How about cutting her a little slack?" I told her one thousand times a day how much I loved her, hoping the words would do the trick, but they didn't. I had to show her love on her own terms, remind her of her kind of happiness. The masgouf was the perfect thing. The only thing.

"Yeah," I lied. "It's a big birthday this year."

"Cool," he said. "Let's see what we've got."

I seemed totally normal for a minute, and, I thought, it had taken me only a million lies to get there.

We spent the next few hours looking through books about New York City restaurants and then books about Middle Eastern cuisine. The most astonishing part of the whole thing was how comfortable I felt. Blot's co-workers walked by and nodded to him and then to me, as if I were someone they knew. And I said "Hey!" to them, not even caring how high or stupid my voice sounded. We sat on the floor. Every so often, he had to get up and go to his desk, to make sure everything was status quo, and when he came back and sat down, I very discreetly watched the space on the carpet—to gauge whether he'd come closer or moved farther off. Also, I devised a way to hold my sleeves in my hands, over my wrists. My whole wrists. It didn't look awful. It looked like a thing. I pretended I was him looking at me. I didn't seem nuts.

"Are you cold?" he asked at one point.

"Always," I said, and felt brilliant. He might want to protect me, I thought. One day, he might offer me his coat.

"Me too," he said. "I'm from Baltimore. The 'South.'" He made quotation marks with his fingers.

I laughed. And though I couldn't place Baltimore on a map, I wasn't an idiot. I knew a thing or two about Maryland crabs and that it had to be a tiny bit warmer there than here.

In the end, there was nothing in the books about the restaurant. There were, however, a couple of recipes for masgouf. One said that you absolutely must catch the fish in the Tigris or the Euphrates and cook it over an open fire using apricot logs. The history books said that carp was used exclusively, but the modern recipes improvised with red snapper and salmon and, in one case, catfish.

"How about the lake in Central Park?" Blot asked.

"I think the Hudson would work," I joked, and he did a double thumbs-up. We found another book that said fish from the Tigris and Euphrates absolutely should not be consumed because of the many bodies that had been dumped in those rivers. Islamic religious leaders had issued fatwas on the poor creatures. Blot gave me a little elbow jab and said, "Wowie." The feeling of his touching me echoed on my skin for hours.

"Your Hudson River idea is sounding better and better," he said, and even my toes blushed.

I tried not to examine him even when I didn't think he was looking. One dimple was bigger than the other. One eye was slightly lazy. There was a tiny divot, like a thumbprint, in the middle of his bottom lip. His eyelashes were not only long but also wet-looking, making his eyes seem brighter, like he'd been swimming for hours in the cleanest, coldest lake.

We learned that the fish must be cut down its back, not its belly. I didn't tell Blot that the only time I'd ever butterflied a fish, my mother had stopped me midway through and told me I was taking too many short strokes. What was I trying to do? Make it into chum? Instead, I told him I had no idea how to butterfly a fish, had never even thought about it. He said, "Let's find out!" And he set off in search of another book that might teach us how. Every time he came back to me, I realized that I'd been holding my breath.

"The restaurant might have been right around here, near Eighty-Fifth Street," I said. "That's where my father used to stay when he came to the city, at this fancy banker's guest townhouse. He had built all their furniture."

It was easy to explain my weird family to him when we were both turning pages, not looking at each other.

"Well," Blot said, "how about this? How about we try just walking around? This neighborhood's full of old folk. Someone must know something."

I was silent. He'd said "we."

"I just happen to be free," he added. For a second, I wondered if he simply felt sorry for me. If he was trying to be nice and was channeling a very fancy great-aunt who had taught him well. But it didn't seem that way. From the bottom of my heart, I swear that it didn't. It felt honest.

I gave out a too-happy puff of air and then sucked in and kind of snorted.

"Want to go after work?" he asked. "I get off at seven."

A chill shot down my spine. I wanted to be close to him. I wanted to tell him all my secrets and I didn't want to tell him any. I wanted to show him my foot, my whole arm, to know if he'd find me disgusting, awful. Just to know. I wondered if everyone had that. The one thing a person always wanted to say forever and ever to get herself out of things and into things. The one thing that mattered the most.

"Okay," I said instead. "I'll come back."

On the street, out of habit, I thought of ways to hurt myself. It would have been so easy to do it then. It was dark out. Our block was always quiet except in the morning, when people sat in their cars as the street sweeper passed through. But now it would be deserted.

All sorts of crazy things went through my head—me and Blot tapping on fish tanks at the pet store; me and Blot collecting lost mittens in the snow; me and Blot tangled in a big coffee-shop chair, reading about Ugli fruit and sharing a cranberry-walnut muffin. I spent what seemed like hours wondering what he liked for dinner. I imagined his apartment with a worn wooden table and huge, rickety windows that looked out onto two, maybe three bridges. I bet he cooked for his cool musician friends, mixing spaghetti and sauce and cheese in one giant pot and folding toilet paper into triangles for napkins. I wondered if he would tell them that there was some crazy girl at work who was obsessed with him. But in my true heart, that's not what I imagined he'd say. I imagined him telling them my name, saying it just like he'd said it to me: *Lorca.* Like the *o* was a bubble that he nudged gently off his tongue. *L. Ooorc. Ca.*

I kept my mind on him, and my whole body felt lighter, like there was some strong, warm current moving around me. And I did nothing bad. For hours, I kept myself in check.

My mother had every other Friday off.

After I got home from the bookstore, I decided to make dinner for her and Aunt Lou. If they were eating or full, it would be easier for me to leave to meet Blot for our not-date. I would bustle around the kitchen and then bustle out the door. Usually, I was on the couch. If I got up for some orange juice, my mother said, "Where are you off to, little girl?" and even if it was nowhere, I'd have to do a whole song and dance.

Pasta arrabbiata. Lidia Bastianich used pepperoncini and prosciutto ends for hers. Me too. I set the table and lit candles. I was happy. I hadn't hurt myself. I hadn't done one thing. I even shaved my legs like a normal person. I'd kept thinking, in the shower, *Look at me! Look at me do this!* I put on clean jeans and socks that matched and I took more than four seconds to braid my hair. I didn't put on music but I found myself humming. I kept thinking, *He'll forget. He didn't mean it.* But actually, in my heart of hearts, I believed he did.

I said, "Dinner's served!" Aunt Lou told me not to shout.

Just when we were all ready to start, my mother looked at her plate and said, "You know what *arrabbiata* means, right?"

I had a feeling about where this conversation was going.

"It means 'angry,'" she said. "Like a red-hot Sicilian woman. Aurelio made it for me the night I left him. He had no idea it was coming. So ironic. So ironic! He took the whole bowl of it and threw it against the wall. That's how much he cared."

Aurelio was a man she'd dated in Italy. That's all I knew about it.

I wanted them to eat. I wanted them to hurry so I could pretend to be busy cleaning up. I hadn't stopped smiling. No one said a thing and I was actually grateful for that: For once, I appreciated it.

"You never should have left him," Lou said, all dreamy, picking out all the pepperoncini and making a decorative little clump of them in the middle of the table. I put them in a saucer and she glared at me.

"I know," my mother said, and she swirled a piece of basil around her plate until I finished my pasta. "I definitely shouldn't have left."

The phone rang. I jumped up and then felt stupid. Blot didn't have my phone number.

"Expecting someone?" Lou said, and I said, "No." I made buckteeth at her. She made them back and then picked up. It was obvious from her smirk that it was Jorge, the married man Aunt Lou sometimes went away with. Sometimes he didn't call for three weeks, and Lou went back on her diet for real, got a wax, and bought ninety-seven pairs of shoes.

She covered the mouthpiece and rolled her eyes. "So needy," she said, and walked into the other room. Yeah, right.

It was the perfect time then. I should have gotten my sneakers and left. My mother put up her feet on Lou's chair. She hadn't had any pasta, and she was on her fourth glass of wine. It had plumped up her cheeks. Her mascara was in little black pepper flakes around her eyes. She let her head fall onto the back of the chair and she breathed out like she was making imaginary smoke rings.

Now.

"Oh," I said. "Crap. I have to pick up homework from school before the weekend. If I keep up with it, I can still get grades for this semester. Principal Hidalgo said she'd leave it with the guard."

Such a lie. Such a big huge lie that no one would notice.

I put on my sneakers and my coat and I was just about to leave when my mother said, "Come, Lorca. Just come here for a second."

Then, very casually, like it wasn't the point of everything, she said, "Oh, you can go. You don't have to stay here with me."

I went back to the table and sat down. She didn't budge. My coat was bunched under me. Her head was still back. When her neck was long and stretched like this, I could see the structure of it, the evidence of lack of sun and air, skin like rungs on a ladder, covered in the slightest layer of dust. She was quiet.

"Let me tell you something," she said. She hadn't had a bite of her dinner. I'd even curled the pasta into a little linguine nest in the center of each bowl. My mother's was still perfect and round and cold. The sauce had darkened.

"This is delish," she said. "But it needs red wine. I tell you because I love you and you should know for the future."

She went on about deglazing and how it brings out the earthy taste of the onions and never use wine you wouldn't drink yourself and a young, robust wine is what you use in red sauces, nothing fortified or dry, for example.

I was sweating in my coat. My stomach was starting to itch. I should have worn an undershirt. I was thirsty. I reminded myself to remind myself to smell my armpits before I went. With her head back like this, every time she took a sip of the wine, her throat looked like a snake that was swallowing a mouse. She wanted to talk about Aurelio some more. She wasn't looking at me. Whenever she talked about other men, I thought of my father. I didn't hate him. There was never a second that I hated him. Sometimes the phone rang and I'd pick up and it was quiet on the other end except for what sounded like rustling trees, which I knew was absurd. It was just the way I imagined him. If no one else was home, I'd say, "Dad. Dad?" But no one ever said anything back. When I called *69, it said the number was blocked. There were a billion other people it could have been, though I'd put us on the Do Not Call list, so it probably wasn't just anyone.

"Your father was never like that," she was saying. "Passionate like that. Can you blame me?" She wasn't talking to me. She was talking to the ceiling.

"I wanted him to fight for us," she said, making figure eights in the air with her glass, and then she gave a sudden punch, like she was in some kind of rally. Some of her wine spilled out and went sailing onto the floor.

"Fight, fight, fight!" she said. "For anything. It didn't matter what."

I said, "I wanted that too," but she didn't hear me. I wanted her to fight for me. I used a paper towel and my foot to clean up the wine puddle.

"I wanted him to tell us not to go and to really take a stand about it," she said. "But he wimped out. Like everyone, he got wimpy on me."

"Then why did you fall in love with him?" I asked. "If he was such a wimp."

She put her glass down, glared at me like I'd misunderstood everything.

"He changed," she said. "I thought I knew what he was after. In the beginning, when I worked at La Grenouille, he sent back my sweetbreads. No one had ever done that. He said rosemary was a moth deterrent."

She put back her head again.

"And he was the first man bold enough to order for me at a restaurant. He was his own person then, so into wood. He used to get totally lost looking at a barstool. You wouldn't believe it. But then, eventually, his interest became me. I was pregnant and he wouldn't get off my back. If it had stayed like that, I would have left him right then and there. But things ebbed and flowed. I'll tell you what, though. If he'd liked my sweetbreads, he wouldn't have had a chance in hell."

I refilled her glass. It was 7:05. She wasn't done. I wanted her to say something about how my needing her was different from my father's needs. I was her daughter. That kind of need was necessary, biological, heartening. There were a million words I wanted to put in her mouth, but she said none of them. At 7:30, she lifted her head, disconcerted, flushed.

"Didn't you say you had to go somewhere?" she said.

"No," I said. "It's okay."

By then, I'd taken off my coat. My back was cold with sweat.

"You go," she said. "I'll be fine."

"All right," I said. I put on my coat. I didn't even want to go anymore. He wouldn't be there. I'd be ridiculous.

As I was walking out the door, my mother called to me. "Lorca?"

I stopped, turned around.

"I must have done something very right," she said. "You're the best little listener."

I sprinted all the way to the bookstore, which was no big deal except that there had never been more people on the street and that made it impossible to run. They looked at me like they didn't know which direction they should go and then they didn't go in either one. They just stood there, with bags of groceries held out like broken wings. Eventually, I started running in the street, staying close to the parked cars and scooting back up on the curb when I saw the lights of a bus.

I burst into the store with my hands tingling from the cold. I raced toward the stairs and noticed that the elevator doors were open, about to close. A walrus of an old man was fiddling with the buttons. I got in.

"Terrible weather," the walrus said, firmly reparting his hair with both hands. His belly was so big that he leaned back even when he didn't.

They taught us in school that if you're ever in an elevator with a pervert, you should shake and scream like you're covered in ants. They said, "Preserve yourself, not your dignity."

Right before I got out of the elevator, my heart started purring. Just for a second; I couldn't help it. Sometimes, no matter how hard I tried to keep my hopes down, they popped back up like a turkey timer.

He was gone. Blot was gone. I could see that before I stepped out of the elevator. I didn't even have to move my head. His desk was right in front of me. No coat. No stray pens or tissues. There was a neat stack of books and a legal pad and his empty teacup, cleaned. I thought, *Maybe there's a note for me.* But there wasn't. Of course there wasn't.

I was standing directly in front of the elevator, blocking everything, and the walrus had to say, "Excuse me, miss," twice to get me to move.

I told myself Blot didn't really want to go with me. I was awful. He'd been laughing at me the whole time. I was part of some bet. That didn't happen just in movies. That was my first thought. Even when I looked at the time and saw that I was forever later than fashionably late, I couldn't convince myself that it was just that: it was as simple as him waiting for me and then leaving. In my head, it was something so much worse. He knew about my cuts. He hated me. He hated me. He hated me. This had all been some kind of setup and here I was, falling for it.

I could have been on the couch, eating sorbet. This was what happened when I got hopeful.

I walked over to his desk. I wasn't going to do anything ridiculous like try to smell a pencil he might have touched. But I wanted to be close to him. He had paper clips stuck to a black magnet in the shape of a house.

Go home, Lorca, I thought. *Enough now. That's enough.* I was about to leave when I saw a *Zagat* from 1986 on his stool. There was a blue Post-it note sticking out. I reached for the book to see if the note was for me. I couldn't believe this. I told myself to slow down. It was like eating a cupcake: you had to eat the bottom before the top. I didn't want to rush everything and have nothing left. I stopped myself. I counted to three before moving an inch.

One haricot vert.

Two haricots verts.

Three haricots verts.

Okay. Enough. I couldn't stand it. I opened the book.

There it was. A restaurant called the Shohet and His Wife at 424 Amsterdam Avenue. The review started like this: "Upper West Siders don't come here for the 'frightening décor.' It is a testament to the food of this 'outstanding,' 'family-owned' 'Mediterranean plaza' that customers get past the door. But once they do, they 'can't get enough.'" On the Post-it, in boy handwriting: *Owners: Joseph and Victoria Shohet, 203 West 112th Street.*

Something dropped inside of me. Disappointment that I hadn't expected. He'd found it. We wouldn't search together. It hadn't even started before it ended. Still, I thought of my mother. I was one step closer. I could see her perfect face. When I imagined it, it was full of sympathy, full of tears, and she was younger. Life with me hadn't aged her three thousand years.

I looked around for Blot one more time. Then I left the *Zagat* on the stool. I wanted to come back for it. I wanted him to be here.

When I got outside, it had started to rain, and I thought, *Of course it's raining.* I thought of putting my face to the sky and opening my mouth but then I thought, *Don't be melodramatic.* From the time I was seven years old, I'd stuck my fingers in restaurant candles whenever my mother turned her head. I'd felt totally alone and unexposed even if we were smack in the middle of Le Bernardin, getting an extra six courses because of her. And even if she'd caught me, she'd never call me on it. My life wasn't a movie.

I walked north. I looked down and watched water flick up against my shoes like angry bees.

And then it came over me. The urge. It was like feeling starved, suddenly. This time, it was my feet that hadn't moved fast enough, that had done nothing right. I wanted to do something terrible to the flabby tops of my feet.

There were certain things I could do that helped, briefly.

For example, I could swallow fifteen times, as fast and as hard as possible. Like a sick cat. One. Two. Three. To fifteen. It made me feel parched and lighter. Like I couldn't coax out the blood if I tried.

If the craving was for something other than blood—for, let's say, the dull aching pain I'd get from banging my head against a cinder block or on the corner of an open drawer—I could hold on to something as tightly as possible until my hand just couldn't take anymore. The exhausting feeling was sort of the same as whatever might have come from banging.

Neither one of these things ever worked for long. Still, I told myself to quit it. *Walk, Lorca. Go. Don't think about it.*

I didn't plan where I was going, but I wasn't surprised by where I ended up.

Victoria

I HAD BEEN DREAMING of our daughter, but what she did in the dream other than just be there, I couldn't tell you. The thing was, the wonderful thing was, she was with me. I wasn't alone.

I woke up to Dottie's mouth by my ear.

"Come, my darling. Come, Toya," she said.

Everything will be all right, I wanted to say. I wanted to be talking to Joseph.

I wanted to tell him I had never loved anyone else, and never would. I wanted to talk to him about our life, how fantastic it was. I wanted to reminisce. I wanted to ask him to forgive me for being gone in that final moment. How long did that moment last?

I allowed Dottie to coax me into the bedroom, into a chair that knew my shape. There were strangers in my house. Anyone could come. Words in whispers. I looked at the clock: 10:56. I couldn't recall when this day had begun.

Then I needed to sign. Our lawyer. He was wearing jeans.

"Victoria," he was saying. "I am so sorry."

Our accountant. His hand on my knee.

"Victoria," he said. "I am so sorry."

Soon afterward, or not so soon, Joseph's friends were opening and closing the fridge. How could they have known so quickly?

Didn't they sleep? Typical Iraqis, always waiting for a reason to party—especially on a Friday. After that, there was the clinking of glasses, the run of the faucet, water boiling, the smell of roasting lemons. A young woman, maybe a sixteenth of my age, lipstick on her teeth, introduced herself as the social worker from hospice.

"I could be your grandmother," I said, realizing the terrible taste in my mouth. She gave me a cup of tea, a very sincere look on her face.

Dottie said to her, "We have everything under control, thank you."

I asked myself, Did we? I would have to write a eulogy. Wouldn't I? I had no idea.

I wrapped my arms around Dottie. She hugged me back, then released me, stood up, and went to my nightstand. She removed a photograph from a frame: Joseph and me—our wedding, at the bakery near MacDougal Street. Just a few years before we'd moved here, to this apartment. She laid it face-down, retiring it.

I knew just what she was doing. She didn't like lingering sadness. She'd pin it on me, say it was to keep me from stewing. But I could stew. If I wanted, I was allowed to stew my head off.

I knew tomorrow she'd want us to start taking ballroom dance.

I wanted to say, *Don't, Dottie. Please. Mind your business for once.* The words didn't come out. She walked around the bed. I watched her place Joseph's silver pen and money clip in her robe pocket like they were hers, casual as can be.

What are you doing? Please. I didn't say that either. She picked up another framed photo of us. We were in Anguilla. I wondered if she'd steal that as well. No. She put it in his nightstand drawer. It closed with a click.

The social worker glanced at Dottie and then at me. I couldn't imagine I could look any more pathetic than I did, but I tried. I needed her help. I couldn't stand up for myself. I couldn't stand up at all.

"I think it's best," she said to Dottie very slowly, as if talking to a temperamental child, "that you leave the reorganizing to Victoria. It is a very long, personal process, which she can begin when she's ready."

"Oh, no," Dottie said in a high pitch. She took the rosemary lotion that I used on Joseph's feet. She rubbed some into her hands and then slipped the bottle in her pocket.

"You understand," she said to the social worker, "I'm helping, of course. It's not good for Victoria to see all these things now. They will make it harder for her."

Words were stuck in my throat like apple skin.

"Why don't you come over here," the social worker said to Dottie. She patted the ottoman by my feet. "I think you can be more helpful by just being with your friend now."

I would have thanked her if I could have.

"Of course, doll," Dottie said and waltzed over. Her hips went *pop pop pop*. Sometimes, if I was in the mood, I'd tell her that she'd strut right into her grave. That was the kind of thing that made her feel like a million bucks.

"Your husband will surely miss you," the social worker said, squeezing my arm. I wanted to ask her to tell me more. I craved the reassurance more than ever, knowing that never again would he tell me anything. Not one single thing.

"Yes. He'll miss us," Dottie said. Her eyes were closed, wrinkly and small.

She had no right. No right at all. I wanted to look straight at her and say, *Excuse me?* I was his wife. He would miss me, yes—the certainty was growing in me by the second—and this house I'd made for him. I tried not to hear Joseph's voice. *Dottie's all alone,* he'd say. *The least we can do is make her feel welcome.*

No, thank you, Joseph. The unwelcoming starts now.

I heard a clanking, something banging against the front door. I wanted to say, *Watch the painting!* I didn't say it. I heard men's voices. I stuck my head out. There was a stretcher. A white sheet. My body lurched. All my organs stopped short. Dottie grabbed me, put my head to her chest. Good God, that was my husband on there. I wanted to say, *No! Let me keep him. Let me be with him forever. I cannot be alone. I cannot live without him.* I said nothing of the sort. I was a coward. I'd always been a coward. I didn't want to make a fool of myself. Instead, I whispered that Joseph had wanted to be cremated, and the social worker nodded at me and then at Dottie, as though the two of them had already discussed it.

"Don't look, Victoria," Dottie said. "This is not something we need to see."

I nodded. I believed her.

Finally, everyone left. The apartment lifted, exhaled. Dottie had been the last, of course, but I'd been angry enough to make her empty her pockets at the door. Lotion, money clip, pen, aftershave, handkerchief with frayed gray edges.

"I just don't want you up all night," she'd said loudly.

"Right," I said. I couldn't fight with her. "Okay."

"I was protecting you," she said, "by taking those things."

"Okay," I said. "I know."

Once she was gone, there was silence everywhere. In the kitchen drawers, between the sofa cushions, in the empty teakettle. You'd think it was because Joseph was gone, but Joseph had never been noisy. It was Dottie. She had been here for years, every day, reading her magazines, making calls to her cell phone company to ask useless questions, using hair remover on her top lip. Tapping her foot, rubbing her eyes, yawning with the screech of a cat. Now I was tiptoeing through the rooms, cautious not to startle myself. I kept thinking of the white sheet, feeling like it was wafting toward me and then over me, and then suddenly, like it had been vacuum-sealed, it suffocated me. I kept thinking of his toes sticking up, but the truth is, I didn't see them. I never saw his toes. I didn't see anything but the dark abyss of Dottie's bosom.

Joseph would have loved that story. *Dottie ruined your death,* I'd say. *She ruined it with her huge old-lady bosom.* And he'd laugh that chubby, delicious laugh. *What did you expect?* he'd say. *What did we expect, my love?*

Now I waited for something to happen. I stood with my hands on the kitchen counter. I was aware that I was still not crying, that I was uninjured, that I was alone.

But of course I was not alone because here was all of Dottie's crap. Her *Reader's Digests* on the kitchen table, her array of nail polish and nail polish remover. The Yellow Pages, which she had left open, had a blue pen—my pen, my missing pen—sunk into the binding. There were cans of Diet Coke—all open, all hers—abandoned. Her things, her shit, everywhere. In the living room, a scarf, a towel, and a package of scented tissues. Between the cushions on the couch was a tube of her lipstick and a compact. I walked through the apartment, gathering item after ridiculous item. A ripped-out quiz, for instance: "What Celebrity Are You Most Like?" I collected it all and put it into a large white shopping bag. There.

This was my home. I did not want to smell her lipstick, the awful perfumey-ness of it. I wanted to make my own mess. I wanted to sit at my kitchen table and spread out my *New York Times* without having to move her shiny fashion magazines. I placed the white bag of crap by the door. It made me feel better, to see her on her way out. Everything else in here was mine or Joseph's. Ours.

Alone in my living room, I imagined my own death. It might happen now, this night. My face would smack onto the floor, cracking my cheek, swarming it with red as if a cranberry had been squashed inside. I'd often wondered about dying alone, knowing that Joseph wasn't getting any better. But I could not die alone, because Dottie would be reading *People* in my La-Z-Boy. She would flail about for the phone, her robe twirling around her like a dog chasing its tail. *No, no, doll,* she would say, voice quivering. *No, you don't. You'll be just fine. You'll see.*

Men with scruffy faces and cold hands would hoist me onto the stretcher and shove me into the ambulance like a pizza going into the oven. A Jamaican woman at the hospital would ask me my name and date of birth and next of kin.

No one, I would say. *There's no one.*

No one longing to cradle me while the warmth of life began flickering out. Alone, I'd be, in a bed with sheets stiff with bleach and a faint smell of apple cider vinegar and no heartbeat beside mine fierce enough to jolt my heart back into action.

I sat down on the floor. Aches and pains and unhappy cracks.

Out of the sky, the buzzer rang. I jumped, clutched my chest. "Shut up," I said, breathless. "Shush."

I didn't need to answer. I was in mourning. Whatever it was, even a gift basket or condolences from some old acquaintance, could wait. But it rang again. And again. The word *emergency* passed through my head but I remembered: The emergency had come and gone. There was nothing left to get hysterical about. *Buzz.*

"Oh shit," I said, finally getting up, not because I cared who was downstairs but because the sound of the buzzer was like an explosion.

"Hm?" I said, just about crashing into the Talk button, out of breath, resting my head on the cool wall.

"Um," said a little voice. "I'm looking for the restaurateurs," it said shakily. "From the Shohet and His Wife? We're interested in having some masgouf—"

"What?" I laughed. I cut her off. "No," I said. "That's hilarious. Masgouf? That's been done for years."

"Oh," the voice said. "Okay. Thank you."

"Wait," I said, my throat suddenly pulled into a dry knot. "Are you? Who are you?"

I inhaled, held it in my mouth.

"It's just that I've heard a lot about it," the voice said earnestly, in a way that was totally unaware of the squall happening in my head. "I heard it was delicious."

My heart dropped. *Of course,* I thought, waving my hands in front of my face.

"Oh," I said.

And then, because I was always proving something to someone, I said, "It was delicious."

I didn't bother to apologize. I thought someone should apologize to me. I walked away, hoping the buzzing wouldn't begin again. But when it didn't, I stopped in my tracks, waiting, even hoping. No one might look for me, need me, ever again. Except for Dottie, who didn't count. There was nothing meaningful in that. The buzzer might remain unbuzzing until someone replaced me here, and there was something worth buzzing about, someone.

I walked through our rooms. Of course I thought of our daughter. Our things, things that I'd once feared would matter to no one, our way of living, might matter to her. We kept dirty laundry in the guest-room bathtub. We left jazz playing for our lemon tree. We had two little fish and when they died we removed them but continued to change their water and put food in the tank. If it mattered to anyone, it would matter to her.

When I went, everything would be delivered to the Salvation Army. Someone else would sit on my sofa, use my jewelry box, fiddle with the knobs on my insured, antique Toastrite without knowing a thing about me. She was my only something. I'd never forgotten her; I had just put the memory somewhere, behind a box, below some clothes. Every once in a while, though, I'd move the dust. I'd come across it and it would just about make me shake. Refusing to love something is the same as loving it. "A quiet conscience," we used to say in Baghdad, "sleeps in thunder." I hadn't slept in decades.

The fact was, without her, I was nothing now. And yet, all those years ago, I was afraid that keeping her would make *me* nothing, no one, to Joseph. I should have admitted that to him, told him the truth: I was afraid he would love a little baby more than he loved me. He would love everything about her that I was not. I am harder to love. I am stubborn. I am not a pretty sleeper. I get bigger, stinkier when I sleep. Red onion clings to my skin. I don't laugh easily. In the supermarket, I never pick the shortest line. I judge everyone. I can't sit through an entire movie. My big toes are unfortunately shaped. The city skyline doesn't thrill me; it petrifies me. I keep waiting for things to go black. And this: She would have loved him more too. They would have been two peas in a pod. I would have been left out, no one to them, like I'd been no one to my family in Baghdad. I would have hated her for it. I could not hate her, my own child. But I believed that I would have. And he would have hated me for that. He would have hated me, but we might have worked through it. I'd refused to ever give him that chance. I told him a million lies: We needed to save money. We needed to become citizens. We needed to do great things, like gamble in Las Vegas and peer into the Grand Canyon. And until then, we couldn't even contemplate the possibility of a child. And Joseph, bless him, said all right, went along with that plan of mine because he loved me, and his love, unlike mine, was not jealous, not insecure.

Years later, when I saw how it had worn on him, how desperately he wanted to care for a child, I nearly gave in. But I didn't. Couldn't. Not then or ever. I'd built such a strong case, I couldn't falter. We came to the States, I told him, to build a life for ourselves. We had to do that first and foremost. But then, when we were established, I said there was more to do. We couldn't stop. We, Joseph and I, were some crucial part of the American dream. Pioneers. Revolutionaries. And yet, all we encountered while forging our way to a new world was the same thing, again and again. The absence. The lack.

Finally—and it felt like it had all been leading up to this—the tears rose into my throat. I began to sigh hard, heavy, determined sighs, but I couldn't stop what was coming. Then, suddenly, it stopped itself. What would the tears do anyway? No one was going to comfort me, bring me tissues or a cold washcloth to put over my face. I'd have to clean up the mess myself, so I diverted it somewhere.

I went into the study. Joseph's mother's locket was on his desk. I turned it over in my fingers. Without him, his things were suddenly grayer, lighter. Like his clothes and toothbrush and the gold lighters somewhere. I had always hated smoking; it made my throat close. But in the last few months, when all he had wanted was an unfiltered cigarette and for me to sit beside him, keeping his hands warm with mine, that smell, like burning dried leaves, had begun to comfort me. I'd find myself letting my head fall back, taking his exhaled smoke into my chest. It filled me with a feeling like the softest sand, and for a moment, I could imagine he was all he used to be again—a humming, sneezing, reaching, dancing person, grabbing life by fistfuls and tossing them like wedding rice into the air.

Everything felt sacred, having been witnessed by Joseph's eyes, and so I didn't want to touch a thing, afraid of ruining some delicate state. One of Joseph's slipper socks was on the carpet and I got down on the floor beside it, picked it up, and kept it to my nose until the smell and feeling of it faded. Then I dropped it into the exact spot where it had been. Where else would I have put it? When I finally got up, my legs were numb, and my knees made a noise so terrible and loud that it scared the daylights out of me. I felt like an intruder on my own life.

From the closet in our bathroom—*my* bathroom, I corrected myself—I took out a clean white sheet and placed it on top of the bed. It felt wrong to sleep the same way I'd been sleeping for years, so I would sleep under the sheet and over the covers. I took one of the ashtrays from his study. It was silver and shaped like a man's palm, deeply lined and shadowed. Something, I thought, that should remain in one's family. The smell survived, though faintly, and I placed it beside my pillow.

"Where are you?" I said to Joseph, and, remembering my promise to him about finding our daughter, "Where is she?"

The next day, Saturday, passed in a blur. I drank plenty of tea, stared at the impossible crossword puzzle, watched television, although if someone had asked me what I'd watched, I wouldn't have had any idea.

That evening, just a day after Joseph passed, the phone rang. It gave me a start. My hope that our daughter might call was ridiculous. *If this is an automated voice,* I thought, *I'll swan-dive off the fire escape.*

"Hello," I said, crossing my fingers that it wouldn't be a sympathy call either.

"Hello, Chef Victoria?" asked a man.

"This is Victoria."

"Chef Victoria?" he said.

"Dottie?" I asked. It was a man's voice. What was I saying? It just came out.

"No," the voice said. "I'm sorry, I must have the wrong number. I'm calling about the cooking classes? The Middle Eastern cooking classes? I'm Robert?"

And then it hit me. Until then, it had totally slipped my mind.

Two weeks before, when Joseph was still alive and being bathed by a nurse, Dottie had barged into our kitchen.

"Yoo-hoo," she'd clamored while I'd ignored her, pretending to page through a catalog. Whenever she had a plan—and her plans always gave me heartburn—she'd try for mystery. She'd stand there so obviously hiding something behind her back, her face swollen with expectation, visibly atwitter. She had the patience of a jack-in-the-box. She'd lasted five seconds before she slapped a bright green sign on my lap.

"Look!" she'd shrieked. "Look what I found!"

"So?" I said, bringing the sign closer to my face, cutting myself off. "What?"

Dottie passed me her glasses and I put them on.

"Read," she said.

"'French pastry classes,'" I read aloud, and Dottie joined in by heart, closing her eyes and nodding her head, when I continued.

"'By Chef Luisa,'" we said.

In the photo, Luisa wore a chef's hat that had buckled into itself. It looked like she'd been smacked in the head. She had a triple chin, crooked teeth, and either a fever blister or a very unhappy mole.

"This?" I said. "Have we stooped this low?"

"We have," she said.

"I don't like sweets," I said, because I hadn't in my youth and would rather admit to incontinence than to the changes in my diet. "You know that. And I'm tired of cooking. Do you see what I've been eating around here?"

I ate Pop-Tarts. My mother, an incredible cook, would have turned in her grave. I liked the ones with colored sprinkles. They were festive.

"Oh yes," Dottie said. "I see. I certainly see what you're eating. It's called carbo loading. Miraculously, you're not a bus. You're a beanpole."

"What's your point?" I said.

I was picking at my lips, taking my unlipsticked skin off in little strips. Dottie swatted at my hand.

"It's really quite brilliant," she said. "I don't know why we haven't thought of it before. It's perfect."

"Spit it out, Dottie."

"Here it is." She said each of the next words slowly and deliberately, as if she were passing out snacks to pesky toddlers.

"I think—"

Long pause.

"That you—"

Long pause.

"Should teach—"

Pause.

"Ready? Ready? Ready?" she said.

"Yes, I'm ready," I said. "Christ."

"A cooking class!" she exploded.

She stepped back, ready to take in my delight, full of emotion.

"Oh yeah?" I said. "And I think you should compete in the Miss America pageant."

"I was almost Miss South Carolina—"

"I know," I said. "You've mentioned it."

"Not the point," she said. "The point is that it would be good for you. You could make a little money. You have a great kitchen. You know so much."

"Like what?" I said. I wasn't in the mood.

"Like eating apples for happiness," she said. "You told me that once."

"Yellow vegetables for happiness," I corrected her. The Iraqi Jews ate according to color. "White for purity. Green apples for hope and prosperity."

She must have seen the look on my face.

"Joseph is in good hands in there," she said. She signaled toward the only part of the apartment she hadn't been to in years. Literally, years. Joseph's wing. Like I said, sickness terrified her. I half nodded. I saw her point.

"I'll make some squash for dinner," I said. "I will."

"Middle Eastern is very in right now," she continued, upbeat. "Those colored silks and the beads."

I'd snapped my teeth at her but she was already at the door, doing a pageant wave. For just a moment, I loved her, her optimism. I appreciated it.

"I have a date with my neighbor friend upstairs," she said, all cheeky.

"Vladimir?" I asked. Vladimir was Russian mafia. We were pretty certain.

"No," she said. "The thirteen-year-old sign maker. He's quite taken with me." She batted her lashes.

"Dottie, don't. You don't even have a picture—"

As the door was closing behind her, she'd waved a shiny photo at me. It had tape curls on the back. It was from Joseph's side of the headboard. He'd kept it there. Dottie must have swiped it while I wasn't looking.

I'd hated that photo. It was from twenty years ago. I was in one of my hostess outfits, all monotone and sheen and unfortunate padding. Mermaid-y. Joseph adored it. There was something nice in that.

It felt like a lifetime had passed since Dottie and I had had that conversation, though it had been only two weeks. And not even a day since Joseph had died. I wondered if time would ever move at a reasonable speed again, if it might ever fly.

Still, I was bolstered for a moment, as it occurred to me that Robert had seen the photo—and called despite it. I wondered if he was almost blind. There could be no other explanation.

"Did Dottie put you up to this?" I asked him now.

"I don't think so," he said. "I don't know any Dotties. I got your name off the flyer? The flyer at the Y?"

"Dottie!" I yelled upward. She tapped her heel. She was in her kitchen, probably watching something spin in the microwave.

"I'm sorry," he said. "I must have made a mistake. Sorry to bother you."

He was about to hang up. But then something came over me. I remembered the buzzing yesterday after everyone left, the asking for masgouf. I remembered our daughter. This wasn't her on the phone now, I'm no idiot. But, for a moment, I wondered if someone was trying to reach me. I didn't want to get ahead of myself, hadn't even thought it through, but I felt that this was my moment. My moment was about to be gone.

"No," I heard myself saying. "No. Don't hang up. This is me. It must be me."

"Ma'am?" Robert asked. "I'm sorry to have bothered you."

He seemed so kind, so concerned that he had taken time out of my day, that tears flocked behind my eyes. If only he knew. Just last week, I'd spent an entire morning poaching eggs, one after another, trying to get them exactly right. I wanted to give Joseph something perfect, to remind him of us. I'd gone through a dozen and hadn't gotten the hang of it. I was out of practice. It broke my heart. For days, the apartment reeked of sulfury hot springs. Before I could stop myself, I was saying, "Thank you."

Don't be pathetic, Victoria, I thought, and I kept quiet so I wouldn't thank him again.

"For what?" he said.

"Nothing. Yes. I am Chef Victoria. About those cooking classes—they'll be held where? What did the flyer say?" I was trying to be professional. I thought again about dying alone.

"Well, it didn't," he said. "That's why I'm calling. It gives your name and number and time—Monday night at seven—and there's a lovely photograph. I believe it's of you. Is it? But there's no location I can find."

"This Monday?" I was shouting at him. I didn't mean to.

"That woman," I said. "I'll kill her."

He laughed like he had a beard. He was a nice man. I imagined children climbing on his shoulders and neck. Her children.

"Yes, this Monday. And obviously," he said, "Dottie put *you* up to this."

"I don't know why I'm surprised," I said. Now I was being casual. Casual was good. "But we'll have the class here, at my apartment. What's today?"

"It's Saturday," he said.

I gave him my address. For a moment, it occurred to me that I could have it all wrong. I *was* getting way ahead of myself. He could have been a con artist. A seducer of old ladies. *Well, then, let him,* I thought. Let him.

Before I knew it, I was taking down the location of the flyer and asking if he'd seen any other ones. And he was offering to write the specifics of the classes on the flyers he'd seen. And I was consenting. I was hopeful.

Later, when I imagined our daughter seeing me in that photo, I wanted to call the whole thing off. It wasn't worth my dignity. Or was it?

I hadn't ever envisioned where she lived exactly, only that it was in a large barnlike house with explosions of lavender and wildflowers everywhere, a place where kids left their bicycles in the middles of driveways and played soccer in the street. But now, for the first time, I wondered if perhaps she lived just down the block somewhere. Let's say in a lovely prewar with heavy moldings and a robin's-egg-colored foyer. She'd always been there. And we—as if we deserved credit for it—had always been here too. With her. For her.

Thinking of the photo, thinking of her, I wished I could have been lovelier in the picture, with a longer neck, in black-and-white, my hand and chin tilted in an artful way. There were women like that. Still, I thought, this was a beginning. Like an anonymous package, a missing-person poster, a message in a bottle. I wanted to be found. And maybe she did too. This flyer, it might be the sign she'd been waiting for. *Here I am,* I thought. *I'm so sorry. Find me,* I thought. *Please.*

Our child, Joseph's and mine, was a girl. The nurse told me when I woke up. They'd already whisked her away. I imagined her as an adult, shiny dark hair getting in her eyes, wiping the counter around her sons' cereal bowls with a kitchen towel as they looked at her adoringly, clamoring for more more more. And now, I wondered if she'd felt it—her father's death. I wondered if she'd suddenly felt less secured to the world—one side of her body lighter, dizzier, refusing to stay put. I wondered where she was when it happened, if she'd been aware of the tiniest zing. *I'm still here,* I wanted to tell her suddenly. *I won't leave you again. Not ever.*

I felt like a fraud. I was more sorry than I deserved to be.

I looked around. The voice on the phone made me feel as though someone had barged in here, opened the curtains, exposed something uncouth. The coffee table, I noticed, was strewn with unopened newspapers and supermarket savings packs. There were empty ripped-open envelopes. Every day, I'd gone through the mail with him. On the way back from the study, I'd drop the envelopes here. There must have been forty of them now. I gathered them up, threw them out.

I had never been this way. I had never lived like this. I had always replaced soap before it grew a film. Everything in the closet faced north.

I found myself in the study, standing by Joseph's desk. I picked up one of his pens, a heavy thing with a complicated ink system. I remembered this one. I'd bought it for him years ago. The first thing he did with it was write me a note: *To the most beautiful woman I know. I'm hungry in case you are wondering.*

I opened the middle drawer and found a lone pill bottle. They really were everywhere. I wondered if I'd put this one here in one of my pathetic, failed attempts to clean up. I'd put a vase in the refrigerator, a VCR warranty in my sock drawer. There was so much stuff. Our possessions grew and grew. Then, one day, they stopped. I wondered if I'd ever buy anything again that presumed life would march on—a plane ticket, a magazine subscription, something decorative for our home.

I dropped a folder, some receipts, and unhinged paper clips onto the desk. There were gum wrappers, used tissues, ancient credit card statements, chandelier bulbs, and blank postcards from Delray Beach. I was making a mess. *I'm sorry, Joseph,* I thought. *I didn't mean to ruin your things.*

There was a recipe for coconut cake, a kitchen timer that jingled when I shook it; there was a movie stub from years ago. I kept going through the things, piling them on his desk, imagining building a giant shape that might resemble my Joseph. *What if you could sculpt the person you loved the most,* I wondered. *What would it be made of?*

Toward the bottom of the stack, I found an oak leaf, big and fingerlike, lovingly pressed between two pieces of wax paper. It looked fresh, brand-new. I hadn't done it. I'd read about this in a craft magazine. It was something Martha Stewart did, not us—ironing leaves for decoration. I found another. A red maple leaf. Then an itty-bitty brown one. I did the ironing around here. When, in all our years, had Joseph ever ironed?

I put them aside, feeling as though I'd intruded on a private moment. Perhaps he'd been planning to give these to me with a very special card. Thousands of things, I thought, were only halfway realized. His juice box had liquid left inside. His clothes remained unwashed in the guest-room bathtub. The Bellow story was dog-eared midway through.

I kept going through his things.

It was while I was cutting up some unused credit cards that I saw the note written on a piece of fabric. It was torn, but not enough. It was there. Right there, on top of the stack on the desk. I'd put it there, not noticing. Front and center. It wasn't even ashamed of itself. And it was nothing fancy, just a scrap of old thin cloth, as though it were a tag that had been itchy and yanked out. White with purple letters, like veins on old skin. It was in a woman's handwriting.

Meet me at the Bow Bridge at sunrise.

I felt like I was going to pass out. I was weak. I was *weak*. I sat down slowly in the desk chair, not wanting to rush this. It felt like this shouldn't be rushed. I picked up the note, delicately, feeling it in my hands. I wondered if something like this should have been heavier, with the heft of a hamantashen, at the very least. I looked at the words and then I didn't. I put it back where it came from. And then I picked it up again. I mashed it in my fist. Go. Vanish. I decided I wouldn't look at it again. It wasn't meant for me. I tossed it into the garbage can. I took it out of the garbage can. I uncrumpled it. Flattened it onto the desk. The letters leaned to the right, poised as if with their hands on their hips.

I sniffed it.

I turned it over. There was a tiny grease stain. From our counter? From fish?

I folded it. It went willingly, like a ballerina being lifted at her waist. Tiny square.

From the Bow Bridge in Central Park, Joseph and I watched the ducks. Sometimes we'd sit in a gazebo nearby and feed them old bread. I didn't like when they came too close. They had ferocious little beaks. Joseph liked to stomp near them and cause them to fly toward my head. I'd scolded him. I'd told him to find someone else to harass. I was always saying things like that.

I'd read that a man was murdered in our gazebo.

Joseph was always up at sunrise, his favorite time of day. He'd go for a walk and return to make our coffee before his shower. Sometimes, he'd walk with Dottie. She was an insomniac and a hypochondriac. He'd tell her it was good for her lungs. She would have drunk parrot urine if she thought it would diminish her frown lines.

For a moment, I thought: *Maybe I wrote this note.* It could have been me. I could have been a walker. I could have liked the mornings. But then, could I have? I liked the afternoons. Sunset, not sunrise. Cooling down, not warming up. I hated walking first thing. It made the system reel. I tried to imagine us. Me, groggy. Him, tugging me along. The air—it never happened. I would have remembered. Perhaps it was Dottie, then. But of course it wasn't. Dottie didn't have the patience to write something down. She just barged in, never knocked, never made polite requests.

And then it hit me: our daughter. I recalled what I'd said to Joseph just after he'd passed, about finding her. I wanted to know where he'd been when I said that—for how long hearing continues to work and when it shuts off. This note, I thought, what if it was from her? What if they had met, after all these years? I always knew that he couldn't let go, but maybe he found a way so that he didn't have to.

It wasn't easy. I will say that. After we gave up the baby, we hated each other a little. I couldn't stand his disappointment in me. I'd wanted to be enough. When I wasn't, I shunned any possible replacement. It's horrible, I know. Still, it's been a very long time. And he, heart of gold, had wanted only something of his own, something to love. I deprived him of that. I know I did. And yet, we moved on. It required silence and shame. It required opening our restaurant just to be something other than non-parents, to watch each other in a different context. They never left us, those feelings, but they dimmed. We grew around the hole. I'd like to think it made us stronger, but I suppose it's impossible to know a thing like that.

Pain in my chest. I wheezed.

I sniffed the note again. There was lead in my stomach. A whole new world had just broken into my house. Then the jealousy surged. Why had he been so secretive? Why had he kept her from me? You *gave her up, Victoria,* I told myself. Our relationship after that—Joseph's and mine—was a delicate hora around that crater. That's the funny thing about loss. Sometimes it's the absence of something that makes everything else appear around it. It's like turning off the lights in order to see.

And yet, I believed we'd moved on. Not always together, but along, past, in whatever way we could. That he'd met her, known her, and for years perhaps, was a betrayal I couldn't begin to comprehend. He had kept her from me, and he'd kept some of himself from me too.

I looked at the leaves. "Did she press these?" I said out loud, waving them in the air. "Why didn't you share them? Her?"

And then I couldn't sit still. Couldn't think. Maybe Dottie had a point—all these reminders were too much. I marched into the kitchen, began collecting used dishes. There were paperweights crouching in a corner next to a tall stack of red manila folders. There was a tissue box impaled and balancing on a little copper giraffe. Our lemon tree was totally dead now. Its smell had been our nostalgia. Baghdad. Now the leaves were brown and shriveled on the floor. I hadn't even noticed.

Moments before, I'd thought: This was Joseph's world, his memory. It all bore such weight. Everything and its dust needed to stay just so. To clean it would be to remove him. Now I reached for his sock. I knotted it for effect and hurled it across the room. "How could you," I heard myself whisper.

I went to Joseph's closet. I yanked things off the hangers. Blazers and coats and merino wool sweaters. I should have been sleeping. A smell of him leaped up, a smell I hadn't smelled for months—garlic and the lavender water I'd ironed his shirts with. In the end, he had stopped smelling like himself.

I knocked his hats off the top shelf with the back of a broom. They scattered like bugs. I pulled his polo shirts out of their drawers. They crumbled onto the floor. I threw his underwear, one by one, into the crouching bag. His handkerchiefs. His undershirts. His khakis bowed into themselves.

I lifted up a pair of jeans, meaning to fold them. I should have folded everything. Brought it all to the Salvation Army. Oh well. I dropped the jeans back onto the floor. I picked up a silk shirt, laid it out on the bed. I saw the shape of it—the wide, bubbled shape of it. This would not do. The intimacy would not do.

Then I was gathering the clothes into a giant hill. I was falling over my feet. My shoulders were going stiff. I was an old, old lady. I put on my leather gloves. I felt criminal.

I set off in search of every half-full pill bottle. The diapers, slipper socks, lotions, ointments, heating pads, urinal, therapeutic pillows, bedpans, baby wipes, wash bucket and its thick orange sponge.

I was outraged. I was hysterical.

I went to the kitchen looking for garbage bags, but there were none. I went to the hall closet. So many odd things. It overwhelmed me. I wanted it all out. I moved the broom to get a better look and the top shelf fell down.

Boom.

Shit.

Immediately, Dottie banged with her heel. She lived above us but heard everything. It was counterintuitive, I often thought, unless she kept her ear to the floor constantly, which wasn't outside the realm of possibility. These flimsy walls were the only things lamer, frailer than me. I thought, *Go away, please.* I rifled around in the closet. Not one single garbage bag in the entire place.

Then, here appeared Dottie. Next to me. She hadn't knocked. She had a headful of pink curlers. She found me on my knees.

"Shit hellfire," she said. "What on earth." I looked up at her. Sometimes, I wondered if she was really from the South or if she just watched too much TV.

"What are you doing?" she asked.

For a second, I was about to tell her everything, about the note, the truth. But when I took a preparatory breath, I choked on some dust. And then I couldn't. I couldn't get the words out. It was my dignity, among other things, that Joseph had stolen when he'd decided to keep his relationship with our daughter from me.

So I pretended that I didn't see her. I moved around her like she was an ornamental plant. She was used to it. She took the hint and vanished. I located some old supermarket plastic bags on top of the fridge. They were small but they were something. I stood on a dining-room chair, fully aware that I could break my neck. "Fine," I said to no one in particular. "Break twice."

In the bedroom, I found Dottie delicately folding some of Joseph's sweaters. Her eyes were full of tears.

My first thought was that she was messing with my mess and interfering. I had already cleaned up after her—her endless piles of crap. But she was making everything smell like her lipstick again—like wet powder, a smell that made me cringe. I did not want to see her face and felt confident that Joseph would not have either. He wouldn't have wanted her all over his things. I had the urge to tell her that this was not a petting zoo.

"What are you doing?" I asked.

I grabbed at the sweaters.

"You're really going to do this tonight?" she asked, and let go. "Let's have tea instead. Let's watch a movie. Come, doll. Let's sit."

"I don't want to sit," I said.

"All right, then," she said. "But you're really going to throw all this out? It's good stuff. Someone would want it, you know. I'll help you," she said.

It was quite comical: Dottie all of a sudden so philanthropic—an ambassador to the poor. *Joseph,* I wanted to say. *Let's call a spade a spade. Has Dottie ever done a charitable thing in her life?*

And then, I remembered what he'd done. *Forget it,* I said to him in my head. *I'm not talking to you.*

I threw one of his shirts at her and she caught it. It hung from her hands by the sleeve, like a small child unwilling to walk. I wasn't feeling well. I was queasy in the throat. I started another bag, stuffing in thing after thing after thing. The bags were thin, some of them already ripped. I began to sweat. Dottie wasn't helping. I looked at her, about to give it to her good. But then I thought of what Joseph would say: *She's alone, she has nothing; it wouldn't kill us to humor her.* But this was extreme, even for Dottie. This needed more than just humoring.

Just then my chest exploded.

"Ouch!" I cried. I lurched forward and crashed. Dottie was there with me on the floor, on her knees.

"Are you all right?" she said, touching my face. "My word. You're pale as a ghost."

The pain was gone, but I lingered. Here was Dottie, I thought. I looked at her. Dottie. In my head, I begged her to stay like that—with me, for a moment. No one else would.

"You look awful," she said.

"I had a pain."

"Sharp?" she asked. "Below the breastbone?" I nodded. She waved it off.

"I get those all the time," she said. "The doctor says it's gas. I say it's lovesickness. But either way, what can you do?"

I looked at her. I couldn't take my eyes off her.

Dottie had her moments. Like just then. Amazingly, she had justified my feelings, my whole life with Joseph. She hadn't meant to, of course, but she had. Dear Dottie. I was lovesick. And despite herself, she understood. I put my hand on her arm, gave it a little squeeze.

"I'll help," she said. We both stood up, arms full of clothes. She was standing there with the same pile and no progress.

We both got down, gathering. We were a team, and we

weren't. We went through one, two, three, seven bags and cleared the floor. We pushed them down by leaning with our elbows. I could smell Dottie's lipstick again. I rolled my eyes. I didn't care if she saw me. Then I held the bag down and Dottie tried to make knots of the tiny bits of plastic that were left.

My body felt like it had been dipped in concrete. It was heavy and stiff. I wanted to quit. I wouldn't give her the satisfaction.

There must have been twenty bags in all. We kicked them out the front door and into the elevator foyer. I asked myself if I was sure about this, and I was. I wanted to feel lighter. This would help. As we waited for the elevator, the bags popped open. One after the other, like lawn sprinklers. I almost fell on the floor, dove headfirst into his coats.

"It's okay," Dottie said. "Let's just get the stuff back into the bags and we'll tape them shut."

It had always been like this. I hated her. I loved her. She was optimistic. I wasn't. She didn't sweat the small stuff. I did. She was uncomplicated. It was as if the American paleness of her skin reflected something from the inside: day clouds or the foam on cold milk. I imagined my own insides but all I could come up with was a steely basement, full of complex mechanisms, functioning and airtight.

We took care of all the bags. Dottie picked up each one and held it while I wrapped, around and around, with tape, which made a loud, screeching sound that I was grateful for, its irreverence.

And then I remembered. "One second," I said to Dottie and ran back inside. I got an old white blouse from my closet, stuck my fingers into the pocket stitching, and began to rip. I couldn't stop. I'd meant to do something small but instead I made a gash nearly the length of the entire blouse, as if I were somehow aware of a certain gasping that was taking place in my chest and was hoping to give it space, a little air. It sounded like a tiny orchestra of cracking bones and I grimaced, thinking of Joseph being hoisted now from the stretcher to somewhere else. Would they see his bones? I wondered. And what color would they be?

"Oh, Joseph," I said, stuffing my testament to our abandoned Jewish faith under my shirt. I went into the study and grabbed the memento leaves from the garbage. I stuffed those under my shirt too, and I raced—using that term loosely—back out the door to Dottie.

I felt like an abandoned ship, rotted and heavy at the bottom of an ocean, and yet as stray and tinny as a can.

In the elevator, Dottie and I were suddenly, obviously still. I could hear our high, wispy old-lady breaths. For a second, I thought I should get back upstairs to check on Joseph. It didn't feel so different yet. For nearly a year, I'd been talking to him in my head, where he was more likely to answer. I'd been reminding myself of him, not the other way around, him reminding me of himself. I was grateful for what hadn't yet sunk in.

Dottie looked awful. I hadn't ever seen her like this. I didn't imagine she'd ever seen herself like this. She'd never given birth. She never exercised. She never cried in public. Black fuzz stuck to the sweat on her face so she appeared bearded. Stray eye makeup had condensed into native smudges above her cheeks. Still, there was something feminine about her. Graceful even. Despite all her hoopla—the makeup, the fur, the high heels—Dottie had always made me question my own looks. Next to her, I was always wrong—too dressed up or down. I was always trying too hard. But Dottie, she knew what to do. She had a vast knowledge of things that I never would. I could say that about plumbers too, I suppose, or nuclear physicists, but that had nothing to do with anything.

We left the bags by the curb between the smeared dog poop and a meter. They made little expanding sounds against the tape.

I threw the leaves into the street, hoping they'd be swallowed by a gutter. I folded my white shirt, the ripped one, and put it on top. Begrudgingly, I wished Joseph rest.

I wiped sweat from my eyebrows. Salt was dripping into my mouth.

Upstairs, I sat on the couch in Joseph's study with the note in my hands. They were old hands, I noticed, and unattractive, like raw meat. The room seemed enormous but darker without all those pale sheets and blankets. For a moment, I considered going back down, carting the bags up again, emptying them onto the bed, folding everything nicely, and keeping the pile in the study. I could have put flowers by it. I pushed the thought away.

It had been like that when we gave her up. Now it was like that again.

But I wanted to find her. No matter what, no matter what Joseph might have told her about me, I had to find her. Or maybe, I thought, she'd find me. Now. Maybe she was already looking. Maybe she knew all about me and when he didn't call her, she would come, knowing that we'd lost him, and somehow we could share just a little bit in each other's hurt.

I went back to his desk. There were no other clues. I spent hours going through the whole house, searching for our daughter in every dusty corner. I found paperwork I thought we'd thrown out ages ago. Despite the hour, I called numbers for the adoption agency, the doctor we'd gone to. I even called the hospital where I'd given birth. At some point, everything in New York becomes a dry cleaner's. Or a nail salon. I came to one dead end after another, and with each failed attempt, I was let down not only because I was getting nowhere but because each moment I spent wondering about her, about who she was, about her relationship with Joseph, was another moment in which she wasn't finding me either.

I made a mental list of the things that I wouldn't do: I would not turn on music. It would make me cry. I would not read the newspapers. They would make me cry. I would not open the mail, put food in the fishless fish tank, use cardamom, or go near the study. I would not cry. I would not wait.

Everything I did was an act against waiting for her.

That's when I remembered the leaves. I raced to the window, but his things were already picked over. The pile was smaller, ruffled up. I put on my glasses. And the leaves, which I'd tossed into the street, were definitely gone. Probably in the sewer system and halfway to Chinatown by now. I stared at the space where they'd been.

Lorca

Surprise, surprise, I couldn't stop thinking about Blot.

Late Friday night, after I got home from buzzing Victoria and Joseph, I was thinking that if I could have gotten my act together earlier, left my mother not-eating her dinner, Blot and I could have both rung the buzzer. We could have been disappointed together. If I hadn't come up with the brilliant idea to cook dinner —a crappy, no-red-wine-in-the-sauce disaster—we could have done the whole thing together. I wouldn't have been by myself. I wouldn't have almost literally killed two birds—Blot and the Shohets—with one stone.

I tried consoling myself with the fact that I was one step closer to the recipe. I'd heard Victoria's voice. But it did no good. The problem was that my happiness was like a soap bubble; it had to be kept in the air, from touching a surface, from popping. I wondered if some people's default was happiness—and what sadness felt like when you were totally sure that you'd be happy again.

The happiness kept unraveling. First, I felt I'd ruined everything with Victoria. I'd pissed her off. She'd laughed at me. Also, Blot might not give me another chance to hang out with him. I'd stood him up. And suddenly I missed my father. I missed the giant size of him. Even his knuckles were the biggest knuckles I'd ever seen. It's amazing to be hugged by a man like that. Sometimes I wondered if my mother missed that too.

"Dad's a super-hugger," I'd told her once.

"If you're in the mood," she'd said. I'd never not be in the mood, I'd thought. Not for a second.

I told myself, *Be happy. Do you want to make it worse? If you were happy, you could have a normal conversation, go for a normal walk, meet a normal boy at a normal time, and do something that might seem totally, one hundred percent normal.*

But willing myself to be happy was like willing popovers to not collapse when the oven door was opened.

When I got home that night, my mom and Aunt Lou were out. So I took a knife and got into the bathtub. I ran the water as I sat in there. I alternated it from all hot to all cold. I took little flecks off the top of my foot, on the flat, turbot-ish part of it. Turbot en papillote; turbot Provençal; turbot with summer truffles; turbot with langoustine, fennel seed, and horseradish.

I imagined Blot saying to a group of friends, all of them drinking beer and wearing vintage T-shirts, *She's totally nuts. She just didn't show up. I bet she was doing some bizarre ritual with goats. I don't think she has a single friend. She's tweaked.*

I didn't completely believe he'd say that. He wasn't like that. Still, I could hear the words. They enabled me.

Eventually, the blood burst. It made tight, stormy eddies around my legs. It made me feel more alive than anything else could, which sounds ridiculous, I know, because it was life withdrawing from me, that blood. Life scurrying away.

A little while later, I put pressure on it. I put on ointment and a Band-Aid. I toweled off and watched to make sure nothing got stuck in the drain.

I made tea and waited for my mother and Aunt Lou. After a while, the warm sogginess of the bath wore off and I caught a chill as I lay on the couch. It was Friday, after all. They'd be out late. But it was so often like this. The waiting. Some days, I didn't take a sip until I heard her in the hallway. I'd try to capture that moment of settling in, just before, so I could be ready for her. Like I'd just sat down for tea. I'd hold my lips to the top of the mug. I'd hover. I'd close my eyes.

"Now," I'd whisper. "Right now. Right now." Usually, by the time she walked in, the tea was cold.

They came home around one from a winetasting, and Lou got right into the shower. My mother plopped down on the couch across from me and threw her perfect feet onto the table. She smelled of sour melon.

I could have moved to her couch—she would have shoved over—if I'd wanted to. I could have held her pinkie finger if I'd wanted to. But it had become part of me, the waiting. I still felt on the brink of something even though we were here like this. I could have reached out and touched her. Each moment—this one and then the next—was rife with possibility, the potential for something good. Better. More.

She was silent and her silence was everywhere. *But in a moment,* I kept thinking, *now, now, now, now, she'll say something, anything, something loving even, about my face or how I'd grown up or did I want to go to a movie, maybe have dessert for dinner, and that boys are difficult, trust her, she knew all about it, but don't be down, I deserved the best. I would be all right.*

Her words would be soft as cream.

Or maybe it was better this way, I thought. What happened after hope?

Then it shot out of my mouth.

"Maybe you shouldn't have left Dad," I said. There was something angry and gusty inside me. She looked at me and then looked away so that I wasn't even sure if it had registered.

"Maybe things would have been different," I said. "Me, for example."

I wanted her to respond, yell. I waited.

Her eyes settled. I watched her watching. I tried to see what she saw. The corner of that brick building? A television light flickering blue black blue red green? Her head trembled ever so slightly, as if she might have been asleep. But she wasn't. She looked at me suddenly, right at my leg where the cut was, though I was wearing pants. I girded myself.

"It's my day off," she said.

I kept my mouth shut for once. It worked.

"You could have been anything," she continued. "Anything but this. It's so hateful."

Everything dropped. The sense of waiting. It felt like I had been in it for hours. It felt like she'd just turned off the lights and everything was suspended by darkness. *Don't, Lorca. Don't say a word.* I didn't. I couldn't look at her. I made the same promise I'd made to myself constantly, daily, hourly, by the minute over the years: I'll never hurt myself again.

"I'll never understand why you do this to me," she said. "I don't know what else you want."

She crossed her legs. Soon, I covered her with a blanket. I kept telling her I was sorry but I didn't say for what. I was begging her. She didn't say anything back. Not long after, she fell asleep. Sleep came easily to her. Me, I had to fight my way into it. Sometimes, going to sleep felt like being punished. I started to cry but stopped myself. I wasn't angry at her.

If I was going to boarding school, I had no one to blame but myself.

The things in my room were keeping me up. The razors, the tweezers, the cuticle scissors, the box of extra-large staples. A car alarm went off a couple of times and I sang along quietly with the sequence of melodies, hoping the humming would comfort my heart.

I thought of all the scars, all the things I'd done to myself.

I imagined they lit up like moonfish beneath the sheets. My knee, my head, my mouth, my belly—like a cat had shredded the moonfish to bits. In the daytime, you could hardly tell. You'd think I'd be covered in scabs and stitches. I wasn't. All those splinters, they came out. They swelled up and then popped right through the skin without any coaxing at all. Still, at night, I thought about it. I had dreams that I was giving birth and the doctor saw the cuts like tally marks on my thigh and proclaimed, "This woman isn't fit to be a mother." My hospital gown went sideways and the nurses said, "Oh my."

The next day, I did everything I could to keep myself from being spineless and needy and running back to the bookstore to see Blot, including writing *I will not go to the bookstore* one hundred and fifty times on paper, until my hand went numb, trying to convince myself of it or to convince someone who might be looking. I even stood naked in my bathroom and pointed out all the terrible things I saw—the new cuts and bruises; the two purple burn marks on my belly, raised and puckered like slugs. I kept looking into the mirror, saying, "Who is going to love you?" But late last night, Aunt Lou and my mother had watched a romantic-movie marathon, and I'd listened to every word. It made me sappy and got me thinking that maybe Blot did want to see me after all. Things might work out.

I needed his expertise. It was a mystery, this whole thing—Victoria being so cryptic and wanting nothing to do with the restaurant that my mother so loved. Something bad must have happened. Something juicy and full of culinary intrigue. Blot, I'd decided, was my only hope. Together, we could get to the bottom of things. Together, we could find the answers.

So I went. It was Saturday and I knew he'd be working. My mother would have said I was asking for it, just begging to be made a fool of. And she might have been right. I had a lump in my throat the size of a bundt cake pan.

I watched him for a full two minutes before he saw me. He was twirling a pen between two fingers and focusing on the computer screen. His eyebrows were drawn together so tightly, they looked like two trains about to crash, and he wasn't smiling at all, but somehow I could still see his dimples. Or maybe I was imagining them. I was sure that there was no one who could imagine my face in a way that it wasn't.

He caught me looking and smirked. My heart was doing jumping jacks again.

"It's all right," he said. "I've been stood up before."

I laughed without thinking about it. Usually, it was as if my laugh had to be unhinged, like the gate into a garden. This time, it broke free.

"Sorry," I said.

"Don't be," he said. "Things happen."

I was hoping he'd say more. Instead, he was waving at someone on the stairs.

Photography? he mouthed and pointed up and to the right.

"Why are you being so nice?" I asked. "To me."

"You remind me of my sister," he said.

"You have a sister?" I said, though that's how I'd imagined it. Blot and three little sisters who loved him endlessly, knitted him things, and painted his toenails red.

"Yes," he said, and I felt very exposed. What if his sister did what I did? I pulled down my sleeves. "And I miss her. She lives with my parents, who are not my biggest fans."

"Oh," I said.

"She reminds me of you," he said. "Little but big."

I tried making sense of that.

"Anyway," he said. "I don't want people to feel they have to go around explaining themselves to me. I couldn't explain myself to anyone."

He shook the *Zagat,* smiling.

"I'm done in an hour," he said. "Wanna walk?"

I must have said yes. I didn't even censor myself. Yes.

While he was getting his coat and gathering his things, I kept thinking, *I should tell him that I've already gone.* But I wanted us to be in on this together—the suspense, the excitement, everything. I didn't want him to know that I'd failed. And so soon. I thought, I shouldn't have ruined our one thing before our one thing had even begun.

"If I were you," he said, "I would have gone already. I wouldn't have been able to control myself."

"I did," I said. His face fell.

"But," I said, a little desperate, and told him everything, hoping that he'd want to help. Hoping it wasn't over—with him, with Victoria. I told him about how she'd laughed at me.

"That's fishy," he said.

"Fishy," I said.

"That's a weird thing for her to do," he said. "Unless she was hiding something."

"You don't think she was just busy?" I asked, to be sure.

"She could have said so," he said, "if that was the issue."

When he said, "Let's investigate," I was pretty much dying: we were in cahoots.

"Onward?" he said.

"Onward," I said, and I imagined his little sister between us, holding our hands, swinging swinging swinging along.

Outside, half-frozen puddles pocked the street like gigantic wads of spit. Whenever the city was like this, I thought of polar bears on ice floes. I couldn't help it. Then I thought of them dying and how much blood might drain and what it would look like from a helicopter. And then I stopped myself. I didn't do that with every animal. Just enormous ones. Horses, elephants, whales. Sometimes, I wondered what it would be like if everyone in the world did what I did—how much blood there would be if it was gathered and poured from buckets into the streets. If that would somehow drain the color from everything else. I wondered how much blood would have to be lost to make the entire Earth buzz. Buzz like me.

"What are you thinking about?" Blot said, and I swear, all that blood swarmed to my face.

"Danish salt," I said.

He nodded.

"What's her name?" I said. "Your sister."

"Greta," he said. He pointed to a poster on the side of a phone booth. It was for a show at Radio City Music Hall, and the dancers were all legs and lipstick.

"We used to come to the city for that every year," he said. "This same week, actually."

Because I'm an idiot, I thought about how he might like one of the dancers especially. But then I thought about him with his family: who he'd sit next to, walk next to, what they'd eat for snacks, and where they'd sleep.

We walked more slowly than I was used to. Much more slowly. Every time I tried to quicken up, I told myself to quit it. I was suddenly aware of everyone on the street. People were looking at us. And there were so many couples, which made me feel like I belonged to something bigger than myself even though most of them looked like they didn't belong together. I wasn't sure what made people match, though I had a feeling that if I were taller and if my hair didn't have the texture of a frisée salad, we'd have a better chance at it. I almost said that to Blot but caught myself in time.

A little girl raced away from her mother and crashed straight into Blot's knee. She looked up at him.

"Hey," he said to her and she grinned, grabbed his leg.

The mother caught up, pushing an empty stroller, carrying bags in both hands as well as a juice box.

"You guys are sweet," she said.

I didn't look at Blot, not wanting to seem thrilled. I thought, *I didn't make this up. I didn't have to.*

I wondered what my mother would have said if she'd seen us. Probably she'd have asked him if he knew why I'd been suspended, and regardless of his answer, she'd have said, *Let me tell you.* And she'd have told him. And I'd have passed out, right there on the sidewalk, my sleeves and coat lifting, my hair swinging away from my neck, my shoes for some reason falling off, exposing me. All my cuts and bruises leaving no room for discussion.

I did that a lot—thought of why I might have to be naked, why people might have to see me. I got run over and they ripped open my shirt. I fell into freezing water and they stripped me down before wrapping me in a blanket. Worse, sometimes I imagined being shoved into a van and men would begin to rape me but then stop, horrified, over my body.

The truth was, telling him about what I did had occurred to me. I hardly knew him, but I'd imagined that in a dark, quiet place, an empty church, maybe, or a neat graveyard, Blot would move his finger along all my ruined parts. It was firm but smooth, like an eraser. It was undoing. He didn't hate me for what I'd done. His thumb was on my hip, on a scar the size of a pea pod.

"Wanna grab a coffee?" he said. He'd put on fingerless gloves. They were gray and woolly, but if someone had asked me to list every detail of his hand, I would have been able to.

"No," I said. "That's okay." Already I was anxious about ordering, about paying or not paying. I'd have taken forever putting whole milk and sugar into my coffee.

"Yeah," he joked, "me either."

As we walked on, our hands kept colliding. He didn't seem to notice, but I did. I'd started a count. Seven. Every time, it felt as if my breath raced ahead over a hill, and I was stumbling to keep up. The wind was getting colder and stronger; it felt like it was kneading against our backs. But for once, the city wasn't in a rush. An old man with a giant yellow hat stopped short in front of us. He laced his fingers together over his head and looked up. We stopped and did the same. The sky was dark gray and splintered like an expensive countertop. Snowflakes had begun to make their way down in inconsistent clumps. It felt as though the sky were shedding its skin.

"This," the man said to no one, "never gets old."

Later, around Ninety-Ninth Street, Blot said, "Why masgouf?"

I'd nearly forgotten the point of all this interaction. So rarely had this happened to me, that the thing itself was more enjoyable than the idea of it, that I was overwhelmed, distracted. Now I didn't know what to say. Every day for as long as I could remember, I'd imagined happiness like this, so much so that the hope took on a life of its own.

"My parents met at the Shohet and His Wife," I lied, horrified by the romance in my voice.

Blot stopped to tie his shoe. "Oh," he said. "That's nice."

A few blocks later, he stopped again. "And you've never eaten masgouf?" he said.

I shook my head. He had a point.

"What if it's really disgusting?" he said.

"My parents are divorced," I said.

"Gotcha," he said.

"Are yours?" I asked.

"No," he said. "Last I knew."

Earlier, I had Googled *Iraqi + Cooking*. On YouTube, I found a series of clips. An Iraqi woman named Violet cooked in her kitchen in Queens. She had a face like a button mushroom quenelle and she kept saying, "Can you smell that in your kitchen too?" You could tell that her son was the one taping her because he said, "Mom, your accent, your accent."

And she said, "What do you want me to do with my accent?"

She threw her hands up. They were covered in egg and flour paste and some went flying onto the lens and he said, "Mom," like he'd just found her lost in the woods.

In one clip, she talked about her husband, who never got out of Iraq. "They thought he was a communist," she said. She was shaking her head, and her son said, "Cook, Mom." She glanced away, embarrassed. She looked like she'd rather stop. But she didn't. After that, she talked about the food. The spices. How they used to make lentils and rice on Thursday and fried fish on Friday and how they prepared sheets of tomato paste or apricots and left them to dry on the rooftops. She was wearing bright blue crumbly eyeliner and silver nail polish but aside from that, everything about her was nutty and brown. She was a sesame seed. In the end, she took a big bite out of these cigarlike appetizers and before she could say anything, her son said, "Don't talk with your mouth full," and she snorted at him and said, *"Bukra fil mish mish."* Whatever that meant.

Then the camera went off.

I decided that I loved her. I imagined having dinner at her table. I bet she'd never sit down. I bet she'd lean over people's shoulders as though she were tending to plants, asking did they try it, like it, want more—and regardless, she'd heap another serving on top of every plate. I wondered how you said *mangia* in Arabic.

I thought about telling Blot all that, but just then I saw something that stopped me. A woman was about to enter a liquor store. Her long neck accommodated many rolls of a camel-colored scarf. She was tall and thin like a saffron thread, and though I couldn't see the details of her hands, there was a feminine quality to them, as if her fingers were the slender tails of many cats.

They curled around the doorknob and she slipped inside. Her dark hair was pulled into a bun, shiny like swirled chocolate butter sauce. The rounded part down the left side of her scalp was unmistakable. My mother.

Immediately, I felt the urge to explain to her, to justify myself. I was doing this for her, you see. I wasn't having fun. I looked at Blot and said that I'd be right back, but when I turned around again, racing to the store window, she was gone. There was no one inside but an Asian man behind the counter. He was writing something, unbothered. I stood there, my breath fogging the glass. *That's why,* I thought. *That's why masgouf.*

"What?" Blot said, next to me now. "Celebrity sighting?"

"Yes," I said. "Bobby Flay."

"I've always wanted to try his blue corn pancakes with barbecued duck," he said.

"Me too," I said.

The lie about the sighting had come easily and I was grateful. I wouldn't have known how to begin.

Blot seemed unbothered. He began walking north again, this time in the street. He tapped his fingers on car hoods as he passed them. He didn't make a scene of it, didn't hurt them, just did *tap tap tap* as if checking for animal life in a tree. Once, I'd closed my finger in a car door three times in a row. To this day, my pinkie looks more like a barkless twig than a pinkie. When Blot walked on the sidewalk, he tapped side mirrors one time per car. He noticed me staring.

"I don't know why I do this," he said, shoving his hands into his pockets and shaking his hair out of his face. "Weird habit."

"I eat cheese and watermelon," I said.

"That's Middle Eastern!" he just about shouted. "I read it in one of those books. It's fate."

I believed him, though I tried not to.

I kept waiting for him to get bored with me, to change his mind. It occurred to me that it was Saturday and he might suddenly have to bolt for a shmancy date or a concert. But he seemed to be enjoying himself, his tapping. I had a sense he'd act the very same way without me, which didn't make me feel awful. In fact, it took some of the pressure off. I didn't have to go through the ABCs of chitchat, which Lou said was every successful conversationalist's go-to. A: ageism; B: belly dancing; C: cabbage diet. After a while, I tapped on the mirror of a parked car and he said, "Excellent choice, my dear."

I could see him smile as he peeked into a minivan exploding with old files. He straightened and then tapped on the mirror. I wasn't thinking about slowing down now—or about speeding up. I seemed to be managing the pace just fine. I wasn't thinking about my mother either. I pretended to look at the trees, doors, dogs, curbs, roofs, street signs, stray pigeon feathers, anything—just so I would stop staring at him. But even in Manhattan, with its thousands of restaurants, windows, and lights, with its millions and millions of people, sometimes it's impossible to distract your eyes from one totally amazing thing.

When we turned onto 112th Street, we became noticeably quiet. Aside from last night, I rarely came this far north. Here, the brownstones were bigger, rounder, redder, and more elaborate than the ones in our neighborhood. The stairs were stouter, sturdier. The doors looked like they belonged in a library. The windows had painted eyebrows and copper lids. One was covered in ivy. Another was made of two different stones, piled one over the other like sandwich meat. It probably never felt busy or like the weekend up here.

I pointed to a building with miniature Christmas trees lined in window boxes on every floor. They reminded me of sunken dwarfs in enormous hats.

"That's it," I said.

The Shohets' building was the tallest. The Washington Irving. It had a wide, grand staircase and pudgy hanging lights. Iron balconies. A carving of a woman surrounded by curtains and flowers. The building looked like it should have a doorman but it didn't. I was strong now and purposeful and tried to appear that way. This was what we'd come for, after all. Otherwise, there was no excuse. I crossed the street, and Blot jogged behind me. I was aware of the way I looked from the back for the first time in my life.

But it wasn't just Blot making me anxious. This was huge. What if they just handed me the recipe? What if that was that? Then what?

I checked the buzzer again. Victoria and Joseph Shohet: apartment 3F. Front. There were Fs and Rs. I walked back across the street again to see if any lights were on. I turned around and Blot stopped short. He'd been on my heels. His face was washed out by streetlight. His eyes were wet and blistery from the cold.

"What?" he said, all dimples and innocence. "I'm just following you. You seem to have a plan."

I realized that I didn't. Of course I didn't. All the research up to this point had been so abstract, far-flung even. When it started two days ago, it had been about one very specific thing, but it felt smoky now, like I'd planned it in my sleep.

We stood next to each other, looking up. I considered ringing the buzzer, trying to explain myself yet again. It wasn't so complicated, really, except that it was. Anytime I said anything about my mother, I became a spinning dreidel. Blot used his finger to count up three stories to her window. He whispered, "*Uno, dos, tres.*" My skin went tingly.

"That's theirs," he said, still whispering. My skin curled again. I could feel his breath on my face. I wondered about the side of my nose. I pretended to be very focused to justify the tightness of my jaw. The Shohets' apartment was dark. No one was by the window. They had long blue curtains, only one of them tied back.

"Hey," Blot said. "Look."

He inched backward and hunkered down on the bottom stair of a townhouse. He crossed his arms over his knees. I followed his eyes. Two women carrying more than they could bear hustled through the door of the Washington Irving. They were dropping things along the way, leaning back for balance and kicking open the door and letting it smack shut.

"I'll get it," one said.

"I'll get it," the other one said.

One was taller. She was wearing heels and a flowing bathrobe. Her legs stuck out, skinny, and her chest too, as she leaned over, dropping the bags by the curb. She stood, fixed herself, let out a huge sigh, and shook out her arms. She reminded me of a pigeon.

"My word!" she said, plumping her hair. "This is exhausting."

The other one without a doubt was Victoria. I recognized her voice.

I stepped back into the townhouse shadow, feeling like I'd been caught. Blot shifted over to make room and I squatted next to him. No air moved between us.

"Do you think that's her?" he whispered. "She looks Middle Eastern."

My heart raced—and not just because of Blot. I imagined resting an enormous platter of masgouf on our dinner table, perfect slices of lemons like happy suns all around. White votives, my mother's favorite, were lit and set in a straight line. Their wicks made snapping sounds and smoked.

The women came in and out, in and out, and dropped bags by the curb, bags messily wrapped with tape and on the verge of exploding. Victoria picked up some stray items from the stairs. Everything about her was quieter than the other one. She dropped a sweater and some socks and a scarf onto the pile. Then she reached into her own shirt, into her bra, maybe, and pulled out something. She folded it slowly and placed it on top of everything else. She put her hand down over it, as if waiting for a burner to heat up. She took it away suddenly, when the other one looked toward her. Then they both stood there, over the things. They looked at each other and then they looked down. They were out of breath. I could see their chests move into and out of the streetlight. They were older. Ancient, actually. For a second, it was like they'd killed someone.

Victoria looked across the street toward us, and I sort of ducked, though of course she had no idea who I was. Blot dropped all the way to the ground like a real pro. At first, she didn't seem to notice. She was looking without seeing. Then, suddenly, her eyes clicked. She saw me. It spooked her. She put her hand to her cheek and then up in a half wave, as if admitting that she scared easily, and it wasn't my fault. It was Victoria. It had to be. It wasn't Violet from YouTube, but she looked like her. The color of her skin, like a grain, her strong eyes and nose. I knew.

"Holy cannoli," Blot whispered. "This is intense."

I wanted to say *Victoria,* but she was turning around already. They both were. The other one was paying no attention and nearly whacked herself against a parking meter. Blot whispered, "Ouch," on her behalf. She fixed the tie on her robe into an even bow. Victoria guided her. They entered the building soundlessly. Victoria turned back for a moment and I thought she'd seen us, but she was just letting her eyes wander, as if scanning for the source of a strange sound or a burst of air.

"Dude," Blot said. "I've got chills."

Once they were gone, we waited for a light to turn on in the window, but it didn't.

"I wonder what Joseph is doing," I said, my voice sounding like a nuclear explosion. We'd been whispering for so long.

"Maybe he's already in bed," Blot said. I imagined a small old man reading, a bowl of ice cream on the nightstand, the covers pulled up to his chin.

"Maybe he's sick of her cleaning out her closets," Blot said.

Don't you dare, I told my mind when it leaped to us as a couple sixty years away.

I crossed the street. I told Blot to stay where he was and keep watch. I looked both ways. I looked both ways again. As it turned out, they weren't her things. They were men's clothes. Heaps of them. Nice things, too, clean-smelling, like rose water. I wondered what my father would have done with a wardrobe like this. He had a couple pairs of wool socks that he washed in the sink. My mother must have had one thousand camisoles. They all looked the same, but she said they were nothing like one another.

There was other stuff too—bottles of pills and sponges and things for taking care of someone sick and old. A seat to go on top of the toilet. I picked up a crumpled red corduroy shirt with snaps at the pockets and showed it to Blot across the street. He gave me the thumbs-up. It undid itself and threw off a stronger smell of lavender. It was for a large man—tall and heavy. I put it down again, just how I'd found it.

I picked up something else—that one item that Victoria had folded so nicely. It was a woman's blouse, silky and white, with a small yellow stain on the collar. Over the right side of the chest was a huge, gaping tear. Someone had ripped it. It wasn't done with scissors. *Keriah.* Bubbie had taught me about that. She'd taught me everything I knew about Judaism, which was basically nothing.

Now Blot came over. He couldn't help himself.

"What's the deal with that?" he said. Tears had risen into my throat. I told myself not to get ridiculous. Joseph was still alive. Maybe these weren't his things. Maybe she'd gotten divorced, never changed the mailbox. Maybe that wasn't her at all. Maybe it was another Middle Eastern woman in the building. Maybe she wasn't even Middle Eastern. Maybe this was a ripped shirt. Just that. Why did I always get dramatic?

I hadn't answered his question and somehow didn't want to betray her. I didn't want to cry either.

Just then light poured out on us from above. We looked up. It was Victoria's apartment. We started to run, but we stopped. She couldn't have cared less. Mindlessly, she was pawing a blue curtain. She rested her forehead on the window. I squinted to see if her eyes were closed.

I was still holding her shirt.

My whole body filled with sadness. She'd lost him. I told myself it was none of my business. That he could have been the rudest man who ever lived. Or maybe he was alive, knock on wood. Maybe he'd just lost weight. That was all. He was over his sickness. All better now. She was just reorganizing.

For a moment, it occurred to me that I might have it all wrong. I could have made something out of nothing. So I took a deep breath and checked the pill bottles. Each one confirmed it. *Joseph Shohet. Joseph Shohet. Joseph Shohet.* This wasn't how I'd imagined it. They were supposed to be a happy, vibrant couple, thrilled to jot down a recipe for me, for my mother.

But Victoria had ripped the shirt down the right side. Her face, the way she'd looked for someone. I was right. I had to be right.

"What?" Blot said. I was trying not to lose it.

I refolded the shirt. I whispered, "I'm so sorry."

I didn't know what else to say.

Blot was going through the things himself now. He lifted up a pill bottle and turned it over in his fingers. "Man," he said. I could hear the pills shifting and shifting like bones in a coffin. He shook his head.

"I get it," he said.

We started back toward the subway.

The snow was really coming down now and everything was

a version of white—from the watery, pearlized pavement to the thickened branch on the tallest tree, as if all of it was encrusted with day-old fat. The sky was a dirty violet color, like a layer of dust on top.

We crossed the street, and something else not white caught my eye. A pink, laminated flyer, giant and bright, taped to the lamppost. It stood out against everything. I stepped closer and noticed a border of cartoonish dancing forks.

IRAQI JEWISH COOKING CLASSES, it said. TAUGHT BY CHEF VICTORIA. And then, scrawled in thick permanent marker: *203 West 112th Street.*

"That's Victoria's address," I said. "Right?"

Suddenly, I wasn't sure. I checked the street sign: 112th Street, yes. I blew on the flyer, sending shoots of water in every direction. It was her picture too. She wore an outfit that looked more like a delicate arrangement of cabbage leaves than clothes and was holding a jar of spices toward the camera. Someone had told her to smile, I could tell. She was pretending to say *Cheese!*

Blot was behind me. "Damn," he said. "It is." He was nodding intensely, grinning.

The class was on Monday, the sign said. The day after tomorrow. At 7:00 P.M. sharp.

"That's our in," he said. "You're golden."

Now I saw that flyers were everywhere—fastened to hydrants, trees, a dilapidated For Sale sign. We crossed the street again, back toward her building.

The lights were off again at Victoria's apartment. Her window rested black and shiny against the warm stone color of the building. I wondered if she was sleeping or if it was impossible to sleep at a time like this.

A few minutes later, we were still there, as Blot was taking down the number for a dog-walking job. A woman walked out of the building. Not Victoria, but the other one. She looked both ways before she descended the stairs. She held one arm out for balance and with the other one she held a large magazine on top of her head, like a shoddy roof. I had the urge to run to her, protect her from falling. It wasn't clear if she was tiptoeing or just unstable on her feet. She moved like she believed she was being watched, though I was sure she hadn't seen us. We were in the dark. When she reached the bottom of the stairs, she stopped and readjusted her robe. A clump of snow fell from a branch and plopped onto her magazine, and she jumped, making a sound like she'd been terribly offended.

She leaned over the pile of Joseph's clothing, opened a bag, and plucked up one item and then another, inspecting and then letting each thing fall to the ground, where it stuck like a lily pad. She did this over and over, rhythmically. Gradually, she moved faster and faster, obviously searching for something. She grew frustrated, her movements shorter and more tense. Though it had seemed at first that she was simply perusing, it became clear that she had lost something and was determined to find it. I could see the snow collecting on her head. She attempted to fling her hair dramatically from her face, but the strands were too short and thin and she had to smooth them back with her hands. I noticed how pale she was. I imagined that in the daytime, her skin looked sickly and lined, like moldy fruit. In the streetlight, though, it glistened, like the inside of a McIntosh.

Finally, she found what she was looking for. She stopped everything. I thought I heard her gasp.

"Now what?" Blot started. I touched his arm. Shush.

The woman picked up a sweater and then, as if remembering herself, turned around and looked up toward Victoria's dark window, dropping it to her side.

She made her way up the stairs, stuffing the sweater into the belt of her robe at the back. It moved side to side with her hips, and one sleeve dangled down, sinister, like the tail of a fickle cat.

"Well, all right, then," Blot said, as if something definitely wasn't all right but he didn't know what. Neither did I.

When we were sure that she wasn't coming back, we started walking again.

Later, I looked up Joseph Shohet online to see if there was anything about his death. There wasn't. Earlier, I had done an image search and found a photo of Victoria and Joseph at a Middle Eastern food festival in Brooklyn ten years ago. Now I looked at it again. Of course it was her, the woman we'd seen. Maybe she seemed older now, but it was still her.

In the photo, they looked content, holding hands and with bent elbows so that the knot of their fingers was by their faces. If it's possible to see conflict in a photo, you couldn't see it in this one.

I printed it out, folded it, and put it into my wallet. The truth was, I'd done things like this before: cut out the saddest article I'd ever read about children getting raped or about animals being skinned just for money. I could use that as an excuse when I didn't have one. I told myself I was hurting so they could hurt less.

Victoria

Five years before, I would have bet my life that I would never work again. We'd closed the restaurant. My feet hurt. I had no more small talk in me. That's what being a hostess is. It's walking and talking. I would have said, had anyone asked, that I wanted to do nothing but catch up. Gather my rosebuds. That I'd like to never ask another person how he was doing, if he needed anything. An extra napkin, perhaps? The check? All the little things I needed to take care of, I'd finally have the time to do: clean out the junk drawer, glue a broken turtle sculpture, throw out ripped stockings, edit our cabinet of spices. The coriander had no flavor. It had been there for years. Chipped dishes needed weeding out.

But Joseph got sick. I told myself that the catching up would have to be put on hold. There wasn't time for it. No room for it. All I wanted to do was wait for him to get better. I hate to be superstitious, because what's the point? You know what they say about a watched pot. I watched him. In Baghdad, they'd say, "A fog cannot be dispelled with a fan." Still, I waited. I would sit for so long my knees went numb. I began delaying my coffee until ten. I found that it was best not to start reading until noon. That way, there was all afternoon to do it. The nurses began to make me lunch. I would sometimes notice that I hadn't changed clothes in a week. I had been waiting. I waited. I thought I'd never have the energy to work again. And yet, when Dottie left with the photo of me, threatening to see the graphics whiz kid upstairs, I didn't run after her. I didn't wrestle her to the floor and yank the picture from her hands. But now, the class held so much weight. Our daughter might come through the door. I wanted to capture the image. I wanted to hold it down in my head and examine it. I wanted to see her face. Of course she wouldn't come. I knew she wouldn't. It was self-indulgent for me to think this way. Foolish too.

But what would she think? I wondered. If she did come. I knew what: *Remind me to kill myself before I end up like her* is what. *Look at her clothes. The moth holes. Everything needs airing out. She must sit in here with the windows shut so tight that she inhales in the evening what she exhaled that morning.* That's what she'd think—and that it smelled old in here. Like someone had been napping with an open mouth. She'd feel trapped. I couldn't blame her.

I opened the windows. I lit a candle. I ran a dishtowel over the hanging pots so they didn't look so dull. I tinkered around with the silverware so that there was sound in the kitchen again. I poured soap all over the sink. There.

Monday morning, less than twenty-four hours before the first class, I woke up at two, anxious to check on Joseph. I turned on the lamp, put on my robe, and got to the doorway before I remembered. It took that long.

It had been just three nights since Joseph died, and there had been much of the same: the same concern shaking me in my sleep, hurling me into a state of groggy paranoia. And then—disappointment. I stood at the doorway, aware of a certain quality about the air. It felt fluid—more than before—and unpunctuated, as if everything swished around between the walls, unchecked. I was alone. I was the only breathing thing. I thought of our daughter. Imagined her somehow here too. She was everywhere now, a fast-moving shadow attached to every one of our things. I thought about Joseph's body, not alive but— No, I wouldn't say it. Not alive. The remains would come soon and then I'd put him in his study, in his urn, next to a photograph of his mother. She was wide-shouldered and stern, almost manly. Her smile was a short, straight line. He would be ashes beside her. Lighter than feathers. She could strew him all over with a snort, a too-brusque turn on her square heel to grab a fleeing chicken.

I wished I could have kept his body, his actual body, for a little while longer. It's morbid but I read about a lady who kept her husband in her garage. She liked to pay the bills with him present. It was something they used to do together. And so, once he was dead, she brought her manila envelopes, her pens, stamps, and calculator to the garage. She sat on a chair and reminded him that the late fee for the electric bill was exorbitant, that they really should switch cable companies. I thought of her when I decided to put the urn on the shelf, where I knew it would get the morning sun. Joseph believed there were two kinds of people: morning-sun people, and the others.

I went into the kitchen and turned on the light. It made the hallway look darker, denser. All of the ingredients were here. I'd ordered them over the phone yesterday and had them delivered to our door. Even flowers. Now I rearranged the flowers in their vase. I cut up some lemons and put them in a Mason jar with olive oil, sugar, and salt. It felt good to be doing this. The lemons were now the brightest part of this house. It was already tomorrow. Seventeen hours until class. The thought made me want to lock the door. If someone rang, I'd just not answer.

And yet, for a moment, I was proud. The citrus slices were

floating in their jar in perfect, consistent rounds. Later, I'd tell the students to do this very thing. *They're great to have on hand,* I'd say. Simply throw one in the pan with your chicken or fish.

Our child might think of me as the kind of woman who prepared, who kept heaps of little meat pies, *sfiha,* wrapped in tin foil in the freezer, who was ready at a moment's notice to whip up a feast. I should have made some *turshee,* or some other pickled goodie that would last. I used to do that all the time. I used to be that kind of woman. Maybe our daughter would feel less sad knowing that I hadn't given her up because I was incapable, a drug addict, a loser. It was because I was smart and deliberate, a planner, a woman who stuck to her guns. Right? Wouldn't it seem like that? I knew what was best for her. The truth was, I hid Pop-Tarts behind the vinegar. Broken bits of wheat crackers lined the couch like a random sprouting of tiny mushrooms.

A wave of tiredness came over me and I started back to the bedroom. I wasn't afraid of being alone until I thought about it. I tiptoed. I checked that the door was locked. I jumped when I noticed the Chinese takeout menu on the floor, forcibly stuffed halfway under the door. I wasn't sure if I was afraid of an intruder or if I felt like one myself. Joseph's father, a great believer in proverbs, used to say something like "At the end of the night, all ghostly cries can be heard." Haunted.

I crawled back into bed. It occurred to me that I might not have enough almonds, that the chickpeas wouldn't have sufficient time to soak, that everyone would be bored, that I wouldn't remember how to remove the lamb from the bone and I'd mangle the thing. I'd had it delivered from the best butcher in town. The extra eighty cents per pound to have it filleted wouldn't have killed me. I should have splurged. *And what if someone asks about chicken liver foam?* I wondered. I was behind the times. I didn't make foam. I didn't want them to whisper. That, I couldn't take.

And yet, I was hopeful.

Four people had called to confirm yesterday. Four people with four different voices, using four different phones, four different pairs of socks on their feet. Actual people, I thought, including Robert. No relation to Dottie. One of them was a woman, the right age. When she said "Hello," my hands began to quiver. Her voice was tugged just slightly by French and I wondered, Had our daughter gone to boarding school in the Alps? Did she ski? I couldn't. I'd never learned.

I didn't dream every night. But that night I did, and I remembered it. There were rows of chickens lined up along our counter. And there was a knife. I sharpened it. I got that far. I lifted up a chicken and turned it over like I was just about to fillet it. I pulled its legs apart. I was in a red apron. But then. Nothing. I couldn't for the life of me recall what to do then.

I started getting dressed four hours before class. And a good thing too. It didn't go well. I was an old lady. A deflation. My knees sagged into rotten peaches. Even my ankles were orbits of skin above my feet. Let us not discuss my neck or chest. God forbid. The clothes looked horrid.

I tried on every hostess outfit I had. They were all too big. Worse, they were highly inappropriate. Worse. In the calculated light of our restaurant, with Arabic music and high heels and stockings, they'd worked because they were ethnic and part of the whole thing. But now they were absurd: shimmery and sounding like crunching lettuce when I walked. I tried on a black dress. Too fancy. A pair of purple slacks and white blouse. I put on my orange corduroys. Old Faithfuls. I'd worn them on the Friday that John F. Kennedy was shot. I was shining Joseph's shoes in front of the television and he was rubbing my shoulders. I dropped the shoe right onto my finger when we heard it. I pinched it so badly that a blood blister formed.

Now I called Dottie.

"Dottie," I said, "I have nothing to wear. I can't even find an apron."

I knew this would thrill her. She'd be flattered to the point of tears.

Sure enough, she waltzed through the door seconds later in a red chenille robe. I made a face and then began to laugh. Her smile disappeared. She looked away.

"If you feel I have so little fashion sense," she said, nose up, turning around, "you shouldn't have phoned."

"I have no choice," I said. "Who else can I call?"

I used to be easy to talk to. I used to say the right things. I was a hostess, for crying out loud. Now I was hateful. And to Dottie? She didn't deserve this. She was all I really had—actually had. Again, it occurred to me to tell her about the note, about our daughter, but I couldn't. All these years, Dottie had wanted to be part of our relationship—Joseph and mine. We were so solid. And it was only because of that that we could tolerate her. My admitting to Joseph's secret, our secret, would unravel too much.

I looked down. I was in a towel. There were two hours until the class.

"Dottie, please," I said. "Look at me. I need you."

She smelled like a cosmetics shop. It made my nose itch.

"You do," she said. "Of course you do. What's happened to you?"

What had happened to me? I looked terrible. I was an utter disappointment.

Dottie realized what she'd done, how she'd affected me. Her face got smaller with embarrassment.

"I'm okay," I said.

"I know," she said.

She took a deep breath and waited for me to follow suit. Inhale. Exhale.

"Go wash your face," she said, quieter, gentler now. "I'll be back."

As she walked out, I noticed toilet paper stuck to the heel of her shoe. I began to say something but stopped myself. Sometimes, enough is enough.

I threw cold water on my face and believed that I smelled, in the threads that dripped off my nose, notes of cinnamon and leather. Joseph's after-shave. I held my breath, willing the smell back. I'd forgotten he was gone. How long did that last? When would it sink in, I wondered, and stop surprising me? When would it be everywhere all the time, like a season in full? I walked out of the bathroom, sat down on the bed, steeling my body against lying down.

I looked again at the only traces I had of my daughter. Here were papers from the adoption agency in New Jersey, unfolded now but with deep, determined lines all through. The phone number of the doctor I'd seen. Here was a little cloth, yellowed and flimsy now. I'd tried to leave it at the hospital. I left my clothes. I left my comb. I left the book I'd been reading with the bookmark inside. I didn't care. I left the cloth I used to wipe my face—or so I thought. Earlier, I'd been looking for my pearl bracelet and found the cloth shoved to the back of a drawer in our guest bathroom. It was among junk—hair clips, broken blow dryers, unused hostess gifts; everything that had no place. Joseph must have retrieved it. I'd gasped. What had I done to him? He'd tried so hard to hold on. Had I ever said I was sorry? That I couldn't remember made me hate him less for his secret.

The papers and cloth were all I had of her. Everything and nothing. Everything important ends up in a tiny space. A drawer, a safe, an envelope, a small jar with a lid.

It was pathetic, I realized, for me to go looking for her now, after all these years. After she'd known Joseph and she'd never wanted to know me. But without me, she'd never know that he'd passed. Or would she? Had he had a plan for this: that the nurse would call her, or our lawyer? Was everyone in on the secret but me?

I went into the living room and waited for Dottie. She came back, her arms weighed down with outfits that I'd never even seen. She put one thing against me and held the hanger above my head, accidentally whacking me with it. Then another. Another. "Yuck," she said, and I was embarrassed. I was awful. That was the truth of it. There was a lump in my throat, like all my organs had been gathered and knotted there. I was weak. This was too much.

But then she found it. Her head bobbed like mad when she put a blue wrap dress against me.

"That's the one," she said. "It's the perfect thing."

"It is?" I said, but she wasn't paying attention. I looked at her, wanted her to know that I had something to say—I wanted to tell her how important this day was, what it meant—but she was fumbling with a pile of tangled jewelry, shaking it, cursing. "Lord Jesus!" she shouted.

As quickly as it came, the urge to speak vanished. You say it and it's no longer yours.

Dottie helped me into the dress. I held on to her. She held on to the dresser. And still, we were shaking.

"Aren't we agile," I said.

"Don't I know it," she said.

She tied a bow at my hip. She came close. I wanted to rest on her.

I sat down to stuff my feet into some slippers. She wasn't going to make me wear heels. I stood up. She bent her knees to get a good look at me. She pulled a chunky silver bracelet from her pocket and shoved it onto my wrist.

"There," she said. "Ta-da."

I was pinching at the fabric, squirming in it.

"Too tight," I said.

"Shush you," she said.

I tried to untie the dress but she smacked me on the hand.

"Don't," she said. "You're perfect."

I acted like I wasn't happy about it because for the moment, I was.

I let her do her thing. Fuss over my hair and apply three different lip-glosses to my mouth. I kept waiting for her to mention the slippers but she didn't. That was the thing about Dottie. Sometimes, she was exactly right.

"Don't come down here during class," I said.

"Oh, please," she said. "I'd double your attendance." She swung her hips, winked with one eye and then the other. I liked Dottie like this. When she was jokey, not taking things personally. She had some stake in this class too, I knew. We were both less futile, less old, for it.

It was seven o'clock and no one had shown up.

It was seven fifteen and no one had shown up.

It was seven thirty and no one had shown up.

Dottie had come down twice already. She knocked on the door. Banged, really. She started yelling, "Victoria! Open the door! It's Dottie!" She singsonged it so the neighbors wouldn't think less of her, or that she was unloved. I didn't open it. I heard her shoes click-clack right back to where they'd come from. Let her pout herself sick, I thought.

The phone had rung once, at about ten after seven, and I'd thought it might be one of them saying the subways were flooded or, better yet, he or she was downstairs but the dumb buzzer didn't seem to be working. But it was no one. I raced to the phone but there was no one on the other end. I kept saying, "Hello, hello, hello." Nothing. "*¿Hola? Soy* Victoria," I tried.

I'd spent too much time hoping. In the beginning, I'd been

skeptical. It's better that way, always safer. It was Dottie's fault for getting me into this in the first place. She hadn't gotten my hopes up though. That was my own doing. I got a little dreamy. It felt nice. I let go. That's the compromise. I forgot that. Happiness is an act of faith. But you can't let it in and be done with it. Emotions come at you from all directions. I forgot to cover my head. It had been a while.

Now, you'd think the sadness would come from something else. From loneliness, rejection, something fundamental. But it didn't. It was from the silly fact that I was all dressed. It took so much effort. I'd clipped on earrings. They pulled. They made my ears hot. Now my earlobes were raw and stiff. In the end, I'd taken off my slippers and put on shoes. Not only that, but I'd put powder in too. I used mouthwash. I cut my hangnails. So much for nothing.

I went back to the kitchen and looked at the stations I'd set up. I'd set up stations! One for peeling and chopping. Another for butchering the meat. Another with the food processor and a spatula. The salt was in the water. The water was in the pot. The pot was on the stove. It would have boiled. There would have been so many bubbles and that smell of starch. I loved that, cooking in the evenings. Basmati rice was my favorite smell in the restaurant. Nothing like it.

Each person was going to have a station. I would have pointed them out, like exits on an airplane. I had baked date-nut bread. The smell still floated in the kitchen. It's the oldest trick in the book.

It didn't surprise me. Or it did, but it shouldn't have. I'd had this feeling it wasn't going to work out. I imagined our daughter getting to her building's elevator and turning around, going back inside her apartment. I imagined her taking off her coat, stuffing it into the closet. I imagined her telling her husband to sit down because she was going to prepare dinner after all; I imagined her kids cheering. She took homemade pizza dough out of the freezer. Together, they all cut the smoked mozzarella, the mini yellow tomatoes. The kids assembled them as they crouched on stools. All the while, their mother hated me. That kind of thinking was a leap of faith too. I was a pessimist. Joseph always said, "Stop hoping the sky's going to fall." It didn't help when he said that, though he had a point.

Just after Joseph and I gave up the child, he took me for a picnic by the Hudson River. We found the perfect spit of grass. We bought hot dogs and soda. We even bought a kite. We were very quiet, the two of us, spinning on separate planes with our thoughts. We hardly said a word for hours, just staring, eyes glazed over, trying to get used to ourselves again. Eventually, it got dark. Joseph held my hand, put a sweater beneath my head, and we lay down to watch the sky.

"What?" I said, finally. "New York doesn't have stars?"

He laughed.

"Come on," he said and nudged me.

But you could hardly see them. In Baghdad they felt so close, like snowflakes on your lashes. It occurred to me that I didn't really miss Baghdad after all. What I missed was the person I'd been when I was with Joseph there—when I'd been happy and unafraid of losing him and unaware of what could happen to a person when she refused to admit to sadness, to a gaping hole—and my former self felt like a stranger insisting that she knew me, absolutely sure of it.

"Look harder," Joseph said. "They're there. Look hard."

Now I began rewrapping the lamb in some wax paper but I didn't have enough. I'd thrown out the butcher paper, not thinking. So I had to use tin foil too. It was a mess, in the end, as if half-ravaged by animals. I couldn't imagine what I'd do with all the food. I might cook the dishes as planned and give them away. But I didn't think I could carry all the vegetables, rice, sauce, and so on. I'd collapse before reaching the front door.

I dumped the lamb into the garbage can. Joseph would have told me about the starving children. "I can't right now," I said aloud. "So cut it out. I just can't."

I poured the water back into the sink. It splashed against the sides and got on Dottie's dress, but what did I care? No one to see it. I told myself that I would never have to get dressed up again. If I felt like it, I could stay in fleece until the day I died.

I went back to the bedroom. I leaned on the wall to take off my shoes. I had to sit down to get hold of the buckle. I untied the dress. The buzzer rang. One shoe on and one shoe off.

I yelled, "One minute!," as if my voice might carry out the window and down to the street. I yanked at the other buckle. I was getting heated. I was getting winded. I yanked so hard the buckle broke. The shoe flew across the room, smacked against the wall, and then stopped. I had to smile. I wasn't dead yet.

"Coming!" I said. I held the dress closed as I made my way through the house, leaving a trail of baby powder across the floor. Things bobbled. My skin had a life of its own. If Joseph could see me now, I thought, he'd jiggle his skin too, in solidarity.

"Coming!" I yelled again.

Dottie heard me upstairs. She tapped with her foot. *Not now, Dottie,* I thought. *Not now, please.*

"Hello," I blurted into the buzzer, panting, letting my shoulders drop forward and my head rest on the wall. The dress was open. I could see my own underwear—and everything.

The voice, when it came through, was garbled, static.

"I can't hear you," I said.

Dottie would have called me a lunatic. I know what she would have said. *You're going to let someone upstairs? You don't even know who it is? And you not dressed? Where shall I begin?*

"Come up," I said, and pressed the buzzer to unlock the downstairs door.

I waited with my eye to the peephole, my heart pounding like an angry fist. Seconds later, a girl emerged from the stairwell, her feet barely tapping the floor. I stepped back, shocked. She wasn't a fifty-year-old lady. She wasn't my daughter. She wasn't Robert either. She was fifteen, if that. Her cheeks were the color of brick. I opened the door. She was wearing a rain jacket, and her hands were hidden in her sleeves.

"Sorry," she said. "The subway was so slow. I got out at Ninety-Sixth Street and walked."

Her voice was deeper than I would have thought. She took off a hat that looked too big for her, all flaps and flannel. She was long-necked, reddish-haired, and freckled, but olive in the skin, as if she'd been shaded. Her eyes were light blue, like ancient sea glass. She took off her sneakers without using her hands and then leaned over and placed them neatly by the door. They were flat as pancakes, with shoelaces that didn't match. She was wearing socks with white bugs on them. She curled her toes when she saw me looking.

"You know they eat them in Thailand?" she said. "Oven-baked with green curry."

"Socks?" I asked.

"No," she said and the sides of her cheeks lifted into a smile. "Crickets *on* my socks."

I squeezed my hands to get a hold of myself. I had to. Otherwise I would have stood there, unmoving, until the sky fell.

Her eyes plucked around the small, unlit foyer while she braided her hair, fast fast fast. She had a cut below her chin. It was nothing big, but what an odd spot, I thought. What might she have been doing? I wouldn't ask. This was the new me: this polite kind of thinking.

"Am I the only one here?" she asked. Before I could answer, she said something else.

"It's okay if I am," she said.

"You are," I said.

I was still fumbling with the dress, like a ninny. The knot had come entirely undone. Here's my bra, folks. Twenty-five cents a peek. Twenty-five years old too.

"Do you need help?" she asked. "My mom has a dress like this."

She unknotted the thing in an instant, careful not to look where she shouldn't. She nearly hugged me as she wrapped it around my back and tied it on the side. She was as tall as me but with lighter bones. Her jacket smelled sweet, like tea with milk. She had long feet. I had long feet too, but I didn't mention it, not wanting to embarrass her. I knew it wasn't the greatest feminine quality.

"There," she said, cinching the bow. When she straightened up, she looked past me. Not at me, though she didn't seem shy. She had a freckle below her eye. Me too. I pointed to it, realizing that I was speechless. I hadn't said a word. She laughed.

"I noticed that," she said. "We match."

I could feel the cold come off her body. What was wrong with me? This was no way to treat a guest.

We stood there for a moment. It was me that was supposed to do something now but I'd been thrown off totally—and then thrown off again. I remembered that the lamb was half wrapped in the trash. What was I thinking?

"Smells like zucchini bread," she said. "Smells really good."

"Date bread," I said. "From my country." Oldest trick in the book: bake something to make guests feel at home.

I wasn't sure what to do then so I began walking into the kitchen. She took off her coat.

"Oh," I said. "How stupid of me. Let me take that."

She crumpled it into a little ball and handed it to me. I unrolled it and hung it on the doorknob. We stopped at the kitchen. I looked at the mess.

"Wow," she said. "This is really nice. Our kitchen is like this divided by four."

She delineated the space with her arms.

"We're always getting in each other's way," she said.

I thought about asking her who *each other* was, but didn't. I wanted to. The truth was, I hadn't had much experience with girls of this age. Any age really. That would have been fine for Joseph. He could have spoken garbage to a garbage can. But I was awkward, overthinking everything. I hadn't taken this into account, a child. I could have known young girls like this. I could have watched one grow. We would have had birthdays for her in the park. We would have brought all the ingredients for falafel sandwiches. Her friends could have made them however they liked and wrapped them in wax paper cones. Pickles or no pickles. Tahini sauce or no tahini sauce. Her birthday parties would have been a hit, I thought. All the kids would have liked them best.

"What's your name?" I asked her.

"Lorca," she said. And I slumped inside just the tiniest bit. I'd never read Lorca. I should have. He'd been on my list.

"I'm sorry I didn't call ahead," she said. "I called a little while ago but I couldn't hear anything. I wanted to ask if it was okay that I showed up."

"Of course it's okay," I said.

I introduced myself, thank goodness, unsure of whether to shake her hand or kiss her on both cheeks, so instead I said my name as I took the meat out of the garbage can.

"I'm Victoria, nice to meet you. This was wrapped," I said.

"Great," she said and I believed her. She was biting her thumb.

She slid onto one of our barstools, as gracefully as I'd ever seen it done. She untied a scarf from her neck and held it to her stomach, slouching in a way that came easily to her. I could imagine her sleeping in the tiniest coil.

"There were supposed to be others," I said, wiggling out my fingers from beneath the heavy meat and putting it onto the butcher block again. "They didn't show."

For a moment, as she turned her head, I thought she was going to suggest that she leave. Then we caught each other's eye. I hope. I hope. I hope. What a pretty face she had, the kind that was unnerving in a child but always would be too. The kind that you could swear you'd seen before, but only because you wanted to. She was a composite of startling things. Cheekbones like you read about. Eyelashes that tickled her brows. A disproportionately large upper lip. She slid off the stool. I thought she was going for her coat.

"No," I began.

"How can I help?" she said and washed her hands in the sink. Child of my heart, she washed her hands. She used the soap and a paper towel, which she folded into a square and put into her pocket.

"Well," I said, "we were going to make *bamia*."

"That's great," she said. "Just tell me what to do."

"Really?" I said.

She looked at me, confused.

"Really?" I said again. "You don't mind?"

She picked up an orange and smelled the skin. I smiled. I couldn't help it. In the supermarket, people stared. I once smelled all the different soups at Dean and Deluca, and a manager came over. He called me madam. He asked me to kindly tell him what I was up to. I said, "Kindly? I wasn't blowing my nose into the chowder." What was wrong with people? Smell is everything.

"Have you ever had a bergamot orange?" she asked.

And I thought, *Here we go.* I knew this was going to happen. She was going to think I was a fake.

"I don't really like them," she said before I could answer. "My mother uses them . . ."

She trailed off and blushed.

"Well," she said. "They're okay, I guess. But I like these better."

"Did you grow up in New York?" I asked. It was a legitimate question.

"No," she said. "In New Hampshire. Nowheresville is what my mother calls it."

"Northville?" I said. "Oh, nowhere. I understand."

I needed to watch myself. I hadn't been around sharp minds for a very long time.

She put the orange back delicately, as if it were glass.

"We went to New Hampshire," I said, trying to be breezy. "Fifteen years ago now. Not to nowhere, though. To the lake?"

I couldn't remember its name. Joseph had planned our trips. I brought my book. I brought loads of bug spray. He did the rest. I remembered the loveliest bakery there, with peach scones. I didn't say any of this out loud and at least there was that. At least I wasn't a babbling duck.

She said, "Winnipesaukee." She'd read my mind.

"That's the one," I said.

"It has two hundred and fifty-three islands," she said.

"You don't say," I said. And then: "How did you get your name?"

She told me like she'd told it before. I felt silly for asking then. It felt like asking her to repeat herself. But I couldn't help it.

"Your mother doesn't like it?" I said. "What would she have named you?"

She was quiet for a moment. Her hands stopped moving. I thought she was going to get mad. She didn't seem like the kind of girl to anger easily, to be jealous and so on. But I thought, *I've gone too far. I've asked too much.* It must kill her to have to talk to me. Stupid me with the stupid accent and the stupid dress that she tied so very nicely.

"It's hard to say," she said. "My mother is sort of complicated."

• • •

After that, I did stop asking questions. I wasn't going to make a mess. I thought, *Kitchen sounds only.* From now on, we cook. I passed her the mint and she was so adept with it, chopping it into a neat little pile. Her fingers moved dexterously around the knife, her motions smooth and steady—and I was thinking: *Don't get your finger, you'll never come back then; if you bleed all over, you'll hate this place,* and, like an imbecile, I'd thrown out all the Band-Aids.

I pointed out the things I was doing. I tried not to sound formal. I was suddenly conscious of my English. She watched me, nodded, but kept chopping. It seemed adult to me, her focus. She didn't flit around. She was calm. Was I calm like that? Was Joseph? It was as if she were at the ocean, her feet rooted deep in the sand.

I opened the can of tomatoes. I regathered the spices: paprika, celery seeds, red pepper flakes, mint, curry powder, ground ginger, salt, and pepper. I asked her to measure out half a teaspoon of each as I cut onions beside her and she said, "Do you know the wooden match trick?" I did, but I said no. And she told me. I passed her the garlic. After a little while, she lifted the grater and the garlic close to her ear and leaned into it. She looked at me as if to say, *Listen.*

"It's so funny," she said, the silence collapsing in on itself. "Doesn't it sound like swishing with mouthwash?"

I put my hand over my mouth. My breath. Was she making a point?

"No," she said, laughing a little. "You don't need it. I just think that. I think it sounds like that."

I laughed too. I laughed at myself. I felt suddenly lighter. I laughed a little more.

"There's no one here," I said, shrugging. "You never know. My breath could be awful."

• • •

We made three dishes that night. We talked about polite things. Lorca was on a break from school for the entire week. She didn't have pets. She lived with her mother and her aunt. She told me that she loved to cook. We loved to cook! And that she'd never traveled except to Florida and went to the bookstore a lot because she didn't have many friends. *I don't either,* I wanted to tell her. *Joseph did but I was never social that way. It's not the worst thing.* I didn't say that, though I wanted to. I didn't feel like a glowing example.

The sky was dark, and Lorca looked out the window. It was as if she were looking through a keyhole, into a fantasy book. Her face was romantic like that. She said, after the *bamia*, hummus *bi* tahini, and cabbage salad, "What's next?" I was tired but not. It was eleven o'clock. I hadn't been up this late for ages.

She said, "Are you tired?" And without thinking, I told her, "No."

My goodness, my word, my heart. No, I'm not. I could do this forever. Please stay. Please stay, little child.

After Lorca left, I shuffled around in the kitchen, where life lingered. It felt like a much-needed rainstorm had passed through. I cleaned up and then stopped. I loved the nest of dishes we'd made. Just so.

I was in a daze as I undressed and put on my pajamas. I felt exhausted, but overwhelmed too. All this was so new. And I couldn't tell Joseph, so the emotion hung about me, like a ringing phone.

I didn't want to get ahead of myself but certain ideas had crept into my mind and were creating an odd sensation in my chest. There wasn't much left ahead of me. It wasn't just the freckle, or the big feet, or even the shadow of Middle Easternness in Lorca's skin—though it was all those things too. Lorca felt so familiar to me somehow. Not like I'd once bumped into her on the street or sat next to her on an airplane, nothing as uninteresting as that. It was something smokier. It was more reflexive too, like being hungry or being stared at or waking up a minute before the alarm clock goes *ding*.

It was wild, what I thought, outlandish even, but I thought it. Saying it out loud would be like trying to explain a dream.

Still, I let myself think that there was some meaning in all this. I wasn't spiritual. I didn't believe in fate. Once in a while, I'd toss salt over my left shoulder but then feel ridiculous. I just kept thinking, *She's supposed to be here. She might just be someone to me.*

"Joseph," I whispered. "Can you hear me? Did you see Lorca? Did you see?"

Silence. More silence. Maybe a creak somewhere. Maybe an ambulance somewhere. Nothing to speak of. I couldn't be sure. I sat there with a sock half on and half off until a car alarm caused me to jump.

"Joseph," I whispered. "I was sad too." And though nothing happened then, no bright light, no crash, I felt a vague sense of comfort that had everything to do with Lorca. Sadness, and then.

Lorca

WHEN I OPENED the door, I found Blot perched on the railing of Victoria's stoop, swinging his legs and whistling. I didn't move; I considered turning around, going back inside, and waiting it out, but it was too late. He twisted his head around, his eyes finding mine, his hair twirling like a straw skirt.

"Good evening," he said. Dimples.

"What are you doing?" I asked, unprepared.

"That was not the greeting I expected," he said. "But I'll take it."

"Good evening," I said, trying for something lighter. *Lecanard-capricieuxhowmayIassistyou* went through my head but I didn't dare say it out loud.

Already I could feel myself soften. I smiled and curtsied, readjusting my sleeves to be sure. Of course, it wasn't that I was disappointed to see him. In fact, if I had made a wish in Victoria's elevator, it would have been for this very thing. But the truth was, I hadn't wished. I'd been distracted all evening, happy. Being distracted was new. Always, real life had been disappointing. I was used to things being better in my head. When life surprised me, I didn't know how to live it, live up to it.

"I was hoping I'd catch you," Blot said.

"You were?" I said.

"Duh," he said. "Tell me everything."

He swung his backpack over his shoulder and stood up. He had on his half-gloves again. He took off one to brush the hair from his face. Feeling self-conscious, I rebraided mine at lightning speed.

"Well," I said and sighed, closing the door gently behind me. I imagined Victoria already asleep, still dressed and with her apron shifted up, her shoes on, her body a diagonal stripe across her bed.

Moonlessness had overtaken the sky; it was so dark that it looked like a lava-cake spill. The sidewalk was slick and I willed my feet not to trip.

Blot was looking at me, waiting.

"That was the longest sigh I've ever heard," he said. "I'm calling Guinness."

"Ever?" I said.

I reminded myself to think before I spoke and to be careful not to come off as an emotional wreck. I was happy but shaky, as though I'd been jumping rope for six hours. Victoria had been everything I'd hoped. I loved her apartment: the faded wall tapestries, vases of dried lavender, art, knickknacks, silver frames balancing on every surface, the smell of baking cinnamon. It reminded me of the inside of a child's fort—a million precious things huddled together. Victoria was wonderful too. She was like an old photograph, feathered and thinned out but mostly unchanged from what, I imagined, she'd once been. She was still unmelted, as if she'd been carved from *pain aux cereales* dough. Her old age wasn't something she did to everyone around her, like Aunt Lou's would be, like her middle age already was. Victoria's smile was mini and maybe could be read as stingy, as though she were fighting against it—but I didn't think so. It seemed more like it was wringing out sadness. When she squinted for a moment just before she spoke, I realized that I'd been doing that my whole life. And when I'd asked her if she knew the wooden match trick, she'd said no, and when I showed her, she'd said, "Fantastic. Just fantastic, Lorca," like I'd built her a house. She'd tried it right then, and she was still for a moment, smushing her lips around the match with determination, holding her face toward the onion, unafraid. I thought, *Even if she forgets me as soon as I leave, this little thing will matter to her.*

Last year when I'd shown my mother the same trick, she'd looked disgusted. "If you can't handle the onions," she'd said, "don't use them."

I'd considered asking Victoria about what I'd seen—the woman taking Joseph's sweater from the pile to be thrown out—but I didn't. I didn't want to say anything that could mess things up.

When I finally spoke, a full block later, my voice hoarse from stifled emotion, I told Blot about the ingredients, one by one, and how we'd cooked them. I recalled measurements and techniques and the funny, elderly way that Victoria peered over her glasses as she chopped as speedily as my own mother. I told him that chickpeas must be soaked overnight, and hummus should be thinned out with brine, not water. I told him that Iraqi Jews didn't eat anything black—even removed the skin from eggplant—because they considered it bad luck. Thankfully, I cut myself off before rattling off the crucial foods for those unlucky in love, which she'd told me too.

"'Give him food so he can grow,'" I said to Blot, quoting Victoria. "It's a proverb. Next class, she'll teach me the Arabic."

I told him that before I went, I'd worried she would find me frightening. My mother always said, "Lorca, don't look so dark." I'd make a big fake grin. She'd say, "Better."

I knew what she meant by looking dark. It wasn't that I was goth. I wasn't. I wore pink sometimes. I wore lip-gloss. It was something about the cast of my face. I had a mole below my eye, and my whole life people had said it made me look like I was crying. My eyes were too light for my face. The peaks of my lips were too tall. My chin was too sharp. I looked like I was squirming out of something even when I wasn't. Of course, what I didn't tell Blot was that I'd prepared for the night by putting Band-Aids all over my arms. That way, if I had the urge to roll up my sleeves, I'd be stopped.

I went silent only when I realized Blot had stopped walking and was looking at me. I let him, though I wasn't used to being inspected—not used to the person I was always looking at looking back like this.

"Before I left, I put on a turtleneck," I blurted out, as if making up for keeping the Band-Aid story from him. "But then I took it off. I put on a sweatshirt. I took it off. I put on rain boots with turtles on them. I took them off. I told myself it didn't matter what I wore."

Blot gave me a big thumbs-up and we started walking again.

The thing was, I couldn't get myself to shut up. I had so much to say. I even told him about the soap in Victoria's bathroom, how it smelled of coriander, which reminded me of a recipe for oven fries with coriander seeds. By the time I mentioned okra, I figured he'd had plenty of time to stop me. Still, I quieted for just a second to be sure.

"What?" he said, making frantic motions with his hands for me to go on, and I did.

I felt smart then, telling him what Victoria had told me. "To avoid slime, we don't wash the okra," she'd said. "We flash-fry it and don't move it around encouraging the juices."

Finally, on Ninety-Sixth Street, I stopped my rambling. Blot's jaw was clenched and muscled. His hands were clasped behind his back and he was pitched forward, heavy. He looked concerned. *Please,* I thought, *don't let me have ruined everything.* I tried to recall the words I'd used. If I'd somehow said that this was the most affection I'd been shown in years, that being with Victoria had felt like standing in a lone coin of sun in the middle of winter. When I'd thanked her for the evening—about to walk out the door—she'd cupped her hand over mine. Her fingers were chilled on the outside but soft like wet petals. After a few seconds, I pretended I'd dropped something and leaned down, just to undermine the moment. I didn't know how else to keep the tears away.

Now I tried to remember if I'd said the word *sad* and made Blot think twice about me. I whispered it, wrapping my mouth around letters. *Sad*. It didn't ring a bell.

"Wow," Blot said and sighed. I waited for more. His eyes followed a pigeon as it moved from a lamppost to a tree and back again. He took off one half-glove and then the other, folded them into two perfect squares. It occurred to me that I'd been totally selfish, talking about myself like this, about all my good things.

"I like slime," he said. "And octopus is in my top ten."

I laughed out loud. I covered my mouth, afraid that I might not be able to stop. A couple walked by and smiled at me smiling. Blot's face was open and unbothered.

"Is that gross?" he asked. "My dirty secret is that I love tripe. Now you know. My grandma was Portuguese and used to make it with butter beans."

I thought of his grandma, pictured her huge and barefoot with a little girl wrapped around her muscled calf. Greta.

"It is gross," I said. "But who am I to judge?"

"Hold on," he said. He actually stopped walking. "Did you get the recipe? For masgouf?"

"Oh, fudge," I said. I slapped my own cheeks. "I totally forgot."

Without thinking, I turned around as if to go back. I had to go back. Though my mother knew nothing of my grand plan, I imagined her with her hands on her hips, and no breath passing through her. *What were you doing with that woman, then, if you weren't getting the recipe? Just hanging out with an old lady? Call your grandmother, if that's what this is about. I don't care.*

"Wait," Blot said. And I turned back to him.

"Next time," he said. "Right? You can just get it next time."

It was something about the stern calmness in his tone that made me not go racing back to Victoria's, made me see that it would have been nuts to go, that I would have been letting myself down and him too.

"I guess so," I said but realized that I wouldn't see Victoria till next Monday: a full week from now. I was suddenly exhausted in my shoulders and knees. For the first time in a few days, I had that itchy, desperate feeling. I'd betrayed my plan. I didn't have time to make mistakes. Worse, I had forgotten my mother.

"Hey," he said, looking at me. Apparently, I couldn't keep my feelings to myself. "It's okay," he said.

We stopped at a crosswalk and I turned away, feeling like I might cry. I needed a moment to catch my breath, get a hold of myself, but just as I moved, he grabbed my wrist. I spun around. For a second, I thought he was about to kiss me. I was ready for it, but also not ready. He wasn't looking at me. He was holding my wrist still, nodding to some dog poop I'd nearly stepped in.

"Careful," he said and I yanked my arm back, remembering myself. I held it tightly to my side. Heat zipped through my body and landed in my face. Suddenly, my eyes were puddles. I tapped at them. I couldn't look at him. I wondered what he'd felt—stickiness or scabs or something like the cool exterior of a hard-boiled egg. I couldn't remember where exactly I'd put the Band-Aids. I put my hand in my pocket. I was shaking. Something sore echoed in my wrist. I must have grimaced. I'd forgotten myself so deeply. I'd forgotten how easily I could ooze out.

"Sorry," he said. "Did I hurt you?" Concern overwhelmed his face. I had to shake off the itchy feeling to tell him. I wanted to, I swear, for a second, I wanted to. I didn't.

"Yes," I said. "No. I mean, I'm okay."

Stop. I used all the strength in my fingers to reach around and feel my wrist for what he felt. It wasn't bloody, at least not yet.

"You sure?" he asked, reaching for me again. I staggered back. His arm was stretched toward me as if he were afraid I might fall backward into a freezing pool. I wouldn't.

We stood there staring. I would have run away but I couldn't feel my feet. I had no idea if they were hot or cold or what shoes I was wearing. I couldn't look down either. I couldn't tell if I was being strong on the outside and concealing what was on the inside, or the other way around. My arm felt leaded, so heavy. Blot's face disappeared into the movement of the city. All I could see were his eyes, sparkling like a candle that had just been lit.

"I have to go," I said. I turned around. I began walking away. I didn't run. My feet were numb-ish.

I thought of my mother, imagined her covering her face, like I'd done it again. I'd not turned out the way she wanted. She'd be heartbroken, I knew, that I couldn't be myself. Any good mother would feel the same.

"See you tomorrow?" Blot called after me. "Come by?"

I turned around.

"Why?" I whispered, but he didn't hear me. He just gave me the thumbs-up again.

"Bye, Lorca!" he yelled.

As soon as I got home and shut the door behind me, I checked my wrist. There were a couple of scars, maybe two scabs, but it was nothing terrible and most of it was covered. It could have been from a kitten. From a burner. From our old radiators. He didn't know. He knew nothing. I was making a mountain out of a molehill. And yet, something about that broke my heart too.

The feeling of his hand on my wrist came back stronger then. It was an empty kind of pain, but persistent, like ringing in your ears. I imagined him really holding it, not saying anything but knowing. And it felt like the opposite of holding. It felt like all the bone and tissue had been removed and my arm was as light as a kite, just about flying.

There was a note from Lou and my mother. They'd be out late even though it was a Monday. Usually, they were at high-class bars with their legs crossed, or at least that's what they told me. But tonight, I imagined my mother on a mechanical bull, and dozens of men staring at her, open-mouthed, tugging at the crotches of their pants. I thought of Blot looking at her. I thought of her looking at Blot. I got queasy.

I tried reading *Saveur.*

I reorganized the condiments.

I flossed.

I put on my pajamas.

I cut up an orange peel and stuck it into the jar of brown sugar.

In some ways, I was being punished for not being successful.

This wouldn't be happening if I had found the recipe.

I went to my room and took a razor from the bottom of a tissue box, careful not to prick my finger. I rolled up my sleeve and sat on the floor and curled over and took it to the crook of my elbow. I had done this before. At first, I thought of what I was doing. I understood. I reminded myself, I was doing this. I wanted to do this. I thought of Blot, of Victoria, tried to think of them harder. It didn't matter. It did no good.

There was the slant of the razor, the pressure, my skin, my tissue, my bone, the counting of something like seconds or heartbeats or steps up a staircase or times that my eyes blinked that became the rhythm, the sound, the rhythm, the sound, the song of it. And then, when it was about to hurt terribly—it took a while—when I felt that my body had been thinned out to something like stockings swinging from a clothesline, I forgot everything. Everything forgot me. Everything escaped and convened at the sting, at that one sensation, but it was so much more than that. It was like my body had evaporated and reappeared at that one single spot. I'd condensed. I was a tiny drop of red liquid, shimmering like a butterfly's wing up close.

I thought of what I was doing until what I was doing took over. I didn't have to push away thoughts. The thoughts let go of me. I leaned back. I dropped the razor. My arm was across me, resting between my legs. There were stripes of blood like someone had just mowed the lawn. You could still see the tracks.

I closed my eyes. Everything slowed. I was weightless. I was a jellyfish. I was free.

Victoria

THE NEXT DAY, Lorca called—she called!—and I let the machine pick up. I didn't mean to. I would have gotten it if I'd known. But I didn't think it was her. I thought, *Let whoever it might be think I'm busy.* No more telemarketers. No more sympathy calls. It had been just four days since Joseph had passed but somehow every collector, insurance company, real estate agent, and estate attorney from here to the Gaza Strip had been notified. I was sitting and tweezing my eyebrows and that was busy enough.

She left a message. I heard her voice, every sentence like a question, and so badly I wanted to pick up. But I didn't. What would I have said? I'd been too slow, too pathetic and old to get to the phone on time? She must have thought I was on the toilet. I bet that's what she thought. Old people are always on the toilet. A little dignity. All I asked for was the tiniest little bit.

Lorca said in her message that she wanted to make something for her mother, who had come down with a cold. *Her mother,* I thought. Her mother. I told myself to not be berserk and to cut off that line of thinking. "No soup though," she said. She said her mother was picky about soup. At the end of her message, she said, "I know our next lesson isn't until next Monday, but I'm wondering if we can do it this evening instead. I only have this one week off and I want to make sure I learn as much as possible!"

My heart flooded. It just flooded over and then I really did have to go to the bathroom.

For a second, I couldn't believe it. I stood up. I sat down. This young girl, whoever she was, so lovely, so adult, wanted to come back to see me. Despite me, despite our apartment, despite Joseph being gone and Joseph being the one whom everyone wanted to visit. I imagined that somehow this would have made Joseph proud and he would have nodded with his eyes closed. *See?* he'd have said. *I told you all along that you're a wonder.* I smiled and moved into a bit of sunlight near the window, where I lifted my face toward the sky. As if he could see me better there. As if that way, he could see me smiling back.

I needed to decide what we'd make—Lorca and I. And quickly. I needed a recipe. I needed something perfect. No soup. No soup. *No soup,* I thought. I couldn't blame her. I liked sweets when I was sick—something light, nondairy, easy to nosh on in bed. So I decided on *shakrlama*. Delicious little almond and pistachio cookies. I didn't even have to shop. I had everything we needed in the pantry and the freezer.

Joseph had loved *shakrlama*. I hadn't made them in ages. Toward the end, I had stopped baking. I started buying Sara Lee. If Joseph had known, his heart would have given out. He would have put his hands over his mouth. *Let me die,* he would have said, *just don't feed me that poison*. He didn't know. He opened up. Said ah.

The Sara Lee cakes had ridiculous names: Chocolate Peanut Butter Thunder, Strawberry Cloud, Seven Layers of Heaven. Absurd. Did they think it worked? People fell for names like that? Did they think we were imbeciles? Apparently. I'd just wanted the calories in him. The more the better. It didn't matter what it was. Bring on the butter. Bring on the frosting. Bring on the

Thunder. In the end, the calories kept him alive. And I told him I'd made the stuff. I know what a horrible lie that was. He couldn't taste a thing. Chemotherapy had ruined his taste buds. Imagine that. I could have fed him canned meat. He wouldn't have known. But he just looked at me, smiling. Some nights, I'd find myself in the kitchen trying a bite of each just to be sure. Just to be sure I wasn't making it worse. I wasn't poisoning him. How he must have missed the taste of cumin. He never said a thing. Breaks my heart.

It occurred to me that I didn't have Lorca's number. There was no way for me to call her back and confirm. It must have been obvious, I thought, and shrugged, that I had nothing else to do but wait for her return. And wait for her I would. She was the only thing I had to wait for except the end.

Lorca buzzed right on time and I told myself, *Don't act like an idiot. She'll want to unfind you if you do.*

I let her in without saying so much as *Who's there?* into the intercom. I knew what Dottie would have said: that I was asking to be shot point-blank in the head. Any last words? No, thank you. I've had two trillion years of listening to my own voice.

Lorca flew up the stairs like there was a fire down below. I heard her before I saw her. I wondered if the hurry had anything to do with me. I hoped. Her feet went *pop pop pop*.

When she saw me, she put her head down apologetically, as if she'd kept me waiting. She hadn't. I wanted to tell her that she hadn't.

"Are you taller?" I asked.

She gave a little laugh, and walked in. "No," she said. "Maybe."

She didn't say, bless her heart, that maybe it was me. That I was shrinking, which I was.

It amazed me how her face changed. Today her hair was back.

Her face was longer. She wore white. Her face was brighter. She had a Band-Aid along the left side of her jaw and she seemed suddenly young—a child who'd fallen off a slide. During our first lesson, as I was salting the meat, I looked at her, her hands in her lap, chin up. She watched me as if peering into a tub of alligators at the zoo. I could have sworn she wasn't a day over ten. But when she was leaving, right before she walked out the door, she zipped up her coat and let out a giant, weary puff of air, like she just had a little way to go, just one more push and then, finally, she could rest.

"Have you ever had *shakrlama*?" I said and my accent came out.

"No," she said. "But I bet my mother will like it."

"She will?" I asked.

"What is it?" she said. Bless her. She didn't want to break my heart.

"Cookies," I said. "Made with pistachio, rose water, and citrus, and each one stuffed with an almond."

"She likes sweets," Lorca said and I sighed out loud. I had no other plan, fool that I was. I was a million miles ahead of myself. *The tables have turned, Joseph,* I thought. Look who can't keep up with her emotions now.

I moved into the kitchen, and Lorca followed. She climbed onto her stool in two graceful motions. She crossed her legs. She folded her hands in her lap, as if about to pray. Already, I was acting like this was our routine. I didn't have the right. I couldn't help it.

I piled two large lemons and one orange next to the juicer. We'd need at least that. I placed a tablespoon next to the rose water.

"Just one of these," I said. "It's possible to overdo it."

From the cabinet, I took out the sugar, flour, baking powder, and vegetable oil.

"We'll need flavorings," I said and then wished I'd thought before opening my mouth. People here don't call them flavorings but spices.

"Spices," I said. "Cardamom first," and I began going through the drawer, taking out one thing after the next. "And nigella. That's the big secret."

"It is?" Lorca said, and when she came around the counter asking if she could help find what we needed in the spice drawer, I felt like letting her in on the "secret" had lent an air of seriousness to the search.

I allowed her to take over not because I couldn't do it myself, but because there was something nice about having someone else in the house moving things that for so long I'd been the only one to touch. After a while, you begin to wonder if your world actually exists. A tree falls in the forest. You smash a light bulb to be sure. I did that once, just to watch a nurse clean it up, and when she noticed me smiling, relieved, she got the wrong idea. "I'm not a cleaning lady," she said and I apologized until my mouth was dry as burned pita.

"Here," Lorca said, proud, holding up the canister to the light. "Nigella."

"Brava," I said and I plugged in the standing mixer.

"This is fancy," she said, running her fingers over its shiny red paint.

"It was a gift," I said. "From my husband. Believe it or not, his first job in America was at a bakery. *He* was the mixer. When we opened our restaurant, we didn't have very much money. We skimped on things like gadgets and expensive tools. Anyway, we were so used to doing all that ourselves. Eventually, we got old and he bought me this thing. It's as big as a car but a miracle worker. I can make anything without my fingers swelling. Pasta, bread, ice cream, sausage, you name it."

"I know," Lorca said. "Some days, my mother uses it to make

giant batches of mayonnaise just because she likes it so much. Hers is silver."

"And then all you eat is mayonnaise for a week?" I said, pretending that discussing her mother hadn't fazed me.

"Sometimes," she said, laughing. "Or sometimes, she'll bring it to the restaurant and add in saffron or currants or anchovies."

"Which restaurant?" I said.

"Her restaurant."

"Your mother has a restaurant?"

"Sure," Lorca said, and she started fiddling with the settings on the mixer.

There was silence as I considered how not to ask her why she was here, then. I wanted to, and, of course, I had a particular answer in mind. But it was obvious that she didn't want to get into it. If she did, she would have. And she didn't. How dare I leap to conclusions when even on a good day I could hardly put one foot in front of the other? I went through all that in my head to prevent myself from ruining a perfectly nice moment and asking her straight out. But I wondered—I couldn't help it—if Lorca's mother was a chef, what did Lorca need me for? Her mother could teach her, couldn't she? Or perhaps, at the very least, one of her mother's friends would be up for it? Surely, I thought, her mother could find someone less pathetic than me for this task. Unless.

And yet, my wild and crazy hopes aside, all this thinking was just a way of nipping in the bud the hope that had recently bloomed in me: that it was because of me, specifically, that Lorca was here. For some unique skill that I could pass along or because she liked me or at least enjoyed the lesson. Not just because she couldn't find anyone better.

Perhaps having children is what makes a person feel needed. And because I'd never been needed by mine, I'd had to find other ways to be needed. First, by the restaurant. Is it terrible to say that I liked nothing more than a call on our day off? "Tell me again," a waiter would say, "how you fold the napkins." I'd flush with honor. Next, by Joseph; I found ways of making myself indispensable, keeping from him the secrets of how I made his shirts so soft, his coffee so thick, his immune system so powerful with my little concoction of herbs. There were times when I'd shove his belt to the back of the closet just so that he—having searched and searched to no avail—would kiss me when I unearthed it.

I couldn't help it. Without Lorca, grandchild or not, I might never be needed again.

"There are some things I know how to cook," Lorca said. "But all very French."

I put my hand in front of my face as if to say there was no need to explain, but when she went on, I took my hand down quickly, hoping.

"And I know nothing about Iraqi food. Or Jewish food, even though I'm Jewish. My grandmother believes that takeout is the best invention since whiskey sours."

"You're funny," I said, because I didn't want to linger on the word *grandmother,* and I wanted her to know that she was funny, and I had a weak laugh. Joseph's laugh made everyone feel like the star of a comedy routine.

"Well," I said. "You're not learning anything just futzing with that mixer."

She put her feet together as if standing at attention. As I took some eggs out of the fridge, I nodded to the citrus.

"First," I said, "we juice."

As we went along, it became clearer and clearer to me that she was the daughter of a chef—so much so that I wondered how I'd not seen it before. I'd not given her the praise she deserved and wondered if I had let her down. She worked with a kind of conviction, I noticed, that seemed well beyond her years.

Her mother must have sat her down with a paring knife and a bag of lemons at age five, I thought. I stopped myself from asking her if that was the case. I imagined her calling me her grandmother.

Today was a quieter lesson than the first. I filled the air with compliments, not knowing what else to do, and I meant them.

"You're excellent with that juicer," I said. "It takes me hours just to turn it on."

But there was a certain shyness that had come over Lorca, or pensiveness, that I didn't know how to break through. I wondered if my asking about her mother had something to do with it.

When the cookies were in the oven and the countertop mostly cleaned off, Lorca sighed suddenly, out of nowhere. It was a giant-size sigh and caused her shoulders to heave forward when it passed. I thought perhaps I'd disappointed her, making something as humble as cookies and not having the right things to talk about. It occurred to me that maybe she'd come for a lesson in Iraqi history or a more comprehensive explanation of Jewish cuisine, but I wasn't sure, and I didn't trust myself to make the material fascinating enough to engage someone like her.

"Well," she started. It was the beginning of an excuse. I could sense it. She had to be home, it was late, or she had studying to do. I dreaded her departure, the thick staleness of the apartment when no one was here but me. Everything about Lorca rejuvenated this place: her quick fingers; her happy socks; her voice, hoarse and deep, but as though it was just growing into itself, not as if it was cracking and decaying and old, like dried cement.

"Are you hungry?" I asked, though I wasn't really asking. Iraqi Jews never really asked. I was already at the fridge.

When she said, "Yes!" I had to turn around and look at her to be sure I hadn't dreamed it. "Starved!" she said.

I felt like I'd cracked the code.

Lorca sat on the stool again and rested her chin in her hands. I got a potholder from below the sink, embarrassed when I had to put my hand on my back to straighten up. I put up the kettle for tea. The burner panted twice before it lit.

I realized that I was hungry too—and exhausted. I hadn't been so aware of myself in years. I took the plastic wrap off the *bamia,* spooned a mound into a bowl, and put it in the microwave. I noticed the perfect, equal shapes of the okra and pointed them out to Lorca.

"No," she said. "They're all messed up. I was just noticing that."

I wanted to tell her otherwise but I wondered if she'd had enough of my bolstering for one night. I folded a napkin, polished a spoon, and refilled the pepper grinder with peppercorns. I turned to the stove, where the kettle had begun to scream.

"My grandmother used to say," I said, "that a hungry stomach has no ears."

I poured the boiling water into our glasses and began stirring even before adding honey.

"Is this," I asked her, "how you make dressing?"

"Yes," she said. "Emulsifying. But I can't do it so quickly."

I slowed down, made myself—for once—a bit less adept.

"Those are juice glasses," she said. I smiled.

"Right," I said. "This is how we drank it in Baghdad."

I put down the steaming glass in front of her and wrapped the oven mitt around the bowl of *bamia* and brought that too, smelling it on the way.

"Heaven," I said.

I watched her as she ate until I caught myself.

"I haven't made this in years," I said.

Lorca lifted her shoulders, cocked her head, asking why.

"I don't know," I said. "I should have. There's a saying in Arabic: *Bukra fil mish mish.* 'Tomorrow, when the apricots bloom.'

Or, in other words, maybe tomorrow. I kept thinking that. I'd do it tomorrow, and tomorrow, and tomorrow."

I was thinking of Lorca, of cooking again. But I thought of Joseph too. No more tomorrows with him.

Lorca picked up her glass of tea and held it for only a second before wincing and nearly slamming it back down again. Her hands fanned out in front of her in a kind of spasm. It was so hot. Her eyes watered immediately.

"Oh no," I whispered, taking it from her, pouring the tea into the thick mug, and passing it back.

"Here," I said. "Don't hurt yourself. Joseph had sensitive fingers too. But you should have seen him fillet a fish. We called him the maestro."

We were quiet. Lorca blew into her tea. Finally, carefully, she drank it. I busied myself folding a dishtowel, checking on the cookies, collecting crumbs, checking on the cookies, readying a small tin with a layer of parchment paper, and checking on the cookies. And all the while, Lorca did not flee.

"Almost done," I said, though they weren't.

Lorca took a very deep breath. I felt like she wanted to say something. I stopped putzing around and tried to relax my face and in some way make myself easier to talk to.

"My mother ate an Iraqi dish once," she began. There was a flutter in my stomach. "She loved it. She never loves anything. It was a long time ago."

"Where?" I said, but I already knew the answer.

"At your restaurant," Lorca said. More flutter.

"What?" I said.

"Masgouf," she said. More more flutter.

"Who?" I said, not meaning to interrupt but following some kind of automatic logic when it felt like logic was quickly slipping away.

"My mother?" she said.

I gasped. I hadn't wanted to leap to conclusions. And yet the conclusion was staring me in the face.

"Your mother," I repeated. "At our restaurant."

I was a little bit dizzy. I squeezed my hands into fists. I leaned back on my heels. I tried to slow down my thinking. There were so many people who passed through the restaurant. So very many faces and different ways of chewing—and wasn't it something that Lorca's mother had been one of those chewers so long ago, and now here was Lorca in my kitchen? The word that came to mind was *relevant*. That we—Joseph and I—were still relevant. The second word was *baby.* My baby.

"She loved it there," Lorca said. "She went often and with my father, actually. She told me all about it. I wanted to tell you sooner but thought you might think I was a stalker, kind of. And I'm really not. I just know the restaurant meant a lot to her."

"It did?" I said.

Until then, I realized, all the lives I'd lived felt very, very far away, once entirely tangible but now remote—like rooms of a bulldozed house. My life had become so small, so gathered in this apartment. When the restaurant closed, there were letters. At first. But then they stopped. There were visits from workers. Then they stopped too. Joseph and I went out less and less. We ordered in. Doctors came to us. I didn't make an effort with friends. I didn't bother renewing magazine subscriptions. The world didn't skip a beat as we hibernated between these walls, as I waited for Joseph to get well again. We mattered to each other. It could be said that was the only real measure of our existence. We didn't leave footprints in any snow. No cars waited for us to cross. Or, at least, very, very few.

"She said that the food was fabulous and the restaurant was really well appointed," Lorca said, changing her tone to imitate what must have been her mother's voice and using her words so I'd know exactly what she'd said.

I felt myself blush. The decorating had been my vision entirely. From soup to nuts, as they say.

"And that's why you're here," I said, controlling myself. "Because you knew about me?"

"Not you exactly," she said. My face must have fallen. "Well, actually, yes, you," she said. "You and your husband owned the restaurant. You were the hostess and your husband the chef?"

"He was the host sometimes. We switched back and forth," I told her. "We shared the duties."

"Right," Lorca said. "Well, my mother said that. And that's how I found you."

"Found me?" I said. "So you looked for me?"

"Only a little bit," she said, getting off the stool and taking a small step backward, her whole body recoiling with only the slightest movements. It was too much for her, my excitement. I was letting it get the best of me. *Take full inhales,* I told myself. *Release full exhales.*

"Right," I said. "Just a little bit. Of course." I acted casual, shaking my shoulders slightly, clasping my hands behind my back.

"I mean, I just looked you up. Or Blot did. He's my friend, sort of. And then we found the flyers. It happened kind of on its own, I guess."

"No problem," I said, like a moron. It was my least favorite phrase and the only thing that came to mind.

"I wanted to know—the reason I'm here—if it would be all right . . ." Lorca said slowly. She shuffled her feet.

"Anything!" I said.

"If I asked you for the recipe? For the masgouf?" she said. Quickly, nervously, she began biting at her bottom lip.

"Oh," I said. I gasped. "Of course I wouldn't mind. It would be an honor."

"It's for my mother," she said. "For her birthday."

"When's her birthday?" I asked. I must have shouted it. Lorca looked surprised, then embarrassed.

"Well, not for a while. It's a long story."

"All right," I said. I would push no further, and the truth was, a part of me didn't want to know. I was living on hope. "A story for a rainy day," I said.

Finally, I could take a deep breath. I felt my feet firmly planted on the ground. I looked out the window to reacquaint myself with the world.

"It's been so long since I've even thought about masgouf," I said. "But it really was delicious."

I wrote the recipe in such careful handwriting that my hands shook. I threw it out. I wrote it again. It wasn't just that my writing had become sloppy and chaotic in my old age, but that it felt like, with every movement of the pen, something deep and visceral was being stirred inside of me. Something that hadn't been shifted in years. There was an overgrowth, a protective layer, and I was afraid of shifting too quickly, setting something loose that was watery and sour-smelling underneath.

As I was finishing up, adding a little drawing of how to cut the lemons properly, it occurred to me that I might never see this child again. If I was totally wrong about everything, totally delusional, and she'd had this very particular reason for coming after all—the masgouf—all she needed from me was right here on this paper. I was giving her the key to lock me in again. Alone. I didn't want to appear sappy, needy, but when I looked up and she was wrapping her scarf around her neck, pulling up her socks, I wasn't sure if I could help it. She'd only taken a bite of her *bamia*. I wrote a little something about the history of masgouf, about the reeds, making a bed of reeds. Finally, I folded the paper carefully. I wrote *Lorca* on the front, biding my time.

"Well," I said. I took a deep breath.

Lorca reached out a hand.

"Here," I said, unable to look her in the eye. "Good luck."

"I'll need it," she said. She began to stand up. My heart had risen into my throat, and my hands were tingling. I had to do something. She couldn't just leave. The cookies were still in the oven. And then it came to me.

"Do you know what's strange?" I said.

"What?" Lorca said.

"Masgouf wasn't exactly our specialty. I mean, it was good. Don't get me wrong. But your mother—she's a chef?"

Lorca nodded.

"I wouldn't say," I said, "it was a very chef-y dish."

"Was it a house special?" she asked.

"It was the tourists who liked it," I said. "It's the national dish of Iraq. It was, you know, ethnic."

Lorca was quiet and probably had no idea what I was getting at.

"If you," I said, "figure out why she liked that dish so much, we might be able to make it just right. We might be able to outdo ourselves."

"Thank you," she said. And then: "That would be great."

She sat down again. She smiled at me. She ate more *bamia*.

"This is delicious," she said and I believed her.

I took out another spoon and fed myself a bite from her bowl, hoping it wasn't too forward.

"Delicious," I said. "Couldn't have done it without you."

She crossed her hands in her lap.

"Would it be all right if I came back on Thursday?" she asked, covering her mouth, which was full. "Maybe we could try cooking some masgouf?"

"Would it be all right?" I said, nearly choking. I smacked at my chest. "It would be marvelous," I whispered.

The cookies, I could smell, were done. I stuffed my hand into an oven mitt and took them out. Lorca lifted herself off her stool and over the bar to get a good look.

"They're perfect!" Lorca squealed. I'd never heard her so happy. "Just look at them!"

After Lorca left, I stood by the stool she'd sat on, tried to take in our apartment as if I'd never been here before. *It isn't so bad,* I thought. I brushed some flour off the table. I threw some over my shoulder. I turned around to see the mess I'd made, and there was something on the floor.

I knelt down too quickly. I wasn't sure if I'd ever make it back up. My knees cracked like celery. But then, it didn't matter. I picked it up—and thought I'd stay there forever. It was a photo of a child, in black-and-white. She had a part curved down the left side of her head, clean as an open book, as if done with a knife. She hadn't yet grown into her limbs or neck but was graceful nonetheless—a human weeping willow. Her eyelids hung heavy, and she had the tiniest pillows above her cheeks. Her hip jutted to the side, and one bare foot was in front of the other. I wanted to hold this little girl in the photograph, wrap a blanket around her tiny, twiggy shoulders, tell her she had nothing to prove. No one had to tell me that she was mine. I was sure of it. Her strong bone structure was all Joseph's, and her thick dark hair, long torso. But her face, an eddy of sadness, was mine. Unmistakably so. I recognized it like I would my own hand if I found it severed, elsewhere.

She was a person, no more and no less than anyone else. I wondered, I couldn't help it, what I'd been doing at the very moment this photo had been taken. Or while she was turning five. Ten. Forty. When she'd given birth. If I'd raised her, I thought, wanted to think, she would have looked at the camera differently, not so defiantly. And though I had no right to think that way, or any way, for that matter, now that she was here, in my hands, I was part of her life. There were no two ways about it. What if I'd folded her clothes? I wondered. What if I'd taught her how to butterfly a fish, to braise and batter?

The truth was, I realized, that I wasn't wondering about her, but about me.

It occurred to me that that is what distinguishes the good parents from the bad ones. Here I was, worrying about how it would have changed my life to part a child's hair, comb it through. A good parent—Joseph, for example—would never have thought that way. He would have wanted to know her for her—not for the experience of knowing one part of himself. But for the first time in my entire life, I truly felt that my giving her up might have been a brave thing to do—and though I would never forgive myself for being the kind of person who should give up a child, at least I could forgive the act that had allowed the child to escape a mother like that. Which was something. And something, anything, was worlds better than all the nothing that had been.

Lorca had left this photo for me to find. The gutsy feeling that I'd been warding off, that Lorca might just be someone to me, someone important, mine, was justified after all. I didn't want to get ahead of myself, but everything was coming together. The very fact of Lorca, perfect as she was, was validation for what we'd done. But that wasn't all. The notion that I'd clung to all these years, that I'd ruined our daughter's life by giving her up, was wrong. I'd gotten it wrong. And now not only was there happiness in that—that she was a successful mother, just fine, after all—but there was a great comfort in the fact that I'd had even less claim on her than I'd imagined. Any illusion I'd insisted upon, that I'd known something secret, sacred, about her, was false. And no part of that was disappointing. Just the opposite. Because it meant that the constant pressure of pushing against thoughts of her, the guilt from that, the fear that all the delicate strings I'd laid and used to walk away from her would snap back and into my face, were based on nothing. She was fine. She had a life and it didn't include me. It didn't include fighting against the pain from me.

What a gift, I thought, and wondered if Joseph had felt the weight of it too.

That night, I went to bed with the photo tight to my chest.

I wondered if Joseph had ever met Lorca, if Lorca even knew about him. I didn't think so. I had a vague sense that Lorca and I were both seeking answers to questions that couldn't be asked simply.

There were so many things I wanted to know, so many ends left untied, but I didn't mind. In fact, they thrilled me. Everything buzzed and blurred together as some strong current pulled me to sleep. I didn't fight it. In sleep, I thought, I might be closer to Joseph. I thought, *Let me come upon him so I can tell him everything and so he can know that I forgive him for having a secret, that things have worked out.*

Joseph

NEW YORK, 1952

In September, Joseph considered writing Victoria a letter. But he feared making a spelling or grammatical error. She'd become such an English expert—a real zealot. Or maybe she wouldn't be able to read his handwriting—distinguish the *e* from the *r*. She'd stop reading. Patience wasn't her strong suit. He thought about taking her to her favorite place, the steps of the New York Public Library—she loved how on sunny days the stone warmed the backs of her legs, and the lions reminded her of those at the National Museum of Baghdad—and talking to her, reasoning with her. But he knew what would happen. Her face would shut down as soon as he got to the point. Closed for business. He knew her eyes, usually bright and discerning, would drain to gray—she would become armored. So this seemed like the best option.

They would go to the doctor's office together. The doctor would talk to them as parents. Victoria would see the possibilities; she would have to. It would occur to her that having a baby wouldn't be a burden. Just the opposite. It would usher her into a routine, a group of friends, lively chats with the pharmacist, the teachers, the cheese lady on Houston. She would strap the baby to her front. She could get out more. Feel less alone. And it would bring them together—not push them apart. She would see. And she could finally quit her hostessing job. Their pillowcases would no longer smell like cigarettes and unwashed dishes.

At three o'clock Joseph hung up his apron at the bakery. He walked home the usual way but was particularly conscious of everything he passed, as if he'd just woken up from a nap in a strange place. He was superstitious. If he went a different way—if he took Third Street instead of Houston—he might ruin everything. He avoided the cracks in the sidewalk. The cashier at the bakery had taught him the song. He walked deliberately and steadily. One. Two. One. Two. One. Two. *This will help,* he thought, *this calmness will matter when Victoria makes her decision.*

He noticed the cleanliness of the streets. The Italians were so proud of their clean streets. He noticed a squirrel, its wild, fluffy tail, and the tiny brown door on Sixth Avenue. The man playing the accordion, bouncing from side to side not quite with the music. His smile revealed very few, very gray teeth. This was the place to raise a child, Joseph thought. This place of all places in the world.

Joseph passed the spice shop on Thompson Street where the Iranian couple worked. They had a baby. And the baby was happy. Isaac brought her by the bakery on his days off. The baby was not pretty. Her face was flat and brown. Like something left on the stove too long, Joseph thought. But she laughed and water bubbled out of her nose. That was something.

On MacDougal Street, he made a right. Almost there. He realized that today was the first day in a long time that he had not sweated through his shirt on his way home. He sweated a lot here. The heat was different. Fall would arrive soon, he told himself. And the sky had begun to change. It felt like it had lowered, come closer to him. Everything smelled metallic. But his hands and toes were clammy. He could feel them. And he had to use the toilet—again. Nerves got the best of his digestion.

He had a plan. When he walked in the door, he would say, *Thank you, Victoria. Thank you for letting me come with you.*

And that would be a good start.

Or maybe, he thought, that was too much. He wanted to say—but how to say it without actually saying it—*It's only right that you're allowing me to accompany you. This is my baby too. This is my decision as much as it is yours. Be fair, please.*

Maybe he wouldn't say anything. Maybe his face would say it all. She always said he had a very expressive face. She could tell that he was hungry, she liked to say, from just looking at his bottom lip. This made her proud. Maybe he should pretend to be starving, for her.

Joseph counted down as he went up the 212 stairs. He reached their landing at 210. For the first time, he had missed two, he thought. He opened the door, and Victoria was standing against the counter, unshowered. She had a spoon in her hand but wasn't holding anything to eat. Her left arm rested beneath her breasts like a broken wing. She wasn't showing yet, but it seemed so natural. She dropped her arm, noticing him. His stupid, obvious face.

"What are you doing?" he asked, motioning to the spoon.

She looked at it, then at him. She disarmed him. He forgot to think about the baby and his plan. He could think of nothing but her face. Her cheekbones were perfect watermelon spears. She looked again at the spoon as if she'd found it peeking out of the sand.

"Don't know," she said and dropped it into the sink.

He'd gotten used to this. Her distance from him, from everything. She hadn't liked New York to begin with, but the pregnancy had made it worse, as if the baby were a magnet drawing her attention inward, to a dark, moldy place. At first, he didn't want to think deeply about what she was doing—or what she wasn't doing. He feared that it would make him hate her, and then what? She'd come all the way to New York for him. He thought of her shivering and thin as she came off the bus, literally tumbling down the stairs with fatigue and into his arms. What kind of person would take advantage of that? If he really wanted to be good to her—and have a shot at changing things too—he'd have to try to understand.

"Are you ready?" he asked. "We don't want to be late."

"Thank you for coming with me," she said, beating him to it.

"Thank *you*," he said with too much emphasis. He knew he should not have said anything at all. She had thanked him. She was being gracious. Being gracious in return seemed like mockery.

"I hope you—" he began but stopped. She looked relieved.

"Come," he said instead and rubbed his eyes with force. "Let's go."

She wrapped a shawl around her shoulders and slipped on her shoes. Was she wearing a nightgown? Some days, she looked like a child, with her large feet and little belly. Some days, he noticed how she'd aged even in the few years since they'd met. Creases puckered the outer corners of her eyes, directing attention away from the prettiest part of her face. Joseph dusted a patch of flour off his sleeve and into the sink. He ignored his urge to use the toilet.

He walked down the stairs with one arm outstretched behind him, reaching for her. She rested one hand on his shoulder and with the other slid a tissue against the banister, making a tiny swoosh as she gathered the dust. Outside, in the milky afternoon light, she opened the tissue to him. It looked like a tiny gray mouse.

"So filthy," she said, to prove a point.

Joseph was elsewhere, imagining Victoria with a red coat cinched around her waist—the kind in the shop windows. She was leaning down to wipe their child's hands with a wet cloth, getting the dirt out of the crevices. In his mind, the child's hand was a little sun, radiant and hot. He kissed Victoria on the head. She looked at him like he'd said something suspicious and strange.

They took the bus to the doctor's office. She kept her fingers interlaced in her lap. When she spoke, she whispered. She still hadn't adjusted to using English in public. She'd been here more than three years but rarely went out except to go to work.

"Are you hungry?" she asked. "I was going to make *fasoulia*."

He tried to imagine her at her hostessing job, the only time she left the apartment—if she was confident without him. He imagined her giving directions to the restrooms, suggesting something off the menu, talking to men. It made his stomach turn.

"I'm not hungry," Joseph said. "Are you? You shouldn't let yourself be hungry."

Red triangles flushed on her cheeks. He knew he shouldn't have. He had been so careful.

"Why?" she snapped. "Why should I be hungry less than you?"

She blamed him for not simply going along with her wishes. He knew that. She blamed him for the horrible things she'd seen by herself: the public hanging of her uncle, for example. She wouldn't mention her own father's name. But Joseph couldn't apologize. Wouldn't. He wanted to tell her to think of his feelings but didn't. He focused his eyes on the back of the driver's head.

They were quiet. This would not do, he thought. This would not help his cause, this anger. He took her hand. She gave it to him grudgingly, unknotting her fingers. A clam.

"Habibi," he said, oblivious. She put her hand on his chest, blocking him.

"A penny," she said, "for that word."

He was looking at her so intently that he no longer could identify her features. He was hoping that something explicit, something radical could happen between them without his even saying anything, but she was busy penalizing him for speaking in Arabic.

Understand, he wanted to tell her. *Try to understand. I want to love you. I want to see you with our baby in your arms.*

She put out her palm. She kept it there for a moment, between them. Then she put it into her lap, embarrassed.

"I'll put in two," Joseph said, taking a nickel from his pocket. "I'm sure to mess up again."

She looked out at the street. A man was being pushed against a building by two policemen. He writhed as they pinned his hands to his back. They pushed their bodies against him. Joseph thought he saw them whispering into his ears. Victoria turned her face away. She was thirteen years old during *farhud,* when the killing of the Jews began. She'd been sleeping on the roof with her mother when she saw the city light up, swell, and splinter with explosion. It was as if, she'd said once, the cries themselves generated the light. "You can't imagine a color like that. Like the insides of a person, ripped out." Joseph had been in Mosul with his rich cousins.

They passed Abingdon Square and moved along Fourteenth Street. He had never been in this part of the city. He did not know where he was going. For the first time, she was the leader of them both.

"You've become a real New Yorker," he said and threw his hands up in mock surrender. "You see? You show me around from now on."

He was trying to empower her. It was clear, however, that the first parts of his plan were absolutely not working—at least, not in the way he would have hoped.

The office was lined with thick wallpaper. The color of flesh, Joseph thought. They waited for the doctor in a windowless room full of tools and small jars. They tried not to look at each other. *Dr. Elliot Espy* was written in fancy lettering on two plaques and four framed papers. Joseph sat on a chair, and Victoria's feet dangled above the floor. She was on a high table with her back like an arrow on a drawn bow. She was wearing a blue gown, and her hands were crossed over her chest. Joseph noticed the bumps on her arms, the dark hairs sticking up. He looked at her until she looked back at him and then he looked to the floor, afraid that she'd say something he didn't want to hear. He reminded himself of what he must do and he hoped the doctor would be on his side. He'd never been to an American doctor. Victoria said the gowns reminded her of white paper napkins.

Joseph wasn't sure how long they'd have to wait. There was a big clock with black hands above the door. He'd never seen seconds move so slowly. The ceiling, he noticed, had no wallpaper but was painted with very shiny white paint. So shiny he was convinced that he could see his own reflection. He felt as if he were being watched.

"It's okay," Victoria said. He wasn't sure if she was talking to him or to herself.

Joseph looked at the cupboards and wondered what was behind the closed doors. Maybe Victoria knew. Maybe she didn't. That made it worse. That Victoria had been in there alone enraged Joseph.

He opened a cupboard. Boxes were neatly stacked according to size. He picked up one, changing the entire formation of things. He shook it next to his ear.

"What are you doing?" Victoria whispered. Her voice was low and tight. "Are you crazy?"

Joseph put the box back and opened another cupboard. This one was less full. A pile of dressing gowns. Some gauze.

"It's not so interesting," he said to Victoria, as if that would matter.

Before he opened the final cupboard, he looked around.

"Don't," Victoria said. "Joseph, do not."

But he couldn't help himself. He had come this far. And he felt he had something to prove. *We belong here,* he wanted to say. *I'm not afraid.*

He pulled on the handle but it wouldn't budge. It was locked. He pulled again, and it moved a little. A light went on inside. He tried pushing it back into the position it had been in. But it was stuck, locked, slightly open and lit.

"Oh," he heard Victoria say. Her hands covered her entire face. He scurried back to his seat and sat down very quickly. The doorknob turned, and Joseph trapped gas from his stomach with a giant inhale.

"Hello, folks," the doctor said cheerily. A tall, red-haired nurse followed on his heels. She nodded to Victoria, then to Joseph. She looked more like a movie star than a nurse, Joseph thought.

"How are we doing?" the doctor asked, resting his hand on Victoria's knee and sticking a silver tool into one of her ears. Joseph moved forward in his chair, wanting to hold her, protect her. A vein flared in her neck. She sensed him. He sat back and crossed his legs.

"Fine, thank you," Victoria said. "How are you?"

"That matters less," the doctor said, laughing importantly. Victoria blushed. She didn't seem uncomfortable, Joseph thought. The doctor looked toward the cabinet and then to Victoria. He was concerned.

"Did you need something?" he asked Victoria. The concern made Joseph angry. She didn't need anything. She wasn't the one who'd been snooping around.

"I did," Joseph said. Victoria looked right at him. Her eyes didn't flutter. In crucial moments, Joseph could never have been so calm. He thought for a second that she would make a very excellent assassin. Then he told himself to stop being dramatic.

"A little towel," Victoria said. "He wanted to wipe his head."

The nurse got right to it. She opened a cupboard below the sink that Joseph hadn't even noticed and handed him a stack of towels, sturdy and thick.

"There you go," she said and smiled to show a set of fancy white teeth.

The doctor's hand was still on Victoria's leg. He put the silver cone into her other ear and looked through it.

"Great," the doctor kept saying as he moved her jaw, opened her eyes wide. "Excellent. You're just perfect."

Victoria didn't move. She let him inspect her like an animal, Joseph thought. Less. In Baghdad, the Hassawi donkeys were like royalty. They carried only watermelon, dates, and honey. They gave birth once in a lifetime.

"You're eating properly?" the doctor asked while opening Victoria's mouth and peering in. "And you've been resting?"

Joseph wanted the doctor to answer Victoria's question: How was he? Joseph hadn't forgotten it. Before the towels, before everything, she had asked him that. Joseph thought a doctor should have better manners than this.

"Yes," Victoria said. Joseph wanted to tell the doctor otherwise, that she refused to give up her hostessing job—four to midnight three evenings a week.

"Have you given any thought," the doctor said, suddenly lowering his voice, "to what we talked about?" Joseph felt like he'd been punched in the stomach. He felt sick. They'd talked about it? She talked to him, Joseph thought, and actually shook his head. The nurse shuffled a bit and cleared her throat. She looked at Joseph. Maybe she wanted him to say something too. This was his chance, Joseph thought. It was now or never.

"We—" he began, but Victoria shot him a look. He went silent. He picked one towel off the stack and dragged it across the sweat on his forehead.

"I have," she said. "I've thought about it a lot."

Joseph wanted to catch her eye. He wanted to beg her to have the baby. He thought of his life without it, just the two of them, and he couldn't take it. Her anticipation, her gloom—it was too much for him. He craned his neck toward her.

"And what does your husband think?" the doctor asked. Now he met Joseph's eyes. Finally.

"We're not married," Victoria said suddenly. They all looked at her—Joseph included—as if they couldn't understand, as if she'd offered to deliver the baby herself. They were shocked. Joseph wanted to shout. They hadn't gotten married because Victoria had wanted to wait until they were citizens, for a nice wedding they could be proud of. It was never an issue. They acted as though they were married because in their minds, or so he thought, they might as well have been. But now, Victoria was using this fact to isolate him. Joseph was determined that it wouldn't. What was the big deal? he thought. These people were not saints. They were in the business of auctioning off babies. Well, he didn't know that for sure. But that was how he imagined it happening, at a red stall with a canopy and a yellow flag—like at the state fairs he'd seen in photos.

Joseph tried to remind himself to be understanding. Her family hadn't been like his. Her father, to whom Joseph, gratefully, had never been formally introduced, was loveless, cruel. Every evening he spent at the Mee-Dan, and even on family nights there, Victoria had told him, he brought just his sons. Her mother was beautiful but sad, desperate. She used to wander around the market, he remembered, looking defeated, lost, like a flower in terrible need of sun. Joseph's own family consisted of just his father and himself, which was why when Joseph left for the States, he was banded with hope. He was sure his father would make it to Israel and things would be all right. That was his father's promise and why Joseph could leave unburdened. If it had been otherwise, he would have stayed. But his father believed that Israel would provide nothing new for his son, so he urged Joseph to flee to the United States. "Go where I could never go," he'd said. "That is the best thing a father can offer his child."

"We are planning for marriage," Joseph said now. The doctor and the nurse turned their eyes to each other and then to the white floor, waiting. Victoria was staring past the doctor, past all of the shiny silver tools and white towels, toward something that Joseph could not see. Wallpaper? Was something there? Joseph noticed nothing remarkable. Not even a tear.

"I want to do the adoption," Victoria said, her voice shaking but determined. "To keep this baby would not be right for me."

"You?" Joseph said, feeling like he was yelling through a hurricane, trying desperately to be heard.

"Doctor," he finally said, no longer able to hold it in. "I don't think that's necessary. I really don't. Do you?"

"Well," the doctor said, putting his hand to his chest as if flattered. "I really don't feel privileged to say."

"But she doesn't want to discuss it with me," Joseph said. For the second time, Victoria put her face in her hands. The doctor gently touched one of her wrists.

"That's her choice, isn't it?" the doctor said. "My opinion? You aren't married. Somewhere, this baby will have a good home."

Until then, Joseph hadn't thought of the baby, exactly. He'd thought of other things. A toddler. A playground. A crib. But a child, a little delicate thing curled into Victoria's chest—that he had left out of his head. Thankfully. Now he saw Victoria's arms with nothing in them and a gaping hole through her body where the baby had been. He turned away quickly. He would have gotten up and walked out if he hadn't feared for Victoria, for what might happen if he left her alone. So he slumped deeper and deeper into the chair. He snuggled his hands into his armpits, away from the itchy armrests. He waited, shutting out all the sound he could, concentrating on the rhythm of his heart. He imagined how fast a baby's heart must beat, pinging like rain on tin.

The doctor wrote something on a pad and gave it to Victoria.

"Your next appointments will be in our uptown office."

He shook her hand and passed his folder to the nurse, giving her a wink.

"You don't worry about a thing," he said. "The baby is going to be fine."

The doctor walked out, his white coat stiff behind him. Joseph felt hollow and weak. He looked at Victoria. Her eyes were set on the door, which was closed again. Her lips were loose with trust for the doctor. Joseph imagined her asleep, so that he could love her again. It embarrassed him, but that was the only way. All of this frustration would be over soon, he told himself. The next phase would be something different. It couldn't be worse. That was the first positive thought that had crossed his mind in weeks.

The nurse underlined various things on a piece of paper. She explained certain points with little movements of her hands and stood very close to Victoria. Every now and then, the two women had a little laugh.

"Some women forget how big their bellies are," the nurse was saying. "They get themselves into the oddest places."

Joseph could tell that Victoria trusted her too. Joseph motioned that he was going to the bathroom. His stomach. As he walked out, he realized he could barely understand what they were saying, the two of them. They spoke in some language he didn't know. He thought of birds chirping to one another. His beautiful Victoria chirping, chirping with this leggy, redheaded American who knew everything that seemed to matter.

Maybe, he thought, *maybe she's my only hope.*

For Joseph, the months after the doctor's visit were quiet, timid ones. Victoria wanted to exercise and so they walked. Often, they took the subway uptown, made a loop around Central Park, and whenever they passed a vendor with an ice cream cart, they bought one or two, as if to prove again and again to themselves that something like that could exist. In Baghdad, you couldn't find a cold drink if you tried, let alone something frozen. Joseph thought of all those days in Iraq when he'd trekked so far west across the city for a dish of non-kosher kebabs. Such delicious sacrilege. He ate it in the shadows of old ratty furniture that would never be sold, careful not to be seen. What he would have done for an ice cream then.

They liked to sit at the fountain. Victoria put her face to the sun, and Joseph could admire her long neck that way. His auntie used to say that a man should marry a woman who had the height of a sail and a neck a yard long. And Victoria did. She had a long, beautiful neck. When she lifted it up and back to look at a fast screen of birds moving across the sky, Joseph felt that he saw a secret in the skin there. That delicate, wonderful skin. And then he'd remember himself. Themselves. They would be one fewer. This buoyancy would not last.

Joseph went to work every morning. Victoria stayed home. She gave up her job, finally, and she didn't seem to miss it. Her belly grew and grew. When she stood, she clasped her hands below it as if lugging a sack of grapefruits. At seven months, she seemed on the brink of bursting. She appeared comfortable though, and more beautiful than ever. Her breasts were rounder, somehow closer to her face. Her lips and neck were plumper, and more pink. She had a new kind of confidence, which Joseph saw as an improvement. He wanted to ask her if she felt less lonely. He wanted the answer in his head to be right. He wondered what it would be like to have another person with you constantly, in your belly. Someone who knew all the secret things you did—crying over some classical music and talking while on the toilet, perhaps. He could never share those thoughts with Victoria. She'd call him sentimental.

She paced the apartment all day, back and forth, tapping gently on her belly to a song she hummed, comforting it. He liked to imagine that she talked to the baby when he wasn't home. He imagined that she named the child something amusing—Mazel Tov or Aloe Vera. Her belly, it seemed to Joseph, was like a friend she hadn't seen in many years who had come along and reminded her of a careless youth. She stood for hours at the window, braiding various pieces of her hair. From the side, Joseph thought, her belly emphasized the knobbiness of her knees and bulbousness of her toes and the way her nose was somehow jumpy. The belly made a pattern out of her—toes, knees, belly, nose. It seemed perfectly natural and right.

One day, Joseph recited the rhyming phrase to himself as he watched her slicing *samoon* in the afternoon sunlight. Knees, toes, belly, nose. Knees, toes, belly, nose. He had just come home from work, and his shirt and shoes were off. The bakery ovens had left a thin, strong sweat all over his body and it had begun to dry and ice on his skin. Victoria's yellow nightgown was tight against her stomach. She was wearing Joseph's boots as she clunked around the kitchen. They slouched around her ankles.

She hoisted one knee onto the stove in order to reach for a jar. Joseph jumped up, lunged toward her.

"I'm all right," she said. "I can do it."

Joseph sank back onto the mattress on the floor. Victoria took the date spread from the high shelf. She winced as she turned the lid. Suddenly, she put her hand to her head.

"Are you all right?" Joseph asked.

"Just dizzy," she said. "I'll be fine."

He had asked Isaac's wife about this. The one who'd had a baby too. She said that everything happened to pregnant ladies. Tiredness, nausea, screaming in their sleep. There was rarely something to worry about. But Joseph couldn't help it. He felt that maybe it was in his blood to worry.

Victoria slathered the bread with thick *halek*. She began to walk over to Joseph with her hand stretched out in front of her, the bread on her palm. Then she stopped. Right there in the middle of the floor. She wavered slightly, then threw her arms out for balance. The bread flipped and fell. The date spread made a quick sucking sound and stuck to the floor. Victoria's face was surprised, and she cradled her stomach from the bottom. She moaned. Joseph got up but stopped, unsure.

The baby had kicked. That's what it was. He wanted to hug her, lift her, laugh out loud. He walked a bit closer to her, wanting to feel it but she put one hand up to block him. His heart sank. She stood still with her eyes shut tight and a strong chin, as if dispelling a terrible fantasy and then waiting for it to rear up again. Joseph rescued the bread from the floor, his hands shaking with denied anticipation. He stuffed it into his mouth whole, dusty, and when the sugar stuck to the sides of his throat he coughed, letting the wet crumbs fly like kamikaze birds.

The next afternoon, Joseph found himself back on the bus, passing Abingdon Square, crawling along Fourteenth Street. It wasn't like him to feel this way, furious, irrational, his feet yearning to stamp, shouts bobbing in his chest. He considered himself a patient person—and understanding. But enough was enough. He'd been patient. He'd been understanding. And where, he wondered, had that gotten him? Any food will go bad, he thought to himself, if you leave it out long enough.

When he arrived at Dr. Espy's office, a woman was behind the desk, leafing through a catalog, licking her pointer and flipping the pages, all drama. She didn't bother to look up.

"Is the other nurse here?" he asked.

She shook her head.

"The one with saffron hair and—" he said, and stopped himself before mimicking her very large chest. He didn't know how else to describe her. "She is very nice," he said.

"Carmen," she said. "No. She's off today."

Joseph dropped his hands onto the desk. This seemed like a very bad sign.

Finally, the woman looked up. That's when her face changed, like he'd handed her a gift.

"Is there something I can help you with?" she asked, adjusting her hair, which let out a lovely scent of flowers he'd never smelled. She stood up, so they were eye to eye, and Joseph wondered if she was going to ask him to leave. But she didn't. Though she'd appeared large before, her waist, wrists, and neck, he noticed, were actually quite slight. Birdlike, even. He wondered if that's what made movie stars movie stars—that gist of grandness. These American women all seemed like movie stars. And this one looked very clean in her white uniform, he thought.

"Well—" he began.

"Tell me," she said. The office was empty. It was late in the day. The woman reached for her sweater.

He was surprised at how easily the words came to him, how directly the woman faced him and with such devoted interest. Her eyes were focused and clear. He realized then how much Victoria had kept him out. She avoided him, eluded him. They hardly made eye contact anymore. They never kissed. And he realized how accustomed he'd become, comfortable even, to speaking to Victoria's back.

Lorca

THE NEXT DAY, my mother slept till noon, like she always did on Wednesdays, and I took the opportunity to rip the place apart, looking for hints and clues about why she loved masgouf so much. I hunted down all the dog-eared pages of her cookbooks, went through all the scrawled recipe notes for a particular love of grilled fish that maybe I didn't know about. I got nowhere. Then I found a website where you put in your favorite ingredients in various combinations and it spit out the "perfect" dish. I listed all the things my mother loved. It came up with nothing even mildly masgouf-y. It came up with pork chop lollipops and rice pudding. My mother would have preferred a sous-vide Christmas tree.

After that, I searched for something about Victoria and Joseph's restaurant. Anything. I looked through a bowl of old matchbooks, most of which must have belonged to Lou because they were from bars near Wall Street, and Lou liked nothing more than a man in a suit. My mother wouldn't have been caught dead in a place like that. I went through my mother's underwear, sock, and jewelry drawers and checked in the freezer, hoping that I'd overlooked something, missed the crucial clue. But nothing. Not a single thing. Meanwhile, in case my mother decided to wake up in the middle of everything, I cleaned the house, made a pot of her favorite white bean soup, and prepared Parmesan croutons on a baking sheet, though I knew she'd never feel like eating them. I made raspberry sauce for vanilla ice cream.

Then, when my mother started to get restless, flinging her comforter off the couch and knocking her knees, I wrote her a note that said I'd gone to a museum to research an extra-credit project that might keep me from getting an incomplete during my suspension. I left for the bookstore.

"Hey," Blot said. I hadn't even seen him. He was behind me, and I swung around.

"I've been reading a lot of Lorca stuff," he said. "I have something for you."

My heart jumped rope. I didn't want to believe him. He cocked his head and did a full-body twirl.

"C'mon," he said.

Only then did I realize it was true what my mother had said: that my feet turned in, that I leaned forward and crouched, that I scurried like a pigeon. He was walking quickly, whistling, picking up a stray book here and there, his body moving like a hammock. He took one step to my two. I scurried scurried scurried alongside of him, taking a giant leap every once in a while so I didn't feel like his midget cousin.

"So," he said. "What's up?"

"Well, I went back," I told him. "To Victoria's."

"And?" he said.

"Well," I said. "I told her what I told you, pretty much, about making it for my mother's birthday."

And then I told him what Victoria had said about the masgouf not being chef-y.

"She had a point," I said. "Because my mother's other favorites include, for example, osetra caviar and wagyu beef tartare from Le Bernardin."

"I don't know what that means," he said.

"Exactly," I said.

"Maybe she liked the atmosphere," he said.

"Yeah," I said, though I doubted it. The review I'd read suggested the very opposite of what she liked. She hated clutter, anything that might collect dust. Even department stores gave her the creeps.

"So did you get the recipe?" he asked.

It occurred to me that if I said I had the recipe, we would have nothing else to talk about. The recipe was something to look forward to, to wait on together.

"No," I said. "And she didn't offer it. I guess the timing isn't right. Yet."

"Understood," he said. "It might take a while."

If I could have patted myself on the back, I would have.

"Here," Blot said and stopped. We were on the second floor, next to a giant display of coffee-table books. Blot pointed at the one at the very bottom of the pile. The spine was black and white.

"There," he said. "That's it."

Unfortunately, it was under a million Marilyn Monroe books. Marilyn was on a chaise, her head thrown back and her knees bent. I imagined myself in that position. I had bony, knobby knees—the kind that would not photograph well. I picked up the book. Underneath that was another copy. And another. Marilyn again and again. Stupid me, I blushed. I was embarrassed about how long it was taking me to move all the Marilyns and put them down gently. I wondered if Marilyn was the kind of woman he liked and if seeing her again and again was making him like me less. I kept waiting for him to say *Never mind*.

"Almost there," he said, dimples so deep you could store almond tuiles inside.

Finally, I got to the bottom book. It was a close-up of Dalí, Lorca's lover. He was half looking at the camera. His eyes were open wide wide wide, and his mustache was so long that it extended past the cover on both sides. The spine of the book showed the little swirl of it, like an escargot. I turned it over in my hands.

"I thought you'd like it," he said. "So I stashed it here. It's the only copy left. One day, when I'm not so broke, I'll buy it for you. For now, it's on hold permanently."

I looked at him, right in his face. His eyes were gray and sort of blue, like the healthiest sardine pulled straight from the ocean. I wanted to tell him that last year, for my birthday, my mother and Lou bought me a slew of stuff from Victoria's Secret—ridiculous things that I'd never wear. They thought it was hysterical. They bought me a book on growing breasts too. It was for eight-year-olds and it said, *Do not try to squash them down. They are healthy. Would you kill a flower when it was just starting to bloom?*

I didn't want to appear sappy. Still, I wanted him to understand what this meant.

"You are too kind," I said, like we were at some stuffy bridal shower. "You shouldn't have." I shouldn't have. I shook my head at myself.

He didn't seem to care. He was smiling for real.

"You like it?" he asked. "It's cool, isn't it?"

"Yes," I said. "It's so cool." I couldn't help it: a billion miles an hour of enthusiasm came through in my voice. I tried to take it back.

"It's nice," I said then. Aunt Lou said that *nice* was the worst word. *Nice* got you nowhere. *Nice* meant "not pretty." "If a guy says you're nice," she'd told me, "you can just about forget it." I should have said *brilliant,* I decided. My mother used that word and it rolled off her tongue like a cherry pit.

We sat down and I paged through it. I knew the paintings. I'd been to exhibits. I kept a catalog of his work on my desk. In the middle of the book, I stopped. There was a postcard. I picked it up and showed it to Blot, thinking I'd found it by mistake. He nodded. It was for me. It was? It was a painting, a black outline of a man's head and neck. Where his brain should have been were clouds. I flipped it over.

I knew the poem. It began: *"Can you see the wound I carry / from my throat to my heart?"*

Nervously, mindlessly, I started itching my arm. I couldn't help it. The pain roused easily, like waking up a cat. But I'm an idiot. I hadn't remembered to put on Band-Aids this morning. I ripped off some scabs from the razor. I had blood on my fingers.

"Shit," Blot said. "Are you all right?" He didn't even go for the book to clean it off or anything like that. He wanted to touch me. "Let me see," he said.

Before I knew it, I was standing up. He stood up too.

"Don't." My face got hotter than hot. I was dizzy, full of something runny, like yolks. *Not again,* I thought. My arms had been hidden. Everything was hidden. I wanted to turn myself inside out. It was nothing. I yanked down on my sleeve.

"It's nothing," I said. "We have a kitten."

He looked down at the book, now half mangled on the floor. I couldn't fix it. I couldn't even move. I felt like I might spill.

"I love that poem," he said. I didn't look at him. He didn't say it like he knew.

"Thank you" is what I managed to get out.

"It made me think of you," he said, picking up the book and holding it open in his arms, and I jerked forward, a response to a surging of something in my heart.

"Think of me?" I said.

I realized then that, with the other hand, the safe one, I was holding the postcard to my chest. I looked down at the book. In the corner of the page was a painting. A woman in a striped skirt looked out a window onto the sea. There was a dishtowel by her side.

I took a breath. He wasn't acting as if he knew. If he knew, I thought, he'd look different. He'd say something. He'd say more. I could be normal.

"Bad kitten," I said, trying to laugh.

He laughed too. "Oh," he said. "I get it. We grew up with Maine coons."

I stood there, unmoving. I'd been right.

"I have to go downstairs," he said. "Why don't you come? You can use the staff bathroom, which smells better than the others."

For a moment, my feet were unresponsive, like something blackened and stuck to the grill.

"Come," he said, and I thought of his sister. I wondered if letting him help me would be doing him a favor as much as me.

"Come," he said again. "I really have to pee."

I fell for it, but he didn't pee when we got downstairs. We went to the lounge area for the workers—green scratchy-looking couches, a small fridge, the kind of instant coffeemaker that my mother loathed, and lots of lots of boxes of books—and I put the postcard in my pocket, keeping my other hand over my wrist in my sleeve, out of sight. I could feel it getting sticky, like dried milk.

Blot pulled out a chair and told me to sit down. He pulled out one for himself. Then he opened a closet and took out a gigantic first-aid kit in a white metal box.

"First things first," he said, sitting down, unlatching the box, and rifling through it. He opened two alcohol pads and held them up. I was supposed to show him my wrist, but I couldn't move—or I wouldn't move. I wasn't sure which.

"Come on," he said, but he wasn't impatient. I remembered my mother sitting me down on the toilet once, years ago, to clean up my knees. I'd fallen off my bike. The gravel felt so good that I ground my leg back and forth against it like a saw. When I got home, the blood was dripping down, and my mother hustled me off the carpet and into the bathroom. She crouched in front of me only long enough to look like she'd eaten something very sour. Then she called for my father. "Paul!" she shrieked. "Your daughter!"

The funny thing was that she hardly ever got queasy. She could skin a rabbit—piece of cake. She'd nail through an eel's head, easy as pie.

"Lemme see," Blot said and opened his hand for mine. Before I knew it, I had given it to him, and looked away. I didn't need to pretend that it made me weak, that I couldn't bear to watch. I couldn't.

First came the alcohol pads, cool and sort of tart-feeling. He cleaned my hand thoroughly. He used a cotton swab to get beneath my nails. When he was done with that, he sighed. I wanted to tell him to stop, but before I could gather my courage, he was taking care of my wrist. His movements were slow and circular, like he was stirring thick stew. He brought it up to his face, as if searching for shards of metal, and I almost explained, but then I felt his breath, a strong, cold stream.

"Does that help?" he asked.

I nodded my head yes.

Eventually, three pads later, I snuck a peek at him, looking for signs that he might suspect me. If he did, he wasn't letting on. He blinked at a very normal pace. I didn't know how much cleaner my wrist could get, but I had the feeling he was warning me against getting hurt again. All this work shouldn't go to waste.

"What do you think?" I asked him finally. I kicked the trash can that he'd thrown the pads in so the bloody things fell to the bottom.

He was opening a tube of ointment and reading the instructions on it.

"Ouchie," he said, like he was hurting for me. That's when I thought of my father, who'd done the same thing. "Ouch,

Lorca," he used to say, the pain drawing his features to the middle of his face.

And then it hit me.

"Duh," I said out loud. "We have to call him."

I took away my wrist.

"Nope," Blot said, taking it back. "Hold, please." And then: "Who?"

"My father," I said.

He was using a cotton swab now to apply dots of gel that peaked like perfectly whipped egg whites.

"I'm not following," he said. "Almost done."

"Duh," I said again and he looked up only long enough to smile at me.

"Because," I said. "He was at the restaurant too."

As Blot cut a piece of gauze into the shape of a triangle and shimmied it along the ointment into the exact right place, it all came together for me. My father: the second thing that made my mother happy. She would have disagreed. She had said that the very thought of him made her want to pan-fry her face, but I didn't believe her. I'd always thought that her only happy time had been when they were together in New Hampshire before I was born. She'd let her hair grow long and kept herbs in clay pots and made raspberry scones for a local bakery and forgotten to take off her oven mitts when she got in the car. Too, she kept these owls on the little side table next to the couch where she slept. They were from him, although she said they weren't.

"Lorca," she'd said when I mentioned it. "Your imagination is something else. I bought these years ago, on that trip when we rafted down the Colorado River."

Not true. I knew it. The owls had lived on her nightstand in New Hampshire, lined up like soldiers. He made them. I knew he did. One had layers of wooden feathers carved into the oak, like ripples in mud. One had tiny pearls for eyes. One had dried crab apples like tiny hearts in a ring around its base. Some were soapstone. Two were concoctions of shells and pebbles. There were fourteen of them. I wanted to say to her now, *He made those. See? He is someone. He's something.*

I liked to think of her throwing her arms around his neck as he lifted her off the ground. Sometimes, if she was in the mood or if we'd just watched a romantic comedy, she'd admit that there were happy times—but mostly before me.

"Crazy love does not a marriage make," she'd said once. Her eyes got glassy. I tried to get her to go on but Aunt Lou had to butt in and ruin everything.

"Forget him, Nance," she said, filing a nail, knowing nothing about anything. "He was never good for you. He was no kind of man."

My mother nodded, curled into herself under a blanket. Then she looked back at me. She was a turtle.

"Men are shit," she said. "You'll see."

But maybe not. Just three weeks ago, I'd found her in the morning cupping an owl in her hand like a quail's egg, contemplating its weight.

I hadn't called my father in two years. The last time I did, the number had been disconnected. I must have redialed a hundred times. Later, I asked my mother about it. We were at the supermarket together, identifying shapes in the swirly sawdust on the floor.

"That looks like a corpse," she said. "A fallen tree, a padlock, spilled milk, a crow."

"That one looks like Dad," I said, and in the same breath, "his number's disconnected."

She looked at me like I'd just made fun of her, like I'd ruined everything. We never played the game after that, and we never talked about it. That was that. If you'd asked me, I'd have said she was afraid of me deserting her. That's why my calling my father felt to her like I'd thrown a strawberry tart with crème pâtissière in her face. But if I told her—and it wouldn't have been the first time—that I wasn't going anywhere, she'd get all stewed.

"You called him?" she said.

"Just to say hi—" I started.

"The world is your oyster," she said. "God knows I'd be the last one to hold you back from your dreams."

And just like that, I never called him again. With her, a choice always had to be made, but there was only ever one right answer.

"Maybe," Blot said, "we could get him to come here."

I was jittering on the inside. It felt a little bit like he'd finished my sentence.

"Dial nine first," Blot said, pulling my sleeve down over his handiwork and signaling toward the phone. I got up as he put away the first-aid kit.

"My password," he said, "is g-r-e-t-a."

I didn't know what to say, so I dialed the password as if it were no big deal—like he'd spelled out d-i-j-o-n instead.

I called the old number. The first time I tried, the line beeped once and went empty. I didn't hang up, thinking that maybe someone was on the other end. "Hello?" I said. "Hello?" Then the beeping started again, and louder, so I hung up. I tried again, hopeful. This time: nonstop beeping. When I looked over at Blot, his eyebrows popped up like done toast. I shook my head.

"Try one more time," Blot said. "Third time's the charm."

It wasn't the charm, and maybe I'd known that all along. All beeps. *Beeeeep.* My father, if he hadn't disconnected the phone line because of the expense, was probably not home, and if he was home, he was probably outside, carving something out of nothing. And even if he wasn't making whatever it was for my mother exactly, he was—which meant that he'd never hear the phone ring, hear anything but the beating of his heart as he whittled whittled whittled what he could, what was right in front of him, what he could hold on to with both hands.

"Well," Blot said. "We tried."

We, I thought. To keep from grinning, I pretended to inspect his handiwork on my wrist. It felt very warm and cozy in there. I never used gauze and tape on myself, just Band-Aids. I could go through a tube of ointment in a week.

"That's more than I can say for myself," he said.

I thought of my mother, her silence. I stayed quiet so he'd continue.

"This is the week that my parents come to New York every year. Right now. My aunt, uncle, and all the cousins too. I thought about calling, but I can't. I haven't called them in a year. But they know where I am. They could call me if they wanted."

I hoped he'd go on, but he straightened his back, coughed twice, and gave me a big fake grin. I knew all about that expression. I used it too.

"So," he said. "What else can we do for you?"

I shut my eyes for a second in solidarity. I wanted him to know that I got it.

"Maybe I'll try again later," I said. "If that doesn't work, I guess I have one other option, though it's tricky. Plan B."

"Plan B," Blot repeated, and he nodded, though he couldn't have had any idea what I meant.

"It's harder than you think," I said. I wanted and didn't want to tell him about my mother, how impossible it was to ask her anything directly.

"No doubt," he said, and I believed he understood.

I started to make my way to the door. "Hey," I said. I stopped. "Thank you."

"For the phone?" he said, smirking, and I laughed.

"Yup," I said. "For the phone."

"May the force be with you," he said. I tapped on the wall for him, twice. Tap. Tap.

And then, like in the movies, he tapped back.

When I was a safe distance away from the bookstore, I pulled the postcard from my pocket. It was flat and warm like a soggy waffle. I'd already melted some of the ink. I read it again and couldn't believe it. I knew those lines. They were in the book from my father. Of course I had them marked.

I stopped in the middle of the sidewalk to read it once more. I couldn't help it. I wanted to sit down right there in the street and keep reading and reading and reading it until I understood what it meant to him, for me. It made me think of love. I couldn't help that either. I moved finally when a stroller whammed into my ankle.

Later, at home, I thought of the last time I'd seen my father.

Four years ago, he came to the city to take me out to dinner for my tenth birthday. He was three months early. We went to a diner on Eighty-Sixth Street. He'd suggested we go somewhere nicer but I told him no, I liked that place best. I knew his bus ticket alone had cost him a week's salary. My mother had told me that, but not in a nice way. He wore a white shirt that I had given him for Hanukkah three years before, when we'd still lived with him. I had stolen it from Mrs. Bennett's house. Her husband died. She paid me to help clean up. She shook so much she broke things. I didn't have to steal it. I could have asked for it. No one would have worn it. The shirt was still in plastic. I stuffed it in my jacket while she was napping with the TV on.

My father and I got there for the early-bird special, which meant a beverage, dessert, and coffee were free with an entrée. I planned on giving him my free coffee.

I'd cleaned my room and refolded all my clothes even though

I knew he'd never come to the apartment. He was the opposite of pushy, especially when it came to my mother. I braided my hair along both sides of my head because he once said that he liked it that way. He looked strange in New York. Somehow too delicate, even though he was big; his hands were covered in calluses, his pants were torn at the ankle, and his beard was so thick it could catch all the dirt that the wind picked up. He looked fuller, like the inside of his skin was lined with bark. His eyebrows had gotten bushy, and his eyes rested in two dark spots.

He was doing odd jobs, he said. Sometimes logging. He looked up at the buildings, almost crouching. He wobbled and grabbed for a parking meter and my shoulder. It made me feel strong.

"I don't know what's happened," he said. "I used to love this city. I guess now it's too much for a country boy like me."

He read the gigantic menu over again and again. I made eyes at the waitress to tell her not yet. I didn't want to embarrass him. He mouthed his order before he spit it out to her.

"Mile-high turkey platter with spinach, no garlic."

His mouth was so dry his lips got stuck on his teeth.

How's school?

How's your room?

Did you make any friends?

He was looking out the window, waiting.

"Dad," I said. "Mom's in the Village with Aunt Lou."

He was startled by what I said and then suddenly relieved, as if he'd taken off a couple of layers. He could really see me then.

Where's she working now?

How's her mood?

Has she changed her hair much?

He closed his eyes like he was crying or dreaming as I told him every detail, hoping it would be enough to fill him. Every time she'd gone to the dentist. Every change to her lemon-lavender crème brûlée recipe. The way she blew on Lou's stove to get it to light. The new shampoo she was trying. I had a feeling he would buy it in New Hampshire, use it himself. She hadn't been on any dates that I knew of. I told him that too, and how often I'd found her with half her body out a window because, she said, the air was cleaner a few flights up. I didn't tell him that I believed she did it to remind herself of my father, of sleeping with the windows open in Cow Hampshire, breathing through both her nose and mouth—his breath keeping her alive too. Or about the owls he'd carved when we were a family, how she'd never gotten rid of them, and some nights, she'd clutch them in her sleep. If I'd told him, it would have overwhelmed his heart.

I did say, "I could have stayed with you." He actually laughed.

"No," he said. "Over your mother's dead body."

For a second I felt flattered. He thought she'd never give me away.

"Your mother is gorgeous as a vase until you knock her over," he said. "Then all you have is a boatload of jagged pieces."

I didn't know what he meant at the time, but I think I do now. He meant that her presence was staggering. That she was commanding, blinding, so much—like sitting in the front row at the movies—and that it was just about impossible to get any real sense of her when you were right next to her, unless you could break her, which he knew I never could. I'd never even try.

When he said goodbye—he took the bus down and back up on the same day—he pressed his rough cheek to my head.

"Send my best to your mother."

His body had gotten more solid.

"I love you, honey."

I pushed down the urge to ask him why. I felt the stiffness of his brown workman's coat for days, its elbow awkwardly jammed into my eye.

At home, I looked in the mirror until I had three eyes and five sets of lips. I wanted to see what it would be like to try to love me. Sometimes, I imagined that my father stood on the corner yelling up to my mother and Aunt Lou that he was going to take me and take care of me, and he was always holding this big white down comforter, like a deflated hot-air balloon. He was ready to wrap me in it.

I'd had a choice, I guess. I could have moved up there with him. Except that I couldn't have, even if he'd offered. The last time I heard his voice was on the answering machine three years ago. I was supposed to be sleeping. He sang "Happy Birthday" like the words were weeping out of him. My mother pressed Delete.

"Damn drunk," she'd said to Lou, and Lou'd said, "That's right! That's exactly what he is."

That evening, after I used the phone at the bookstore, I searched for hours on the Internet for something about my father. As it turned out, there was only one mention of him anywhere, crediting him for the millwork in a historical bed-and-breakfast in Cow Hampshire. I thought about calling the place but then I came up with a better idea. If he was anywhere at this hour, he was at a bar. It was too late for him to be working. So I went online again and found the names and numbers of the three pubs in our old town.

Aunt Lou was watching *Jeopardy!* in the living room when the phone rang.

"Get that!" she shouted. "If it's Jorge, tell him I died."

I raced for it in the kitchen, even though the phone was just feet from Lou.

"Hello?" I said, picking it up and making my way to the couch.

"Yup," my mother said to me. Then she was silent. I was too. I was wondering why we were on the phone if she wanted to say nothing at all. For a moment, I wondered if she somehow knew I was getting ready to call my father. Then I imagined she'd called because she just wanted to be with me somehow, to protect me from myself—that it was her way of holding me in her mother arms. We stayed like that forever.

"That's it?" she said finally. "That's all you have to say for the trouble you've put me through? I can't focus at work. I can't do a single thing right."

"I'm so sorry," I began, aware that this was out of the blue but feeling horribly guilty nonetheless. I wondered if she'd found a razor or had a camera somewhere or had met Blot, but asking would get me nowhere. I wanted to tell her all the work I'd been doing, how desperate I'd been to find the recipe for her, but I knew how stupid it would sound. I'd wasted so much time.

All I could get out was "Is there anything I can—" before my mother was gone. The phone line was deader than langoustines in pea risotto. I sat there, brimming with emotion but motionless, wanting to take a nap but too tired to even move. When I finally did, it was only because the phone was beeping that it needed to be hung up.

Lou stood up. She was shaking her head. "Naughty, naughty, naughty," she said.

"What?" I asked.

Lou rolled her eyes.

"We used to hope and hope and hope, your mother and I," she said, putting her palms together as if praying, "that you wouldn't end up like your father."

"Stop," I whispered but Lou didn't hear. She loved to trash-talk my father. She loved it almost as much as building up my mother, but not quite.

"You know, silent but deadly," she said. "All nice on the surface but really taking a knife to everything."

I imagined my father racing around Cow Hampshire with a knife, going at the hammocks, the black ice, the fences, the flies, the fluorescent lights at the gas stations, but I couldn't imagine his face. He wasn't like that. He used to rescue moths.

"Maybe we didn't hope hard enough," she said.

She sat down again on the couch across from me and looked at something between her toes.

"This is not going to make your mother love you more," she said. "You doing those things, it makes her feel like a bad parent. This isn't the way to get attention."

"It isn't about her," I said. "I don't do it so she'll notice. I try to make sure she won't."

"You think that," she said, "but everything you do is about her." She repeated the word, drawing out the syllables: "Ev. Ree. Thing."

"That's not true," I said. "I have a life."

"Oh yeah?" Aunt Lou said. "Prove it. You don't have friends like a normal teenager. You don't have hobbies. You don't do drugs. You don't do anything because you're afraid you might miss her."

"There's this guy—" I began.

"Oh Christ," she said. "You're like six years old. You tell that to your mother and she'll chain you to the fridge.

"You think," she continued, "that maybe one day she'll be home and she'll want to take you to Les Halles. And if you're out with your friends or you're getting laid in a museum bathroom, you'll miss out on being with her. I know. I get it. Don't feel bad. Nancy has that effect on people. When we were kids, everyone wanted her to sit in the middle of the table at a birthday party—even when it wasn't her party—just so they could be a part of what she gave out."

It happened right then. It started in my shoulders and made its way down. It was like traveling ants. The question I wanted to ask Lou was if Les Halles was my mother's new favorite restaurant. It used to be, years before. But what else didn't I know?

"So just live your life," she said. "If she's going to be happy, it won't be because of you. I can tell you that right now."

"I'll take Mobisodes for two hundred," said *Jeopardy!*

I tuned out.

Then: "What is *The Sopranos*?"

"That is correct!"

"I knew that," Lou said, and clapped her hands in front of the television.

When Aunt Lou was on her third glass of wine, and my mother was in the middle of dinner service at the restaurant, I closed the door to the bathroom and called the Hinkley Pub. The line was busy. At McSorley's, they knew no Paul. I was starting to feel like this was the stupidest idea in the world when I called Frosty Bear Tavern and asked the final time for Paul Seltzer.

"Paul!" said the bartender. "It's for you."

I had to do a little dance with my lips to keep them from sticking together. I swallowed hard.

"Hello?" said my father, whose voice was more careful than I remembered, and higher.

"Hi," I said.

"Hi," he said back.

"It's me," I said. I wondered if my voice had changed too. I closed my eyes and crossed my fingers that he'd recognize it anyway and that if he did, it meant something.

"Hey, you," he said, clearly unsure. My heart dropped.

"Oh, you!" he just about shouted. "Lorca?"

"Yes, hi," I said, relieved. "I was just calling—"

He cut me off. "What's wrong?" he asked. "Did something happen? Is your mother all right?"

I sort of laughed. It was a question I didn't know how to answer but that I should have been prepared for.

"I know you're busy," I said, wanting him to say something about his never being too busy for me or that he'd been hoping I'd call. Instead, he got defensive.

"I am busy," he said. "You can tell your mother how many calls I've gotten lately about my work. The inns around here are throwing dozens of projects my way all the time. Every day." He paused. "Just about every day."

"That's good," I said. At that moment, I realized that I didn't miss him anymore. I thought about dying in an accident: I'm in the back seat of a car, and he's far away. I imagine my mother calling him, sharing the news, and him clutching his stomach, about to rip the phone out of the wall and then not, not wanting to lose her. Her. All the while, the seat belt is still across my chest, and my mouth is open, attracting flies. The police are circling around the car, making a brown ring of footprints in the snow, just waiting for someone to show up. It gets dark and no one does and finally, hours later, I just disappear. The seat belt is still buckled and the car is a tin can, but I am gone. No one ever claims me.

On the phone now, I had the urge to tell him that something was very wrong with me. I was very very sick.

"Honey," he said. "I'm really sorry I missed your birthday. Like I said, it's been busy up here. But I thought about you. Had a pistachio ice cream in your honor."

I believed him. Pistachio was still my favorite.

"Is that why you're calling, honey? I'm so sorry. What can I do?"

That was exactly what I'd hoped he'd say.

"Remember," I said, "that restaurant?" I went through the whole song and dance about the Shohet and His Wife. I told him all the things I knew—and added some made-up details for atmosphere. Like about how in love they'd been and how he probably picked up my mother's fork from the floor, put his hand over hers, knocked his knees against hers, and had bought her flowers, which she kept sniffing all through dinner. I told him about how beautiful she'd looked. That part, I didn't need to make up. That was always the truth. I kept going—about her hair and her thick fans of eyelashes and her long legs, too long for any table, and about her perfect teeth. I told him that she broke her rule for him—she put her elbows on the table so she could be closer to him. I told him about the delicious masgouf.

When I was finished, my mouth was dry, and the line was silent.

"Hello?" I said. "Dad?"

"Is that what she told you?" he asked in a tiny voice. I could barely hear him.

"Well, sort of," I said.

"It wasn't me," he said. "Honey, I've never had that fish in my life."

Victoria

FOR OUR FIRST couple of lessons, I'd ordered in the groceries. They arrived at our apartment, boxed and fresh, at a designated time, requiring no more than a signature. The deliveryman brought the goods into the kitchen and put them at waist height, so I never even needed to bend.

On Wednesday, I considered the same convenience for our next lesson and was just beginning my phone order when Dottie barged in.

"What are you doing?" she said. "Go outside, for crying out loud." She grabbed the phone from me and hung it up. "Go out," she said, more quietly now. "When was the last time you got some fresh air?"

I nodded toward the kitchen window, which I'd opened.

"That doesn't count," she said.

She had a point. And yet, the idea of going into the world, seeing all the people, burying the unbearable feeling that they had no sense of what I was going through, of Joseph, felt like an affront that I wasn't prepared for. It had been only five days since he'd gone.

Too, I'd turned on the news in the morning. The temperature had suddenly dropped to well below freezing. What was the point?

As if hearing my thoughts, Dottie started in again. "Don't talk to me about the weather," she said. "You're the one who always goes on about the cold being good for us."

"In theory," I said.

Dottie had already made her way to the front closet, where she was mining for who knows what and huffing. Seconds later, she returned with my geriatric snow boots and a triumphant grin on her face. She dropped the boots down in front of me.

"Why don't you come too?" I said, more for effect than anything else.

"I have a hair appointment this afternoon," she said. "I've got to get ready."

She walked away, leaned against the wall, took a Diet Coke from her robe pocket, and cracked it open. Her robe was silk and mint-colored with ornately stitched Asian dragons down the back and arms. She was wearing heels and stretch pants, which made her legs look a mile long.

"That stuff will kill you," I said.

She hesitated before she put the can to her lips. We chuckled. "Good," we said at the same time. I picked at some lint on my knee and accidently made a hole in the fabric. Secretly, I wanted Dottie to ask me about the cooking lessons. I wanted to tell her all about Lorca, to gush. But Dottie stayed true to form, pressing for only the news that might pertain to her or be worthy of her pity. She excelled at pity. Anything that might require her to offer some form of congratulations or appear impressed, she didn't want to know about.

"Are you okay?" she said.

I looked up. For some reason, it felt like she'd punched me in the chest. Not because it was so typically Dottie or because I probably wasn't okay and wouldn't even have to admit that since it was apparent all over my face, but because it occurred to me that I hadn't really thought about it, and that felt suddenly like a big, fat betrayal of Joseph. I was going through the motions—but more than that. Lorca had been here, giving me a kind of happiness I hadn't experienced in years. Despite Joseph dying. Perhaps even because of it, though that thought was too much to bear.

"What's okay?" I said.

"It's—" Dottie began, and stopped. She looked out the window. "I don't know," she said and sort of snorted a laugh.

It was a sincere question she'd asked. I could tell. She was worried about me. She was good at worry and had ample reason for it. Look at the facts: I'd just lost my husband of a hundred years. I hadn't been outside in the five days since he'd died. And yet the really worrisome part was that there was nothing tangible for me to worry over. No cancer. No heart disease. No husband on the cusp. In the end, that's the price you pay for taking such good care of yourself—for eating well, shunning artificial sweeteners and antibiotics, taking echinacea and vitamin D and evening primrose, and keeping your head warm in winter. I ended up, for all intents and purposes, all right. And alone. Any real damage, any signs of distress were holed up and shifty on the inside, and unless I was willing to deal with them directly, to press and press on them like an old bruise, I was okay.

"I'm not as good as I've ever been," I said. It was all I could think of.

"As bad?" she asked.

Now I looked out the window.

It occurred to me that in my happiest times—falling in love with Joseph, for example, and bustling around on Saturday nights at the restaurant—I couldn't imagine being any happier. But in my saddest, I'd always imagined it could get worse. I wondered if perhaps not everyone was like that. *Stop waiting for the sky to fall,* I told myself. The voice in my head was Joseph's.

"It's hard to know," I said.

"Of course it is," Dottie said. "That's probably as right an answer as there is."

Getting dressed for the cold is always a task. At my age, it's an undertaking. It requires not only layers, protection from wind and wet, and comfort, but also planning in regard to the more subtle issues of balance and bladder control. Getting dressed after Dottie left took me a full forty-five minutes.

As I buttoned up a wool sweater, I thought about how odd it was that Dottie had become the closest thing I had to a friend. There was no one else here, was there? I'd grown apart from all the other women I knew: the Iraqi Jews in Great Neck, the wives of Joseph's backgammon partners. It took effort to maintain those relationships, and effort I wasn't willing to give. Effort went to the restaurant. Effort went to Joseph. It's possible, I thought, that other people simply had more effort to begin with, that it was genetic. Or maybe you could store it up, increase it with good karma. But that wasn't me. After a time, I stopped craving travel and culture, new experiences and chitchat. My life was a potted plant.

Dottie and I were friends out of convenience. Friends only to a point. Over the years, we didn't exactly listen to each other. One of us spoke, and the other responded with a physical reaction rather than an emotional one. She told me to get dressed, and I did. I told her to go away, and, for the most part, she did. Rarely did either of us answer a question with a question. I'd never needed it. She mustn't have either.

I finally dragged myself outside and down the stone steps. I stopped, took a deep breath, prepared myself.

"It's cold," I said to no one in particular.

"You ain't kidding," said a man walking by. "It was in the sixties last week."

"Right!" I said.

Not wanting to overdo it, I walked only one block before hailing a cab. "I know, I know," I whispered to Joseph. He believed in the subway like one believes in flossing. You do it because it's good for you.

"On the way back," I said, lying to him and pretending that he knew that too. Somehow. "I'll take it on the way back."

Sometimes, it feels like New York City is doing you a favor. Perhaps it's a matter of expectation. But on this day, when I walked so carefully, afraid of slipping, of missing Joseph, of the enormous and bleak possibility of going anywhere, anywhere in the entire world, of falling into some crack in the earth and having that go totally unnoticed, everything seemed to snap to. A taxi stopped for me immediately. The driver didn't drive like someone was holding a gun to his head. The traffic lights were on our side. Fairway was not horribly crowded, and the persimmons were perfectly ripe. Though there was only one other woman on line at the fish counter, she suggested I go ahead of her.

"Really?" I said.

"Yes," she said. "I'm feeling indecisive." She moved aside and consulted her shopping list.

I kept thinking, *The world goes on.* I kept thinking, *Does it look like I've just lost him?* I kept thinking, *Is anyone else as sad as me? Of course,* I told myself. *Of course.* But the thought didn't make me feel any better.

As I passed the dried-fruits section, I ran my fingers over the bulk apricots. Joseph's favorites. How many bags, I thought, had I filled for him over the years? So many times I had watched him place three or four of the apricots on his tongue, letting them rehydrate into a sticky glob and then chewing them endlessly before swallowing. "The sweetest thing you ever had," he'd say, mouth full.

I plucked three apricots from the bins without using the tongs. I placed them on my tongue. I closed my eyes, leaned on my shopping cart, and waited for that surge of sweet.

The next day, I spent hours preparing for Lorca. I tidied the house. I threw out every condolence gift basket that had been gathering dust on the dining-room table. I kept only the dark chocolate and herbal tea selections, and I schlepped everything else to the curb. I bathed. I used hair remover on my upper lip, moisturized my elbows, overdid it with the rose water. I made myself a shot-glass-size screwdriver with some ancient vodka, just to loosen up the joints. By the time Lorca buzzed, I was so exhausted that I was nodding off on the couch.

"Coming!" I shouted, but my knees had a different plan. They'd stiffened up as I'd slept and I just about went face-first into the desk.

"Coming!" I said again.

As I buzzed, I checked in the mirror. A trail of drool on my chin shone in the evening light. "That's fantastic," I said out loud, and used the sleeve of my blouse to wipe it off.

I opened the door. I waited. I waited. Lorca never took this long. She was a gazelle up those stairs, an Olympian.

"Hello?" I said into the hallway. I didn't hear anyone. I cursed the buzzer and poked at it again and again, thinking maybe the dumb thing had finally met its Maker.

Seconds later, the elevator doors opened.

"Nice to meet you too," Lorca said to someone before stepping onto the landing. Her face was vibrant with cold.

Dottie leaned out of the elevator. She wiggled her fingers at me.

"Good evening, madam," she said. She was all made up and her hair had been done. The word that came to mind was *buoyant.* She had a mink coat dramatically wrapped up to her chin.

Lorca turned around to wave at her.

"Bye, Dottie!" she called.

Reluctantly, I waved too. Bye, Dottie.

I felt violated. I shouldn't have. I should have known that Dottie would find a way to insert herself into my relationship with Lorca. She couldn't help it. She had to be a part of everything. I wondered how long she'd waited in the lobby for Lorca to show up.

"She's so nice," Lorca said, closing the door behind her and taking off her hat.

I made some singsongy noise with my mouth shut and held out my hands for her coat.

"She let me in downstairs," Lorca said.

"She did, did she," I said.

"She says you and she are the best of friends," she continued. I knew those weren't Lorca's words. *Best of friends*. As if we had other friends from which to select the best.

"We are, are we," I said.

Lorca shrugged.

"That's just what she told me," she said in a way that meant that she didn't believe everything she heard.

"Right," I said. She followed me as I hung up her coat in the hall closet. I heard Dottie turn on the television upstairs. *Go pick on someone your own age,* I thought. *Your hair looks stupid.*

As far as I knew, Dottie hadn't done any damage. Yet. The issue was that she couldn't simply let me have my happiness. *My* happiness. She couldn't go find her own. For as long as I'd known her, she'd relied on us in a way that could only be considered inappropriate. And it wasn't just for happiness. When we went to the post office, she'd throw in money for stamps. If we had our floors refinished, she'd do the same. On holidays, she'd show up at the restaurant and sit for hours. Joseph and I would take turns keeping her company. She insinuated herself into every nook of our lives and, in doing so, diminished whatever preciousness, whatever joy, whatever sadness, even, was finely balanced between Joseph and me. In cooking, one poaches in order to keep something delicate from coming apart. In life, it means stealing the delicate thing away. And Dottie was a poacher of the highest order. The only secret we'd ever kept from her was the story of our daughter, and somehow, I realized, the fact that Dottie didn't know about her made it seem like she'd never existed.

You'd think such feelings would grow irrelevant in time: the jealousy, vanity, hate even. They don't. They simply find fewer occasions on which to present themselves and when they do, it's as if they've multiplied in the dank, unlit place where they've been dormant. In my case, the occasions almost always included Dottie. Again and again and again.

"I'm so excited for our lesson!" Lorca said. It was then that I realized I was still wearing my slippers. Dottie hadn't been here to dress me. I hated her. I loved her.

I kicked them off and allowed the cold to quickly infiltrate my feet.

"Me too," I said.

Lorca waited for me before making her way into the kitchen, as if afraid I might not follow. But of course, I did. To be with her. As we walked, I found myself wanting to hold her hand, but I couldn't. Instead, I awkwardly touched the middle of her back. And like this, I forgot about my anger. Like this we went.

"Masgouf is a simple dish to make," I explained as I moved a glass out of the sink. "It's a humble dish, but it has a lot of history."

"I read that," Lorca said. She wore layers today, maybe even more than I could count. A hooded sweatshirt on top of a thermal, with some black ribbed thing popping out from underneath, along with a half-dress/half-shirt, gray and stretchy, pulled down below her waist. She had on blue socks and jeans stitched with yellow thread.

"The rivers in Baghdad were a place of life, of happiness," I said. "Am I boring you?"

"You just started," she said, so earnestly that I laughed.

"So I did," I said.

I went on about the Tigris and the Euphrates, the fishermen on the banks and how they hauled out the carp, made a fire, split the fish from head to tail, seasoned it with salt and oil, and speared it so it cooked, open and on its side, over a smoky fire.

"It took a couple of hours," I said. "We didn't have these fancy grill pans."

As I began to lift ours out of a bottom drawer, Lorca came to my rescue. And thank goodness. What strength in such a tiny thing, I thought.

"What is amazing," I said, "is that no one will ever eat this meal that same way again. As we did, growing up. With all the dead bodies in the rivers, they've declared a fatwa on the fish."

Masgouf merely scratched the surface of all that never would be again. Life: never again.

"Everything is changed," I said, staving off sappiness. "Not just the food. We use red snapper here."

"Have you been back to Baghdad?" she asked. She was sitting at her place at the bar now, her head propped up on her hands.

"No," I said. "We never went back. We never could, legally or safely. We had to give up everything to come to the United States. And the Jews have no place there now. We were once the majority, the intellectuals, the sophisticates. But that changed quickly because of the Nazis. And when Joseph and I came to America, we promised to make this our home."

I realized how strange it must sound to anyone, much less a young girl, to abandon a life, to move forward with such determination. *Leaving is the easy part,* I wanted to tell her. It's moving on that one gets mired in. It takes years. Decades, actually. It takes tragedy and drama and the most painful part: the haunting feeling of what's lost when it finally starts hurting less. And yet to this day, if I close my eyes I can smell where I grew up. Burning vegetable skin and floral tea. It pulls the tears out of me, as if it's the scent itself coming through my nose and rushing down my face.

"We had to love America more than we yearned for Baghdad," I said, wanting to defend myself, "or we couldn't have loved America at all. I don't know if that makes much sense."

"It makes sense to me," Lorca said. It was obvious: she too knew what it felt like not to be understood.

I unwrapped the fish, which was still in its brown paper. I did it slowly and noticed that Lorca had lifted herself just slightly off her seat to watch. This seemed like a good thing.

"The monger has butterflied the snapper for me, you see," I said. "But it is not so complicated to do it yourself. My hands shake," I offered as an explanation, and then wished I hadn't. "I bet you have a very steady hand."

Lorca blushed and shrugged. She pulled her sleeves all the way over her fingers and sat on them.

"No, no, no," I said. "Your turn. Come."

Lorca came around to where I was, delicately revealed her hands, and began washing them in the sink.

"We oil the fish first, and then season it," I said. "So the spices will stick."

I took out some new salt I'd bought, fancy flakes that seemed impressive at the time but now appeared overwhelming and rough. As subtly as I could, I shoved it to the back of the cabinet, taking out my trusty sea salt instead.

"Olive oil?" Lorca asked.

I feigned shock.

"Of course olive oil," she said. "Stupid me."

"No." I laughed. "Not stupid."

I would have to be better with my behavior, I told myself. I would have to be so careful with this little girl. *She's as sensitive as I am.* Instinctively, I looked toward the study, as if Joseph would be standing in the doorway in a thick cardigan, corduroys, and slippers, on the same page as me, nodding. But of course, he wasn't. Not standing there. Not on the couch. Not anywhere yet. His remains had been ready since yesterday. They'd taken only five days to "process" is what they told me over the phone, and I could come by to get them. But I couldn't bring myself to go out the door and do it. What would I carry him home in? I wondered. A shopping bag? A cashmere shawl? What could bear the weight of him, of everything he ever did? Nothing felt right. For the first time, elaborate funeral processions made perfect sense to me. Without one, without the fanfare, there was life and then dust. And I couldn't bear the thought of him like that—like almond meal, cake flour, or sand. He was the love of my life. The world to me. But until I went to the funeral home, I had no idea where he was, really. I had no idea where he went. I'd come home from my walk that night and all that was left was the shell of him. The rest had slipped away somewhere. Would you believe I checked under the bed? I considered lifting his head, the pillow, as if it might have been trapped beneath there. Until then, even when he was sleeping, despondent, nearly catatonic from a morphine drip, there had been something between us, sustaining us. What is inside a person is unknowable as anything. That's not life. Life is the dynamic, silent buzz humming around us, like static. And when it's over, there's none of that. All I could feel, as I stayed with him before Dottie helped me away, was the lonely echo of my own life, myself. A vacant, one-pitch hum. It was worse than feeling alone. It was being alone.

Lorca salted the fish. The word *remains* played over and over in my head and took shape as something else: a glass container of leftovers in the fridge. I shuddered and kept my eyes on the study again, as if willing him there. *Did you see that?* I wished to say. This child *was* as sensitive as me.

"And now?" Lorca said. She was talking about the fish but it felt like she was ushering me along.

For her, and for me, I kept on.

As it turned out, the assembling of the masgouf took much less time than I'd imagined, and hoped. So before putting it in the oven, we pickled some onions, made mango chutney with a rock-hard mango, and I let her in on the secrets of making Iraqi flatbread. Perhaps it was Lorca's nimble fingers, or maybe her excitement, which seemed to fuel her motions, but she was brisk and confident today. Purposeful. That, ever so slightly, broke my heart. I thought, *We might make the masgouf and then I'll be obsolete.* I was giving her the secret to living without me. And yet, how could I not?

For some reason, it occurred to me that that might be the key to parenting: rendering oneself obsolete. It was something I rarely thought of, parenting. It was something I had no business considering. But here I was. I hardly knew her. I had to remind myself that I hardly knew her at all.

I wasted time doing some dishes. I was distracted, thinking of Joseph, of Lorca never coming back. As I wiped down the countertop, circle after circle after circle, it was as though I was trying to wipe my mind clean of worrying. It didn't work.

"Shall we put this in the oven?" Lorca said. My heart sank. When she started fiddling with the lemons, I was bolstered. More time. More time. The relief went as quickly as it came.

"I did such a poor job with these," she said.

"They are perfect," I said.

"They're not," she said.

"No regrets" is what came out of my mouth. It wasn't what I meant to say—the phrase being nothing I lived by, or even thought very much about.

Lorca glanced at me. You could tell just by looking at her that she knew too much about the world. Something in her eyes—perhaps the depth and sheen of them, how they seemed to summon the world around her and refract it like an artifact window—aged her in a way that had nothing to do with years. She was a gorgeous combination of ancient and brand-new.

"It seems like that for you," she said. "It seems like you live a life you don't regret."

I had to take a moment to swallow back sadness. She wasn't altogether wrong. Joseph liked to bask in the feeling of how far we'd come. I never made time for that. I never made time for anything, and yet it was the regrets, not the pride, that snuck through regardless.

"Oh, heart," I said. "There are so many things I'm not proud of: things I did, or didn't do, and sometimes the person I was. And worst of all, the person I wasn't and hoped to be. Also, I wish I'd learned to tie-dye and run long distances and play the piano."

"You could still learn," she said. "Why not?"

"I'd have no one to play for," I said. I realized then how very much I'd done for Joseph. How much of what a person becomes is because of the person she loves. If I'd ever taken up piano, which I hadn't, it would have been to show him. That I didn't learn, and wanted to, in some way weighed on our relationship too. It kept dawning on me that Joseph's life would no longer punctuate mine. Or mine his. His life, our life, was a series of notes until his death, which shocked those notes into a song, full of symmetry, full of meaning. Something to behold unto itself. To behold it now was the most I could hope to do. We'd never reach for each other again.

"I gave up a child for adoption," I said suddenly. "It was the biggest mistake of my life."

I expected Lorca's face to fall in some way, for her to be disappointed by this person who'd revealed her deepest secrets to a somewhat stranger, and a child at that. I expected that nothing nice could be said about what I'd done. Instead, she became altogether still.

"My mother is adopted," Lorca said.

"Your mother?" I said. It felt like I'd just jumped into a frozen lake. My breath was very shallow. *Calm down,* I told myself. *Take it easy. She's not suggesting anything.* I took a glass from the cupboard, filled it with tap water, and chugged it down. All the while, I kept my eyes on Lorca, trying catch a glimmer of something covert.

"But it's not because she's adopted that she is who she is," Lorca said. She was talking casually, drying her hands on a towel. I had the distinct feeling that this was a subject she'd talked through at length, perhaps with someone older, perhaps with a professional. "If her biological mother had kept her, that woman's life would have been ruined like my grandmother's, and my aunt's, and my father's. My mother does that. She's kind of like a tornado but people don't know to run when they see her coming."

The word *biological* ran and ran and ran through my head.

"How do you know so many things?" I asked.

"I mean—" she said. The question made her self-conscious, but I wasn't sure why. She shoved her hands into her pockets. "I guess I've thought a lot about it. About my mother."

"That's nice," I said. So stupid. As if it were a good thing.

"Sort of," she said. "I just mean that you never know. Your child could have an amazing life and so do you and maybe that's because you're apart."

It wasn't clear if Lorca was getting at something or just stating the facts. The questions I wanted to ask vibrated in my mouth, but I told myself to be patient. Be smart.

"I understand," I said. "And if her life isn't amazing—"

"You can't think that way," Lorca said, cutting me off.

"Is she ruining your life?" I said.

"Oh," Lorca said, and she straightened up suddenly, shaking her head as if I'd misunderstood, though I was sure I hadn't. "It's not like that," she said.

I looked out the window and noticed that it had begun to snow a gorgeous, slow-motion snow, like something showing off. Every now and then, a flake would stick to the window and then drip down.

If there was something Lorca wanted to tell me, it wasn't going to be told now. She had shut down and I couldn't blame her. My body felt heavy, as though some protective mechanism had cut off my nerves to keep them from overheating, and everything was weighted, stagnant inside.

I put the fish in the oven. "Want to go see it?" I asked Lorca and motioned to the window, surprising even myself. Spontaneity shows its face less and less as the years go by. But for the first time in a very long time, the thought of standing in the snow didn't seem like a horrific assault on my joints. I needed some fresh air too.

"Come on," I said. "The fish will be a little while."

We took the elevator and then the stairs to the roof. When we opened the door, the wind charged at us and I tottered on the top step. But then here was Lorca's hand on my back, prepared to catch me. I was wearing mittens, a hat, two sweaters, and two scarves and feeling a bit like I'd been stuffed into a sausage casing. Still, I was thankful for every layer. The cold chilled me right to the bone, and fast.

Lorca's coat looked expensive, all diagonal pockets and reflective patches, something a lot of technology had gone into—but it was too big for her. The flakes snuck into the neck.

"Can I give you a scarf?" I asked and pulled out an extra one—the cleanest and least handmade-looking that I could find—from my pocket, hoping to be a hero.

She laughed. "I'm okay," she said.

"Oh, right," I said. "Your circulation still works."

Our building was higher than most and we could have seen for at least a mile in every direction if it weren't for the weather. Tonight the city was purplish, washed out, fuzzy but for the flares of streetlights and traffic lights.

"The first time I saw snow," I said, "I was older than you. I was afraid of it, thinking it might sting, like a spark."

Lorca was holding her hand out in front of her, her palm open and flat. Her cheeks had taken on a sudden glow not unlike something cooking in an oven.

"It doesn't," I said, teasing out a small laugh.

"My mother hates the snow," she said. The slightest mention of her mother seemed to suck the air out of her. She shrank, tightened in the face and shoulders.

"And you?" I asked, though the answer was obvious.

"Well, I love it," she said softly.

"That's very brave," I said.

Lorca's face wasn't giving any clues as to how she was feeling, what all this talk about her mother meant to her. So I looked up at the sky, thinking that perhaps something would come to me—some morsel of wisdom from Joseph, some appropriate words that might make more sense of our conversation than our conversation was making to me. Instead, phlegm dripped down the back of my throat and I had a minor coughing fit.

"I'm fine," I kept saying as Lorca tapped her hand gently against my back. "Just fine!"

We stood on the roof long enough for Lorca to point to the

general vicinity of where she lived, went to school, had taken ballet lessons, shopped for groceries. And then me: where I'd found a hundred-dollar bill, seen the Clintons, witnessed an armed robbery, been hit by a cab. With her foot, Lorca drew the formation of her apartment: living room, kitchen, bedrooms, bathroom. With mine, I drew the house where I'd grown up. Both floors. Lorca drew her childhood home in New Hampshire. I drew the countries of the Middle East. Together, they looked like a deformed mushroom. I pointed to Israel.

"Most people went there," I said. "The great majority of the Iraqi Jews. But not us. Not Joseph. He had his heart set on the United States."

"I don't blame him," Lorca said.

"Thank you," I said, moving my boot around the snow of Baghdad until I hit on a glimmer of something. A penny. Lorca reached down for it.

"Lucky," she said, and slipped it into my pocket.

Many minutes must have gone by because by the time we opened the door to go back inside, my hands were stinging, pulsing with cold—and the smell of something burning fumed all the way up the stairs.

"Oy!" I said.

"Oy!" repeated Lorca, more upset than I thought she'd be.

"I can't believe I did that," I said. Lorca was passing me, taking the stairs two at a time, the earflaps of her hat flopping against the sides of her head as she made her way down.

"It's okay," she yelled back. "Maybe we can salvage some of it."

It took what felt like a month for me to get down those stairs, though I was moving with all my might. I just couldn't bring myself to wait for the elevator.

• • •

In the end, we couldn't salvage a thing. I found Lorca flicking off the skin and then the meat in black swaths like small dead bugs.

"This is terrible," she was saying, still zipped up in her coat. She looked as though she was about to cry.

And me, I was useless, so bundled I could have smacked into a brick wall and been all right. Puddles leaked onto the floor beneath my boots, and for a brief moment, I considered my bladder.

"Hm," Lorca said. She washed her hands and pursed her lips; she moved them from side to side. She began picking at them fiercely as she stared, just stared, at the fish. I wanted to beg her to stop. I'd messed this up horribly, been a poor teacher and so on. But there'd been a glimmer of hope that it wasn't just about the masgouf. Now it was obvious that it was.

"I was going to make the masgouf for my mother tomorrow," she said. "But I don't know how it's supposed to come out."

I had nothing good to say.

"It's okay," she said. "It's fine."

I didn't know if she was talking to herself or to me.

"I should probably go," she said. "I can help you clean up first."

"No," I said. "This is nothing. I'm awfully sorry."

I took off my hat. I needed to think of something or I would lose her.

"We can try again," I offered. "Or we don't have to."

Lorca looked at me.

"You're not sick of this?" she asked.

I actually laughed.

"Tomorrow?" I said. "I'll get more fish."

"Maybe we could butterfly together," Lorca said. "I'd like to learn that for myself."

"Of course," I said. "There's nothing to it."

"Your mother's birthday isn't tomorrow, is it?" I asked. There was a buzzing in my chest. "Isn't that why you wanted to make the masgouf?"

"Oh, no," Lorca said, as if she'd forgotten. "It's not tomorrow."

"That's a relief," I said, because it was.

Lorca

I SAW HIM BEFORE he saw me. Blot was waiting for me again outside Victoria's on Thursday, alternating between a jumpy foot shuffle and tapping on the hood of a car, looking away from the building and out toward the street. He was anxious or excited or both. I took a deep breath before finding out.

"Hi," I said. He swung around, threw his hands up like he'd been standing there forever.

"You!" he said. I held my breath.

"Hi," I said again.

"I called them," he said, racing to the steps, sticking out his half-gloved hand to help me down. My fingers went immediately clammy. My first thought was that he'd called my mother and Lou and that I was going to have a lot of explaining to do, although I wasn't sure about what exactly.

"My parents," he explained. "I called them after you called your dad yesterday. It got me thinking."

"Oh," I said, but it sounded more like *phew.*

I put on both of my gloves before reaching for him, as if the cold were my concern. There was more snow than not on the street now. Little bits of pavement and metal and trees and car parts peeked out as if they were afraid of getting caught. But otherwise, white. Even Blot's hat was coated in a thick layer that looked orangey in the streetlight, like a Creamsicle. I didn't tell him so.

He helped me down the stairs and sort of directed me to face him. His hand was as strong as something marble. Then he let go. We were standing very close to each other, but it didn't feel particularly intimate. It felt urgent. Necessary, more than romantic. Like things had to be said, and in this manner exactly. Maybe, it occurred to me, that was romance. I tried not to obsess about it and not to breathe too much in his face.

"I stared at the phone for forty-five minutes," he said, "before I could even pick it up and dial. And then when I did, I was so nervous that I couldn't speak, and my mom's saying, 'Hello, hello, hello.' And I'm trying to tell her it's me but I can't."

I thought about my father. About those calls we used to get maybe once or twice a week when no one would say anything. All you could hear was trees rustling or maybe just phone fuzz. And I'd whisper, "Dad," so he'd know that I knew that it was him. Dad. Dad. So he'd feel less lonely. Then he'd hang up.

"And then what?" I said.

"Well, then finally I said something. And my mom wasn't not nice. She was fine, which isn't all that surprising. I haven't been the greatest to them either. I haven't called in over a year. Which is not a decent thing to do to one's mother."

His voice had gotten very stern, grown-up.

"Noted," I said.

Being this close to him was overwhelming—because of me, because I had no sense of what I looked like, smelled like, but because of him too. He was giddy and I wanted to match his mood, not overdo it and not underdo it either. A smile had replaced his usual expression, and it was as though everything—his mouth, eyebrows, dimples even—was teetering around trying to accommodate it. I wanted to ask him what he'd done, why his parents didn't want him at home. But I didn't believe it was his fault, and I didn't know how to phrase it to get that across so he'd know that I wasn't blaming him for anything. I wanted him to think I understood it, whatever it was.

"I haven't told you the best part yet," he said. "Are you ready?"

"I'm ready," I said. I shook my shoulders a bit to get them ready too.

"Greta's here," he said. His sister.

"Where?" I said.

"In New York," he said. "Somewhere. Probably midtown. My parents didn't come this year, but my sister came with my aunt and uncle. They brought all the cousins for a couple of days to see that show and ice-skate and shop and I don't know what else."

"That's amazing," I said, wishing for something more descriptive. "Brilliant," I tried. My mother's word. It sounded dumb, but he wasn't listening.

"They're going to Radio City tomorrow afternoon," he said. "But my mother promised she'd ask my aunt and uncle to drop off Greta with me afterward, so we could have some time. Just us two."

It didn't feel strange to me that his parents trusted him with her. And some part of me liked them for that. It seemed like good parenting to know, intuitively, the lines that one's child would never cross—and that Blot, no matter what, no matter what they were angry with him for, would never do anything to hurt his sister, even if he hadn't called home in over a year.

"I think my mother was relieved," he said. "To know that I'm okay. And that I still want to see Greta. Maybe my parents thought I'd forgotten all about her, which I haven't. Obviously."

For some reason, I felt flattered that he was okay. As if it had anything at all to do with me.

He started walking, first a few steps ahead of me and then backward, looking at me with his hands clasped behind him.

"It's so good. It's so so good," he said.

I remembered what a sour mood I'd been in just a few moments earlier. Victoria and I had ruined the masgouf, which meant that we'd have to try again before I could make it for my mother. The days were getting away from me, and I was afraid that if I didn't do something soon, I would lose my chance and be sent off to boarding school forever. It occurred to me that I might smell like burned fish skin. I tried to sniff my arm without him noticing.

"Hydrant!" I said and Blot turned around just quick enough to keep himself from tripping over it.

"She could be anywhere in the city," he said.

I stopped, turned around. Looked up and down. Did a spin.

"She's not on this street," I said.

"Good," he said. "Nine thousand four hundred and eighteen streets left to go."

I was only the tiniest bit envious. Not enough to ruin anything. Just enough to make me ache a little. His enthusiasm, his love for her, was so huge. So so huge. It endured years and a long distance—all the way to Maryland. I wanted some of that for myself. I imagined it made a person feel toasty to always know that someone was out there, radiating support. My father, warm as he could be, deferred to my mother on everything. Whenever I'd asked him to visit, he'd said, "Oh, honey, did you ask your mother?" As if I should have known better. So it didn't matter if he was radiating ever because my mother got right in the middle, blocking.

"I had to tell you," he said. "I figured you'd be here. Sorry to stalk."

I bit my cheeks so I didn't smile too hard.

"It's okay," I said. "What will you do together?"

"I've been saving these books," he said. "Four of them. I was going to send them but now I can give them to her. Face to face." He made fists with his hands and shook them like he'd just scored a goal.

I did the same thing. Solidarity. Score.

"We'll probably go to the coffee shop next to the bookstore," he said. "I'm supposed to work anyway. Someone's going to cover for me, but it won't be the worst idea to show my face at the beginning and end of the shift."

"Right," I said. "Great idea."

I wished I had something more important to say. Something that would make him feel proud that he'd told me, justified. I wanted to ask him why he'd waited so long to call his parents, and if he thought of Greta, wanted to be in touch. But I didn't ask him any of those things. I thought of how I got in my own way constantly. I couldn't even ask my mother a simple question.

"Gret-idea" is what I said. "*Greta* and *idea*."

It just came out. I was an idiot.

"Genius," he said. "I'm going to tell her. She'll love it."

He paused. "Unless she's too old now. For that."

"She's younger than me," I said. "Isn't she? And I love it."

"Okay," he said. He held out his hand, palm up, and like a genius, I understood. I mimed putting the gret-idea there. He closed his fist and put it into his pocket.

"Thank you," he said. I nodded.

"And you?" he said.

I didn't want to tell him about the masgouf, not even that Victoria and I had tried to make it, because it meant that the quest for masgouf was one step closer to over. And the quest was still our thing—mine and Blot's. So I told him we'd made some salmon and that we'd burned it horribly.

"Nothing worse," he said, shaking his head gravely.

I was careful not to give too many details, afraid he'd figure out that I was lying, and then we'd really have nothing to talk about. I asked him to tell me more about his sister so I could listen to his voice.

"When she was a baby," he said, "she used to call me Blah because she couldn't say Blot. Like, blah-blah-blah. It's humbling to be called that. Take it from me."

I had been right, kind of.

"But why is your name Blot?" I said.

He pointed to me and smirked.

"Million-dollar question," he said.

He stopped just in front of me so we were face to face and unwrapped his scarf from his neck. He unzipped his coat. For some reason, I felt like I should look away, but I didn't. Couldn't. Getting undressed seemed so private. He wore a thick navy sweater in a tight knit and he pulled the neck of it all the way to one side and shimmied it down his arm as far as he could. Below that, an old T-shirt with a ripped collar, thin as phyllo. He pulled that down too. He pulled down more. There, on his chest, just below his collarbone and off center, he had a birthmark, purple and flat and the size of a portobello cap. He moved into the light.

"See it?" he said. Suddenly, he was covered in goose bumps. After a second, they went away.

I nodded.

"I see it," I said.

My fingers tingled, wanting to touch it; I wanted to close my eyes and press on it as if on a secret door. My throat went dry and metallic. *Mine,* I thought. *I want to show you mine.* My wrists, my stomach, my feet, behind my knees. But he was looking down at his chest, his chin pushed into his neck. His shoulder was square and firm as an ice cube. The top muscle in his arm flickered and made me blink, self-conscious. I took a step back and looked past him so the wanting would fade. He shrugged his shoulder to redress himself, and zipped up his coat.

"I was born with it," he said. "My mother said that from the first time I caught sight of it in the mirror, I couldn't leave it alone. I'd take a towel, blanket, tissue, newspaper, rock, anything, whatever, and blot it. Blot blot blot on it, as if it were a stain. She said it must have been an instinct somehow—that it shouldn't be there. She didn't ever remember blotting anything for me to learn from. I just wanted it out, she said. Off."

He sighed, shrugged, starting walking again, as if it were nothing.

"The name stuck," he said.

If I'd stared too intently at his arm, it didn't seem to bother him. I wanted to stare at it again. It was whiter than mine, his shoulder. His skin thinner, tighter, like something in an ad for perfume. I realized that my hands were in fists.

"What's your real name?" I said.

He laughed.

"Logan," he said.

Logan and Lorca are almost the same, I thought, and it felt like that was important somehow.

"I never say my real name out loud. I only write it. And that's normally only when I'm in trouble."

"Logan's good," I said.

He shrugged.

I told myself to stay quiet, hoping he'd say more.

"I'm fine now," he said. "But I had a drug thing. A problem. Big or little means the same with drugs. I left home four years ago. I was fifteen. I lived with my grandparents, then a girlfriend in Puerto Rico, then with an old teacher, and then the great-aunt of that teacher. My parents paid for rehab last year and I fell into this house-sitting situation, which is how I get to live here now."

The word *girlfriend* got caught in my head and I could imagine her in vintage photos: Californian, with long legs and hair and moving like a tall tulip. Like him.

"I'm fine," he said. "Now."

I nodded.

"And the drugs are done," he said. "Technically speaking, I mean. Never really done. Always a fight against the craving."

"Craving," I said, as if I didn't know what the word meant. But of course I did. I'd just forgotten it as it pertained to me. I hadn't craved in a while. Three days since the razor. I asked myself if I was craving right now. I wasn't. For the moment, I wasn't. The gauze he'd used on my arm was still attached. I'd showered carefully, kept it intact.

"Go," he said. "Your turn."

"Um," I began.

"I'll walk you home," he said. "But you have to promise to do most of the talking from here on out."

I said all right. I said that I'd try.

As we went along, the snow turned to hail and then to rain, but we didn't mention it. I didn't say the word *cozy,* but it occurred to me. I told him the details of the evening. About Dottie and Victoria and how we'd been right about them when we saw them putting out the clothes: that they were friends and not friends.

"Dottie's such a character," I said.

"Like from a musical?" he said.

"More tragic than that," I said. "Off-Broadway." I'd never seen anything off-Broadway in my life.

"Got it," he said. "And Victoria?"

"From a book," I said. "Strictly fiction."

He nodded.

"I'd say Dottie's up to no good," Blot said.

"Probably," I said. "But I don't want to think about it."

Not thinking about it made me want to hug Victoria.

I told him about what she had said about giving up a child. We were waiting to cross Ninety-Sixth Street.

"I can't imagine what that would be like," he said. "Like, I have absolutely no sense of it."

"Me either," I said.

Then we were quiet. For the first time, I felt the same age as him, though I wasn't. I wondered if parents constituted an age group of their own. Victoria and my mother in the same age group, I thought. Dottie: not. Victoria had told me that Dottie had never had children and somehow that made sense to me. A certain kind of dull seriousness, like slate in their bones, settles into parents. No one else.

I tried not to count the seconds during which we were silent, which was hard only when Blot unfurrowed his brow. Other than that, he seemed intent, thinking deeply about something that had to do, I thought, with me. And I liked that.

When he began with "Obviously, I don't know your mother," I felt flattered. In a way, I thought, it was like he was saying that he did know me. "But doesn't it strike you as strange," he said and stopped walking again.

"Wait," I said. It came to me quickly. I knew what he was going to say. He didn't have to finish and I didn't want him to. If the thought was going to become fully formed, I wanted it to develop in me. And I didn't want him thinking that I was stupid.

I would have come up with it on my own. I might have. But it's the way I do things: eating the uninteresting bottom part of the muffin before the perfectly compact top, eating the French onion broth before having anything to do with the cheese and bread. Good things, I have to save. I can't look straight at them. And if I do, sometimes they feel prickly, as if I've been sitting in front of a fire for too long. This felt like that. I knew what was coming. It had been itchy but I couldn't tackle it head-on. It felt like I needed to do a little dance around it first or it would bite me square in the face.

"She might be my grandmother," I whispered.

"Right," he whispered back. "I mean, I thought maybe she looked like you. From what I could tell."

I didn't know why we were whispering.

"It's a stretch," I said. "It would be crazy." *Crazy* didn't even begin to describe it. I put my hands to my face. "My grandmother?" I asked him.

"I know," he said. "Crazy. But."

We went quiet again, thinking.

"How did you say you found out about the masgouf?" he said.

"I overheard my mother talking," I said.

"Right," he said.

"It would be bananas," I said.

"Greta's here," he said, as if it were evidence of how things could be bananas—in a good way. "Of all the days. Of all the gin joints."

"My mother always quotes that movie," I said.

"Eh," he said. "I prefer drama in real life."

I held out my hand. He mimed catching the drama all around us and then putting it in my palm. I closed my fingers around it, blew on my fist, put it into my pocket, and zippered it up.

I thought it was better to be safe than sorry, so Blot and I stood across the street from my building to say goodbye. To say that I felt funny didn't scratch the surface. I felt like my body was carbonated and there was cotton candy filling my head. It was a miracle, I thought, that my feet were still on the ground. I wanted to ask him what had happened tonight, as if his spelling it out for me might make it all more real. But it wouldn't. Just his standing there felt unreal. I hardly knew him and I wanted to ask him how he knew me so well, the crux of me—and how had he figured it all out, and who was he really, and where did he come from. That the answers would never do the questions justice felt like magic, when they talk about magic in that way.

As we looked at each other, I wanted to touch him. I wished I could just squeeze his arm, but I had no idea how. I couldn't pin down the timing. So we stood there, quiet for a few moments, shrugging, nodding at each other. Finally, I bent down, filled my hands with snow, rolled the snow into a ball, and gave it to him.

"Here," I said.

"*Magnifique,*" he said with a gasp, marveling at it as he held it in front of his chest.

"Good," I said. "Okay." I turned, started to walk away between the parked cars.

"If you want to come by after I see Greta," he called, "she's getting picked up at the bookstore tomorrow night at ten."

I tapped twice on the roof of a car.

When he left, he marched. Really marched. He held the snowball in his half-gloved hands at a distance, as if it were a fancy dessert on fire, like bananas flambé, or something he'd present to a queen. I watched him for as long as I could and he kept on like that, not even looking before crossing the street, just marching and keeping his eyes on the snowball in his hands. Left right left.

I opened the door of our building imagining that the snowball wouldn't melt. That Blot would take it home and put it in a vase, and it would stay just so. Intact and glistening and clean.

Upstairs, I thought about going to see him tomorrow when he was still with Greta. Not to meet her, just to watch. Ever since we'd moved away from my father, I'd been obsessed with families. In Central Park. In Times Square. Ice-skating. I stared at so many families that I was always being passed a camera to take a group shot. I took my time, getting it from all angles, letting them joke with one another about smiling, and standing up straight, and sucking in their guts. I loved it when a little girl—maybe she was carrying a blanket and chewing on her hair—leaned on her mother's leg and got one hundred times stronger, daring the world to mess with her. Or when a father pulled his son's head onto his shoulder, all roughness and warmth, and the son's head bobbed up just for a second, independent, before he let it rest again. And the mother winking at the father over their pack of kids. Or vice versa. Whatever. I loved that. I loved all of that.

It made me wish so hard that I could remember being young, remember being so unable to be on my own that my mother had to carry me everywhere. Touching so much. But we weren't stronger when we were together anymore, my mother and me.

I imagined Greta would make Blot stronger somehow. Prouder. He'd already done that for her. I was sure.

I would go to Victoria's for the lesson early, I decided. My heart did a pancake flip as I thought of what to say to her. If anything. Should I say anything at all? I had no idea.

After that, I'd go find a place to watch Blot where he wouldn't see me but I could see him. And Greta. Little Greta, now big. I bet she was beautiful and I bet she had no idea how very much she was missing, being far away from him. Not knowing how strong his shoulders were, how he could protect her from everything—and wanted to.

I undressed and lay down on the couch and waited for my mother to come home. But I didn't hold my breath. I imagined the snowball in the vase and Blot watering it before bedtime and in the morning saying "Holy shit!" when he saw it had doubled in size. I craved that. That's what I craved.

My mother came home very late. I knew just what I was going to say. I'd written it down.

She was softer when I was sleeping, even when she was mad at me. It was like she could imagine me before I could talk, and it filled her with mothering emotions. She took off her earrings, massaged her earlobes. She smelled like gardenias and gin. Her mouth was dry, and the clasp of her necklace was in the front.

She leaned over me.

"Come," she said. "Let's get you to bed."

Very sleepily, I did it. Like I'd been dreaming about it.

"Mom," I said. "What was so special about that masgouf you loved? The one at the Shohet and His Wife?"

She didn't remember that she hadn't said it to me. That it was Aunt Lou she'd told a week ago.

"The people, I guess," she said. "It was so warm there. You've never seen such a family place."

"Family?" I said. My heart came to a very vigorous boil. I wondered if she could feel it even though she wasn't touching me.

She smiled like she couldn't help it, and because of that I knew. I knew why she loved the masgouf. And why she loved that recipe, despite her chef-y-ness. I knew why she was always scanning the obituaries. I knew why she was so lonely—not only because of what was inside of her, splintered like dried-out marzipan where all the joy could slip through, but because Joseph and Victoria were out in the world, not-dying without her. They were making beautiful, delicious food. The only way she could love them, I thought, was for her to eat it and hope that it would fill her up.

It was just like Blot said. She had wanted me to hear what she'd told Lou. What he didn't know was how it felt to have her count on me in such a profound way. She needed me, her little Lorca. Her little helper. In my head, I told her I was on it. I wouldn't let her down. And I swear she nodded at me, though I hadn't opened my mouth.

"Yes," she said. "Family." Her eyes welled up.

Then, so softly, "Oh, Lorca," which only affirmed how right I was. I was in on the secret now too.

She took off the blanket and folded it over the arm of the sofa. She pulled up my socks as if she were about to stuff my feet into snow boots. When she kissed my forehead, I could tell that a smile had crept into her cheeks.

"I've never met anyone who asks so many questions," she said.

"Thank you," I said, like it was some kind of compliment,

and even though it wasn't—at least, not exactly—I knew that it would be soon, that I'd finally cracked the code and was on to something after a million years, after my whole life.

I thought about rushing to Victoria's, telling her everything, and having her reach for my hands, pull me to her, hold the back of my head, and tell me that this was the best moment of her life, but I decided against it. First of all, I had no idea how I might react to big emotion like that; it scared me—I might pass out, or break out in hives, or vomit endlessly into her kitchen sink. Second, though Victoria said that giving up my mother was her biggest regret, I couldn't help but wonder if there was a reason for her doing it. If there was something I didn't know yet about her or, worse, if there had been something dangerous, sly, or hard about my mother even when she was the smallest baby, something that frightened Victoria, pushed her away so immediately and so forcefully that she'd vowed to never look for her daughter, even when she wanted to find out what she had become. Everyone who loved my mother spent his or her entire life trying furiously to get over her, to win back the emotions that my mother seized. I wondered if Victoria was entirely sure that she wanted to be found. After all, she hadn't looked for my mother. I had looked for her. And also, I didn't want to lose Victoria yet. I imagined her desperate to meet my mother, to be with her. And my mother would be cold to Victoria, elusive. I wanted to protect Victoria from that, but I was afraid too that Victoria might only look me in the eye and ask me how, how on earth, she could get into my mother's good graces. What was the trick? Surely I must know.

For a moment, I considered telling Victoria that I'd been lying all along. That my mother had died and that's why I'd come to her, to find the family that my mother and I never knew. And I'd spin her a beautiful story of my mother—of how she was meant to be a mother, born to love and care for a child. Victoria could feel proud that she'd had something to do with that quality. But it was a hateful, horrible thought and it repulsed me as soon as it popped into my mind. I repulsed me.

The next night, after my lesson at Victoria's, during which I'd kept my mouth shut for once, didn't say anything about my mother, and tried to just let things happen as they might, I headed to the bookstore, figuring that Blot would still be at the coffee shop next to it and I'd get a glimpse of him and Greta together. I put myself into position across the street and tried to see in, which I could. Easily. But he wasn't there. Neither was Greta. I crossed the street and walked by briskly just to confirm it. I was right.

I had two options. I could wait an hour and a half in the freezing cold until I was supposed to show up and hope that they would turn up at the coffee shop, or I could go inside the bookstore now. I was sure they'd be in there. I wouldn't let him see me. I'd hide behind the Winter Favorites table. And on the off chance that he did see me, I could simply say that I wanted to do some browsing and figured he'd still be at the coffee shop. But he wouldn't see me. I wouldn't let that happen. I'd be sneaky. Easy as *tarte à la poires*.

At first I was cautious, peering into the aisles before making my way through them, running my fingers over the book spines halfheartedly, just in case. Eventually, I moved faster, more carelessly. I couldn't hear Blot. The bookstore was very quiet. And when I found him in *libros en español,* not with Greta but restocking a shelf, I wasn't terribly surprised. He was all dressed up in a nice shirt, blue with buttons and tucked in, and he wore different khakis than usual: slimmer and ironed and belted against his very straight stomach. He had a silver pocket chain, which swung against his leg as he moved. His hair was back in a ponytail and a gray headband. And for the first time I could see his whole jaw, and it made the insides of my cheeks hurt. His man jaw, man neck, man chin.

"Hi," I whispered.

He turned. The left side of his face smirked and his dimple responded.

"You had a feeling too?" he said.

I shook my head.

"No," I said. "I was just walking by."

I realized I didn't have my story straight.

"Well," he said, before I could make a fool of myself. "That's that."

I wanted to tell him that I was sorry. That I knew all about waiting for someone. And waiting. And waiting. I knew all about not being able to stop waiting, even when it became ridiculous to keep on. I knew that he probably still hoped—even now—that Greta would show up somehow, running toward him, all limbs and hair. But she wouldn't. It was too late. But I understood how impossible it was to cut out that hope. It would die inside him. Scar tissue. I understood.

"Hungry?" I said instead.

I held out a takeout container of *bamia,* which I'd brought from Victoria's.

"So he's not your boyfriend?" Victoria had said when I told her I was going to meet Blot at the bookstore. I left out the part about Greta and about my plan to spy on them.

"No," I said to her, definitely blushing. "Not my boyfriend."

"But you're going to all this trouble?" she said. And then, when I didn't respond, "I see." And it was very clear that she did, which felt flattering and thrilling at the same time.

"I could eat," Blot said now. He sat down and put the books next to his feet and slumped against the bookshelf. His legs fell to either side in a pose that looked like yoga. He took off his headband and wrapped it three times around his wrist. His hair fell into his face, and he pushed it back, held it firmly against his head, and took a deep, long breath.

I wanted to tell him about Victoria and me. And not. I knew it wasn't appropriate. And yet, I was aching to share. Aching for his advice. I had done as I'd planned and not told Victoria anything yet. I hadn't let on. I wanted to be totally sure first. I wanted the moment to be just right. I wanted to tell Blot how careful I was being—and I wanted him to feel in on the plan, crucial to it. *Patience is a virtue,* he might say and give me the thumbs-up. I sat down across from him and gathered my legs so as not to intrude on his space. His face was sapped of color, like tuna poached. I passed him a spoon, a napkin, and then the container, which he held up to the light.

"I'm guessing this is not masgouf," he said.

"You guess right," I said.

He pretzeled his legs, opened the container, and balanced it on his ankles, then used Victoria's spoon like a shovel to bring the food to his mouth. He stared at a spot on the carpet as he ate, blinking slowly, at a particular pace. I didn't ask if he liked it, though I wanted to. It was clear that he didn't not like it. He was eating heartily. I winced at the irregular okra shapes. Every time he took a bite, he leaned all the way forward, folded himself entirely in half so he wouldn't spill. I considered helping, holding the container closer, but (a) he didn't ask for my help, (b) I'd never seen such a flexible boy before, and (c) he seemed so deep in his thoughts that I was afraid of what might happen if I said anything. I imagined the stew flying everywhere. They say never to wake a sleepwalker.

"Let's not talk about it," he said. For a moment, I felt selfish, not knowing what he meant: Greta or Victoria.

"Let's talk about you," he said. "What do you think?"

I took a deep breath.

"You were right," I said.

He put down the spoon, moved the *bamia* aside.

"You asked her?" he said.

"No," I said. I was smiling.

"Well?" he said, and shook his hands at me, like *Out with it, young lady.*

"It's just that she asks so many questions," I said.

"How many?" he said.

"A lot," I said, wanting to tell him about my mother too, but he wasn't through.

"Per minute?" he said, and took out his pocket watch. On your mark, get set. "Go," he said.

"When did we move to New York," I said. "Did I know that my parents were unhappy. Had my mother met anyone else. Did I have a relationship with my grandparents. Did my mother. Were my aunt and my mother close. Did I cook with my mother. How long had she been working at Le Canard. What is my favorite thing to cook. What is her favorite thing to cook. Did I go out to dinner with friends. What are my friends like. My school. What is for lunch at school. My mother never packed me lunch for school? My mother slept till ten a.m.? What did I like for birthday cake. Had I ever tried tongue."

Phew. I exhaled. Blot stopped timing me.

"There's something else," he said. "Tell me."

"Well," I said. "I asked my mother last night about why she loved the masgouf, and she said it was because it reminded her of family."

"Family," he whispered and then put one hand over his mouth. He shook his head in disbelief. He wasn't faking it. And seeing his emotions, I felt my emotions suddenly surge. The enormousness of the whole thing. The alarmingly bizarre way that it had happened, and how quickly. I reached out and grabbed his arm. I couldn't help it, was so excited. And before I could get embarrassed, take it away, he slipped his hand around mine and held it in the air between us. He squeezed it. The muscles in my thighs clenched. Soon, though, his eyes glazed over and I knew he was remembering Greta. He let go. My pulse returned to its normal rate. I tried not to make a noise as I exhaled.

"You're lucky," he said.

"I know," I said too quickly, not wanting him to hate me.

"Go on," he said. "Tell me more."

I could see that he needed me to talk now, so that he didn't have to, so that he could be reminded of something better. That it was my story, my family, that would provide this kind of comfort felt very strange. A little bit like I was lying, actually. His eyes were glued to mine, so intensely that they almost shook. But I couldn't say anything. Words were not forming in either my head or mouth. I was the burned bits that adhered to the bottom of a pan, stuck.

Blot shifted his legs so they were under him and he was kneeling. He was more alert this way, and taller than me. He folded his hands to his chest, and when he spoke, he spoke slowly.

"Okay," he said. "Start from the beginning. You said that your mother never looked for her biological parents."

I nodded.

"She told you that?" he said.

Finally, my mouth worked. "No," I said. "My aunt told me that."

"But your mother did look for them, right? And she found them at the restaurant?"

"I guess," I said. "But the thing about my mother is that she'd never fully reach out. She likes everyone to come to her. Wait for her. I bet she sat at that table at the Shohet and His Wife thinking that if they didn't somehow recognize her, she wouldn't go any further."

"Your mother is nuts," he said.

Without thinking, I burst out laughing.

"She takes playing hard to get to a whole new level," he said.

"I know," I said.

"You must," he said. "So it's not really her birthday, right?"

"Right," I said.

We were quiet for a minute. Blot had begun nodding, looking very sternly at the books behind my head, and wouldn't stop. "Okay," he kept repeating. "Okay okay okay okay."

"Okay what?" I said.

"I'm just making sense of it," he said.

I tried to do the same but my thoughts were bouncing around, refusing to stay put.

"What do you like for birthday cake?" he said out of nowhere.

"Sacher torte," I said. "Chocolate, hazelnut, raspberries. You?"

"Anything with a candle will do," he said and winked. "The candles give me such a sense of accomplishment these days. Stop me if I get morbid."

"No," I said. "I won't."

Victoria

It didn't seem as though Lorca was ready to discuss what needed discussing: that we were, in fact, related. That she was my granddaughter. And I couldn't say that I was altogether upset. It occurred to me that in a million ways, she was a stronger person than me—stumbling upon my class, figuring out who I was, being prudent, being smart—and the truth was, more than ever, I had no idea of where to begin. What would I say to her? There were no words that I knew of that would suit the emotion, all of the emotion. So, despite wanting desperately to hug her, tell her how grateful I was that she'd found me—and, of course, meet her mother—I took comfort in waiting. I've waited years, I told myself. A few more days won't kill me. I knocked on wood. I decided I would let her go first. I'm a coward, I know, forcing a child to take the lead. But part of me wondered if she wasn't a bit relieved too that we hadn't yet broached the subject. It's a lot for a little girl to handle. Strong and capable and perfect as she is.

We'd had four lessons in all, and one since I so horribly burned the masgouf—but what a wonderful lesson it was. We made the masgouf successfully. Excellently. So much so that I lost all inhibitions and said to Joseph with Lorca standing there next to me,

"Little Lorca's a better cook than you! Than me!" I wasn't kidding. She was. *Pride* is the word that came to mind. *She's simply astonishing,* I'd told Joseph when she left. *And so adult, and so beautiful, and so kind.* I imagined that he couldn't be happier either.

Yesterday, Friday, Lorca had suggested that we meet tonight —again!—so that we could go over the butterflying of the fish once more. It was time she made it for her mother, she said. I saw a little twinkle in her eye and I tried to match it. I tried not to make a fool of myself. I'm a horrible winker, but I like to think I can twinkle with the best of them.

"Super," I said. And then: "Fabulous." And then: "Great."

I had a feeling it was going to be the big day, and I practiced my oh-my-gosh-it-is-you face in the mirror a hundred times.

Lorca brought over some dry, pallid-looking no-name fish that she'd gotten at a Jamaican market.

"We won't eat this," she said. "I just need it to practice butterflying."

"We definitely won't eat it," I said, and I had to fight the urge to open a window and surely embarrass her. It smelled like trash.

I was right. Lorca did have an incredibly steady hand and she cooked with her whole body. Like a pro. As she cut the fish, she leaned forward, moving her shoulders and arms so that the knife didn't depend on just one muscle as a guide.

"Perfect," I said. "Not too much pressure and not too little."

She was a quick learner and I told her so.

"You don't need me for this," I said.

And very sternly, she looked me in the eye and said, "I do. Yes, I do."

Whatever feeble breath I had left was taken away for quite a few seconds.

When we finished with the fish, Lorca, the most conscientious child in the world, used bleach on the cutting board and in the sink, making sure there wasn't a whiff of anything rotten as we moved on to *zingulah* and then my favorite on ice cream or toast: mango and nectarine jam.

"I'm just going to bring this garbage to the basement," she said.

"You don't need to be so careful here," I said, but she had already taken off down the stairs.

When she came back, we moved on to the baklava, which Joseph liked with plenty of fresh butter. Into a bowl, we added three kinds of nuts, warm spices, lemon juice, rose water, and honey. Lorca held the measuring spoons and I passed her what she needed with instructions of how much of each. We went along like this, smoothly, methodically, until I remembered: my secret ingredient.

"The vanilla!" I said. "How could I forget?"

I didn't use the liquid, never the liquid, but the pods. Our spices guy would bring them to us in giant canisters and I would use them in everything: coffee, desserts, even soups for just a touch of earthy sweetness.

"Now, where could it be?" I said. I looked in all the ordinary places; I was sure one would turn up. Eventually, Lorca helped too.

"Maybe you don't have any?" she said.

"No," I said. "I never don't have any."

From a drawer, Lorca took out an old remote, some batteries, a tin of cinnamon from twenty years ago. She flipped a piece of paper from one side to the other, but the words were faded or never there to begin with. She was making a small pile on the counter. Suddenly, she stopped. It went quiet. I spun around, thinking she'd seen a rat or mouse.

As it turned out, it wasn't an animal she'd seen. It was nothing that could be trapped.

It was Joseph. It was from a newspaper. It was in Lorca's little hands.

"Is this him?" she asked. I thought I heard some shaking in her voice, but it could have been me, the shaking in my system.

In the photo, he was a stranger. It wasn't just the suit he was wearing, how it made him taller and more definite, or how much time had passed since it had been taken, or even how little he'd resembled this version of himself toward the end. It was that he'd kept such a secret from me. He'd met our daughter. He'd never let that fact slip. It grew like a body of dark water between us. It made his memory elusive and him somewhat unrecognizable. I noticed now the sharpness of his chin and wondered if I'd ever considered that before. Lorca's fingernails were the tiniest cubes of ice. I imagined them melting against my old, stiff skin, jolting me, soothing me, coaxing my blood to snap to. I wanted to be robust again for her.

The photo was from the *Upper West Side Chronicle.* They did an article on the restaurant and we'd framed it, though you couldn't have paid me to find it now. All we had was the photo. What happened to things? I wondered. How did they disintegrate, change color, go stale, fall to pieces, turn inside out, open and close, move across the apartment without my knowing? For so long, I'd felt like I was the only one here, the only one with a real handle on this house. Joseph had done so little. He'd been so sick. And yet, I thought now, so much had happened without me. So many changes had snuck in as I'd been downstairs, on the corner, reading newspaper headlines in my pajamas and an overcoat. He'd known our daughter. The leaves proved it. They'd spoken to each other. He could recognize her voice, the shade of her hair. He knew whether her eyes reflected the colors of Central Park. And what else? It didn't even matter. That was plenty. So very, very much.

Memories knocked the wind out of me suddenly, as if they'd been stored for decades, airtight and sealed on the shelf above the stove, and my focusing on them now had popped the lid, sent them shooting out, fierce.

That night, when the people from the newspaper came, we'd put sunflowers on every table.

I'd cleaned the toilets with a toothbrush.

I'd chopped so many walnuts that my fingers were blistered at the tips.

We'd hired a band.

We looked sunburned from twirling eggplant over the flame for hours, making baba ganoosh and more baba ganoosh.

It had been an enormous success. True, a wineglass had shattered. The sunflowers drooped faster than you could say *salamat.* The *halawat sha'riyya* was too sweet, and there were not enough pistachios. But the newspaper people hadn't seemed to mind. They loved every bit, they said. And I believed them, as they'd asked for fourth helpings, another napkin, a definite yes to cardamom coffee and desserts.

At the end of the night, one reporter asked if he could take a photo and I'd said, "One minute. I don't know where Joseph is." I looked all over for him. No one had seen him. I raced around and raced around again.

As it turned out, hc was outside. I should have known. He had his hands stuffed into his pockets, his face to the sky. His eyes always watered in the spring, and a single tear was slinking down his cheek. He never cleaned them up but let them fall, stain his collars, the pockets of his shirts. Perhaps he was reabsorbing his emotion, doubling it, as if for the both of us.

"Remember the sky in Baghdad?" he'd asked me, right in the middle of everything. I told him not to get schmaltzy. I told him to come inside. I was so excited. This was a big night for us. A very big night. They wanted to take our picture.

"Come on," I must have said. And he did. He tipped his head down, put one foot in front of the other. He followed me because he knew it mattered to me. What mattered to him we left outside—the charcoaled, blotchy sky, which looked as though the moon had bounced around, restless, before finally settling in. In

Baghdad, the stars burned so bright they were like deep holes, not at all transparent. When Joseph came inside, everyone wanted to be around him. Wanted to know where he'd been. People loved him, wanted just to touch his arm, his shoulders, be close to that big, warm head. But I was angry, refolding napkins like my life depended on it. I remember that I was suddenly, stupidly fed up with him for always thinking so much, feeling so much.

I'd worried about the flowers—that the petals might stain someone's dress shirt or jacket, that the stains might get yellower and deeper as the night went on, as clothes came off, slumped discarded on chairs. Joseph's feelings made me embarrassed about my own brain, which was no bigger than a bird's. His feelings were glass between us. Decades later, I hadn't gotten over our differences. Still, I wondered why Sunday mornings had never made me giddy; why musicals couldn't bring me to tears. I believed in karma because I'd been selfish. Joseph didn't waste his life not living it.

I tried to remember the rest of the evening but couldn't. A couple sleeps together so many nights. It occurred to me that I could remember very few. It's like driving by cornfields. I wondered if Joseph had been different from me in that way too, or if his memories were a tightly packed box. Perhaps he'd known where our child was even then. Maybe our restaurant had been across the street from her apartment and he'd stood outside just waiting for a glimpse of her.

My quiet lasted a very long time because I snapped out of it only when I heard Dottie making unsubtle tapping noises upstairs with her shoe. I knew what she was doing. She was trying to get my attention. She wanted me to invite her down.

Lorca didn't seem to notice.

"I would miss him too," Lorca said. What a wonderful, feeling child she was. I so wanted to know where her sadness came from—if it was specific or innate. I felt responsible, somehow, though I shouldn't have. I was entitled to nothing. And yet, she was so much like Joseph. She didn't wear her sadness like a hat. It was buried deep within her, hungry worms below the dirt.

I studied Lorca, trying to gauge what this meant to her, seeing her grandfather perhaps for the first time.

"Okay," she said. "And now?"

"Well," I said, trying for levity. "Now, now, now."

I turned around. I started fiddling with the stove. I made a little drama with my hands. I was terrible at making light of things. I couldn't laugh at myself. Lorca put the photo back and closed the drawer with a civilized click.

"Found it," she said and held up a vanilla pod, shriveled and dark. "What else do you need?"

I heard her like I was underwater. It took time to process. I put my hands to my face to remember me. I wanted to say the right thing to her—and to thank her. I wanted to tell her our stories, to know hers. But how she was reacting made me unsure. Maybe I'd misunderstood everything. Though I hadn't. I thought of the photo; of the freckle on Lorca's face; of her mother, the chef. I couldn't have been so wrong.

As Lorca skimmed the vanilla from its pod with a knife, I put everything into a small pot and began stirring over low heat.

"Like this," I said, but it wasn't right. The mixture gobbed like dry concrete. I needed a backhoe to get through it.

"Strange. It must be the weather," I lied.

She nodded, as if I might have a point, then picked violently at the sides of her nails. Soon she shuddered and stuffed her thumb into her mouth. I was making her anxious.

"Sorry," I said.

"Sorry," she said.

I wished Joseph had been there. He would have known what to do. He wouldn't have been awkward or embarrassed. He made the most of things.

I turned off the burner. I needed to think.

• • •

"I have to ask you something," Lorca said quietly.

I walked toward her, holding on to the counter for strength. I had been waiting for this moment, hoping for it. Lorca was lifting the bowl of dough, turning it slightly, and putting it down. Around and around. Again and again. I put my hands over hers, stopping her. She wouldn't look at me directly, but I couldn't take my eyes off her. I didn't know a lot of young girls, but I was sure that this one was perfect.

"I know," I said. "It's all right."

"Well, the thing is," she began. She shuffled her feet on the floor and bit on the side of her lip. I wanted to tell her to stop. She didn't need to worry. She didn't even need to speak. "When I first came here, I came for the recipe. Because of my mother. It's complicated. But then you said some things that got me wondering about why my mother mentioned masgouf in the first place. I'd never heard of it before. And then Blot, the friend . . ." She paused. I nodded.

"The one I'm friends with," she said. "He really put things together for me. Said something that made me think that there was a very significant reason for my mother to mention the masgouf. And then I asked my mother about it—"

I cut her off.

"I know," I said. I closed my eyes. "I know who you are."

I was holding her hands and I wasn't sure if they were shaking or if it was just her pulse consuming her, fluttering like a million butterflies from the inside out.

"You do," she said, half asking, half telling.

"I do," I said. I opened my eyes.

There were tears the size of grapefruit pits rolling down her face and when she finally looked up at me I noticed that her irises turned a pale gray when she cried. Like a peaceful bird. Like mine.

In that moment, touching her warm little fingers, I didn't ask myself why or how I loved her, I just knew that I did. It had nothing to do with need or comfort, which is more about the feeling than about the object itself. That was my terrible truth about love: I loved my mother because it comforted me to need her, and I loved Joseph because I needed love. Eventually, I loved who Joseph was, but that was always secondary to the act of loving him.

But this was different. I hadn't looked for Lorca. I hadn't even known to wish for her. Her turning up was a heartening confirmation that not every good thing had been sucked into that jagged hole between Joseph and me, me and all else. She was here, feet on the ground.

It occurred to me that everything, every single moment up until this one, I could have imagined. Brushing teeth, paying bus fares, hearing "Happy Birthday" sung to other people at restaurants, never returning to Baghdad, falling asleep at the movies, sickness, health, and sickness again, even Joseph's death, even my own—all of that, I could have foreseen. Some things a person fears; other things, one wishes for.

But this, this moment with Lorca: I never.

And that's what love is, I suppose. The one thing that is most worth hoping for, and the one thing that's most surprising when it lands. Because it's better. It exceeds hope, makes hoping nearsighted. For me, and forever, Lorca was the world's evidence of love.

"I think I have to go to the bathroom," she said suddenly, breaking the shell of my trance.

"Are you all right?" I asked, afraid that she might throw up, that all this was, in fact, too much for her.

"Sorry," she said, shuffling down the hall.

"What for?" I asked, but she was moving away and didn't turn back.

I felt foolish standing in the kitchen alone, like it had rained but only on me. I wasn't prepared for Lorca to walk out so abruptly. I told myself that I shouldn't have expected anything. It would have been overwhelming for anyone—all this emotion—and even more so for a young girl. If there's one bit of good news about getting old, it's that the surges of feeling stop taking you by surprise. And physical pain, even the terrible kind, never feels catastrophic. It's bound to happen. Everything tastes the same if you cook it long enough. This moment with Lorca, of course, was different.

There were questions I wanted to ask her—so many questions. I wanted to know about her mother. But now didn't seem like the perfect time. I reminded myself of Joseph, of not waiting for the sky to fall. This should be enough, I told myself. Enough.

Just then I caught a glimpse of my reflection in the window. I was haggard, like someone no one could stand being related to. I searched around for a tube of lipstick and found one of Dottie's. I covered my teeth with my finger in an attempt at a decent application. I reorganized my hair. I smacked at my cheeks to subdue the emotion.

Lorca was still in the bathroom. There was nothing but silence between here and there. Like an idiot, I glued my eyes to the door, waiting for her to reemerge. *Snap out of it, Victoria.* I pumped my hands at my sides.

To keep myself busy, I cleaned off the countertop. I wondered what Joseph would have done if he'd been here. He wouldn't have applied lipstick, I thought, and he would have laughed at me for doing so. I tried to laugh at me.

Well, Joseph, I said without speaking, *what shall we do now?* I took out the newspaper clipping again and looked at him.

Hm? I said, again in my head. *Any thoughts?*

Silence.

"Me too," I said out loud.

Lorca was back. I put the clipping away.

"Can we still make baklava?" she asked.

"Of course," I told her. Of course.

I tried to contain myself when at the very same instant we began to roll up our sleeves.

That night, I was too excited to sleep. I was imagining the rest of my life with Lorca and my daughter in it, and trying desperately not to imagine the rest of my life with Lorca and my daughter in it. Just in case.

So, I watched some TV. I listened to three shows on the radio. I made myself a cup of lavender tea. I watched some more TV. I stood by the window and counted cars. I listened to a couple have it out across the street. They were speaking Russian. Eventually, I tried warm milk with honey. I turned on the white-noise machine. Then, probably around two o'clock, I shut it off. That my bladder wasn't used to so much liquid wasn't helping anything either.

Eventually, bored and feeling productive, I flossed between every tooth and then between every tooth again. I gargled with salt water until my gums burned. As I brushed my teeth, I fake smiled at myself in the mirror, trying to get a sense of how I looked to someone else. It was something I hadn't wondered about in years. I paused. I really looked. As it turned out, I looked very different than I'd imagined. Older, of course. Everything had slumped into the wattle of my neck. But changed too. For most of my life, my reflection had come as a shock to me. My nose was always smaller than I thought, and my eyes larger, farther away—even now—from my brows. But those were little things. What struck me now was something more significant and subtle. I leaned my head to one side. Then the other. I inspected my profile as best I could.

Then it hit me. I was American-looking. Not like a cowgirl or a WASP, but like a New Yorker. Like someone second-generation, with parents from Italy, Greece, or Spain. Maybe born in

Brooklyn. Maybe Queens. But certainly, I thought, I didn't look like a Baghdadi. My skin didn't have a uniquely olive cast. My eyes were no more almond-shaped than anyone else's. It couldn't even be said that I looked Jewish. I wondered when these changes had happened. Whether it was a particular haircut that had redefined me permanently. Or the diamond studs from Joseph that I rarely took out. Or whether the linguistic shift from Arabic to English had altered the curve of my mouth, so that when the lines and wrinkles grew around it, they grew around my American voice. Or whether I really never had a sense of myself to begin with.

When, exactly when, I wondered, had this taken place? Had Joseph seen it too? How could I not know myself yet? Was it my appearance that had changed? I wondered. Or me, considering my appearance? There was no way to know, and yet neither possibility should have come as much of a surprise. The truth was, I hardly stopped to consider myself, the state of my physical affairs. For years, I'd stayed busy. Kept going. Kept on. So much fancy footwork involved to keep myself afloat and from thinking too deeply about the marriage I'd damaged, about Baghdad, about loss and change despite loss. And then Joseph, so sick. I couldn't think about that either. Not for a moment had I allowed myself to wither into sadness. Wouldn't. It's impossible to know when sadness ends. It's a string I feared I'd keep on pulling until I unraveled the carpeting of a million rooms. So I'd told myself—all along I'd told myself—that every negative thought I indulged in nudged me one step closer to a very dangerous ledge from which I would one day slip and fall. Holding things together is what I thought I was doing. Keeping the sadness out. Not falling. And this was done by never analyzing change. Never even considering it. Never looking too hard at my reflection and wondering. But of course, fighting against sadness never kept me from feeling sad. It just moved things around. The ledge, the endless hole below it, bore itself inside of me. The only thing I avoided was the sensation of falling. I couldn't avoid the gorge. And I was nothing more than the delicate rocks on either side.

I suddenly became conscious that Joseph might be aware of these thoughts, so I said out loud to unworry him, "Not anymore, Joseph. It's all all right now. We have Lorca. We have her to love."

Joseph

New york, 1953–1954

On a particularly warm day in March, Joseph considered rolling down the window in the taxi but then thought better of it, not wanting to upset Victoria. It was just the two of them. Joseph and Victoria, Victoria and Joseph, as it hadn't been in nine long months. It was the two of them and no baby, just the heavy, leaded absence of it. Of her, Joseph thought. His baby was a she, they'd told him.

They weren't speaking, the two of them, but Joseph felt they were communicating. He hoped that. He needed it. Victoria sniffled. He coughed back. Victoria scratched her forearm. Joseph crinkled his nose. He kept his right hand beneath his leg, hiding. It was beginning to go numb. He was holding a small washcloth. A nurse had given it to him, thinking Victoria might want it. It was hers. But of course, she wouldn't. She wanted no part of any of it. She'd even bought new clothes for the occasion and had thrown the old ones in the trash—she went that far. But this washcloth was something. Joseph kept thinking: It had been in the room. It had been there. It had touched his baby. Joseph kept it wound very tightly in his fist as if it were cutting off a valve that might make his eyes burst. He felt like a wall of glass, just smashed though still suspended.

He watched as Victoria put her hands on her knees and tucked her chin to her chest. She was wearing a new dress, baggy and shapeless, beneath a large brown overcoat. Her legs were bare and pale. A pair of men's socks pooled around her ankles like spilled milk. She pulled them up and then let them slink down again. Then she looked at her belly. Her face loosened. She reminded Joseph of a child who had made a mess. To see her that way made Joseph ache. He wanted to hold her. He missed her. But he knew—he'd gotten used to it—that if he tried, she would retreat from him. So he didn't try. He tightened his grip on the washcloth. He coughed, ridding himself of the impulse as if it were an irritating fleck of dust.

As they sat there, the two of them in the back seat, Joseph couldn't help but think that he'd given up long before—and it made him feel awful. Months ago, when he'd convinced himself that enough was enough, and there was nothing else he could do for Victoria, he'd given up. And then, each time Victoria didn't reach for him in his sleep, when she was furious with him for not abandoning the idea of keeping the baby, he gave up a little more. When she didn't hold his hand on the street, didn't smile when she looked at him, didn't put honey into his tea, so compulsively ignored every aspect of her pregnancy and rejected his having any part in it at all, he kept giving up. He gave up until his sympathy was entirely given away, and he felt he had nothing else to give. That's when he'd found himself at Dr. Espy's office, ready to be given to. Ready to take. Now he'd been taking for months, on most weekdays after work. He told Victoria that he'd been given additional duties at the bakery. How strange, he thought to himself, to call it a "duty."

And now, he felt horrible. He felt sick. He was sorry but couldn't say so. He wanted to be sure that the affair hadn't been the final blow to ensure this—this lack of baby. This everything. Maybe if he'd been more loving, if he hadn't lost hope so quickly, so easily, things wouldn't have turned out this way.

Victoria could have changed her mind. But he couldn't be sure of anything now. He'd done what he'd done. Everything, he thought to himself, every feeling about the baby from now on would be wrapped up in the fact that he'd found someone else for a while—because of that, and despite it too.

He opened the window, stuck his head all the way out, and gasped for air. The driver honked, and Joseph jumped, nearly broke his neck. Victoria crossed her arms over her chest and shuddered. Joseph almost asked her if she was cold—the words were on the tip of his tongue—but he decided he'd better not do that either. He decided that he wouldn't tell her. Couldn't. And if he didn't tell her about the affair, he had to do something kind, something selfless to make it right. He was afraid of what his voice might convey. He kept his eyes set forward on the traffic, the splashes of red light. It was rush hour. This was going to be an expensive ride. Joseph was making calculations in his mind until he caught a whiff of baby powder, and he was back in the hospital again, where, for just a few moments, he'd been a father.

Joseph wound the washcloth around his hand. He stuffed it hard into his pocket and ripped the seams of his pants. He pushed harder and through. He felt his own leg. He pulled a hair. He pulled another and gave himself the chills. He wondered if he was in shock or panicked or numb or what that sensation was, like he was balancing just above the floor. He wished, impossibly, for the feeling to be relief but knew it wasn't. Relief meant that something was over. He thought of the baby. He would always think of the baby. It would be on the streets, in the sunset, when he looked down at himself in the shower. Here it was in this very back seat, occupying all the spaces in between. And yet, that was the least of it.

For the rest of his life, he realized, he would have a relationship with something that was what it wasn't. It was what wasn't sleeping in his arms. It was what wasn't being breastfed in a rocker in the middle of a night. It was what wasn't splashing and grinning and splashing and sneezing in the bathtub. It was what wasn't in framed photographs squished and happy between himself and Victoria. It was what wasn't reaching for his hand before crossing the street. It was what wasn't asking if murder was killing a bug. It was what wasn't going to school from their stoop in the morning, to school with a lunch box, to school in an ironed uniform, to school at a university with giant evergreen hedges and red bricks and books stacked a mile high, making this father so proud, so very proud, the proudest ever. He wondered how he could ever live with what wasn't, and harder still, how couldn't he?

He continued to blame himself. If he hadn't given up, things might have worked out. If he'd taken her to the Statue of Liberty or Macy's or he'd saved his money for a horse-drawn carriage ride through Central Park or even for a nice shawl, things might have been different. If he'd kissed her harder, rubbed her feet, helped her to wash her hair and braid it, they might not be here. But he hadn't done any of those things. After a certain point, gestures like those didn't even occur to him. He covered his mouth and felt himself choke.

The cab stopped quickly and stalled. The driver cursed and started it up again. Joseph pumped his knee, still trying to undream himself. Victoria let out a little sigh. Then he did too.

"Don't think of it," she said. "Think of anything else."

Often, he'd wondered if this was as hard for Victoria as it was for him. He'd wanted to keep the baby, after all. She hadn't. But her voice now, the way it teetered, nearly broke, left him feeling reprimanded. Of course it had been hard. Of course it had.

He thought about the space below Victoria's heart, empty now—and how her heartbeat no longer harmonized with another's. As if hearing his thoughts, she put her hand, warm and swollen, on his. He looked at her but knew she would never indulge him in big, weepy feelings. Instead, she squeezed his fingers. He fought back tears. He hated his emotions. Sometimes he wanted to wrangle them to the ground like a wild animal. Couldn't he, just for once, have been the steady one, been strong?

She squeezed again, as if telling him she understood.

In the past few months he'd found himself missing her, even when she was an arm's length away. Now he looked at her. She was touching him. Still, he missed her. She looked at him. He missed her less.

He squeezed back. He squeezed to feel her, to feel himself, to feel her, to feel her, to feel her.

Upstairs, at the apartment, Victoria paused in the doorway as if searching for something she didn't want to find. Her hands were clasped in front of her. Joseph eased her coat off her shoulders. When he saw a platter of pignoli cookies (Mrs. Messina must have been here) next to the bowl of crushed almonds with honey and sugar that he'd prepared—an homage to his mother, a healer, who fed the almonds to women who had just given birth, to ward off the evil eye and encourage happiness—he used the coat to cover them. It felt inappropriate. No one would have thought that this was how they'd come home. With less than what they'd left with. Fewer knees. Fewer bottom lips.

"Are you all right?" Victoria asked, swinging around.

He coughed to make light of it, swallowed hard. He shook his head that he was fine. He was fine. He wanted a cookie. Hell, he wanted the whole plate.

Victoria walked to the mattress and dragged her feet, not lifting them but shuffling, as if trying to scuff something off her soles. On the bed, she folded herself onto her side, toward the wall and away from everything. She rested her head on her arm. She kicked off one shoe and then the other. They fell next to each other, organized. He imagined her face—twisted like a street pretzel, crying. But as much as wished he could, he couldn't go to her. Was it written all over his own face, he wondered, what he'd done? It was only then that he remembered how well she could read him, how she could tell from the lines around his eyes if he was unsatisfied or tired or nostalgic. He relaxed his jaw, trying to erase any hints at all about his feelings, keep them from sneaking out. He held his breath.

Joseph thought of all the ways he'd seen her body lying down in the past months. Long, leaflike, silhouetted this way and that—below the windowsill, on the bench, on the floor, on her elbows, on her back with her belly pointing up like a dune. He couldn't remember her height beside him now, though he tried.

"We're going to be all right," Victoria said. He could hear the smile on her face.

"All right," he said in a voice he hoped would carry her closer to sleep. He was too exhausted to talk. "All right," he said again and then once more in his head.

Joseph put on the pot for tea and stood with the safety of the counter between them. She would be asleep before the water boiled. The little washcloth was still in his hand. He opened a drawer they hardly used and pushed it to the back. He went to the table and reached for the plate of cookies. He ate every one of them, without a sound, hardly taking a breath. And then spoonful after faithful spoonful, he finished the bowl of almonds too. If he couldn't breathe, he thought, he couldn't cry. And if he couldn't cry, he couldn't feel sorry for himself. And if he couldn't feel sorry for himself, he could perhaps convince himself that there was nothing to be sorry about. If he could convince himself of that, he could convince himself of anything.

And yet, the next day, everything changed.

Joseph thought he knew what to expect. After Victoria's pregnancy, he would need to nurture her, restore her, because some part, he had to think, would undoubtedly have been lost. And he was prepared to take care of her—feed her yellow vegetables, and the ground almonds with honey. He was ready to be flattered by it, by being needed in that way again. It would be a fresh start. It wouldn't be perfect, but it would be something.

Together they could discover the city in the manner he had originally hoped. She might look at him like she had in Baghdad. The first time he'd ever seen her had been years before they'd officially met. They were at the market. She'd dropped her bag and he'd lifted it for her, held it open while she dusted off a persimmon and put it back in.

Now he watched her. She hadn't moved all night. She'd kept tight to the wall, her back guarded and hard. There was a darkness about her that he hadn't known before, as if an angry stranger were standing beside her, refusing to disappear. Then she turned around. He took a step back, but she wasn't angry. She was smiling. Her face was pink and flooded him with a sudden, alarming warmth.

"Good morning," she said.

"Good morning," he answered, breathless.

When Joseph came home that afternoon, the apartment was sparkling. Spotless. The linoleum floor was a lighter shade of gray. The windows were clear, ungreased. Victoria stood in the middle of the room with her sleeves rolled up and her hair rebelling from her face in wild wisps, as though she were a flower in the wind. She had a toothbrush in one fist. She motioned to the countertop. Finally, he thought, finally she was upright, undelicate. It had been so long since he'd seen a flush in her cheeks. He'd forgotten how it made her eyes brighter. Her face was glistening with sweat. But then he remembered, was filled with a sudden rage. Had she forgotten already? What kind of person was she?

"Let us sit," he said, taking Victoria by the elbows. "You need to rest."

She resisted him. She snatched her arms away.

"I cannot sit anymore," she said.

He tried to remember how he'd once felt about her. They were the same people, weren't they? He believed in chemistry. He believed in love. And he believed that he still loved her; was determined to. More than anything, he wished they could start over. He imagined a crisp white canvas coming down from the sky and rolling out in front of them. He realized that in order to love more, he would have to feel less. This was what it meant to love, he thought. It required a certain degree of forgetting, of loss; it was like rushing into freezing water, jumping with your eyes closed into a dark hole, not making a sound.

Victoria held the toothbrush in the air like a flag. When she smiled, he was surprised to see the beautiful symmetry of her teeth. Her nightgown was long and sorry, and it now appeared incongruous on her, as though the very idea of napping had forced itself on her, against her will, all these months. She scratched one foot with her other foot, not moving her arms. As she stood in the afternoon light, Joseph noticed two silver hairs on the right side of her head. They hadn't been there before. And yet, he was grateful to them. At least, he thought, he'd not been the only one grieving for months.

He went over to the countertop, put his face to it, and licked. She clapped and raised her hands in the air. She threw her head back with laughter.

"Isn't it clean!" she said. "It's clean!"

"So clean," he said, and he could feel himself begin to laugh too.

As the weeks went by, Victoria continued to do things. She went to the Fulton Market every morning, despite how dangerous she knew it was. She stayed there for hours. When she got home, she cooked. All day, she cooked. She cooked and hummed and kept the windows wide open. She knelt on the floor and peeled cucumbers into a dishtowel. She cracked pomegranates and squeezed out the juice with cheesecloth. She made all the things they ate in Baghdad: *kba, tershana, kitchri* and *ambah, sambusak ab tam'r*. She made extra for the neighbors. She used all the money they had on spices and pans, and when Joseph couldn't pay the rent, he didn't tell her. He asked their landlady to take pity on them. And because he'd also told the landlady what had happened, she shrugged and said, "You good man. You bring me money when money come."

Everything was different. Joseph woke to the sounds of the stove clicking on. He was happy. Victoria made him cardamom coffee and he brought it to work. It kept him thinking all day of her bare feet. Flat feet, moving around the apartment with purpose. In the afternoons, he walked all the way home with his body pitched forward. Getting there faster faster faster. Some days, from a block away, he could see a crowd gathering outside his building, looking up at his window toward the dark, orange flavors of Victoria's cooking. And he felt proud walking through the front door. He felt important.

And just like that, he never went back to the meeting place by Dr. Espy's office, never leaned on a hydrant, waiting. Never ventured into that dank, sticky bar for midday drinks or shared the weight of his body with someone else. Letting go came naturally, as if the weather had suddenly changed. The day after the baby was born, he'd gone to the pay phone to call. His hand hovered over the dial, but he couldn't remember the number. For the first time in months, he simply couldn't recall it. He laughed out loud at himself. He hung up.

As he headed back to their apartment, he imagined himself and Victoria as a small but unshakable unit, walking under an umbrella together as the world tornadoed around them. How could it be any other way? Their accents, their apartment, their memories—it bound them, kept them. They'd met at a market in Baghdad. They fell in love. They would be all right.

Later, he asked her to squeeze his hand. And she did, smiling, only half mocking him. He had to close his eyes to bear it. *This,* he thought, *is the only way forgiveness can be effective—when both people have regrets and hope, both.*

The year that followed seemed to Joseph the happiest and saddest of his life. It was the kind of year that had no beginning or end. The seasons made their way open-mouthed from one to the next. Joseph and Victoria anticipated them in a way they never had before. They looked forward to things. They went on walks in the evenings, embracing the weather and changes in the trees. It was during that year that they saw the Statue of Liberty, Macy's, and Central Park. It was like it had been before. The two of them and the city of New York and everything else mostly behind them, quiet but tender, like delicate scars.

Just as there was incredible happiness, there was fierce disappointment that Joseph couldn't shake. At night when Victoria lay sleeping, a resentment would stir in the pit of his stomach, all acid and bile. The longer he watched her, the angrier he became. How could she sleep, he wondered, if she knew the pain she'd caused him? And yet, just as his anger reached its pinnacle, her face would quickly clench and release, as if her insides had been seized by some invisible hand. He'd feel sorry then. The resentment would wane, and the anger would realign against himself. He was so much at fault too.

It went like this. Back and forth. On and on.

It was during that year that Joseph suggested Victoria cook for the bakery. They sold her food on Fridays. Her breakfast bread went faster than anything else. Her almond *malfuf* were gone by noon. They had to make a sign: ONE PER CUSTOMER, PLEASE. They were gone in ten minutes, five minutes; a woman offered triple the price for the whole lot. Soon, Victoria was cooking every day of the week. Some days, she came to the bakery and stood outside just to watch. Her face oohed and aahed as each of her items flew off the shelf. It made Joseph laugh. He'd never seen her so full of herself. It even seemed she'd grown taller, her body less stiff. He bought her a turquoise necklace. She wore it everywhere and moved her chest forward like a peacock.

Still, some nights he woke to her sitting, legs crossed beneath her, dabbing at her breasts as tears spilled down her face. Her nightshirt was stained like drenched soil. Some nights, he sat up too. He consoled her. Other nights, he pretended to be asleep, only half immune to the sadness of the thing.

One day in the late spring, Victoria was frying eggplant. Joseph stood next to her by the stove. He leaned around her, trying to pluck a piece of eggplant from the pan, but the oil kept popping and he drew back his hand. Victoria didn't help him, didn't take one out with her fork. Usually, she did. A lump grew in his throat. She was thinking of something. He was afraid of it. Maybe she was going to want to talk about the baby. But finally, things were good. They were happy. Victoria had taken to washing his face in the morning, holding a steaming towel with one hand, the other hand on the back of his head. Or, what if, he wondered, she knew what he'd done? What if she didn't think their failures canceled out the way he had so doggedly convinced himself that they did?

Now she was looking at him, her eyes set like two rocks in a glass. Joseph's throat twisted. *Please,* he thought. *Do not ask me.* Quickly, he found something to say.

"Are you remembering Baghdad?" he asked.

"No," she said. "Why?"

"I don't know," he said. "You looked like that."

She smiled. Her eyes became sharper. Whatever she had been about to say, she was now sure of. He had made it worse.

"I'd like to have a restaurant," she said. Joseph didn't say anything. He was relieved and he wasn't. Once again, he felt himself wondering about her—about her capacity for sadness and, if not sadness, empathy, at the very least.

"The people enjoy my cooking, don't they?" she said. "They ask for more."

She was swinging the wooden spoon in her hands. Her mouth was wet with excitement.

Joseph knew: he had to move on. He didn't have the right to hold this over her forever. Not even just in his heart.

He realized only then, as he burned his fingers on a fragrant piece of eggplant, that forgiveness was born from loss. It required giving up and moving past dark corners where grudges, wrapped in dusty clothes and stacked like corpses, lay idle, unmoving.

"They love your cooking," he said and took a deep breath. He realized that he missed her already. He felt like she'd just returned to him. But, he thought, he'd done what he needed to do. Now she could do the same. And no one ever died from missing, he told himself. He was quite sure.

"So," he said. "All right. Let's."

Lorca

TWO HOURS AFTER I found out I had a real grandmother, a biological grandmother, my mother announced she was going through menopause.

"Let's just say," she said, "it's the end of being a woman."

"It is?" I said.

"All the great parts about being female," she said. "It all ends now."

She crossed her arms into an X in front of her, and then uncrossed them violently. Done.

"One day you'll understand," she said, leaning her head against the back of the couch and tracing her hairline with her fingertips. Her eyes were closed and fluttering. Her chest inflated, deflated.

"You're far too young to understand. But learning how to be both feminine and powerful is the best thing a woman can do for herself. It's an art, really. It's the only reason I survived."

Usually, I'd be killing myself to get to the heart of what she was trying to say, hoping that something important could be attributed to me. But now I was distracted, away somewhere. It felt like I'd had seventeen café au laits, though I hadn't had a single one. Part of me was terrified that the secret was written all over my face and my mother would see it, and it wouldn't go according to plan and all my hard work would be ruined. Off I'd go to boarding school. Another part wanted to tell her sooner rather than later, before she found out some other way, but I dreaded it. I wanted to mull things over, talk to Blot, enjoy Victoria before I had to give her up to my mother. Another part still was disappointed that I hadn't been able to match Victoria's emotion the way I had hoped. But when she said she knew who I was and she looked at me like she was going to cry, it felt like a very heavy foot was standing on my chest.

Formations of words collected in my head and then slipped away like spaghetti on a spoon. There were some food magazines on the table and I paged through them slowly, just to keep from being idle. I stopped at an article on celeriac, left it open, pretended to be very interested. All the while I stayed quite still, as if my mouth were packed with soda bubbles and too much sudden movement would result in a giant, delirious explosion of words, all of them wrong, all of them ruining what I'd been trying so hard to perfect.

"When I was your age," she said, now smiling, "I had so many boyfriends. A lot of them were older, much older."

I was about to say something about Blot.

"Which is not right for you, cookie," she said. "You're not ready for any of that just yet. You're very, very young for your age. You'd be taken advantage of. It's okay to take your time."

She looked at me, her eyes not interacting with mine but like confident periods at the ends of her sentences.

"Look," she said. "What I'm trying to tell you is that I'm thrilled. I gave you a life that no one gave me. I gave you time to grow up and to grow into yourself. And just look at you!"

I looked at her. She looked genuinely proud for exactly one second.

"A life of leisure," she said, as if the term had just dawned on her. "I'm not saying that you've taken full advantage of it. You haven't. And actually, I'm quite angry about that, but that's not the point right now. The point I'm making is that I've done well by you. As a mother."

I was starting to get itchy in my chest. I flicked a table lamp on and off four times and pinched the backs of my knees.

"So," she said. "Maybe my job as a woman is done."

Her eyes were on me, her face too bright.

"Right," I said. "Yes. It's been great. Everything!"

She was waiting for me now, waiting for more. Her silence was an uncovered manhole that I fell into every time. She knew something was up.

"What if," I said, straightening my posture, flattening the wrinkles on my sweater, "I knew a really big secret?"

She cocked her head but didn't seem intrigued. She breathed in and out and blinked slowly, like I was five and had woken her from a nap.

"A secret," she said. And then: "Okay."

"Well," I said. I crossed my hands in my lap as if holding something inside: a magic bunny or a special key. "What if I knew *two* really big secrets?"

"One isn't enough?" she said.

I refused to let the disappointment stick.

"One secret has a lot to do with the other," I said. "They're not entirely separate but they're both brilliant." Her word.

"You're pregnant!" she shouted and erupted into laughter.

"No," I said patiently, trying to bring her back.

"Okay, okay," she said. "I'll be serious."

I was waiting for her to ask me about the secrets, paw for them.

"I'm confused," she said. "Am I supposed to be guessing?"

I realized that I wasn't sure. It hadn't been my plan to tell her like this. But that's how these things always played out with her.

I wanted there to be a big reveal, something dramatic, lots of buildup so that my mother could gasp when I finally said, *I found the recipe. And not just that; I found them. For you. For you, Mommy.* In real life, I never called her that.

"I don't know, Lorca," she said. "You got a tattoo that says you love me?"

"No," I said. I tried to compose my thoughts. "Did you have family dinners as a kid?" I asked. She looked intrigued.

"Does it count," she asked, "if we didn't like each other?"

"Yes," I said.

"Okay," she said, a little disappointed in me. "Then, yes."

"And what did you eat?" I asked.

"TV dinners," she said. "Gummy, sloppy things. All disgusting."

"That must have been terrible for you," I said.

"I guess," she said. "It was gross. Yes."

"Okay," I said. "And what did you talk about?"

"Lou talked," she said. "Mostly."

"What did Lou—" I began, but she cut me off. She was done answering questions. I wasn't done. I felt like I was gaining speed.

"Lorca," she said. "C'mon, now."

Suddenly, I was angry at her. Not at anything other than her. It might have been the first time ever. And I forgot where I was going, where my big interrogation was supposed to lead us.

"Why don't you ever cook for me?" I said. I snapped it. You could tell, my mother wasn't used to this—me, like this. She sat up as if she'd seen a bug on the ceiling. For a second her face was very hard and I was sure she was going to explode, but then she softened, got too soft.

"Oh, Lorca," she said. "Is that what you want? Is that all this is about?"

I wasn't sure what I wanted. I slumped onto the couch, lay down, defeated.

My mother stood, picked up a blanket from a chair, and covered me with it as I stared right at her, not smiling or crying or anything, just trying to figure out if this was real or fake. In real life, I didn't get angry at her. And I couldn't make sense of her either, couldn't tell if she was furious or disappointed. She wouldn't look me in the eye. She started at my feet, tucking in the blanket beneath them with both hands, gently lifting me and then dropping my weight as she made little shoves with her fingers until I was airtight. She moved all the way around, up one side of me and then the other, and when she came to my shoulders, she looked past me at the pillow as she lifted my head. I let it go heavy in her hands. She tucked the blanket under there too. Everything was pulled taut around me; even my arms were bound to my sides, but I left them. I didn't squirm. I didn't fight anything. I let myself be pinned to the couch.

When she was done, she left.

I heard her go into the other room and close the door and that was that. I didn't hear anything else—not the TV, not her voice on the phone, not nose-blowing. I didn't even hear what was happening outside. I don't know what happened next. It might have been the emotion, the fear of being awake and angry at her; or it might have been the way she'd instructed me to relax by tucking me in; or it might have been that she'd just shown me more attention, moving around my feet and legs and sides and shoulders, than she had in years, as long as I could remember, and I could still feel the sensation of her fingers under my head—but it knocked me out. All of it. I fell asleep just like that, just like her.

I woke up to something amazing: the smell of chicken in half-mourning, a favorite of my mother's, done with black truffles, Madeira, garlic, and loads of butter. She was taking it out of the oven. I raced to stand up and help her. She plopped it onto the counter, took out one knife and one fork. The chicken was steaming, the color of expensive wood.

"There," she said. "*Bon appétit.*"

I wanted to capture this moment just as it was. It was the moment, I thought, just before I told her about Victoria and Joseph. And here we were, like this, like a normal family. A mother cooking for her daughter as she'd napped.

I took out two plates, thinking she'd cut it and we'd eat together. She and I. But instead, she went to the bathroom, came back with the tweezers and a magnifying mirror, and sat herself down on the windowsill, though it was dark out and the window let in an ugly, orange light.

"You're not hungry?" I said.

"No," she said. "I'm just not."

The sensation of collapsing poured through me but I kept standing. I ate as much of the chicken as I possibly could—one thigh, two drumsticks, a very large breast—though I wasn't hungry either. At first, it felt like I was eating away the space between us, but when I came to my senses, I kept eating, just to have something to do with my hands.

The phone rang. I raced to it, wrapped a paper towel around the receiver so I didn't cover it with grease, and passed it to my mother. I wanted her to look at me, make sense of what had just happened, but she wouldn't.

"Hello," she said, singsongy, like she'd just come in from a swim.

She put the tweezers on the counter, sauntered away from me, and reassembled herself on the couch. She folded her legs beneath her.

"Paul," she said. Her voice was calm, expectant even. I wondered if he'd ever called her before, begging—though I wasn't sure for exactly what. And if she'd just sat there, queen of the world, taking it in, like dough rising.

"Paul," she said with just as much patience. I could make out my father's voice now on the other end, sounding wild even through the phone. Anxiety gripped my throat. I hadn't expected him to stand up to my mother about the masgouf, about her eating it with someone that wasn't him, especially now when he was already so far from her. It had been so very long. I hated myself for having called him, for not thinking of how it would come back to bite me.

"Paul," she said, and her cheeks went red.

She picked at a burn on her finger only for a second before slamming her feet down on the floor.

"Excuse me?" she said, her voice trampling his.

"No," she said and kept repeating it over and over, becoming calmer and calmer—her own personal lullaby. "No no no no no no no."

She let him make a scene. I could hear him. Then, with her eyes closed, she said, "You are right. We were together then. But I didn't go to the Shohet with someone else. I went by myself."

She paused, and I heard my father's voice, but it was softer now, and I wondered if he was apologizing already. For a moment, I could see them as a couple again, after all these years. For some reason, I could still imagine it—not in a certain place or doing particular things, but just the two of them, holding on to each other and floating. He was the only one she allowed to touch her, really touch her.

"I told Lou that I went with you because it's what Lou needed to hear. If I'd told her I went by myself, she would have asked why, and I didn't need to tell her. That wasn't part of our conversation."

My stomach soared into my throat. I leaned forward. She was about to tell my father about Victoria and Joseph, that they were her biological parents. I had the urge to shout that I knew it. I'd known it first. I'd done so much work, but I could barely open my mouth. My jaw was locked.

"Mom," I whispered.

"And I have to say, Paul," she said, "that it's really amazing that you decide to be jealous now, to give a shit about something now. It's way too late to get possessive."

"Mom," I said again. "Wait." I started to make my way over to her, but she put up her hand, shut her eyes tight, as if defending herself from a terrible stench. I stopped, sat down, and slumped to the floor. Wait.

My father said something else and she stood up, stepped over and around me. She took a breath. I imitated her. In, out. She rubbed one foot on top of the other and tucked the phone between her shoulder and her ear so she could stretch her arms in twenty different ways.

"I found my parents," she said. "Just before I went to the Shohet, I'd found them."

Now I stood up. I covered my mouth. I opened it. "Victoria," I said. She shot me a mean look, like what was I talking about, and why did I need to say anything right now.

"Victoria and Joseph," I said. "Mom." I was loud.

"In the obituaries," she continued, turning away from me, looking like she had absolutely no sense of what I was trying to do. "I did all this research and ran around for months like a chicken with its head cut off, trying to find where I was from. Finally, I found their names, their address. And just before I was going to go see them, I found them in the obituaries. The man had crashed his jet flying to Nantucket, and he was survived by no one, it said. His ex-wife had died sixteen years before."

I had to remind myself to shut my mouth, which was still open. Now I picked at a scab on my neck until it bled. She had other parents. The man. The ex-wife. I repeated the whole thing in my head. I turned around once. I turned around again. I wanted to yell. Instead, I shoved my fingernails as deep as I could into my palms.

I sat down on the floor again and replayed what she'd just said in my head, faster and repeatedly. The part that made the most sense was that they'd been wealthy. You could always tell just from looking at my mother that she came from kings and queens. There were constants about her that I imagined had everything to do with fancy blood: perfect skin, white nails, hair that looked blown-dry even when she'd just come from the shower, correctly shaped teeth. Even the way she walked was wealthy. Put her next to Lou and there was no denying it.

"But he was important," she said. "Always in the papers and with his picture taken at fundraisers. He'd lived in Boston. A patron of the arts."

My father said something that made my mother smile just briefly. So badly I wanted to know what. For a second, it felt like he'd won.

"Anyway," she said. "Right after I saw the obituary, I went to that restaurant and had the masgouf. We used to walk past it all the time, remember? It seemed like such a family place. Everyone was so nice. And so not like people from Nantucket. And so not like the people who adopted me. And so not like people from culinary school. And I wanted that. Not forever. But, you know. I kept that obituary in my pocket for weeks."

She paused for a second and stood up taller, as if pulling taut whatever emotion had become loose and runny inside of her. When her posture returned, so did she. She spoke fast.

"I burned it," she said to my father.

As my father spoke, softly now, my mother sat down, crossed her feet, pushed the hair from her face.

"I didn't want to explain all that to Lou," she said. "Get it now? I didn't cheat on you."

He said something else.

"They made good fish," she said. "What else do you want from me?"

When she got off the phone, she looked at me.

"I'm waiting," she said.

"It's not a big deal," I said. "It's not like I call him all the time. It's nothing."

"And what were you saying while I was trying to explain? Trying to defend myself?" she said.

"Nothing," I said. "I was just saying nothing."

She didn't sit on the floor with me and she didn't touch my head. Instead, she lay down on the couch, used her foot to knock the blanket over herself, let out a big heavy sigh, and said she was exhausted, would I mind waking her in twenty. She wasn't looking for an answer.

I felt fogged in, everything too wispy to get a hold of. Even my mother, inches away from me, seemed a little bit like a ghost. My feelings were dull. I had to keep going over the events of the past few hours just to try to comprehend them. Victoria was my grandmother. Victoria wasn't my grandmother. I wondered if I'd somehow willed her to believe that we were related, if I'd tricked her into it. I felt as though I'd taken advantage of her. I desperately didn't want to tell her that things weren't as she believed. I wanted her to think of me as family, regardless. I wanted to be her granddaughter. I wanted her to hold my hands again and to one day sit at my graduation from somewhere, clapping, beaming. Even though I hadn't had the right reaction before, I would. I could. I was sure of it.

It occurred to me that my actual grandparents were strangers to me. More than ever, and dead. And fancy. And I didn't care.

It struck me that Victoria was nothing like my mother. And yet, surprisingly, I wasn't angry at myself, at my hope. *Please, let's keep pretending,* I thought. *Please.*

"Tell me a story," my mother said after a while. "Something really happy and nice."

I'd been standing at the counter, cleaning up, holding on. Now I took a deep breath.

"Okay," I said. I went over to her. I sat on her feet.

I told her one of the few stories that she'd told me of myself as a child. We'd gone to a park by a lake. I was no older than two. Me, my father, and my mother. There was an enormous tree with branches so long and droopy that my father moved the picnic table from underneath it. He was always afraid of me getting crushed. My mother believed that kids had stronger bones than grownups.

"There's more calcium in her forearm than in an entire dairy farm," she liked to say.

That day, my mother had made roasted tomato and goat cheese sandwiches with salmon she'd smoked herself, and I ate, she said, double my weight of it. She was complimenting me when she said that. I always wondered if eating so much was my best way of complimenting her.

The story went that all through lunch I kept pointing at a gaping hole in the tree, reaching for it, waving it at. My parents thought it was just that: a hole, one that had been filled with fall leaves, stiff and brown, by some kind of ferrety animal. But I wasn't satisfied with that explanation. I wouldn't give up.

"What?" my father kept asking me. "What do you see?"

I ate my sandwiches, drank my sparkling hibiscus drink, and refused to take my eyes off the hole. "It was as if you were flirting with it," my mother said, "the way you smiled and all."

Finally, I squealed, "Butter fire!"

Some honey upside-down cake went flying from my mouth.

"Butter fire?" they asked me. "Butter fire?"

"Butter fire!" I yelled, pointing, reaching, waving.

They couldn't understand. There was nothing interesting about the leaves in the tree. They wondered if I'd seen a squirrel.

"Chipmunk?" they asked. "Owl?"

I shook my head fiercely. No. No. No.

"Butter fire!" I screamed so loudly that I sent hundreds of the tightly packed monarchs that my parents had mistaken for leaves exploding into the air in an eruption of lava-colored flames.

They went soaring wildly, first in a vibrating clump and then as tiny careening postage stamps, floating through the sky.

They were proud of me that day, my parents. My father for my recognition of an animal so delicate and precious, and my mother because I'd used a food word, regardless of what I'd actually meant.

As I told her the story, her eyes closed and she nodded only slightly, enough for me to recall that was something she did, had always done, since I was a child. She disappeared to me. It occurred to me that Victoria wasn't the kind of person who disappeared like that.

A little while later, I called the bookstore, wanting to talk to Blot. I had no idea what I was going to say and hoped that he'd know who it was when I said my name. I hoped he wouldn't say, *Who? Laura?*

No, Lorca, I'd have to explain.

But when they transferred me to his section, the phone just kept ringing. And ringing. And ringing. I tried only one more time and then I took it personally. He was avoiding me. Of course, I thought. I imagined my mother saying that she'd told me so—though I wasn't sure about what, exactly—and of course.

Victoria

I HAD NO IDEA how a grandmother might act. But stew seemed like a grandmotherly thing to make. So I decided we'd make *kubba* with squash. What I wouldn't make—I'd made a very serious promise to myself—was a big fuss about anything.

Lorca arrived on time on Sunday. She took off her coat, and I held out my hands for her thick brown scarf, which she had wrapped around her neck, but she didn't remove it. Instead, she stuffed her hands inside of it, popping her fingers out the top as if to keep her wrists warm. She was so endearing that way, always trying to make herself smaller, more compact.

Only then did I notice how very tired her eyes were, glassy, and as if they'd been rolled around in rose sugar.

"Are you all—" I began but Lorca's heavy nodding cut me off before I could finish. I was overwhelming her. I was doing it again.

To keep myself in check, I started talking and walking. I explained the mechanics of *kubba*. I told her more than she ever wanted to know.

"I came from a good family," I began. "Not *good* like 'nice,' but *good* in terms of status, and so we used only a bit of semolina flour around the meatball, or *kubba,* rather than stuffing a small amount of meat into a doughy dumpling."

I turned around only to make hand motions to show the dumplings. Lorca nodded and smiled slightly. Her lip caught on the side of her tooth.

"Today," I said, "we will make a *kubba humudh,* which is a tangy sort of stew and with citrus. Sweet, or *hulou, kubba* isn't my favorite."

I wanted to ask her if that was all right, but I kept walking, stopped fussing.

Lorca was following me into the kitchen, her only noise the tiny sweep of her socks against the wood floor. I was afraid to look back at her again, to see her exhausted with boredom. I'd told myself that I wouldn't ask about her mother, wouldn't ask to see her or anything of the sort. If she wanted me to see her, she would tell me. There was a reason that Lorca was the only one here.

"When I say *tangy,* I don't mean like candy," I said. "I mean we use some citrus. For *kubba humudh,* we make an oblong *kubba,* like an American football. Sweet stews incorporate baseball-shaped *kubba.*"

I wanted her to be proud of my American analogy but realized that now wasn't the time to be asking for reassurance.

"Yes," Lorca said.

"Hm?" I said and she just shook her hands in front of her face and nodded. I noticed now that it wasn't just her eyes that lacked color but her entire face.

I stopped in my tracks. We must have been quite a long time with me looking at her because finally she said to me, "I'm fine. Really."

I took a deep breath.

"You must be hungry," I said.

In the kitchen, I poured her a glass of almond milk and filled a bowl with nuts and raisins.

"Eat," I said. She sat on her stool. She ate.

I wondered if I'd done something to upset her but didn't quite know how to ask, so I kept on about the *kubba*. On and on and on, like I was recounting some stupid, nonsensical dream.

"It's not traditional," I said, "but Joseph and I like to make our *kubba* with chunks of meat as well as the dumplings, so as to flavor the stew with its own stock—" I cut myself off. Joseph and I *liked,* I said to myself. Not *like. Liked* and no more. But now was no time for fits of sadness. Lorca was here.

"Liked," I said. "Excuse me."

Lorca was holding the milk close to her mouth.

"*Kubba* can be frozen," I said. And then: "If you make them for your mother, you can freeze them."

That's when she looked up. She had a piece of walnut just above her lip. I'd said something very wrong, very inappropriate, and I knew it. I'd invaded a sacred area. Her mother was hers. I had no right.

"That's a good—" Lorca said, but I didn't let her finish.

"Never mind," I said. "I didn't mean to make you uncomfortable. Let's just focus on these *kubba* now. And the squash. You and me, *kubba* and squash."

Finally, the girl smiled. *Inshallah,* I nearly said out loud. *Inshallah!*

All the ingredients were ready. I'd done some chopping and measuring ahead of time in case Lorca had other plans. I couldn't ask her to stay with me forever.

"At our restaurant," I said, "our customers loved *kubba* with pumpkin. We served that in the autumn, but it was a little sweet for me."

"I prefer savory too," Lorca said.

I had to remind myself that we knew we were related. I didn't need to constantly look for clues to prove it anymore.

"How about this?" I asked. It was as if we were doing crafts. "I will begin, and you join whenever you're ready. Finish that milk. It's good, isn't it?"

I'd done it again.

"Yes," she said.

I put oil into a pot and as I waited for it to sizzle, I poured Lorca more milk. I uncovered the meat. I dumped it in with the onions and peppers and cayenne. I kept myself very busy. Cutting things smaller than they needed to be, washing my hands repeatedly. I didn't want her telling her mother that I was unclean, that my cooking technique was lax.

"We add beef stock instead of water," I said. "I have some prepared."

Lorca looked at me like she was about to say something. I stopped stirring. Her mouth was poised. Then she looked past me.

"Hm?" I said but as quietly as I could.

"Well," she began, but I could see her changing her mind. I didn't move. I wanted her to tell me. But then she was getting off the stool. She came and stood next to me, very close. "Let me help," she said.

"Of course," I said.

We went along, stirring, browning, adding stock, and so on. Lorca kneaded the dough and put the filling inside. She made the most perfect dumplings and I wasted no time in telling her so.

We were having a very lovely evening. There was quiet and not quiet. We danced around each other without the least bit of awkwardness, which I know for certain because when she bumped me, taking the tray of *kubba* from one side of the sink to the other, I shifted more than she had expected. I really moved, and she said "Whoops!" so sweetly and then apologized, laughing a little.

"Osteoporosis-schmosis," I said to her. "I think my end will be when I can no longer keep my feet on the ground. I'll lift off like a balloon."

"That's nice," she said. "That wouldn't be so bad."

We were happy.

She washed a bowl.

"Oh," I said. "I nearly forgot. Will you dissolve some tomato paste in water?"

She went to the pantry shelf. I turned on the sink. It sputtered and then nothing. I tried again. A dribble, if that.

"That's strange," I said.

"Let me try," Lorca said. But our luck didn't turn.

We shook the faucet. Lorca got under the sink and must have looked at the pipe. Finally, when we were all out of options and beef stock, I knew that I had no choice.

I took the broom and banged up to Dottie. I wanted to see if she had water. I knew from experience that we were on different water lines. She'd come right down. For a moment, I wondered if she'd been the one to sabotage our faucet, hoping for this very thing—that I'd call her, need her help, for anything. And then she'd stay forever, asking Lorca one thousand inappropriate questions, ruining our whole evening.

"She has nothing better to do," I said to Lorca, banging again.

I imagined Dottie upstairs with her ear to the floor, her satin-covered tush high in the air, her slippered feet curled under. She'd been waiting for this moment. I banged again.

"She's never doing anything important," I said. "She leaves the door half open, hoping that someone will stumble in."

Again. Nothing. We waited.

And then my heart sank. Not Dottie too, I thought. I imagined her open-mouthed in her chair, smelling of sleep, and worse. I imagined her freckled bosom stilled. Oh, Dottie. I realized that I'd never thought about losing her. Lorca tensed too. She understood my fear immediately.

"Want me to go up?" she asked, but she'd already turned around. My, she could move. She breezed out the door.

"Be right back," she called.

I stood with one hand on the faucet, the other cupped beneath, waiting for water that wouldn't come. The pipes made the breathy noise of lack. I saw my reflection in the window across from me. When one reaches a certain age, seeing oneself becomes an exercise in disbelief. It's like waking up from oral surgery, distorted and full, and then looking in the mirror. It takes a moment to compute that you are who you are. Maybe, I thought then, it's because of everything that isn't. My reflection was no longer an image of what was—cheekbones, lips, a husband, hope—but of what wasn't anymore. And yet, I was still here. I had to leap over a gaping mental chasm just to live.

It felt like hours before I heard Lorca upstairs, and then Dottie's voice—high and defensive as ever. She was alive. Both my arms collapsed into the sink. How much more could I take? I thought. I began fanning my heart with my hand. Joseph had died. It occurred to me that if I was ever going to be happy again, it would have to be despite that. He'd died.

The tables had turned again, Joseph. I was Dottie now, listening for more, wanting to hear exactly what she was saying to Lorca, Lorca to her. For the first time, I hoped Dottie was being Dottie. That she was being a ridiculous fool, telling Lorca some stupid story, showing her an album of prom photos from 10 BC.

I couldn't just stand here, alone, not celebrating life. I wanted to wrap my arms around Dottie, tell her that we were going to be all right now. I raced up the stairs. What they say about adrenaline is true.

Her door was only halfway open and I kicked it with my foot, ready to exclaim. Then I stopped. Dottie's face was white. It wasn't a normal white, but a very ugly white—a shallow, greenish, bloodless kind of white. Dead-bone white. The kind of white that you see only under something fluorescent, a policeman's flashlight, for example. She was sitting on her thick, woolly yellow chair smack in front of the door, watching TV with her feet up. The smell of popcorn hung heavy. She didn't move. She always moved. Her eyes flicked from me to Lorca to her lap to me. For a second, I thought Dottie was cradling a baby. She was leaning back slightly and her right shoulder rose tight to her chin. A smile was stilled on her face. But of course, it wasn't a baby. It was a sweater—Joseph's sweater. One that I had left out on the street. One that she'd folded. One that she'd apparently stolen. She was holding it dearly, as though it had just fallen off to sleep. She sat there for just a second longer, and I wondered if maybe she'd gone blind or deaf.

"That's Joseph's sweater," Lorca whispered, not looking at me. A granddaughter, I thought, protecting her kin. A sudden feeling of pride slipped into my confusion.

"What are you doing?" I shouted at Dottie, grabbing the sweater as if I were taking it from a naughty child. Nervous laughter slipped out of me. I was embarrassed. Lorca wouldn't understand what kind of woman Dottie was, that her cradling a man's sweater—Joseph's, no less—like it was a living, breathing being was just Dottie. She was needy and lonely and ridiculous. She did things like this. She was half senile, for crying out loud, older than a dinosaur's great-aunt. She'd probably pretended the sweater belonged to some sailor who'd died years ago at sea while missing her desperately. But Lorca didn't know that. And Dottie didn't say anything. She just sat there, not defending herself.

Lorca hadn't lifted her eyes from the floor. I could tell she was growing more disappointed in me by the second. I couldn't find vanilla in my own kitchen. I couldn't use the faucet properly. I sent her into the apartments of kooky old bats. But that wasn't it. I realized that Dottie didn't look so stupid. She looked like a person who'd just lost her friend, who was heartbroken, who was mourning. And me: I looked cruel, unloving, unsentimental, prancing around the kitchen just after my husband's death. Lorca's grandfather's death. *Thanks a lot, Dottie,* I wanted to say. I didn't.

"This is normal behavior for Dottie," I began to explain into the chaos of quietness. "Joseph was very kind to her."

Lorca nodded without moving.

The longer I stood there, the more enraged I became with Dottie. What did she think she was doing, embarrassing me like this? And keeping mum? When had she ever been mum in her entire life? I wanted to shock her out of it. I wanted to be so much better than her. So much better than her stale apartment with the peeling wallpaper, the bleached-out velvet couch, the color of decay. She'd embarrassed me. She'd made me into a fool. But I had something she didn't, couldn't ever have.

"Dottie, this is Lorca," I said suddenly, full of meaning. "This is my granddaughter."

It's not what I'd meant to say. My voice quivered, failed at the end into breath.

Lorca looked at me. Dottie looked at me. They had the very same expression on their faces, like it was something about my identity I was revealing, not Lorca's.

"Wait, I—" Lorca began. Dottie interrupted. I wanted to know what Lorca was going to say, but Dottie had taken over.

"Sweetheart," Dottie said to me slowly, carefully. "She couldn't be. You know that." She was talking to me as if I were the child.

"Wait, I—" Lorca began again, but I cut her off.

"Why, Dottie?" I snapped. Dottie knew nothing. "You have no idea about this," I said.

"Your baby was born still," she said as if trying to piece it together herself. "A stillborn baby."

Lorca covered her mouth. *Wait* is what I think she said but it could have been *what*. I couldn't be sure.

"Oh, Dottie," I said. "Shut up. Stop this." I shook my hand at her, waving her off. "You didn't know us then. You didn't know anything about us. And you still don't."

Dottie shook her head fiercely, fighting emotion.

"Wait," I said. Her words were starting to sink in. "What did you say?"

"Joseph told me," she said. "He never wanted to hurt you. He knew how much you'd been through already. But I thought you knew. I always thought that a mother must know."

"A mother does know!" I said. "And you don't. You're just a neighbor. The nosiest neighbor in the world. Joseph was only nice to you because he felt bad for you, because you were so lonely. You don't know anything about our child."

"I do," she whispered. "He told me."

The world went wispy, pale.

"You," I said slowly. It snapped into focus. "He told you. You and Joseph. You knew Joseph. You took him. You."

"Me," Dottie whispered, head down.

The word fell flat, like chewed-up gum, and stuck to the floor. The end. I'd thought that my relationship with Joseph could have no more bumps, no more sharp turns. Joseph had lived two lives, but when he died they converged into one. And I wouldn't know the half of it. The secret had been so valuable, so enormous when he'd been alive but was now just that little word—*me*—barely audible. His life had been closed with a click. *Click.*

"Please," Dottie said. "I'm sorry. It wasn't what you think. It was nothing. Just a couple of moments. And after the baby, he couldn't. Everything ended."

"Stop," I yelled, but it emerged like a growl from the low, dingy place where hunger lives. "I can't."

For just a moment, I didn't believe her. She made things up. She had to, for attention. She was a sad sack. And yet, the earnestness with which she was looking at me was something I'd never seen before. *Of all the everything ever,* I thought to myself, *this she means to say. She knows this.* She knew Joseph before she knew me. They had a world apart. A world unto themselves. They were them.

As the moments went on, the truth continued to braid itself together, one section at a time. Joseph told her. Her. She. Dottie. The sweater. The note. It was her handwriting. I should have known, though I hadn't seen it for years. Nobody makes loops like that but Dottie and teenagers. It was her loop, her note. He was her Joseph. The note had nothing to do with our daughter. I should have known that too. Joseph, if he'd ever met our child, wouldn't have been able to contain himself. Why hadn't I thought of that sooner? He was a good man. He would have kept only the bad stuff from me. He was like that. Still, I could no longer say that if I knew one thing, I knew my husband.

And our daughter was dead. I hadn't known that either. Damn Joseph for never telling me, but that wasn't all. I was the worst mother in the world. To not know. To not have any sense at all that she was gone. It had never even crossed my mind. I'd never felt it in my gut.

My hands were shaking. My back was sweating. I was freezing. I was broiling. My stomach made a horrible, wailing noise, the sound of death in the walls. I wanted to lie down on the floor and catch my breath. But the sadness would have to wait. All I could muster was anger.

"I can't," I said. "I can't. I can't." The phrase fell like sneezes.

"Can't what, doll?" Dottie said, and she began to get up but I stopped her, looked her right in the face.

"It smells horrible in here," I said. "It's making me sick."

The first thing I felt was not sadness, not even anger, but jealousy—not because of the affair but because of the closeness. Dottie, it occurred to me now, *had* been more reverent than me. She'd kept something of his because she'd cared for him, loved him. I was horrendous, paralyzed by affection, disgusted by grief. I had thrown him away.

All these years, I'd thought Dottie had been the dense one, acting like a fool, being made fun of from all sides. The words *subtle* and *Dottie* belonged in different universes. And yet, she'd been a master of discretion, which somehow made sense too. Every person knows how to whisper. She was smart enough to get attention—why did it never occur to me that she'd be smart enough to sustain it too? I wanted to know what covert name they'd called me. And, worse still, what they had called each other.

Loneliness. Their affair meant that both of them were total strangers—except to each other. I imagined secrets as silent illuminators, visible only to those who knew. When they saw each other, they saw the truth spark around them like fireflies. They glimpsed all the things that mattered. And I knew nothing. That night the photo was taken at the restaurant, I wondered, had she been outside too? Had she been hiding somewhere with her shoes off, the back of her hand against her mouth? Had she watched us from behind as we walked home? Had she hoped that he wouldn't reach for my fingers? He reached first. He always reached first. Maybe she knew that as well—and she scoffed at the particular kind of thrill that it gave me. I wondered if he scoffed too.

Maybe when I'd looked at him, I thought now, for years and years and years and years and years, all the things I saw were the unimportant, gray things: on the outside, a mere veil of skin, human hair and bones and teeth. And it was on the inside that he was a blushing, rocking, stained-glass thing, full and delicate as a peony, strong and vital as a lighthouse—and all that was them. It gave them joy, sustained them, matured and nurtured them. He was her secret light. She was his. I knew merely the casing of him, and never even knew to peel the damn thing off.

I had no idea where their love began, where it ended. It was resignation I felt as it occurred to me that the details made absolutely no difference. What was was. Joseph was and was no more. It would do no good to fight about what he'd done, discuss it, move on. We couldn't even try now.

"Come on, Lorca," I said, wanting to get her downstairs, to explain. I wouldn't put all my stock in Dottie yet. But Lorca wouldn't look at me. She knew something too. Somehow we were no longer in this together. That much I understood.

"I'm so sorry," Lorca said. "Victoria, I meant to tell you before. I believed we were too. But we can't be. I just found out that my mother's parents died. I just found out too."

"All right," I breathed.

I began to back myself out of Dottie's apartment. I couldn't look at Lorca. She was completely different to me now. If I'd recognized her from somewhere, it must have been from the bus stop. Or from the neighborhood. Or maybe she'd been one of those schoolgirls I'd been particularly appalled by, one who'd made a scene, flirting, carrying on, outside our bank. I wanted to like her, but what was left? Why should I? We were nothing. She had kept me in the dark. I was a fool. And I couldn't take care of her, whatever she needed, whatever she needed me for, whatever reason she had come to find me. I didn't understand it. Didn't care to. Not now.

"Would you like to sit?" Lorca asked and I shook my head. I was at the door. I just had to make it downstairs, but my legs had begun to shake. It felt as though I'd been swimming for days and days.

"How about some water?" Lorca said. She disappeared into Dottie's kitchen. I needed to rest.

I don't know how long we existed there, Dottie and I, saying nothing, but the room full of our static. Thoughts ran through my head faster than they had in years but felt distant—it was like being on a plane: the actual speed at which the aircraft moved had nothing to do with the woozy pace of things inside the cabin.

Dottie started fidgeting with her hair, her clothes. She pretended to see something important under her fingernails, which were painted pink. Her robe was flag-colored silk. She had lipstick on her teeth. *Cosmopolitan* was on her coffee table. *See,* I wanted to say to Joseph, *she never could have survived in Baghdad.* And yet, she'd survived the loss of the man she loved. We both had. And that, it pained me to admit, was far more difficult.

"He didn't want to hurt you," she said. And then: "Please believe me that neither did I."

I didn't care if I fell down the stairs. I left.

Soon, Lorca came down and collected her things. I didn't even get up from my chair to say goodbye to her. I couldn't bear to look her in the face. As lovely as she'd been, she was no one to me now. I'd put all my eggs in her basket. For a moment, I was sorry for her—that she too was so very, very lost—but then it struck me that it wasn't my job to find her. She had her own mother, her own dead grandparents, and I had no idea of their story. There was nothing left for us. She'd be another girl on the bus. All girls from now on would be just girls on the bus.

"Wait," I said, just before she walked out the door. "I think you dropped that the other day." I pointed to the photo of my not-daughter, which I'd tucked behind a throw pillow.

"Oh," she said, putting it in her pocket without examining it. She was waiting for me to say something else. When I didn't, she said, "Thank you. I didn't mean to leave that here for you to find. I didn't even know I'd dropped it."

It only half broke my heart.

"I just found out too," she said.

I put up my hand for her to stop.

Three hours, two glasses of Shiraz, and one very emotional shower later, there was a knock on the door.

"I'm not coming," I shouted from the couch. The knocking stopped.

Only when I heard her clanking back up the stairs did I manage to get up. I looked through the peephole first. There was no one there. I opened. The air was cold and still, and smelled like burned butter. I looked down. On the floor, folded like a flag on a soldier's grave: Joseph's sweater.

Tears poured out like paint when I leaned down to pick it up.

I put it on the couch in his study. I rolled it lengthwise, then folded it in half, tucked the fold into the crook of my arm. I sat down. I sniffed it. It did not smell of Dottie. It was my turn. I cradled it. I waited for emotion to flood in. I waited for a while.

I'd never imagined I'd be left with so many questions, so many answers to questions I hadn't asked.

It was too late to feel excused for my faults, if that's what I'd wanted. And the truth was that even when Joseph was alive, it was too late. I'd posed the challenge to him silently, constantly: Love me, despite. Despite my heart of mud, love me. Despite my distrust of New York, love me. Despite my anxiety, love me. Despite my anger. Despite my fear of losing you, love me. Despite what I do not say. Despite what I would not give you, what I wouldn't do for you, what I stole from you, love me. Despite the way it was so easy for me to give to everything else, nothing to you, because nothing else mattered like you did until the end when I was so sure of you. You couldn't get out of bed, my love.

Love me despite all that. Despite who I was, who I am, love me, Joseph. Let me see you try. Because if you love me hard enough, strong enough, I might just believe that you've forgiven me for who I am, the hideous, selfish thing I am. But the truth is, you did that years ago. You found Dottie and did what you had to do so you could love me. Does this mean I can forgive myself? I just want to catch up.

Still, no decision is entire of itself. Swindling my husband of his greatest joy was only one part of it. There we were every day, waking up, going to sleep. I was who I was and I was what I'd done, with every living breath, no reprieve. That was the intolerable part. You are the decisions you make. You die with them. And the person you love the most is testament to that.

But now.

Of course, I thought. *Of course.* I asked him to let go of a child, but in order not to let go of me too, he needed something. He needed support from somewhere. I'd never been a sympathetic listener. I ended hugs too soon. I never liked to be picked up. I'm not sure I allowed myself to be lifted, ever. Not ever. Joseph—he'd been the opposite of that. He found love in the oddest places. And if he had to find love, at least he'd found love with someone who needed it. He was always giving people what they needed.

And he'd done all that for me. He'd let me live with my decision, had saved me from the truth and more pain, the burden of trying to make sense of something that could never make sense, that I could only be sorry for. He didn't punish me for it. He lived with it too. He loved me, despite me—which, actually, when you think about it, means because of me.

Joseph

New York, 1968

It had been exactly ten years since they'd opened the restaurant. An important occasion, Joseph thought. Something to be proud of. Something to celebrate. Joseph planned a big night. He wanted to get things back on track. Ever since that day at the hospital, Joseph had expected a big shift. Victoria and Joseph. Joseph and Victoria. A pair. A couple. Two birds on a branch. He'd hoped for her to need him. Really need him. And she had, for a short time. But a few years later, they opened the restaurant. And it offered Victoria all the feelings that Joseph had wanted to give her: confidence, focus, happiness. All that he had wanted was funneled away from him and right into the restaurant. It made her giddy. It became everything; everything around them and everything between them. When they slept, he reached for her. She smelled of kitchen, of the burned bits dumped in the trash. She slept soundly, sealed in, heavy as tar. They'd married at City Hall and never made time for a honeymoon. Still, his father always said, "Life without a wife is like a kitchen without a knife." And in many ways, it was true. Marriage had given Joseph confidence in Victoria—that he wouldn't lose her and he wouldn't lose himself, again.

• • •

"Remember what tonight is," he said to her in the morning as he spit toothpaste into the sink and reached for a towel.

She put her hands to her face.

"Oh no!" she said. "The restaurant is reserved for a private party. The Turk's birthday! I completely forgot about the anniversary. Another night, we'll celebrate it. We'll just do it another night. I promise."

She went down to her hands and knees to look for a missing shoe. She kept huffing but it had nothing to do with what Joseph had just said. She was just trying to get dressed. Nothing else seemed to matter.

That night at the restaurant, she was a firefly, bustling and twinkling and flitting around. Joseph felt he had never seen her so light. So carefree. He sat at the bar and watched her, proud but abandoned. He had a drink. He had three.

An hour or so later a woman walked in. Her mouth was unmistakable. It was the shape of a heart. He clutched his chest. For a second, he was sure he'd stopped breathing. He had thought he'd never see her again. He'd counted on that. Mostly, he'd hoped.

It had been nearly fifteen years, but he would have recognized her anywhere. Seeing her now, he noticed how bland she was, an untoasted hamburger bun. American women no longer thrilled him, or even made him pause. That he recognized her, he thought, was more a reflection of him than her. He'd obsessed over the affair for the years that he and Victoria had been deeply happy, hated himself for what he'd done. In the more tenuous years, he hated himself too, but not for the normal reasons. Not because of his actions, exactly, but because of what they stood for. Victoria had deprived him of such joy, and by getting back at her, he'd deprived himself of his upper hand, of his righteousness, and, most important, of the opportunity to hold against her what she'd done to him. They were even, he thought, for all practical purposes. And, for a while, that changed everything. He'd never gone back to Dr. Espy's. Or met Dottie on a street corner. Or for drinks. He'd never called. Never seen her. Partly because he hadn't wanted to, exactly, but mostly because he'd been determined to regain Victoria's love and maintain the even playing field. He didn't consider himself a saint.

Now Joseph stood up. He held on to the bar. He started to make his way to the bathroom, sure that she hadn't yet seen him. He could hide. Just then, Victoria called, "Dottie! Welcome!"

He stopped. He tried to sit back down but nearly fell off the stool.

"Holy shit," he whispered. "Holy shit shit."

Victoria hurried over to Dottie, all generosity and charm. She wrapped one arm around her and guided her from the entrance to Joseph. He swallowed hard. For a moment, he wondered if this was some sort of trap.

"This is Dottie," Victoria said, stopping in front of him and pulling out a stool. "She's our new neighbor."

"Our what?" Joseph said.

"At the apartment," Victoria said. "She moved in upstairs."

Dottie's face was getting redder by the moment, and yet her mouth was wholly still. It was stunned into a rectangle, no longer a pretty heart. Her chin quivered.

"Pleasure," Joseph said and went to kiss her on both cheeks, be normal, but she stepped back. He was left hovering.

"This is Joseph," Victoria said, not missing a beat as she took Dottie's coat. She gave Joseph a look like *Don't mess with the customers.*

"Please, Dottie," she said. "Have a seat, a drink."

Dottie sat down. Joseph couldn't. He imagined he could hear the exhales, from the two of them, slam into each other, unmeshing, unalike.

Holy shit, he said again, but this time only in his head.

"My word," Dottie said, finally. She took a deep breath and looked past him. "This restaurant is simply beautiful."

Victoria clapped her hands and turned around. "I have to get back to work," she said. "Joseph will entertain you for a while. It's a pleasure to have you as our guest."

Dottie laughed to herself. It broke the makeup on her cheek.

Joseph was still attempting to reassemble himself onto his stool. He kept moving it back and forth, somehow unable to find solid ground.

"Holy shit," he said finally, and kept standing.

He rubbed his eyes. The hysterical pulse in his throat was making it hard for him to focus. He touched his chest, to be sure of himself.

"Breathe," he said out loud. In, out. Out, in.

Dottie wouldn't look him in the face. She was making a production of noticing features of the room and nodding at them in approval. A painting, the gold-colored molding, the many glasses stacked into a pyramid behind the bar. Joseph nearly asked her if she'd become interested in interior design. He had the unfamiliar urge to be cruel.

Finally, after many moments of aching silence, Joseph forced the words from his throat.

"How did you find me?" he asked.

She looked like she'd been smacked.

"Find you?" she said and then lowered her voice. "You said you lived on MacDougal Street. I didn't know you moved. This is as much of a shock to me as it is to you. You're despicable."

It was obvious she didn't mean it. Tears mobbed her eyes. And it was because of that, the fact that she seemed as horrified as he did, that Joseph believed her when she said that she'd just moved in. She'd had no idea he lived beneath her. She'd gotten a deal on old Mr. Pinalta's apartment. His walls were streaked with cigarette smoke. A suitcase full of Mexican dresses had been left in his closet.

Joseph went silent. He found himself counting the seconds. With each, he imagined a raindrop pinning him between the eyes. Ping. Ping. Ping. Ping.

"I'll move out," she said. "I'd be happy to. Believe me. I've hardly unpacked."

He almost said yes but then Victoria caught his eye. She was presenting a whole snapper to a table of German tourists. There were lemon slices all around the fish, and they didn't budge, nothing did, in her careful, capable hands. She put it down, full of grace, slipped her hand from beneath, rested it on a customer's shoulder. The customer looked at her, all trust. She pointed to the best piece and he nodded.

Joseph touched his own shoulder. He had missed Victoria. Now he remembered those times he'd lain with Dottie, years ago, and how sometimes he'd missed Victoria to the point of tears. He'd seen her just hours before, but still, lying there, he found himself missing her woman smell, like something fresh from the ground, and the odd shininess of her fingers, delicate, like a just-watered plant. Sometimes, he didn't miss her until later, when he was with her at their apartment on MacDougal Street. Really, that was when he missed her the most.

He felt sick.

Dottie kicked Joseph lightly in his shin.

"Well?" she said. And then, angrily, "Pearls before swine."

"Move?" Joseph said. "No. Of course not."

"It isn't so bad," Dottie said, clearly relieved. "Just pretend I don't live there. Pretend we never met. Pretend we were never anything."

Joseph closed his eyes and tried to imagine it, the life of pretending. Instead, he couldn't help wondering what he'd have to do to make her, his Victoria, touch his shoulder. Reach out to her, hold her hand there until she stopped trying to budge.

Sometimes, even now that things were better, great even, he felt it would be like suffocating a fish.

Soon, Dottie was drinking whiskey sours. She had opened up. Her sass was entirely restored. Victoria was immune to it, Joseph noticed. She was the opposite of sass. Sass didn't agree with her, which might have been why, after his sixth gin cocktail, Joseph put his finger on Dottie's pinkie fingernail. It was painted a light tan color and was a perfect oval. It reminded him of something on a poster, the sheen and shape of it. And smooth, it was smooth. It didn't move. It didn't even flinch. But he did. His whole being flinched. After a moment, he took his finger back. Away.

Lorca

I'D FELT HOPEFUL. Then I'd felt like I'd had the wind knocked out of me. And then the wind knocked out of me again.

I'd believed that I might actually be Victoria's granddaughter. And she thought that too; she believed it too. I wasn't being ridiculous. Not by myself, anyway. And I let her, even after my mother told me about her real parents, because I didn't want to be disowned. Not so quickly. I wanted Victoria to be mine. I wanted to be Victoria's. But then, of course, she wasn't. I wasn't either. And not only that, but she wanted nothing to do with me. I reminded her of something that wasn't, I guess, of something that never was. I didn't want to cause her pain. Her face, when Dottie told her about her baby, stillborn, had turned a color I'd never seen before. White with red on top. Not pink, but like a foot in the snow, nothing blending, nothing right.

After that, she couldn't look me in the eye. *Please,* I'd said in my head but I couldn't put it into real words.

That night, after I left Victoria's, it started snowing. I tried to just stay in bed and keep my sheets warm, except there was an expectant feeling in my chest that refused to quit, and so I peeled the skin off my elbows. I burned my tongue with a match. I pulled out some hair. Usually, that little white stamp of scalp would fill up what was lost. But now after I did it, I still felt all wrong. I still felt responsible. It occurred to me that it had nothing to do with loss. My whole life, I'd been trying to fill an empty space, to feel full, complete—but I could only ever feel less empty. And even then, only for a moment—because, though the pain filled the emptiness, it *was* the emptiness too. It was where all good things got stuck.

I took the surgical tweezers to my gums. Images of Blot broke in only briefly. Then I thought of how he was avoiding me and how I would be a disappointment to him too. He'd think I'd failed. Or worse, he'd think I'd made the whole thing up for attention, for his attention. And I had nothing to show for myself. There was nothing else to look forward to. I imagined going to the bookstore and telling him, and that once he knew I'd failed, if he didn't vanish immediately or say something awful right off the bat, I wouldn't be able to muster any enthusiasm, wouldn't be able to say anything nice—and he would realize he was tired of me. Soon, just to have something to talk about, he'd point to my bloody gums, and he wouldn't be kind about it. He must be fed up. And it made me so angry, just thinking of him like that. And the anger told me to go ahead, go hurt. Blot could never understand, I told myself. He wouldn't understand me. So what was the point?

That Sunday night, my mother came home late. She sat down on my bed, where I'd been pretending to sleep. Snow twinkled on her hair and eyebrows. She took off her gloves and balled them in her lap.

"Tomorrow evening I talk with the dean at the boarding school," she said out of nowhere. "I just have to give him the okay. He's holding your spot. I'm going to do what they suggest, Lorca. What else can I do?"

It didn't surprise me that someone was holding a spot. He was doing a favor for my mother. Another favor for my mother.

I pulled down my sleeves over my wrists. I tucked my feet into my pajama pants. I had a cut below my chin and I sat halfway up, just to get it out of the light. It wasn't that I'd forgotten about boarding school; I hadn't. Everything had felt very slow lately.

I didn't want to be sent away and yet, when I watched my mother now, I didn't miss her, wasn't waiting for her to face me, take me in. My whole life, I'd wandered the earth looking for her, roaming between the trees like a lost cat—even when she was right next to me. But something was different.

Still, if I wanted to stay, I had no choice. This was my only option. I took a deep breath.

"Will you be home for lunch?" I asked her, praying that there was still hope in the masgouf. That even if I couldn't bring her family to her, perfect and proud, or my father, perfect and strong, there could still be magic in the masgouf. I could bring her magic. I could remind her how family felt when it was what you were looking for, even when it wasn't your own.

The good news was that she looked more surprised than disappointed. She shrugged. She said she guessed so.

The next morning, the snow hadn't let up. I raced around getting the ingredients on the recipe Victoria had given me. I started making the dough for the Iraqi pita, which Violet on YouTube said would need two hours to rise. I used whole-wheat flour, though I'd never seen my mother touch anything but all-purpose or cake; I wasn't taking any chances. I'd do it right. I went to three different bodegas before I finally found mangoes for pickling. They were small and as hard as rocks, but I'd try leaving them in a paper bag with a dozen apples to hurry up the ripening. If that didn't work, I'd read something about microwaving them until they were soft, but I was a little worried about ending up with mango mousse. I bought Meyer lemons, thinking the sweetness could be nice, but as soon as I got home, I thought of my mother, her mouth shrinking into a knot: *You used Meyer lemons?* Like she'd never understand why I did the things I did. I went back out, got snowed on again, bought real lemons on the corner, and then went home and pickled them with ginger, paprika, garlic, and salt. I hoped they'd taste like they'd been marinating for months but I was starting to have a bad feeling. Things weren't exactly working out.

I cut myself twice, accidentally, trying to use the mandoline to slice the onions "as thin as a breath." I made a bed of them that looked like a lattice. I sprinkled thyme on top. The whole thing looked like the side of a house in Scotland where roses grew like weeds. I hoped my mother liked Scotland, but I'd never asked her. I minced garlic until my hand was shaking.

When I'd cut things with Victoria, I realized then, I hadn't thought about the cutting exactly. I'd been normal, relaxed, for a little while. Distraction can give you a new life. But it was different now. I felt like I was back to where I'd started. My hands were trembling, itching for the soft pet of the knife. Twice I went into the bathroom just to take a few deep breaths, avoid myself.

It occurred to me that I'd never paid Victoria for the lessons I'd been to; I wondered if I should call her. I could drop off an envelope, but that didn't seem appropriate. Would I ever ever ever see her again?

I set and reset the table. I ironed the tablecloth and napkins. I made napkin rings out of old covers of *Food & Wine*. I pretty much taught myself origami by noon. I put white votives on beds of kosher salt in Mason jars and tied sprigs of rosemary to the outsides with cooking twine. I wrote our names—mine and my mother's—on little cards that I'd cut into the shape of fish but that looked more like balloons than fish because I'd forgotten the fins. I redid them, though, until they couldn't be anything other than fish.

My mother was walking around the house, not grumpy but unsure of what to do with herself. She kept peering over my shoulder and then walking away like she didn't really care. She was barefoot, and the floor didn't creak beneath her. If she'd asked, I would have told her that she couldn't help. But she didn't ask. She just kept shrugging and saying, "Interesting." She wanted to see what I was capable of too.

When she saw the votives, she picked them up, turned them around, and gave a smirk. "Thank you," I said and she laughed. It was the best when she knew how tough she could be.

Finally, she plopped down on the couch and stared at me.

"Yes?" I said, not being unpolite.

"What?" she said. "I'm not allowed to watch my daughter being lovely?"

I looked up. "Me?" I said, choking on my own spit. This was too much.

"You know what I love about you?" she said. I didn't, but she wasn't waiting for an answer. She reached above her head in a lion stretch and yawned. She rubbed her eyes and crossed her lady feet.

I was waiting.

"You're a fighter," she said. "My little fighter."

I'd always wanted to believe I was strong. *More,* I thought. *Tell me more.*

"So determined to make me happy," she said.

I looked right at her, wondering if maybe she was joking. She was examining her toes: point and flex and point and so on. A few weeks ago, I wouldn't have been disappointed. Something collapsed inside of me now like a flower tricked by the light.

"That's what I fight for?" I asked. "Is that what you mean?"

She closed her eyes. She made her hands into fists.

"Impossible," she said. "I can't say a single nice thing."

She went into Lou's room and closed the door.

"Thank you," I whispered, relieved. For a moment, with the door closed, it was just that: a closed door. It wasn't as if she'd reinvented this room by going into another. It wasn't as if she'd abandoned me again, like always, with yet another chunk of the universe to make sense of in her wake.

I was a fighter, I thought. But not in the way she meant.

I butterflied four English cucumbers before I even touched the fish, just to get the hang of it, like I had with Victoria. Smooth, smooth. It had to be smooth. I was nervous, not at all confident in myself, though I'd read about it, practiced, and watched a video clip that made the whole thing look like a cinch. I got out the fish.

One.

Two.

Three.

"Lorca!" my mother shouted, and the knife skidded straight into my hand. She came out of nowhere. The door had been closed. She'd been quiet in Lou's room. I dropped the knife. I couldn't believe my eyes. It hurt. It hurt.

"Ouch," I said. The blood sprang like a sudden rose bloom in my palm. If I held it open, it made the most perfect circle you've ever seen.

"Lorca!" she screamed. "Don't do that."

"What?" I said. I hadn't *done* it. She had. She'd scared me, appearing out of nowhere like she did. The blood was coming faster now, and I leaned against the counter. My ears rang like tin bells.

"I didn't," I said, but my voice was weak. "I didn't do it on purpose."

She came over to me.

"You did," she said. "I just saw you. I can't believe you."

She opened the drawer, took out a dishtowel, and passed it to me. I wrapped it around my hand as tightly as I could. The red burst through instantly. I watched her, waited for something motherly, neighborly even. I hadn't done it on purpose. I hadn't.

"Yuck," she said. "But I've seen worse."

She tossed the knife into the sink. Blood and skin stuck to the tip like wings. She took another knife from the block and finished butterflying the fish in one perfect stroke.

"You'll be fine in a minute," she said. And then, her hands gliding as if she were playing the violin: "Like this. You do it in a single clean move or you don't do it at all. Don't butcher the thing."

"What if I won't be fine?" I asked her, meaning it. "What if I won't be fine?" Ever. Again.

"Don't be dramatic," she said. "You're not dying. It's a little nothing."

Maybe the most amazing part about my mother was how tidy her thoughts were, so much like a perfect recipe that would suffer from even the slightest excess of salt. Years ago, she had decided not to indulge me, and she hadn't. Not for a second. To give in, she'd decided, would ruin everything. Except that it wouldn't have been indulging, I realized. And the masgouf, of course, was hopeless. The recipe was something she created for herself in order to survive. A place where happiness lived and died, and against which everything else paled in comparison, which was why even she, with her most discerning taste buds in the world, could never replicate it. And much less could I. I hated myself for even trying.

When she was done filleting, she poured herself a vodka, removed a seed from one of my lemon rounds, and dropped it into her glass.

"Thanks," she said. And then, like we were making plans for later, "Now do you understand why I have to send you away?"

"I'm not fine and won't be," I said to her. "And sending me away won't fix that."

"You have two legs," she said. "Two arms, two eyes, two ears. Everything works. What's the issue?"

"What if I'm just not okay?" I asked her. "I'm not."

"Then it's your problem," she said, pointing to my head. "You get in your own way."

I closed my eyes. Words bounced off her like rubber balls. They kept hitting me in the gut. She stood so tall, like an emperor, and her words were so deliberate that I wondered if she'd known all along what I was going to say. If she'd been planning this discussion for years.

"I've lost my appetite," she said. "Let's rain-check."

"Right," I said.

I was too dizzy to fight her on it and I wouldn't have anyway. My body was heavy, like wet cardboard.

She went into Lou's room. She closed the door, like she'd always done in one way or another. Or another. And me, I stood there, the towel getting thicker and redder around my hand, like a small carcass, my pulse swinging like a pendulum against my palm.

Later, in my room, I took out the photo of my mother. I hadn't ever looked at it. It had been in my hat, at Victoria's, and here again. It said something, I thought, that it hadn't been priority number one. And yet here I was, holding the photo close to my face.

She was a cold war, my mother. It occurred to me that I didn't know that kind of self-sufficient feeling that she had and the slipperiness that grew around her because of it. She daunted. I was daunted. She asked to be challenged. I asked to be forgiven. Her chest dashed forward with pride. Mine sidestepped. Sorry. She would never have sat here like this, I thought, feeling sorry for herself.

But then I looked more closely. I rotated the photo again and again. I squinted and moved to find a patch of light. What I'd thought were her fingers fanned in front of her mouth was actually two fingers and a cigarette, lit and long and drooping with ash. Her bottom lip curled down. She was maybe eleven years old.

I choked on my own breath.

At first, they looked like smudges, maybe, plays of the lens, shadows of clouds, even dust perhaps, the marks up and down the inside of my mother's left arm. The photo was old, I told myself. Not everyone was like me.

But she was.

Seven perfect burns marked my mother's little-girl skin. They were round like buttons, dark and furious like tornadoes under the skin. Four on her upper arm, three on her lower, at equal distances apart. At first I wondered if someone had done that to her, but that would have been a source of pride for my mother, something she'd wear like a badge of honor—a testament to all she'd been through. I would have heard about it, I thought, if the story had gone that way.

But it hadn't. It was clear from how she held her arm with the cigarette that she was hiding something, hiding the inside of it, as she had it folded into herself like a broken wing across her chest. And the other arm, the giveaway, was in motion. You could see from the cocked intention of her wrist. She was about to move it, turn it around, hide. About to. She hadn't been fast enough. She hadn't meant to be caught. Someone like me could identify something like that easily.

My mother was like me. There'd never been an inkling of it as far as I could remember. But it made terrible, perfect sense.

And for once, instead of worrying about her, I was filled with rage. All the things she could have said, all the ways she could have comforted me, had bored an enormous hole in my life, just waiting to be filled. It was a parent's job, I thought, to give. Again and again and again until a child had grown-up hands and muscles. A grown-up heart. Even Victoria, I thought, who'd planned to give her child up, tried to give something, tried to give her child a better life. Even my mother's real mother knew how to give. Now I hoped for a second that my mother would find me here, seeing her like that in the photo—and for once she did what I wanted.

"What are you doing?" she whispered.

Then: "Lorca, what the hell are you doing?" she shouted. She grabbed the photo out of my hands. She had spit on her lips. A vein in the center of her forehead quivered like a branch in a storm.

"Where did you find this?" She was shaking it at me.

I just looked at her. I looked at her. And I looked at her. And I looked at her while she said nothing. There was everything to say.

I imagined the blood coming out of my mother like it came out of the polar bears, the horses. I imagined what she was like weakened. If her chest would ever deflate. I didn't want to hurt her.

And yet, I went over to my bed. I knew what I was doing. I felt like I was watching myself in a dream having nothing and everything to do with myself. I took a lighter out of my pillowcase. I knew just where it was, between the zipper and the seam. It was clear purple and full of fluid; like a plastic liver, I thought. I sat down. I lit it. I held it up in front of me and saw my mother next to it. When it flickered, it cast her out. In one swift maneuver, I stuck it to the inside of my arm. It licked me like a dog.

Soon, I lifted the lighter and moved it, an inch closer to my elbow. I did it again. It felt like being pulled under by hungry waves. I did it again.

My mother staggered back.

I tried to keep watching her but could keep my eyes open for only a second before the pressure closed them. Still, in that second when I couldn't see her, I saw her. It was as if she'd been struck from behind. Her neck was pushed a little bit forward, her face a little lifted, like she was about to cry out. And yet she didn't. Her mouth was open in the tiniest *o*. If she'd let her voice burst, it would have made the sound of something huge crashing into an unfilled pool. Something unfamiliar, a little bit absurd.

But the thing was, there was dead silence. She should have screamed. She should have held me. She should have told me that everything would be all right. She should have raced for an ice cube. She should have cursed herself. She should have shared the story of why my name was Lorca, and that it was a beautiful name for someone like me. She should have. She should have. She should have. She should have. And yet, as I should have known by now, her doing any of that would have been the most unlikely, most alarming thing that could have happened. She never ever would.

She covered her face. "I see you," she whispered. "Okay? Enough now."

"Enough?" I said.

"I won't stand here and watch you," she said. "I won't condone this kind of thing. So just stop. I don't know what you want me to do."

She reached for the doorknob and left, closing the door behind her silently, like she'd just put a child to sleep.

"Anything," I said and the word ricocheted off the door.

I stayed in my room for hours. She didn't come back in. I

heard her turn on the TV, turn it off, put on her coat, drop her keys, and then pick them up. Go.

After that, I really couldn't stop.

It's impossible to know when enough is enough until it's too much.

Victoria

WHAT HAPPENED NEXT was that I felt feverishly sorry for myself—and it didn't end there. With every moment, I felt more entitled to feel sorry for myself, and so I did, until I couldn't remember what I'd felt sorry about, and then it started all over again. I did dramatic things like huff and shake my head, cry out. I tossed and turned in bed and shoved my face into a pillow, sitting up only when I was left gasping for air. I listened to sad songs on the radio and wept until something cheerful came on and I felt embarrassed and inappropriate. I ordered in, didn't wash dishes or change my socks. I had Joseph's ashes delivered—they came in a giant cardboard box surrounded by lots of bubble wrap—and had the man put them into Joseph's closet directly. I tipped him generously, as though it were hush money for my strange behavior. I locked the door so Dottie couldn't even attempt to pop in. I did not think of Dottie and Joseph as a couple. I did not. I did not. I did not think of all the lies that grew between Joseph and myself, like mold under a house. I watched the snow from the kitchen window. I rested my head on the glass. Every once in a while, I thought of how dismissive I'd been to Lorca, how I might never see her again because of it. But rather than punish myself or—God forbid—actually do something about it, I felt sorrier still.

If I really wanted to reach the bottom of my sadness, I'd remind myself that all this was entirely moot. I could cry myself to death and no one would stop me. I could lie down and kick and scream until I hit my head on the radiator and knocked myself out. Out and out. It could have been Lorca who held my hand at the end, but now it wouldn't be. Not ever. To make it even worse, I'd never been one to believe in the kind of loving that led to losing. Why had I tricked myself? I would have rather, if I'd had all my wits about me, kept my expectations to a minimum.

Days later, my buzzer rang. I hoped it was Lorca being braver than me. I gathered my bones and raced to the door. I buzzed her in. I would apologize first. There was no question about that. I should have made cookies, lit a candle, readied some tea, just in case. I should have tidied up. Still, things might turn around.

Instead, seconds later, a boy who merely looked like a girl was at my door.

"Have you seen Lorca?" he asked, out of breath. His cheeks were red, and his eyelashes thick and dark as spider legs. "Hi," he said, as an afterthought.

It took me a second to process. Not Lorca. *About* Lorca. *Come on, Victoria. Snap to.*

"No," I said. "Not since—" I began, but he was impatient and interrupted me. Young brain. Young love. It was obvious. His face was plump with young hope.

"When?" he asked.

I tried to count the days on my fingers. One day collapsed into the next. What was the difference? The difference was that each day I was a little less sure of which day it might actually be.

"Who are you?" I asked him.

I told him to come inside while I looked at a calendar, but he wouldn't. He stood on the threshold, twitching in a thousand different ways, holding the door open and waiting for me. It made my heart race.

"Come in," I said again. "You're Blot."

He nodded. I moved my finger through the calendar boxes, through the tiny closets of emotions that had been the past week.

"Five days," I said finally, venturing a guess.

"What happened?" he said. "Something must have happened."

"How much do you know?" I said.

He nodded again.

"I'm not her grandmother," I said.

"Shit," he said.

He was itchy, just standing there. Looking at me, looking at my feet.

"Are we going somewhere?" I asked him, knowing the answer. As I leaned down to shift my socks, Lorca's face emerged as it was just before she'd left. I'd done something awful to her. I'd known that at the time. But I'd been beaten, exhausted. It was my excuse—and I'd reveled in having it. In having an excuse to have an excuse. I'd been selfish. Again.

Joseph was a giver. He'd minded the weaker ones. "That's what you do," he'd said. And not just with Dottie—though obviously with Dottie too. He passed a tissue to a crier on the subway. He asked tourists if he could take their photo for them. He put trash where it belonged. And I—one thousand years old—was still afraid of what empathy might do to me, how it might weaken me, which was why I'd pushed Lorca away. And yet, how much weaker could I get? I wondered. How much stronger?

Lorca was a child, I told myself. It didn't matter whose.

I put on my coat and gloves as this young man, Blot, stood there.

"I think she's hurt," he said.

Believe it or not, he helped me with my boots. Still, I've never moved like that. I had someplace to go. I moved. I surprised even myself.

We climbed into a van cab that smelled of spearmint. Salt made rings on the rubber floor mats. Blot buckled up. Feeling strangely important, I did too.

He told me about how they'd looked for the masgouf recipe together.

I told him about the restaurant.

He told me that she hadn't been going to school.

I told him that she'd called it vacation.

He told me that they'd seen Dottie and me putting Joseph's clothes on the street.

"What a first impression," I said and he shrugged.

I told him, hating myself, that I'd ignored her until she went away because of something that wasn't her fault but mine. And because of my pride. It didn't feel any better admitting it out loud, but Blot just nodded and I was grateful for that.

I should have put it all together—the cut on her face, the too-long sleeves, the way she always sought her own shadow, as if afraid of shining through. But I was blinded with hope. At least, that's what Blot said. He was trying to be nice. It didn't help.

"Self-harm is what they call it," he said, and I covered my mouth. "Self-abuse, self-mutilation, self-injury."

The words made something funny happen to my skin.

I had to ask him to stop. I was feeling weak.

"But how do you know that's it?" I said. And just to hear the things I wanted to believe, I said, "Couldn't she just be back in school now or studying or watching television? Maybe she doesn't feel like talking."

"No," he said. "She bled on a book once. The scabs on her arms were like fireworks. I saw them. She said she had a cat."

"She never told me about a cat," I said, as if I knew everything about everything.

"Another time . . ." he said. "Well, never mind. You can just tell."

"I know," I said.

I knew nothing.

I'd read about it years ago. Back then, I couldn't understand. It was during the Gulf War. What audacity, I'd thought, to hurt yourself for the hell of it. How about those death plows? How about being killed as your surrendering arms shook above your head? It was guilt I'd felt then, for the lives that I wasn't living—but only for those who were worse off. It's amazing how guilt doesn't work in reverse and how empathy can be like walking a tightrope.

The cabdriver caught me in the rearview mirror. I was rubbing my lips to keep myself from crying.

"Are you sure you want me to come?" I said. I swear, I wasn't looking for a compliment.

"You have to," he said and left it at that.

Lorca lived in an ugly white building with too-small windows not far from our old restaurant. We made our way up the four steps to the buzzers. I gripped the handrail for dear life. Blot was scanning the names and corresponding numbers, wiping away snow just to see.

It had begun to hail and the wind was picking up, hurling the tiny pellets into our faces like it was some kind of nasty child flinging fistfuls of jacks. My legs were wobbly. My energy was waning. We were the only ones out. But the weather was the least of it. It wasn't that I wanted to be home. I didn't. I just didn't know if I could bear rejection again.

"Do you have a plan?" he asked.

I gave him a face, like he must be joking. Hadn't he been the one to come get me?

"What if she doesn't want us to help?" I said, but as soon as the words came out of my mouth, I wished I could take them back. I knew the answer to my own question. "Never mind," I said. "I'm sorry."

Just then, a woman came out in a hurry. Her scarf was wrapped halfway up her face but she was unmistakable, her thick eyebrows, the part in her hair. Of course. The woman from the photo. I couldn't move. And yet, I wanted to say something to her. She wasn't my daughter, but I'd dreamed about her. For a little while, this woman had been everything. But she was moving very quickly. She was brisk, hardly one for chitchat. You could tell just by looking at her.

"Hey," I said, surprising myself by catching the door. For a second, I held her gaze, but then I couldn't. Her eyes were piercing, insulting without her saying a word. It was too much like trying not to blink during a sneeze. She was waiting for me but not really waiting. It made me lose my courage. I couldn't imagine what we might find upstairs. Lorca's mother was all ice. And Lorca, dear Lorca, wanted nothing more than to warm her. *It's so grossly unfunny,* I thought, *how self-satisfied a person can be. You'd miss your little girl,* I wanted to say. *You have no idea how much.*

"Hold the door for an old lady," I whispered instead, but she was already on her way. Blot held the door and held on to me as we went in from the cold. He checked the mailboxes. I realized that I didn't know her last name.

"Goldberg / Seltzer," he said. And then: "Ladies first. Up we go."

We only half knocked. The door was unlocked.

The place was a mess, but only in a superficial sense. You could tell that someone kept things organized. The books were neatly stacked on shelves. The pots, the ones still hanging from the rack, were arranged by size. There were hooks by the front door for keys with a little note in silver marker that said *Don't forget me!*

"Hello?" I said, all wheeze and breathlessness. "Lorca?"

There were two doors, both closed, in front of us, and a noise came from behind one. It certainly wasn't an answer, more of a swish, and suddenly I was afraid we were in the wrong place. Someone could be waiting to attack. I turned to Blot but he continued to move us forward, pointing to a chair with Lorca's hat on it, perched like a well-behaved raccoon.

"Oh," I whispered. "Okay."

Blot opened the door on the right, and then, as if having almost entered a girls' bathroom and not wanting to make a scene, he moved out of the way. I went in. There was Lorca, on the other side of the bed, kneeling on the floor with her head bent forward and her braid like a spear pointed down her back. She didn't look at us, didn't move. I held on to the door frame to get on my tiptoes and see what she was doing over there. What was she doing? She was still.

Her hands were upturned and her elbows tight to her sides. With her like this, I could see how long her legs were, endless, even when folded like a horse's. She wore hardly anything, just a yellow undershirt and loose-fitting shorts, though the window was wide open beside her. Sleet reached in and attached itself to her hair, catching a silvery light. She was shaking slightly. And her face, what little I could see of it, was colorless, like a dried-out plant.

"Hi," I said quietly, afraid of what might happen if I made too much noise. The way she sat there, so delicate and yet so clearly loaded with pain, caused me to think of what it must be like to find a bomb: not wanting to get too close and yet desperate to get close enough. Great concentration just before a finale. Sometimes, I wondered what horror had happened in the living room where I'd grown up since we'd left Iraq. It was a different world now. I had dreams about a bomb being found there while I was sleeping on the roof. I imagined gore on the rug.

Then I said, "It's all right," inching toward her. She followed me with just her eyes but when I came around the side of her bed and I could really see her, she looked into her hands, as if I'd disturbed her from reading. Though her palms were very white indeed—so much so against the rest of her, red from cold, that they seemed incongruous, like a book or like two beached jellyfish found miles from the ocean just after a hurricane—her left hand was just a little bit cupped and held a pool of blood. The way she wasn't moving but looking at it reminded me of a child carrying a dead bird.

I gasped.

The cuts were all over her arms. It looked like she'd been splattered with someone else's death. It was impossible to imagine such violence from inside her, turned against her, like a rabid set of Russian dolls had occupied her belly. This room too, though bleak, seemed so unassuming. This happened elsewhere, I thought. So much gore, elsewhere. There was an eerie pattern to what she'd done to herself and I searched for some method to it, as if that would explain something, whatever she was trying to get at, what she was trying so desperately to open up. The lines on her arms were short and dark, as if very bitter, strict little mouths had crawled out of her and now refused to budge.

"Don't look," she whispered, her voice a ghost of itself, barely language. Still, she didn't move.

"Here," I said, picking up a blanket and wrapping it over her shoulders. Her skin was cold as glass. I didn't know what to do with her hand. I just looked at it. If she moved, the blood would go everywhere. Then here was Blot. He took off his hat, a wool thing, lifted her hand, and put it inside. He put his coat over her legs, tucking it under her knees.

I could tell by her face that this wasn't normal, even for her. She looked terrified. She was leaning on the wall just to stay up.

There were a million questions I wanted to ask her. But all of them, I realized, would have been for me. All I knew was that if I'd had a daughter, I wouldn't have left her like this.

"Let's go," I said. Finally, I felt I was coming to. We helped her onto the bed. She didn't protest at all. Blot arranged her feet and arms as I rummaged around in her drawers to find pants and sweaters. We tied a bra around her palm, using the little padding as a sponge, and put the whole thing back in his hat. We bundled her up, her body only moving when we moved it. Her limbs felt loosely attached. Her neck, too, floppy as a hose.

It was while I was putting on her socks, running my fingers over thick, slug-like scars on the tops of her feet, that she finally said something. I thought she was about to scold; I shouldn't have stared so.

"Okay," she said instead. "Okay." The sound was so gentle, as if she was trying to comfort me. For a second, I put her foot to my cheek. Only then did I feel the warm tears on my face. She was. She was comforting me too.

Blot carried her in his arms down the stairs, into a cab. He kept her on his lap. She kept her hand close to her, still in his hat. She was shoeless and her feet turned in, covered by two pairs of bulky socks. As the cab made its way, dodging squats of snow, she bobbed along as if all her blood had been drained and she'd been left weightless. She was a shadow in a storm.

I gave the driver my address, and Blot sat up straighter. "Hospital?" he whispered, but Lorca wasn't stupid.

For just a second, she got hysterical. I put my hands on either side of her face. I promised her we'd do no such thing. I had a plan.

At home, I used the broom to tap on the ceiling.

Dottie, a million years ago, had been a nurse, a doctor's assistant. She'd quit because an inheritance fell from the sky and she didn't feel she was the working kind.

But when she walked into the apartment now, all purpose and charm (Blot had gone upstairs first to fill her in), it suddenly occurred to me that she might actually have been very good at her job. And it was a shame, for more than one reason, that she so easily gave it up.

She followed me into the bathroom. It took some time, even for her, to get onto the floor. She winced but made no sound. She examined Lorca, who was in the bathtub and who'd barely opened her eyes since we'd left her apartment.

Now Lorca looked at me, and then at Dottie.

I laughed out loud just once. I put my hand on Dottie's shoulder. Like I've said, I'm a thousand years old. I can barely hold my head up. Do you think I can hold a grudge?

"It's all right," I said.

"It will be," Dottie said. "I'll need a Waterpik. And a candle, bucket of ice, needle and thread."

"Joseph used a Waterpik," I said, walking out of the room.

"He did?" Dottie said.

"Yes," I said. A wife knows these things, I thought to myself, if not everything.

Lorca

❈

We didn't have wooden stakes in the ground. We didn't have burning brushwood either. We didn't have fish from the Tigris or the Euphrates.

We did have fresh red snapper from Citarella, which I butterflied down the back; tamarind paste from Fairway; hand-skimmed olive oil from Tunisia. We had a small fire when Victoria's sleeve brushed past the stove. And when I threw a glass of water at her, we had a fit of laughter so overpowering that I had to help her into a chair.

We brought the food outside and sat on the stoop of Victoria's building and ate with our hands. The fish rested in aluminum-foil boats with grilled lemon rounds that floated like life rafts in the olive oil inside.

It was freezing, but Victoria said she wasn't cold. And I wasn't either, though my eyes were watering, the insides of my cheeks were stiff like tin roofs.

Blot showed up just in time. He brought Victoria the old copy of *Zagat*. He brought me the Dalí book. He put it on my lap. My hand was still wrapped in gauze; it had healed a bit in a week, but not completely. That would take a while. Victoria passed him a foil boat.

"Thank you," I said.

"Thank you," she said.

"Thank you," he said.

The snapper flaked into tender, charred pieces, and the bitter tamarind cut the richness, unperfecting the dish in a way that I wasn't used to—but in a way that I loved.

"This is even better than the last time," Victoria said.

"Hear that, Joseph?" I said, and Victoria leaned toward me in thanks.

We ate messily, the food getting stuck beneath our fingernails, the oil plumping our lips. But it didn't matter. We ate more. And just before we finished most of the fish among the three of us, eating nearly two pounds each, Victoria yelled up to Dottie. She came to the window.

"It's freezing down there," she said. "If you were offering hot toddies, I'd whistle a different tune."

"Absolutely, you make better *turshee* than Joseph," Victoria said after a while, leaning back, taking a shallow breath, putting her hand over her stomach. "Bless his heart."

"That's the best fish I've eaten," I said. "Ever."

"I hate fish," Blot said. "I loved that."

He said he had to get back to work.

"When do you leave for school?" he asked me.

"In two days," I said. "It's just an hour north of the city."

"And we can come visit on Saturdays?" he asked, gesturing to Victoria.

"Of course," I said, maybe with a bit too much excitement. "If you want to, come the second weekend. My father's coming the first."

When he left, he kissed Victoria on both cheeks and then me. It was a different kind of butterflies I felt now. The only word that came to mind was *faith*.

• • •

Victoria and I sat there for an unreasonably long time, eventually growing so cold we had to move our feet to get the blood flowing. But we were close enough to warm each other. Our shoulders, elbows, knees, and toes were touching. We were blocking the wind.

"Tell me something," she said out of nowhere. "Why did you do it?"

I'd been waiting for years for someone to ask, and yet I didn't have an answer, really, not one that I wanted to share.

"Because it felt better," I said.

"Better than?" she said.

"Better than nothing."

"Better than this?" she asked. She took another bite of fish, passed some to me.

Like I said, I'm not used to life surprising me. I shook my head no.

"I know," she said, and though I didn't, at least not exactly, I put my hand on hers. Her bones awakened to my fingers.

"I would never have thought," she said, the words less audible than the cracks in her voice.

"I know," I said.

I leaned into her but it didn't feel like I was giving in to something stronger or that I was too weak to hold myself up. It simply felt better than not.

I didn't think this was the beginning of my life or that I'd been given another chance or anything like that. I knew that I was made up of my choices, the things I'd done, and whom I'd loved and how. I thought only that things felt like themselves, but different. This was happiness, I realized, when I was pretty sure that I'd be happy later on, again and not, and then again.

It wasn't snowing and though it was dusk and slatelike all around us, the sunlessness pouring into the folds between the hungry, reaching branches of the trees, there was lightness in the sky behind the buildings that caught our attention, both at once.

There was a bright blue color, like a very heavy, tired eyelid with a sliver of pearl at the bottom—the crest of a wave about to rush through. It seemed impossible that the day was on its way somewhere, or had come from somewhere else, unless its intention had always been to show off the sky just as it was then.

Later, I would go home. Soon after, I would book a ticket and kiss my mother and hail a cab and take a train and carry my own bags and maybe I'd get a job at the kitchen in my new school. Maybe not. I'd have to see.

We sat there and watched people go home and leave home and when I wondered about their dinner tables, I wasn't jealous. We sat there until well after we'd finished. All that was left were bones.

Masgouf

INGREDIENTS

Whole carp (or other white fish, such as red snapper, sea bass or sole)
Equal parts turmeric, tamarind, black pepper
Olive oil
Lemons
Rock salt
Optional condiments: pickled onions, ambah (mango cured in turmeric, lemon, and salt), or diced tomatoes with garlic

DIRECTIONS

Ask your fishmonger to butterfly fish and leave the skin on. Otherwise, do it yourself: clean and scale fish, and slice all the way down the back so it can lie flat.

Brush both sides of fish with plenty of olive oil.

Cover the flesh with a thin layer of the spice mixture.

Season both sides generously with salt.

Indoors: Place the fish skin side up in a shallow baking dish covered with tin foil. Cook under a preheated broiler for 7–10 minutes, or until the skin is crispy. Flip the fish and cook just until flesh is opaque, about 2 minutes.

Outdoors: Impale fish vertically on wooden stakes and put directly into fire pit or place the opened fish, tail down, head up, in a well-oiled wire grill basket and cook until done, turning now and again for even heat dispersal. Cooking will take anywhere from 45 minutes to a couple of hours, depending on size of fish and intensity of fire.

Serve on a platter with grilled lemon rounds, a sprinkling of parsley and lemon juice, and choice of condiments.

Acknowledgments

So very much gratitude is due.

First, and foremost, thank you to Stella Jane, who is simply the best kind of mother and person and whose love of good writing is contagious, or genetic—and inspirational, for sure.

Then, from the beginning: Blanche Boyd, Julia Fierro, Margery Mandell. Next, Peter Carey, Nathan Englander, John Freeman, Nicole Krauss; Scott Cheshire, Alex Gilvarry, Liz Moore; and, of course, Colum McCann, who believed in me first. After that, dearest Claudia Ballard: I didn't know to hope for such things from an agent. Raffaella De Angelis, Eric Simonoff, Cathryn Summerhayes. Brilliant Jenna Johnson, who made everything, everything, better. Lori Glazer, Tracy Roe, Taryn Roeder.

And finally, my deepest gratitude to Alex for all the tea, green juices, my desk, my pens, heated blanket, faith and encouragement and patience. This is nothing without you.